LIVING WATER

A Novel

OBERY HENDRICKS

HarperSanFrancisco
A Division of HarperCollinsPublishers

To my parents, for their legacy of love
and
For my children, to whom I bequeath it

The scriptural quotations regarding Hokmah are found in chapters seven and eight of the biblical book of Proverbs. Both the International Version and the Revised Standard Version of the Bible are used in this text.

HarperCollins books may be purchased for educational, business, or sales promotional use. For information please write: Special Markets Department, HarperCollins Publishers, Inc., 10 East 53rd Street, New York, NY 10022. HarperCollins Web site: http://www.harpercollins.com

HarperCollins®, ■®, and HarperSanFrancisco™ are
trademarks of HarperCollins Publishers, Inc.

FIRST HARPERCOLLINS PAPERBACK EDITION
PUBLISHED IN 2004
Designed by Joseph Rutt

Library of Congress Cataloging-in-Publication Data
Hendricks, Obery M. (Obery Mack).
Living water : a novel / Obery Hendricks. — 1st ed.
p. cm.
ISBN 0-06-000088-0 (paperback)
1. Samaritan woman (Biblical figure)—Fiction.   2. Bible. N.T.—History of
Biblical events—Fiction.   3. Women in the Bible—Fiction.   I. Title.
PS3608.E535 L58 2002
813'.54—dc21   2002032838

04 05 06 07 08 RRD(H) 10 9 8 7 6 5 4 3 2 1

As a young woman, who had known her? Tripping
eagerly, "loving wife," to my grandfather's
bed. Not pretty, but serviceable. A hard
worker, with rough, moist hands. Her own two
babies dead before she came.
Came to seven children.
To aprons and sweat.
Came to quiltmaking.
Came to canning and vegetable gardens
big as fields.
Came to fields to plow.
Cotton to chop.
Potatoes to dig.
Came to multiple measles, chickenpox,
and croup.
Came to water from springs.
Came to leaning houses one story high.
Came to rivalries. Saturday night battles.
. . . When he called her "'Oman" she no longer
listened. Or heard, or knew, or felt.

From "Burial" by Alice Walker

There came a woman of Samaria to draw water. Jesus said to her, "Give me a drink." For his disciples had gone away into the city to buy food.

The Samaritan woman said to him, "How is it that you, a Jew, ask a drink of me, a woman of Samaria?" For Jews have no dealings with Samaritans.

Jesus answered her, "If you knew the gift of God, and who it is that is saying to you, 'Give me a drink,' you would have asked him, and he would have given you living water."

The woman said to him, "Sir, you have nothing to draw with, and the well is deep; where do you get that living water? Are you greater than our father Jacob, who gave us the well, and drank from it himself, and his sons, and his cattle?"

Jesus said to her, "Every one who drinks of this water will thirst again, but whoever drinks of the water that I shall give him will never thirst; the water that I shall give him will become in him a spring of water welling up to eternal life."

The woman said to him, "Sir, give me this water, that I may not thirst, nor come here to draw."

Jesus said to her, "Go call your husband, and come here."

The woman answered him, "I have no husband."

Jesus said to her, "You are right in saying, 'I have no husband,' for you have had five husbands, and he whom you have now is not your husband; this you have said truly."

The woman said to him, "Sir, I perceive that you are a prophet. Our fathers worshiped on this mountain; and you say that in Jerusalem is the place where it is necessary to worship."

Jesus said to her, "Woman, believe me, the hour is coming when neither on this mountain nor in Jerusalem will you worship the Father. You worship what you do not know; we worship what we know, for salvation is from the Jews. But the hour is coming, and now is, when the true worshipers will worship the Father in spirit and truth, for such the Father seeks to worship him. God is spirit, and those who worship him must worship in spirit and truth."

The woman said to him, "I know that the Messiah is coming (he who is called Christ); when he comes, he will show us all things."

Jesus said to her, "I who speak to you am he."

Just then his disciples came. They marveled that he was talking with a woman . . .

(John 4:7–29)

His blood glistens red in the dim light of the stone hut, though not as red on his berry-brown skin, held taut and shining by labors and prides and hatreds and taunts, as on her cinnamon. It gushes from the neat gash staring from his fleshy throat, from beneath his thick woolen beard, in rhythmic bursts, the first high and angry and terrible, then those that follow coming slower, without the heated immediacy of the first, like angry breath mollifying. His thick back is pressed against the rough-hewn stone wall of the hut, and his tunic and sash bunch on its jags as he slides down slowly, still leaned against it, to half-sit on the hard-packed dirt floor. The purple linen tunic with its brocade and appliqués that minutes earlier he'd flaunted at market is now dirt-splotched and reddened, its fringe dripping crimson onto the dirt. His blood pools around him, like the issue of a spilled pot. As his strength drains with the pulsing stream, he stiffly thrusts a meaty hand into the clotting dust to brace himself. The little of the afternoon light that seeps through the hut's cloth entrance falls upon his outstretched legs and hard, sandled feet, which do not move now.

He does not wince, though he sucks the air quickly and unevenly. His eyes are open, but flutter now more than blink. The corners of his dark mouth turn upward, yet not in their usual sneer, or even as the expression of pain. Rather his lips, ample and quivering slightly, wear something of a smile, like sheepishness or a prelude to weeping. Yet it is a smile, a very faint, wisping smile that, with a rueful, almost imperceptible shake of his head, bespeaks his realization of the great irony that clarity should finally come to him at the very moment he can do nothing with it.

"I shoulda . . ." Only now does he raise his hand to staunch the flow of blood. His words are a hoarse whisper.

"I shoulda . . ." He coughs a dry, weak cough.

"I shoulda . . . loved you better." He coughs again and breathes hard, as if to cry.

Her eyes begin to soften, then they abruptly harden again. She does not move, has not moved since the red cascade began. She is standing with her back to the rear of the hut, her body half-turned his way. She does not look at him. Instead she stares, brown eyes unblinking, into the close dusty dimness of the hut, past the clay pots of beans and soaking lentils, past the stacked bunches of coriander and dill, past the pungent strings of onions and garlic and drying figs hung from the coarse ceiling of dried reeds and clay; past darkness, past light, past everything ever known or said or made or done, at something, at nothing. Her head covering is askew, exposing a neck the color of cinnamon ground and sun-drenched, and thick, tight ringlets of dark hair. Her red sash is missing, her yellow linen tunic with its careful stitching is torn at the shoulder, exposing the drab undertunic. She blinks blood from her eye, lightly strains against the swelling to open it. Her head is throbbing, as is her jaw. The taste of blood still taints her mouth, and drops of it hang, half ooze, half coagulant, from her chin. Her fists are clenched as if she is still unsure if she is safe.

The crimson is a faintly pulsing trickle now, very slow in coming, as is his breath. His head wavers as though his bones are dissolving. He lifts his face, slowly, as if death is pushing down upon it.

"I wisht I had."

His voice is almost too faint, his breath catches in sobs, but still she hears him.

"I wisht . . . I had."

He mumbles something she does not hear, then sobs twice, thinly.

His breath rattles and stops. His bones leave him, his chin falls loosely to his chest and lies like it is planted there.

She has not moved, does not move until she realizes that no breathing stirs the dimness save her own. She shuts her eyes, exhales sharply, reopens them and steps to the entrance of the hut, pulls back its covering and stoops through it. She does not look back.

The sudden freshness of the air and the late sunlight fall upon her like kisses, like the long-ago kisses of Ma Tee, like the unknown kisses of the child she never got to hold. Only now does she speak.

"You should have," she says aloud, as she steps forth to face the frenzied throng arrayed outside. She does not look back, neither to the dead husband in her hut nor to the four before him who so flailed her spirit and tore at her soul. Neither does she see the angry men she has known from birth standing before her screaming her dead. Her gaze is elsewhere, upon another time in this place of suffering. There, in that distance, is a girl. She has no name, yet she is loved.

Part 1
WOMAN

"Ma Tee!" The little girl with cinnamon skin runs, frowning and breathless, into the half-dark of her grandmother's windowless stone hut, panting as she looks into the old woman's lined face, struggling to speak despite the demands of her small lungs.

"Ma Tee!" she gulps. "I . . . I got a question!"

She has run all the way from the shrub-enshrouded outcropping of rock jutting in the midst of the greening fields of labor where stooped and grunting parents loose their little ones to play amid feather-leafed tamarisks and cheery bougainvillea within easy sight and fussing distance. Past the moss-written stone markers announcing the limits of the particular plots of this small slice of the land of Samaria from which whole families spend their lives coaxing their subsistence and struggling to survive the greed and brutality of the legions of Caesar. Past the palms and sycamores and poplars and the pines. Past half-parched barley and half-parched wheat and half-parched plots of half-grudging produce on the stately sloping hills of green and almost green. She rushes down hard, dusty paths hewn by generations resolutely tramping to toil, flinging polite, rushed greetings to each stooped figure she passes. "Shalom, Mr. Laban!" "Shalom, Miss Elisheva!" "Shalom, Mr. Zelophehad!" "Shalom, Miss Rutheline!"

Through rivulets of midday sweat the women offer smiles that are faint yet heartfelt, each waving with more energy than she cares to spare, yet willing it to the little girl nonetheless as a ritual of love that is casual, yet required to offset the daggers that masquerade as the village men's eyes.

"Stay with her, Hokmah," they whisper. "You know how men are about *gibora*-mindedness."

Pausing to retie their work scarves, or again to tuck the frayed hems of their drab tunics into coarse sashes, transforming them into the makeshift pantaloons more suitable for field work than their garments left free-flowing, the women watch her pass and reminisce sadly of long-ago times when their own feet flew like freedom and their own hearts soared like air.

For their part, the men glare disapproval at her that is studied and decided.

"Look at that girl, running around like she's a boy," one yells through lips curled with disdain over his field of cucumbers and beans. "It's not godly. Here we are trying to raise our girl-children up right and her daddy don't pay any more attention than to let her run around smiling and laughing like she ain't afraid of nothing. I sure wouldn't let no female whatsoever dishonor my name like that."

A field mate calls back over knee-high wheat. "Me neither. Cause when I got through waling her with this here 'teacher'"—he holds up his fist and grins—"if she even thought about acting gibora, she'd slap her own self."

The men laugh heartily. Swiping at their sweat with hands gloved in field dust, they return to their toil, satisfied with the crassness of their humor and the sure righteousness of their sentiments.

"Somebody needs to talk to him about this," the first man calls out in afterthought as he pulls a stubborn weed from a freshly hoed furrow.

His field mate raises up with a vigorous nod, as if his jawing partner is looking at him rather than at the dark soil. "You're right. But don't worry. Gibora-minded as that girl-child is, somebody's bound to. You just watch and see." He turns his face back to the earth beneath his feet. "You watch and see."

The prepubescent boy toiling beside him looks up with a quizzical squint. "What's gibora, Daddy?"

The man grunts and answers without interrupting his work. "Something shouldn't no woman ever be, son. Or no girl-child either. Better for a woman to be deaf, blind, and not able to speak a word than for her to be gibora."

He feels the boy's questioning gaze. "See, son, the last thing any man wants is a gibora woman. They're nothing but trouble. They have more mouth than Caesar has soldiers, and generally they're too hardheaded to listen to anyone—except another gibora woman. A gibora woman just don't want to let a man be a man. They're always keeping some mess going, arguing about this and questioning that. They're just more trouble than they're worth."

Gibora. When applied to a man, this Hebrew word *gibora* is a good thing. Evocative of strength, bravery, and boldness, in the scriptures it anoints men as heroes and is even used to praise the strength of God. But when applied to a female of any age, gibora is not a pleasing thing. For a woman to be called gibora means that she is "mannish," that she does not know her place, that she speaks up and talks back, and that she is committed to the blasphemy of daring to claim the same standing before God as men.

A woman is not to be gibora in any way or form; to do so is to bring dishonor upon the man whose chattel she is—daddy, eldest male relation, or husband—and to invite upon herself the almost invariable violence that such dishonor blindly demands. When applied to a girl-child, it means the same, and one thing more: that she has neither the sense nor the home training to be slow and earthbound; that she runs and climbs like a boy when everyone knows that in God's creation girls are meant to walk, leaving soaring of whatever kind to males of whatever station. That is why she, this running, climbing, laughing little brown girl has been called gibora-minded, as invective and indictment, by one person or another since her first steps. Rather than being celebrated by all, as would be her lot if she were a gibora boy, her loud quick laughter, her unabashedly ready smile, her love of running and skipping and climbing and, especially, her questions, have elicited disapproval at every turn instead.

Even the busy band of little girls who are her playmates parrot the village assessments of her, though none of them knows what gibora means. Of course, it is not yet theirs to know, not really, for this is grown folks' business and they are girl-children, to be seen and not heard. Still, each has already learned to gauge the curl of her father's lips in the full fuel of testimony, to read the fury or resignation in his gesticulation, to listen for the "uh-huh" of his approval or the "hummph" of his condemnation. And it is clear to all that gibora in a girl-child is always a "hummph."

It is in this, the listening, the hearing, the internalization of the hard judgments of their fathers that her playmates learn to be complicit in the slow strangulation of her spirit, and the gradual shackling of their own. If she displeases any of them by winning a race, or by walking some ground they fear to tread—climbing a sycamore or jumping from one of the many pocked limestone boulders rising from the rocky landscape like sentries—the girls sneer at her spiritedness with the vivid sentiments of their male forebears.

Their leader in her torment is little Izevel. Chestnut-brown with pleasing features, taller and more calculating than the others, Izevel thinks it is her right to be the girls' leader and the constant center of their attention. Izevel's spirit carries the twin poisons of youthful jealousy and adult rejection of female exuberance. It is always Izevel who snorts "hummph" and lashes out whenever in their games the girls' attention turns to her rival with cinnamon skin. Izevel is unfailingly diligent in her faultfinding, never missing an opportunity to drive a wedge in the girls' camaraderie.

"You all can follow after her, acting all gibora, if you want to," she says dramatically, as she turns to leave with a sniff. "But see if all that climbing and running races is gonna get you a husband. Hummph!"

The little girls' games always end with Izevel stomping off and the others tripping behind her, cowed by her hoisting the specter of their fathers' disapproval, stealing ambivalent glances at their stunned playmate, who is left grasping for meaning as her companions depart. It seems so clear to everyone, like the nose on her face or the fresh scab on her elbow, that what is she, a child with few defenses, a child with little sanction to believe in herself, to do but accept as real the thing so offensive to so many? Little by little the small voice that usually befriended her instead began to admit a growing decay in its humor, a taking of anxious breaths that now whispered only cancers to her. *Something must be wrong with you. With you.*

It came to her in the droning quiet, then louder and more frightening when the prickly frowning eyes of grown folks turned upon her, then it was a swelling hum, a whispering chant, an ever-increasing pitch of doubt speaking to her without invitation or welcome. Yet as she runs through the fields this day, she hears none of it, thinks none of it, feels none of it. Today the ugly voice is silenced. Because today all her mind holds is a question.

Down the rock-strewn path she runs. Past the prosperous *nahalas,* or family compounds, of a few well-to-do villagers, with their penned-in livestock, their expansive fertile fields, their several stone dwellings of extended family and live-in workers proudly arrayed in a ring, sprawled upon the best lands of her village like fat arrogant hounds. She stops to admire one of them, and momentarily to catch her breath. Then off again. Now past the nahalas of the less prosperous, like her own, tiny stone huts set off from the village as well, but with smaller fields than their prosperous cousins, their dirt yards hosting perhaps several chickens, a bony goat or two, a small garden, and invariably a rude earthen oven.

Off to itself, a small hut stands amid neat arrays of sleeping melons, knee-high vegetables and blooming flowers. A white-haired man stoops, wrist-deep in freshly turned earth. Huge hands at home with arms of still bulging sinews, a barreled chest competing with a big man's belly, movements slowed yet recalling great power—these belie the long length of his years. Except his face. His face bears his age without deceit or apology. It is earth-colored, rich, like the dark, lush soil he has fingered almost from birth, with deep lines in his forehead and around his eyes from long seasons of smiling at life and squinting at the hard farmer's sun. Thick hair white like undyed wool frames his weathered face, both beard and crown. His name is Mr. Ishmael.

A widower and childless, Mr. Ishmael has lived alone for the many years since the death of his wife. He associates little with the village men, who think him strange because from the day of his betrothal he treated his wife as his equal before God. Because he argues that every man should do the same, they consider him a troublemaker as well. In old age, his physical strength is still formidable, yet he is gentle and kind enough to befriend this small girl. At the telltale pat-pat of her scurrying feet he raises his large proud head.

Silently kneading the soil in another part of the garden is a second old man. He is compact, slim-waisted, with a small head of hair that was once copper but is now shot with gray. His face is impassive, unexpressive, dedicatedly silent; his hands, though, are ever busy. His name is Phinehas, although everyone but the straitlaced Mr. Ishmael calls him Mr. Pop. A bachelor, for most of his life Mr. Pop has been a fighter in the guerrilla armies that sprang up to rid Samaria of its Roman colonizers. In war he was a dedicated soldier whose impetus to make battle was not hatred or rage or lust for blood but a faithful zeal to establish the *malkuth delaha,* the sole sovereignty of God, God's kingdom of justice on earth as in heaven. He never entered battle without a leaf of the scriptures in the leather pouch around his neck—which once blunted the thrust of a Roman sword in combat, sparing him from serious injury—and he never slew a foe if he could subdue him. Before every battle he recited from the Book of Exodus:

> *I have seen the affliction of my people . . . and have heard their cry because of their oppressors; I know their sufferings, and I have come down to deliver them . . .*

When the various rebel armies were finally vanquished and scattered by the superior Roman might, Mr. Pop was already an old man. He returned to the village to live out what was left of his days on the nahala of his childhood friend. In the village environs, the fortitude and discipline he had displayed in war he now placed at the service of his neighbors. Each day before sunrise, before even the morning mist appeared, Mr. Pop worked his neighbors' fields, chopping firewood, watering livestock, all without words or formality. At first light, just before the workers left their huts for their fields, he quietly tramped back to the nahala of his friend, avoiding the effusive thanks of his grateful neighbors with their inevitable fawning and offerings of gourds of cool water and hot barley cakes. He was said to be either the craziest man in the village or the holiest. When asked why he served in secret, indeed, why he served folks at all who thought him so odd, he replied, in one of his lengthier discourses, "That's just the way things supposed to be."

"Shalom, Mr. Ishmael. Shalom, Mr. Pop," she calls as she passes the old men without stopping.

Mr. Ishmael pushes to his feet, smiling. He is noticeably unstooped for his age. Mr. Pop silently waves and continues his work. For him this is a lavish gesture.

"Now wait a minute, little friend-girl," calls Mr. Ishmael in an amused, grandfatherly tone. "Where's my sugar?"

The little girl slows, casting him that earnest look of childish impatience. "I gotta go, Mr. Ishmael. Honest. I gotta go ask Ma Tee a question."

The old man beckons her to him. His demeanor is pure gentleness. "Now, you know I'm not going to let my little friend-girl run past here without giving Mr. Ishmael his sugar. How are you going to be my little friend-girl and pass right by here and not give Mr. Ishmael some sugar?"

She saunters back slowly, sighing extra loudly and stopping every few steps to pat her foot and roll her eyes. He watches with amusement as she approaches in that slouching posture of pained childish protest, kicking at the dust with her soft-edged attempt at reluctance. "Awww, Mr. Ishmael. You always be wanting some sugar."

"Uh-huh. I sure do. And you know why, don't you?"

She rolls her eyes again, but this time to hide the smile that is blooming despite herself, the same smile Mr. Ishmael's loving presence always elicits from her. Dutifully and reluctantly she recites the old man's everyday rationale for his everyday hug.

"I know. I know, Mr. Ishmael. Cause I'm such a sweet little thing." She turns up her nose. "Alright, I said it. Now I gotta go, Mr. Ishmael. I gotta go ask Ma Tee a question."

Her fuss is only a dance, for both know how deeply she loves his attention, his affirmation, his expansive expressions of love and care. Mr. Ishmael, she knows, is her friend. Unlike everyone else, he tells her neither to slow down nor to quiet down. He does not have the hard eyes of judgment that glare from the heads of other adults. His eyes are soft and friendly and laughing and accepting. He reaches down and scoops her up in a noisy hug.

"Ummm, uhhh." It is the same lush love-filled hugging sound he always made.

She feels the pleasing coarseness of his beard against her cheek. Her little arms encircle his neck like vines round a tree. She squeezes hard, trying to make the same warm sound as he. "Ummm, uhhh."

"That is s-o-o-m-e good sugar," he laughs as she crinkles her face to hide her delight. "Now what's this question that got you running through the fields like a house afire?"

Normally she laughed at his folksy descriptions. But not today.

"This is my question." Her head is cocked, her expression intense. "Mr. Ishmael, what's a *erwat dabar*?"

The old man's face flattens with surprise. His eyes lose their laughing edge. He sighs heavily. "Ummm. That's sure some question you're asking." He pauses to regain his smile. It is less bright now. She does not notice.

"Yessir," he says, stroking his beard. "Seems like a grandmama question to me. I think you were right the first time; that's definitely something you should ask Ma Tee. I believe she can answer better than me."

He pats her head softly. "Well, since I got my sugar for the day, guess I won't keep you anymore. Go on and find your Ma Tee."

He bends at the waist and kisses her forehead. "Bye-bye, sweetie pie."

"Alright, Mr. Ishmael. Bye." She is already on her way. "I'll tell you what Ma Tee says," she calls through the faint curtain of dust that again trails her.

Mr. Ishmael watches her depart, then sadly calls to his friend. "Phinehas, I sure hate what's happening to this village."

"Ain't right," says Mr. Pop.

The hard-packed, rocky path brings her stumbling into the village. Hers is a *kefar,* a "little village" of the traditional form of communal living in the land of the Samaritans and the Jews. As with most villages of her time and place, it is a weathered stand of windowless, mostly one-room stone huts loosely ringed by the outlying nahalas. Without breaking stride, she scampers through the muddy narrow alleyways that separate the rude basalt dwellings. Darting around the clay humps of the communal ovens that populate each alley, she runs into the open courtyard at the center of the village, a brief expanse of hard dirt with few patches of green, dusty and raw and open. The courtyard serves as the marketplace and the general site of gathering, gossiping, and tale-telling. Several male elders whose worn backs can no longer bear the strain of the fields hold court, squatting on flat stones and smooth-topped stumps, or reclining on the bare ground beneath the terebinths and sycamores on the edge of the courtyard, telling tales and talking various gradations of righteousness talk about the goodness of the Lord, how much they love the Lord, how they live now only to serve the Lord, what the Lord has done for them. But each round of testifying ends always with the same complaint: how hardheaded their women have gotten to be. By the unpleasant looks these men give her, the panting little girl senses, without knowing why, that she is viewed as a glaring example of that very grievance they curse as the greatest plague of their lives—that is, after their ongoing debasement at the hands of the Romans. She is well winded now, but she musters her last strength to flash past the scary, squinty gazes of the fussing and spitting old men, hoping to avoid the ire that even a glimpse of her would raise. To her relief, not one notices; each is much too busy being righteous to discern the frightened scampering as hers.

Finally she splashes through a muddy walkway to rush, as at a finish line, through the coarse cloth that covers the open entrance of her grandmother's hut. Sweat-drenched, her thick wavy plaits are plastered to her face; the question is hot in her mouth.

"Ma Tee!" she pants. "Ma Tee! I . . . I got a question."

Breathless, she looks into her grandmother's lined face, her little head in an exaggerated tilt, fingers splayed on her narrow hips like the grown women in her village when they discuss serious woman business. Not yet nine years old, she is the color of cinnamon and honey mixed with a bit of fresh cream. Her hair is parted in squares and plaited into a headful of thick, wavy braids covered with a light scarf. Her coarse woolen tunic is tied loosely at the waist and hangs just above her sandled feet. Its bottom is frayed and torn from tree-climbing and frequent games of hide-and-seek in the foliage and underbrush. She is exuberant and brave without knowing it.

Undisguised pleasure blooms in the old woman's face as she pulls her panting granddaughter onto her lap. With her tattered skirt she wipes the beaded sweat from the little girl's face. Hugs her with exaggerated grandmother hugs. Smothers her with smacking grandmother kisses.

"Ma Tee!" The girl protests through furious giggles. "Ma Tee! I got a serious question for r-e-e-a-l! Stop, Ma Tee! Stop!"

Ma Tee grabs her own head in mock pain. "Oh, oh. Not another question." She leans back in mock trepidation. "You and those questions. Oh Lordy, we're in trouble now."

With pretended disgust she slides the child from her lap and mimics her, playfully, lovingly. "'Ma Tee, why Mr. Moon have such a big head?' 'Ma Tee, why Mr. Sun always shining in everybody's business?' And my personal favorite, 'Ma Tee, why boys are so uu-gg-ly?'"

"Ma Tee!" The little girl squeals with delight. "You know I didn't say nuthin about no Mr. Sun and Mr. Moon!"

The child's laughter is fuel for her grandmother's fun.

"'Ma Tee, why do I have feets?'" The old woman stomps her feet. "'Ma Tee, why do I have a nose?'" She honks her nose. "'Ma Tee, why do I have this little bitty booty?'" She turns in a little dance and shakes her rump.

The child convulses with laughter, grabbing her grandmother's hands in laughing protest. "Stop, Ma Tee! Stop! I mean it. I got a question to ask you."

Ma Tee cannot contain her delight with this "nervy" little girl—her youngest grandchild and her favorite—who asks questions like her life depends upon it. Yet she is painfully aware that a girl with too many questions is headed for trouble. That the way things are is bound to ride her. Ride her right into the ground. And break her. Since That Day she has seen it too many times. Bright eyes become dull because the feelings that light them are little valued. Bouncing steps become plodding apologies for the least unsanctioned movement. Laughter and airy banter become speech carefully measured and controlled. She has seen it too many times.

Yet even knowing what awaits her granddaughter, for brief moments Ma Tee cannot help but delight in her perkiness and spunk. Her gibora. If only the world loved a spunky, brave, question-asking girl-child. But it does not. So she will yet again answer this inquisitive child, but this will be the last time. After this, she will discourage the questions in earnest. And do something about her gibora-spunk before she ends up broken. But for now, she cannot resist the burning urgency of the child's plea.

"Alright," says Ma Tee, lifting the braided bundle onto her lap with a stiff smile. "Come on, Miss Busybody, and ask your important can't-wait-another-moment question before it gets to be next week."

"Ma Tee," she says in her most grown-up tone, "what's a erwat dabar?"

Ma Tee is used to this child's questions. All kinds of questions. About everybody and everything. Embarrassing questions. Exasperating questions. But this—she is not prepared for this. This is no question. This is torture. This is bleeding rashes and weeping skin boils, hot coals dumped into her bosom.

The old woman's face, usually placid and calm, is drawn into a sudden weariness. Her countenance is a pained visage of stinging memories, memories filled with suffering so deep it would prostrate if left to its work. Instead, as she has so many times before, Ma Tee embarks on an imagined journey to a life in which she is valued for more than her willingness to do the bidding of others. She floats there, between rapturous visions and the true harshness of her life, and prays to fly. Fly to a world where the softness of her heart is a known and honored thing. But the sky is not her home, and her flesh is not meant to fly. So her thoughts return to their place beneath the clouds, like the time-dried leaf when the breeze has died, like the vanquished heart when its hope no longer stands. There, beneath the sky, beneath her dreams, Ma Tee drops her head, clears her throat, smooths her tunic, wets her lips. She does not wish to betray that the thing this child asks holds such pain for her that she has to flee to the momentary succor of illusions before she can answer. She pauses, as do those who must speak what their hearts would wish away, then raises her head. Clouds still hang in her face. Sorrow and exasperation swirl in her voice.

"Child . . ." The baldness of the pain in her utterance surprises her. She clears her throat. Her voice is calmer now. "Child, you know this is grown folk's business you're asking, don't you?"

"Yes, ma'am. But I wanna know."

"'I wanna know. I wanna know.' Why do you always have to know? Why it so important for you to know this, baby?"

"Cause it just is, Ma Tee, that's all. I wanna know why it be making my mama and all those other grown-up ladies cry and act mad and scared and everything. I wanna know, Ma Tee. I wanna know."

The old woman gathers her strengths, draws them around her like protective raiment, yet she feels exposed, she feels vulnerable, she still feels the painful knives of memory thrusting at every turn. This is a hard thing, but she will answer honestly. One day this child will be a woman. She has to know sometime; she might as well begin to know now.

Ma Tee's words are measured. Her eyes are sad. "I don't know if you can understand all of this, child, but grown folks do a lot of things that don't make good sense, and some things that just seem to be pure evil. I don't know much of the scriptures, so I'm not sure which one this erwat dabar is—without good sense or just plain evil—but if Ma Tee had to choose, I'd call it evil, pure and simple. How it found its way into the scriptures I just don't understand."

"Erwat dabar is in the scriptures, Ma Tee?"

"Yes, baby." Ma Tee's voice is grave. "Right in the book of Deuteronomy."

Although women are not allowed to study the scriptures, Ma Tee has heard men wield this passage so often she knows it by heart:

When a man takes a wife and marries her, if then she finds no favor in his eyes because he has found some erwat dabar—*some "indecent thing"—in her, and he writes her a* sepher keritut—*bill of divorce—and puts it in her hand and sends her out of his house . . .*

The little girl is wide-eyed. "Send her out of the house she lives in with her family and everything?"

"I'm afraid so, child."

"How, Ma Tee? Why?"

The old woman hesitates. She means to say little, but her seasons of pain goad her to say more. "Well, all her husband has to do is say she's committed an erwat dabar; all he has to do is just say she did some kind of 'indecent thing.' No proof, no nothing. Doesn't matter what the wife says; the scriptures treat the husband's mouth like he has a prayer book in it. And it doesn't matter who he is or how low-down he might be. If a man says it, his word is treated like law. The woman has no say-so at all. After that, all the man has to do is write up a sepher keritut—a bill of divorce—and the woman is put out of her own home."

"Where the wife go, Ma Tee?"

"Used to be she could go back to her family. Used to be that if her husband divorced her, the woman could take her *ketubah*—her dowry— with her. When men stopped honoring that, the woman's father would turn at least some of the *mohar*—that's the bride-price her husband pays her father for the right to marry her—into a ketubah and give it to her so she could have something of her own. That was the custom of our people, and it still is in a lot of villages. But after That Day the men's hearts became as cold as stone, and the women's daddies or their elder brothers or whoever was the head of their family started keeping for themselves the ketubah and the mohar, too. Wouldn't give the poor put-out wife anything, like being put out was her own fault. Nowadays most families—most men, that is—look at divorced women like they're a failure and a disgrace, so they don't want anything to do with them.

And because the man is the *rosh*—head—of the house, his word is law. If a man says a woman can't come home, then she can't come home, pure and simple."

"But what about the little children, Ma Tee? What happens to the little children?"

"The man has the right to keep them all, if he wants to." A sudden bitterness invades Ma Tee's voice. "But most men only keep their sons. Sons are real important to men. They think the more sons they have, the more of a man that makes them." She sucks her teeth bitterly. "Nowadays they seem to only want to keep their daughters if they're good-looking enough or obedient enough or good enough workers or have good wide hips for birthing, or whatever makes men think they can get a big mohar for them. But mostly, girls have to leave the house with their mothers."

The child blinks hard. "So where they go, Ma Tee?"

"Outdoors, most of them," the old woman sighs. "They live outdoors, outside the village. On the edge of the fields or in the woods or in a cave or wherever they can."

The little girl's eyes are big as saucers. "You mean like those raggedy women and little children that live in those raggedy tents way out past my daddy's fields?"

"Yes. That's them."

"They're all raggedy and boys be throwing rocks at them and people be ignoring them and everything!"

"That's them."

"Just because of that old erwat dabar?"

The absurdity of injustice is best seen in the eyes of children. It is hard for innocents to fathom. The little girl looks at her grandmother as if part of the story has been left out.

"This erwat dabar must be a real bad thing, right, Ma Tee? Cause don't the wife have to do something real bad first? I mean, to be put out the house she live in and all?"

Ma Tee hesitates. She does not know what to say but she knows she must speak; her granddaughter might rephrase the question, but she will not stop asking.

"Baby, this is more than a little girl can understand. This is grown-up talk. Let's wait till you get a little older, and we'll finish this talk then. Just like grown folks. Alright?"

"No, Ma Tee. I wanna talk about it now. I wanna know now, Ma Tee. P-le-e-e-se Ma Tee. I wanna know."

The old woman is pleading now. "But you're nothing but a child. Why should Ma Tee tell you about grown folks' business?"

"Cause it's women's business and one day I'ma be a grown-up woman, too."

It is her eyes. Insistent, so insistent. Needing to know like breath itself. Ma Tee might deny her words, but she cannot deny her eyes.

"Alright, baby. Alright. But it's a hard word to hear, because this erwat dabar is a terrible thing. And it's not just one thing. Wouldn't be so bad if it was one sure thing, then women would know what they're up against. But an erwat dabar is anything that a man wants it to be. Seems like if anything displeases a man it can start him to accusing, 'Erwat dabar! Erwat dabar! You did an "indecent thing"!' If you don't give him children, especially sons, he can frown up his face and call that an erwat dabar and divorce you right out of your home. Don't keep his house clean like he wants, he can call that one, too. Miss cooking one of his meals, or cook it too done, or don't snuggle up close enough to him in bed, or don't seem religious enough for him, and all those things are erwat dabars, all of them are 'indecent things' if he wants them to be. It seems that everything is an 'indecent thing' to these men if they're upset with a woman, or tired of her." She shakes her head ruefully. "It's just this simple: when a man doesn't want his wife anymore and he's ready to give her the sepher keritut, he can declare anything she says or does an 'indecent thing.'"

Ma Tee sees the horror in her granddaughter's eyes. "I know it sounds hard, baby, but it's true. Much as I hate for you to hear it, I guess now is as good a time as any. You're young, but you might as well know about this devilish erwat dabar, because someday you're going to be faced with it. So you have to learn to mind yourself and not cause any trouble. And most of all, you have to be careful how you live."

Ma Tee's face is solemn and somber. "Always," she says with grave intensity. "Always be careful how you live. Always."

Be careful how you live. All her life she'd been told to be careful; she was used to it. But the dangers she'd been told to avoid had always been clear. Snakes. Swirling currents in the deep part of the river. Roman soldiers offering sweets. Yet this careful was different. Careful of what? Not to displease men? Were men ever pleased? It seemed that all she'd known her young life was men's displeasure. Her daddy. The old men squatting in the courtyard. The teasing boys who waylaid her at the edge of the fields. She knew this displeasure. But how did women displease men so much to cause them to just throw women aside? And would that be her fate?

She wraps her arms round Ma Tee's wrinkled neck and squeezes hard. "Don't let that happen to me, Ma Tee. Don't let nuthin like that ever happen to me."

The old woman holds her close. She would give anything if she could promise her spunky grandchild the cloak of protection from the coldest seasons of womanhood, from the direst winds of the whims of men, but she knows she cannot; she has not even been able to protect herself. So she does what she can: she holds her close, this child frightened by the specter of the life that lay in wait for her, and prays to be her protector.

Into the abyss of the little girl's questioning creeps the ravenous self-doubt that eats at too many women from girlhood, subtly, quietly, until they come to regard themselves as forever unworthy of the fullness of life.

"But why they do that, Ma Tee? Why?" she cries. "Why men treat women like that? Don't they like women? Sumpin wrong with women? Don't they think God loves women same as men?"

Ma Tee settles the weeping child into her lap and gently rocks her.

"I don't know, child. I just don't know. Ever since the Romans came in here That Day, nothing's been the same . . ."

For all that happened, for all that could be named and remembered, that is how every soul in the village knew it, simply as That Day, a shorthand for horror too great to need elaboration. Say "That Day" and everyone old enough to remember recalled the very spot upon which they stood when the soldiers exploded upon their peace, the exact task in which they were engaged, the poise of their limbs, the angle of their bodies as they turned to look, the peculiar, frightened catching of their breaths. Mention "That Day" and eyes begin to tear, heads bow in shame, mouths twist in unrequited anger and barely suppressed curses. Infants flinch instinctively at the hurt they hear in its phrasing, begin to fuss and wail, grow fearful and melancholy.

It seemed that every soul in her village was marked by the horror. On That Day the little girl with the cinnamon skin was barely in her fifth year of life, yet its trauma and ugliness remained for her a memory vivid and raw, as if seared into the depths of her young psyche; as if seared into her remembering flesh.

Her elder sister, Oholibamah, though married now and a mother herself and who, since her own wedding day, had been kept from the life of her younger sister by the off-putting meanness of their father and the daily demands of her husband, was then twelve, a year from the traditional age of betrothal. Oholibamah usually worked the fields like all the older children, but she had fallen awkwardly while pulling a reluctant weed, so her task while her painful wrist healed was to look after the littlest children while their parents toiled toward dusk.

This day Oholibamah had brought them from their everyday play space by the rock outcropping in the fields to run free in the village courtyard. It was then, as the children laughed and chased one another through the open yard, that they appeared in a clotted horizon of driven dust and drumming hoofbeats: Roman soldiers, a cohort of them. She could still see them, seated like kings and conquerors astride snorting steeds, some holding spears like scepters, all with swords hung menacingly at their sides. The soldiers galloped into the courtyard, their horses swaggering, scattering the children crying for their parents and shrieking in terror at the strange pale-skinned men atop their monstrous beasts. Little ones tripped over one another in their terrified scrambling. The little girl remembered falling in the dust, lying in frightened whimpers until Oholibamah scooped her up in one running motion.

When the soldiers came, the able-bodied of the village, both women and men, were in their fields of work or at the swirling fishing pools at the elbow of the river, as on every day except the Sabbath. Those left behind—the elderly, the infirm—hastened to help Oholibamah gather the children to safety as best they could, while at the sound of horses and the cries of the children, every worker rushed madly from fields and nets, desperate to snatch their little ones from the danger each knew to be the soldiers' occupation. The men shouted, "Get back, woman!" as they ran, claiming rescue and protection as their duty alone, but the women ignored them and ran with the desperate urgency of mothers, not slowing even as their sandals flew off in their scramble and rocks bloodied their feet.

By the time the frantic parents reached the village, Oholibamah and the elders had herded the children into one of the narrow alleyways that separated the stone huts. In the alley sat the squat oven that was shared by the houses flanking it. The children crouched behind it whimpering, fearfully peeking at the goings-on.

The workers called frantically as they reached the village. "Where are the children?" they cried. "Are the children alright?"

From their alley the elders shouted reassurance. "They're alright. They're here with us."

The panic began to ease. Assured that no little ones were caught by Roman hands, and finding no tiny bodies crushed beneath the hard hooves of horses, the frantic shrillness of the voices dropped to a low murmur, then to a forced dry rustle as every tongue, freed from their desperate pantings, stilled with ominous expectation.

The long strides of Big Shim'on had brought him into the courtyard before the others. Big Shim'on was called that because he was big. Big and blustery. In fact, he was the biggest man in the village. A full head taller than most, his broad face was the deep brown of ripe figs. A thick, pointed beard hung to midchest and a long, straight nose with nostrils so large they looked perpetually flared gave him a threatening appearance. His eyes were large and slightly bulged, and one always seemed to look away, the vestige of a childhood feat of daring gone awry. Coupled with his exaggerated swagger, his bulk and overgrown features conspired to give Big Shim'on a look of menace. Although he was known to throw his weight around in wrestling, good-natured fisticuffs, and contests of strength, Big Shim'on was no bully, for bullies lack real courage and Big Shim'on was a brave man. Brave and honorable. In the men's friendly competitions, this meant that he never struck an opponent harder than he had to, and never struck a man at all that was not at least shoulder-high to him (these he simply held in excruciating embrace until they surrendered or passed out). In everyday life, this meant that his greater endowment of size and strength obliged him to care for the safety of his neighbors.

Big Shim'on stood before the mounted soldiers, feet apart, a subtle defiance written across his broad face. When he stepped forward to address them several of the village men stopped him.

"Big Shim'on, you know you should let Abba Samuel do the talking," said Mahali, a short, chubby man with eyes that twitched nervously.

"I know, but Abba Samuel is up in years," Big Shim'on answered. "What if they decide to make an example of him like they did with Yoram? How would we protect him?"

Yoram had been the village rosh, the respected head of the village *knesset,* or council, when Roman soldiers besieged them last. By nature a gentle and conciliatory man, he addressed the soldiers with respect and deference. More than that, after seeing the steel in the soldiers' eyes, Yoram counseled his compatriots to cooperate with their demands without dissent. But after enduring months of rebel activity in the northern province of Galilee, the soldiers had brought with them the strategic desire to remind everyone over whom they ruled that Rome was still serious about the business of subjugation. It was for this reason that as the soldiers mounted to depart, their booty in hand, with a sudden signal they abruptly seized the surprised and gentle Yoram, keeping the shouting village men at bay with drawn weapons and the threat of wholesale slaughter. The soldiers half-dragged Yoram into the hills where they beat him and, to punctuate their disdain for the people of Samaria and the power they held over them, stripped him and repeatedly raped him.

The next dawn the village men, searching for what they expected to be Yoram's lifeless body, instead found him naked and bleeding and deliriously praying for death. Awakened from his stupor by the men's footfalls and their murmurs of horror and pity—"Aww Lord, look what they done to him!"—Yoram was awash in tears and anguish that death had so callously refused to befriend him. Denied the grace of the grave, at that very moment he began to ponder how he would live out his disgrace, and where. Humpbacked with shame, he knew he could not return to the searching stares of the village, especially the women, their eyes filled with pity and disgust, either of which would break his heart. Instead, he chose to remain there in the hills, at least until he mended, beneath the makeshift tent of old woolen cloaks and threadbare blankets that the sad-faced men hastily raised for his convalescence, which they outfitted with a pallet for his comfort, a jug of wine for his drinking, and wooden bowls of aloes, madder root, and mint oil for his healing. The men took turns sitting with him, reading the scriptures, trying their best to assuage the hatred crusting over him and to allay his bitter mortification.

When Yoram finally recovered, when he was again able to walk without every few steps pausing to grit his teeth, wincing and cursing Caesar's name, at last he settled on the only choice he knew to escape his shame and dishonor: he borrowed—that is, his village compatriots gave him—a donkey and enough bread and wine and dried dates to last for a week, and grimly prepared to set out to lose himself in the distant seaport of Caesarea, where he would live out his life as one wounded stranger among many, forfeiting forever his family and every earthly possession. His eyes were flat and lifeless when he told the men his intentions as he prepared to depart.

"Why you want to go to Caesarea, Yoram, a whole city named after Caesar? Seems like that would be the last place to go if you looking to get away from Romans," said Pasach, a tall, thin man who wore a perpetual look of befuddlement.

"Can't kill them if you not around them."

"Kill them?"

"Kill them. I'm going to kill every Roman the good Lord sends my way."

"You know the Romans will just as soon kill you as look at you."

Yoram flashed a bitter smile. "They already killed me."

"Well, you can't kill all of them."

"I know. But I'll kill as many as I can. Don't matter if they're soldiers or not. As long as they're Romans, I'm going to kill them." He barked a short, hollow laugh. His new language of ferocity was chilling.

"But you can't make all Romans guilty for what Caesar and his soldiers do."

"Why not? Isn't Caesar's kingdom against God's kingdom? Don't Romans walk around with their noses in the air like they're God all by themselves? From the moment they're born, doesn't every Roman benefit from Caesar's evil in some kinda way? Tell me true, have you seen even one Roman ever say, 'Caesar, please don't treat them Samaritans like dirt; they're people just like us'? Have you heard even one of them fix his mouth to say, 'No, Caesar. I don't want to live better than them other folks just because I'm Roman'? Have you? No. If they benefit from the evil, but don't try to stop the evil, how can they not be guilty?"

The men looked for one among them to speak, but they knew that none could refute Yoram's logic. After a few whispered statements among themselves, they silently produced two daggers and a short sword. They tied Yoram's few provisions tightly on his beast, reluctantly handed him the weapons, chanted a prayer for his safety, and sent Yoram off with sad embraces, watching him amble away for what they knew would be the last time. Not one of them ever told Yoram's grieving kin that he had survived his abduction, nor was it ever again spoken among them that his flesh had been so heinously abused. The men's parting gesture of fellowship to Yoram was to keep intact his silence, his secret, and what he defined as his honor.

"It's better if one of us does the talking," said Big Shim'on. "If they try something, we would have a better chance of . . . of . . ." His voice trailed off, and for the briefest moment the men recalled Yoram lying face down beneath that tent.

"Alright," they quietly agreed. "You speak then."

They caught Abba Samuel's eye and respectfully but firmly gestured for him to remain silently in the crowd.

But I am the rosh of this village, Abba Samuel thought. Then he looked at his wrinkled arms, his gnarled hands, heard his own wheezing and reluctantly resigned himself to the men's judgment.

"Alright. Now stay calm," Big Shim'on said to his compatriots. "We don't want no trouble with these crazy Romans." Then he turned to the commander and spoke with a loud, flat tone. "What do you want?"

The villagers were by now silent and still. Puffed up by their fearful, rapt attention, the commander gestured to his attendant to unroll an official-looking scroll. As the attendant held the document for him, with great ceremony the commander read from it with an eloquence usually reserved for more formal occasions.

"People of Samaria, hear and obey. His Excellency Pontius Pilate, governor of the imperial provinces of Samaria, Judah, Galilee, and all of Syria, appointed by his Majesty, the mighty Caesar, emperor of Rome, by imperial sanction and decree has empowered the cohort of soldiers of the imperial Roman army under my command to expropriate and confiscate any and all supplies and foodstuffs as we deem necessary to the efficacious conduct of the business of the imperial Roman army." He reared back upon his horse like Caesar himself. No one responded. No one moved.

The little girl remembered whispering to her sister, "What that mean, Oholibamah?" and one of the elders answering, "That means those old dirty Romans are getting ready to take from us whatever they want. Again."

Big Shim'on addressed the waiting commander with a tone that was forceful, yet measured. "Sir, we're just hardworking people trying to take care of our families and mind our own business. You Romans come here, steal our crops, and call us criminals. You take the fruits of our everyday labor, and call us shiftless and lazy. You even blame us for being poor. Why don't you just leave us alone?"

The commander answered with great impatience and condescension.

"This is not thievery, you fool. This is an honor, allowing rabble like you to serve the good of the Roman empire."

"But we don't know a thing about the Roman empire. All we want is to be left alone to raise our families in peace."

"And that is the purpose of the empire, you ignorant peasant, to establish and maintain throughout the world the Pax Romana, the peace wrought by the magnificence of Rome."

"But we had peace before you Romans came. All we need to have peace now is for you Romans to leave us alone."

The commander was losing what little patience he'd brought with him. "You sure are uppity, aren't you, boy?"

The Samaritan drew himself up to his full height. "I'm not sure what you mean. And my name is Shim'on."

The commander smiled a grim smile. "Oh, it is, is it? Well, that's just your Samaritan name. Your Roman name is 'boy.'" The listening soldiers looked at one another and relaxed into the knowing posture of those who are about to be entertained.

Big Shim'on had not yet let his eyes meet the gaze of the commander. He knew Romans counted eye contact from their subjects as insolence, and he wanted no trouble. But he was deeply stung by the insult, and he looked at the commander without thinking. "I am not a Roman," he said with fierce restraint. "And my name is Shim'on."

"I know you're not a Roman." The commander looked to his men and laughed. "Not with your ragged tunic and your nappy beard. No, *boy*"—he emphasized the insult—"you're a Roman subject. You are an inconsequential little speck of a beaten, conquered people. You are our subjects and we Romans are your superiors."

In addition to his usual impatience, the Roman's face now wore a smug, self-satisfied look. "Superior to you in every way. In intellect, in physical beauty. We have great libraries and great centers of learning, while you people sit on the ground reading parchments scribbled with prayers and superstitions. Our noble aquiline profiles are immortalized in busts, great statues, magnificent mosaics, while no one even thinks to honor your dark and stubby features, not even to portray them in chalk."

His men chuckled with an air of self-satisfied superiority.

"And compare our modes of living," he rhapsodized. "You live in these muddy villages, and what you call the *cities* of Samaria are at best dusty little towns. Rome, on the other hand, is the greatest city on earth. Great palaces, expansive plazas and streets paved with cut stone;

coliseums, aqueducts that carry water hundreds of miles for our drinking. Romans rule the world. You Samaritans are nothing to us. We extract tribute from conquered peoples like you every day. Clearly, we are your superiors."

Big Shim'on scanned the soldiers before him, dirty, hair scraggly and unkempt, some with mouths full of rotten teeth and skin pocked with scabies.

"Yes," he said, turning to the commander with a barely stifled laugh. "We can see how superior you are."

Muffled laughter rippled through the villagers. Big Shim'on's face hardened. "But if being superior means being better at murder and thievery, then I think we Samaritans are glad to be inferior."

The commander could not believe his ears. This arrogant Samaritan was mocking him. He replied in a voice dripping venom and authority. "Let me remind you, boy, that not only are we Romans your superiors in every way, we are also your imperial masters. That means that you will do what we tell you. Now speak your name, boy."

Big Shim'on was silent.

The commander recognized in Big Shim'on's posture the proud stance of the unvanquished, for Big Shim'on meant it to be understood in just that way. He looked at Big Shim'on with momentary boredom. Spurring his horse slowly toward him, the Roman stared, frowning, into the Samaritan's face, offering him the opportunity to accept defeat and bow to his authority by lowering his eyes in at least ritual capitulation. The commander was tired; he did not feel like drawing his sword today, so capitulation would be enough. But Big Shim'on stared back in defiance. This brand of open rebelliousness was not new to the commander; he encountered it in every village of every subject people it seemed. At every turn, men of particular bravery (or foolhardiness, in his estimation) sought to challenge his power by very public shows of resistance and spleen. Without exception, he crushed every one. Thus, tired or not, the commander knew what he must do to retain his authority over the villagers and the respect of his own men: this Samaritan was publicly defiant, so he had to be publicly broken.

The Roman rode closer, so close that Big Shim'on and the Roman's horse shared the same breath. "Don't you know what we do to rebels and rabble-rousers? Haven't you heard what happened to those troublemakers down in Judea? At Sepphoris in Galilee? And surely you heard of the routing of Judas the Galilean and his rebellious rabble?"

Big Shim'on answered in an even tone. "Yes, we know what you do. Our elders still talk about how you Romans enslaved those thirty thousand Judeans at Tarichae, how you slaughtered all those folks at Gophna, Emmaus, Lydda, and Thamna. Lynched two thousand folks at Sepphoris and left their bodies to rot, and killed anyone who tried to take them down for a decent burial. Yes sir, we know what you brave soldiers do."

"Well, then you understand why you'd better watch your uppity peasant mouth," said the commander. His face wore a chiseled cruelty and his voice a new haughtiness, as if he were speaking to no one in particular. "And by the way, we did not 'lynch' those rebels, boy. They were crucified for the crime of insurrection against the Roman empire. They disobeyed their imperial masters, and they died a painful death for it—like you are very close to doing right now. No more talk. Speak your name!"

The Roman dismounted and drew his sword, quickly and pompously. Several grinning soldiers jumped from their horses in rapid, acrobatic motions, as if to showcase their desire to do harm to somebody, anybody.

"They going to hurt Mr. Big Shim'on!" Oholibamah whispered.

"Shhh!" said one of the old men holding the children. His eyes were wide with fear. "We don't want to do nothing to set these crazy Romans off."

The commander held his sword menacingly before him as his soldiers surrounded Big Shim'on. Everyone was tense with fear. The little girl remembered asking Oholibamah, "Why don't somebody do sumpin?" and one of the elders whispering, "What can we do? Them is Romans." She distinctly remembered that he spoke as if Romans were gods, invincible. And it seemed to her at that moment that to everyone in her village the Romans were invincible. For no one spoke. No one challenged them. Except Big Shim'on.

Big Shim'on was glancing at the crowd now. The eyes of some urged resistance, but most pleaded submission. He avoided the gaze of his wife and children, whose fear he knew would only cripple his resolve. Several of the men in the crowd urged, "Go on, Big Shim'on, say it. Ain't nothing but words."

But acquiescence was the last thing on Big Shim'on's mind. A bitter anger spiraled within him, filling him with fire, fed and stoked by the mistreatment at Roman hands that he had seen and heard and endured all his life.

The commander raised his sword. He was shouting now. "Say it! Speak your name!"

Big Shim'on faced the Roman, his body stiff with anger. The two men's eyes locked in furious intensity. The air was thick with rage and anticipation. The Samaritan tensed for battle, his eyes narrow, his teeth on edge. Just when he seemed sure to explode, his shoulders suddenly relaxed. For wrathful moments he had thought of nothing but vengeance, but his honor reminded him of the slaughter he could cause if he offered the wrong response, or even the wrong tone of voice. So he willed himself into a sudden calm. He turned to the villagers with an unmistakable confidence, then back to the seething commander. His head was high as he spoke.

"Whatever you say. My Roman name is . . ." He paused and looked the Roman full aface. His voice was firm. "It's 'boy.'"

"I didn't hear you. Did you say something?" the Roman said, sneering and baiting him.

The villagers held their collective breath. But Big Shim'on did not lose his composure. In fact, he felt more powerful than he ever had, certainly more powerful than the scowling soldier before him. He answered louder and firmer this time. "My name is 'boy.'" Big Shim'on paused for a brief moment, then turned to take his place in the crowd of villagers.

The commander looked back to his troops. They hooted with laughter. "Good boy!" he shouted. But he was not fully pleased. This Samaritan had spoken the humiliating words, yet he clearly was not humbled. A hateful anger came over the commander. With a quick skip he viciously kicked Big Shim'on in the buttocks. "Now get out of my sight, boy!" he bellowed.

The troops hooted louder.

It happened so quickly that no one could stop him. Someone called out, "No, Big Shim'on!" but it was already too late. In a rush of rage Big Shim'on was upon the commander before he could raise his sword again. He was already clutching the Roman's throat when the soldiers grabbed him, shouting as they pulled him off, "I'm tired of you Romans coming in here grinding us down into dust. My name is Shim'on, son of Anaiah! That's my name! I'm not a boy, I'm a man! And my name is Shim'on!"

Somehow he broke free. The enraged commander lunged with his sword. Big Shim'on sidestepped the blow but fell into the soldiers. With their fists and the butts of their swords they rained blows upon him that sounded like the splitting of ripe melons. The village men pressed toward Big Shim'on's thrashing figure, but the heavily armed soldiers kept them at bay.

"Stop!" they shouted. "He's had enough!" But the soldiers could hear only the sound of their own savagery.

Blood now freely flowed from Big Shim'on's mouth and nose. Still he fought, and somehow again he broke free. This time the soldiers pounced upon him with real savagery, fists flailing, cursing, swarming like beasts on a kill. When he fell beneath their onslaught they stomped him with murder in their limbs. Finally Big Shim'on lay still. The commander spat upon him and turned to the assembled crowd.

From the alley where she crouched the little girl had noticed a small man at the back of the crowd who seemed particularly agitated from the Roman's first words. He seemed filled to bursting with fury, straining to break free of several older men holding him fast. Avram was his name. A young man, thin and wiry, Avram was known to have a short fuse. Since his childhood, when the Romans had taken his family's entire store of grain, badly maiming his father and trashing their hut in an "officially sanctioned" raid just like this, Avram seemed always to be angry and ready to fight. Folks shook their heads and declared, "One day that boy's temper is going to get him into trouble." And indeed, his temper was his master from the moment the Romans' turgid hateful dust appeared in his sky. He'd rushed toward the village cursing and swearing, his work hoe in hand like an instrument of death, vowing to send many Romans to hell that very day. Before he could reach the village, he was tackled by several men and relieved of his makeshift weapon. They held him to the ground, covering his mouth with their callused hands while his father implored him to keep his violence at bay.

"Boy," he said, "if you run in there going for bad, those Romans are going to kill you, and a whole lot of somebody elses besides, maybe the whole village. You know I hate Romans, too, after the way they crippled up my arm, but you can't stir them up, because we can't win the fight. We just can't. And Romans don't mind lynching anybody—man, woman, or child."

Avram stilled and quieted, but his eyes held their fury. The men let him to his feet and together rushed to the courtyard, but their eyes told one another to hold close to Avram. They stood with him, shouted and winced and shook their heads with him as Big Shim'on was beaten. Held him as he squirmed, hushed him when he took breath to curse. But it was when the commander spat upon the motionless, bloodied form of Big Shim'on that Avram exploded. In the spiteful arrogance of that spittle he saw the leering Romans as they had barged into his hut, as they'd pawed his mother and sisters, as they'd beaten his father almost to death. Avram pulled free of the restraining hands with strength forged in years of festering bitterness and ran headlong toward the Roman commander.

Avram's fury was like lightning: its heat was overwhelming, yet it lasted but a moment. He got neither revenge nor satisfaction, for when he rushed the surprised commander a soldier stopped him with a spear thrust to the ribs, dropping him to his knees. Then another pierced his back. Then another. Avram keeled to the ground, yelping in agony with each thrust, as the soldiers continued their frenzy unabated. The villagers were paralyzed with shock and fear; no one moved but the mother of Avram, who dropped to her knees in breathless horror, and his father, who rushed to his son shouting, waving with his good arm, the useless arm dangling at his side.

"Stop it! Stop it! In the name of God, stop it!" The butt of a spear knocked him to the ground. He lay sobbing in the courtyard dust, not even in reach of his dying son.

The commander remounted. "Now look at this." He pointed to the lifeless Shim'on and the nearly lifeless body of Avram. Their blood was dark as it mingled and seeped into the yielding earth.

The Roman cleared his throat and spoke with such malevolence that it made the little girl's skin crawl. "You, the people of this village, have resisted a decree of His Excellency Pontius Pilate. For this you must be punished. If any of you resists further, all of you will be summarily executed for sedition against the empire of Rome."

The villagers' thoughts turned to Sepphoris, to Gophna, to impaled men, women, and children, and the air became thick with their moans and plaintive wails.

The commander seemed invigorated by the sounds of terror. He turned to his troops and barked crisply. "Round up the men," he said with a grim smile.

Women and children screamed and clawed at their husbands, their fathers, their sons, their brothers, as the soldiers dragged them to the center of the courtyard. Old men, the able-bodied, youths with only the faintest signs of facial hair, all stood together, trembling with anger and fear. The commander raised his hand for quiet. Only the fearful sobs of the women and the whimpering of children broke the hush. The men stood in strained silence waiting to hear their fate.

"Now strip," the commander barked. "Remove your clothing. All of it. Now."

The men stared in dazed dismay. The commander raised his sword. "Undress. Now!"

They looked each to the other in riotous unbelief. One of the younger men, Binyamin, broke their silence. With tear-filled eyes he crossed his arms and huffed, "I'm not taking off nothing, in front of these women and children and all. Nothing. Not one stitch. They're going to have to kill me first."

The others whispered to him with desperate fierceness. "You better get your clothes off like everybody else, and save our families."

Silently, purposefully, the men disrobed. There in the middle of the courtyard, before the women and the children whose respect they so coveted. They stood naked, heads bowed, shameful tears burning furrows in their cheeks. Then the soldiers surrounded them. And beat them. Beat them long and hard. And cursed them. And mocked them. And spat upon them.

Of all the horrors of That Day—the slaughter of Big Shim'on, the butchering of Avram—the beating of the men was her most vivid memory. She could still feel the terror of it. The sickening *thunk!* of clubs and spear shafts against skulls and upraised limbs. The singing lash of whips cutting naked flesh. The screams of the men. The shudders. The moans. The grunt-punctuated entreaties.

"Don't let the children see! Don't let them see!"

She could still see her father struggling to protect himself with one arm while hiding his privates with the other. But mostly she heard it. For the women did cover the children's eyes, and although their hearts felt every blow, they refused to participate in their men's humiliation by watching it.

The Romans beat the men of her village until they tired of it. Then the commander dispatched the soldiers to their work of confiscation so they could continue their business of conquest on full bellies. While the men lay moaning and bloody and defeated on the blood-reddened ground, the Romans went house to house. They took grain and cattle and cured meat and stored vegetables, and oxen and ox carts to carry their booty. And then came the real horror. Women. They seized women. Wives, daughters, mothers. Weeping, begging, struggling frantically, desperately looking to their fallen men for deliverance. Seven in all. Some taken for immediate sport, some to be sold as concubines, none ever to be seen again.

The powerless men lay broken in the dust watching their world torn asunder. Children screamed for mothers, husbands screamed for wives, fathers for daughters. They called for angels, for ancestors, the strength of demons, the wrath of God, for anything to raise them whole and healed to kill these monsters and free their loved ones. But there was no bolt from heaven, no intervention from demon or angel. The

Romans departed unaccosted, as arrogant and powerful as they had arrived, the shrieking women held fast in their grasp. The village was never to be the same, nor could it.

The beating was for her more vivid than anything and everything—everything but the hollow, vacant, defeated look in the men's eyes that was its aftermath. For weeks thereafter, men limped through the somber village turned inside themselves, their heads hung, wearing a humiliation so deep it seemed to replace their own skins. All of them walked like men nearly dead, silent, grunting when they spoke at all, save when anger and shame gathered them in the shade of the trees skirting the courtyard or beneath the willows and sycamores and poplars overhanging the bend of the river, to drink palm wine and curse the Romans to hell.

Yes, her memory of That Day ran deep. But what the little girl did not remember, because in her youth she could not have understood, was what it did to the men, how it murdered their spirits, the self-loathing it birthed deep within them.

These proud men, the proud seed of fathers who had stood against Assyrians, dispatched Babylonians, chased the Persians from their hills; men who, with little more than staves of wood, withstood the practiced thrusts of Greek swordsmen, battling with stones and farm implements when their weapons gave out; these proud men who heartily welcomed strangers while in the same breath apprising them that disrespect toward the women of their village would earn knots on their heads and bruises on their backs; these honorable men who knew the one true God, kept the Books of Moses and added nothing to them, slaughtered the unblemished lamb and called God's name in deepest awe; these just men who held no slaves, worshiped no opulence, drank no blood, engaged in no debaucheries; these steadfast men who prided themselves as guardians and cherished their families' certainty that they would never become prey to bandits or to blasphemers; these tender men who nourished their young, respected their elders, loved their wives, and held midwives in high esteem; these proud men who had shielded, sheltered, protected, and secured, suddenly were no longer proud men, no longer confident, no longer unfaltering, but something else now. The pride that had once animated them, nourished them, strengthened them, sustained them, was now beaten from them. It bled through their skins, seeped from their psyches.

Yet worse was what bled from their spirits: the precious marrow of their love. Love that had been earnest, steady, calm. Love that had eaten goat curd and honey so the children could have meat. Love that went threadbare so the suckling and its mother would know no chill. Love that worked through broken bones, through torn and infected flesh, through fevers, through nausea, through pains too numerous to name or to number. Love that coaxed crops from rock-filled soil and built sturdy shelters with stones, mud, sticks, and stout river reeds. Love that prayed for the dead, pulled stumps from neighbors' fields without invitation, and delivered calves from the choking grasp of breech births. Love that called old folks "ma'am" and "sir" and deferred to their pronouncements no matter how cantankerous, infirm, or beset they were by senility. Love that contested with wolves for the lives of lambs, if only to fulfill their fathers' pledge that nothing in their village would ever become quarry—it was this love, spilled by the clubs of tormentors, that crusted now and hardened in the cauldron of the men's humiliation. Their sense of duty remained, although that was at best the dry husk of a dormant love. But love that could be seen and touched and felt and heard, that was gone. It had left the men with such quiet and such finality that most did not recall that it had ever been. And so the men of her village, who once thought themselves proud, who once thought themselves protectors, now cleaved to one another in the desperation of defeat. The hopes, the fears, the dreams that dawned within them they now shared only among themselves, and there evolved among them a cheerless fellowship of emotional insularity through which they meticulously avoided the fearful tyranny of what their hearts might have felt. In this barren emotionality of their own construction, there was still sex with their wives, but now no affection; births, but no celebration; worship, but no communion; talk, but no real sharing.

For if they could not protect those entrusted to them, how could they love? If they could not shield them from the bloodstained grasp of pale hands, the arrogant toss of uncoarse hair, if they could not keep them from alien harm and stupidity and ensure that nothing but the hand of God would take them, how could they risk to love? Even the thought was an agony, reeked of too much loss and fear. So love became a place their hearts could not visit. Only in their fellowship of detachment and complaint did they allow themselves to admit the worlds of feeling that throbbed within them. Only there did they give voice to the pain that elsewhere was unspeakable. Yet even there, seated on lean haunches beneath night-blackened skies, or gathered at their haven at the bend in the river, hardened feet sunk in the cool grit at the water's edge, even there every word was weighted with tears and reproach. Even there, between guzzled drafts of palm wine and strong barley beer, even there soliloquies of contempt wafted through their spirits, swirled in rushes of self-abhorrence, gave their blood its tepid color.

With their hearts hidden in that sequestered circle of suffering, the presence of the women and the anguished uncertainty of what they now thought of them hovered over all that the men spoke, felt, or longed for. Unable to face the women in their shame, the men cursed them in their absence.

"Every time my woman smiles at me I know what she's thinking; I can see it. She's saying, 'He's weak. Goes around acting like he's so much man, but I saw the Romans beat him like a child.' I can see it. Either she's laughing at me or she's smiling to keep the pity from showing, like now she's better than I am."

"Yeah," said another. "I should've just come right out and told my wife to stop her lying. I should've said, 'Woman, don't tell me you're crying because I took a stomping to keep you and the babies from being killed like Big Shim'on and Avram. You're crying because you're ashamed. You're crying because you think I'm not man enough to protect you anymore. That's why you're crying.'"

"And that's why I can't stand the sight of these women," said the other. "They always expect so much from us, expect us to be strong every minute. But how can they know what it is to be a man in a land ruled and run by folks who do everything they can to make you feel like nothing?"

"Yeah. Seems like every time there's a crime they blame it on us. A Samaritan man is guilty from the womb. And if we say anything about it we're flogged, crucified, lynched just for breathing."

"Ain't it the truth," said the other. "They come in here stealing our goods, and call us thieves. Rape our women and call them loose. Take our crops, then when we can't pay Caesar's tax, or when they've taken so much from us that we can't pay back the loans we took to pay the tax in the first place, then we got to decide which of our babies to sell into slavery. How is a man supposed to do that?"

"That's the worst thing, that we can't even do the honorable thing and sell ourselves, because if we're gone, who's going to feed the babies left at home? Who'll make sure the crops are planted, the harvest is in, the jackals are kept from the door?"

"And we got to stand still and take it just to keep our people alive."

"But do these women appreciate us? No!"

"Never have. Ain't nothing we do is ever enough."

"And that's why I can't stand them, cause we're walking around carrying this naked pain like a bunch of hot coals, and they don't have a clue and don't want none."

"Should be on their knees daily thanking God with gnashing of teeth that they have men willing to keep on going just so they can have decent lives, even if it means us dying a little every day."

"Should be praying right now. But these women don't appreciate nothing."

"You know it's true. And that's why I can't stand them."

A part of each man knew he was being unfair, that their women had been their partners, had stood beside them, encouraged them, suffered what they suffered, struggled to withstand the oppressors' onslaughts on their own spirits with comparable stoicism and strength. A part of each man knew he was being unfair; it was just that none of them could believe their women still loved them simply because they felt themselves unlovable. So they mistook every woman's smile for a smirk of derision, and gestures of nurture for displays of mocking pity. From That Day, other than the Romans, the only thing the men of her village despised more than their defeated selves was their undefeated women.

It was in the weeks following the men's beating that her father, Aridai, first assaulted her mother. Before, this would have been unthinkable. Like his fathers before him, he had never been particularly demonstrative, never spoke of love, never dispensed kisses or sought them for himself. Still, in his own way he was a loving man, but his was a love tempered by the emotional reticence bequeathed to him by the centuries of his people's tribulations. For long before That Day, the generations of their battles against those who would count their children as chattel had increasingly sapped the emotional vigor of men and their sons, and their generations of subjugation had grown in them a sense of powerlessness that they could not shake. There seemed always to be a surprise on the horizon, something ugly and unforeseen, something insidious and out of their control. In this plague of uncertainty each generation of men felt less and less free to speak of love, until by her father's day, except when read aloud in scripture, *love* was a word no longer used by men at all.

Rather than talk about love, rather than share their vulnerabilities, their passions, their fears, the men forged them into a rugged zeal to protect, to shelter, to feed. In this new conception of their world, callused hands were no longer for tender touching, but for defense, and sinews were no longer for holding loved ones close, but for the holiness of work. It was work, struggle, protection, dry shelter, and adequate food that became the articulation of their love. They did not hug, they protected. No words of romance, yet they stood guard until dawn. They never spoke of love, they just toiled from can't-see in the morning to can't-see at night. They paid no compliments, displayed no strong passions, cooed no affection. They simply worked. And struggled. And offered the integrity of their lives and their willingness to die for their kin as all the love that even God could ask.

Despite the wordlessness of their love, however, or maybe because of it, never for a moment did their families doubt their devotion. And with Aridai it was no different. The breadth of his love was evinced by his daily struggle to keep his loved ones from want, by the solitary smile the contented purr of their full bellies called to the corners of his mouth, by his quiet delight at their laughter and carefree banter in the secure world he helped to shape with his labor. And they loved him back. Showered him with their playful attentions, called his name as though the mere sound of it made all things right, prepared his meals as if for a special visitor, and to honor his willingness to die to keep them safe, took not a bite until his first mouthful had disappeared. Their hero, their rock, they were as proud of him as he was of them.

Yet despite the depth of his commitment to kith and kin, after his beating at the hands of the Romans a spirit of seething meanness took residence within him. He did not change all at once. Rather, pieces of him withered gradually as the malignancy of his shame and unavenged anger rotted the deepest core of his feeling. He seemed to lose touch with all emotion save resentment and anger, and wore a perpetual countenance of insulted honor and offense easily taken. The once cherished laughter of his children now struck him as a nuisance, and flashes of warmth at the graceful form of his wife curved over pots or grinding stone, cooking the vegetables they had harvested together or kneading the wheat they had threshed, were replaced with sudden frowns and ill-thought words of undue harshness and scalding disapproval. As the best parts of him fell away, he who had been his family's hero became their bully, and he began to beat his wife like an enemy, like the enemy he could not beat, like the enemy that had beaten him.

If the mistreatment of her mother had only been physical, and if it had ended before her flesh had known real insult, there might have been space for her healing and reclamation. But because all her life she had known only kindness and security from the presence of men, she had no defense for the meanness that enveloped her now. And because she had never had reason to distrust her husband before, she knew only to trust him now. That is why she could do no other than believe that if Aridai was displeased, it must be she who was displeasing. So rather than challenge his cruelties, in the face of them she became more pliant. With neither defenses nor champions with which to question, resist, or fight him back, her pliancy became self-abnegation, and her desire to please became a raging self-contempt. She agonized over his denigration of her intentions, reproved herself for her mistreatment, and was gradually crushed by a cruelty whose contours she never learned to fathom.

Of course, she did not have to submit to his rancor. She could have railed in defiance or attacked him in his sleep. Instead she shrank back in the abiding hope that his hardness would pass and she would have back the satisfying life she had known. That is why when he struck her, she knew only to blame herself for vexing him so.

"If only I were a better cook," she said through flowing tears. And when again he struck her she cried, "If only I did not aggravate him so," as she daubed at the blood in the recesses of her mouth. And when he struck her yet again she sobbed, "If only I kept myself up better," as she bound her latest wound.

When she finally became aware of the terrible decline of her own life, it was already too late to reclaim it, for she was already too weakened, too depleted, already less than a wisp of the woman she had been; the best parts of her, the parts of her that threatened Aridai most—the parts of her that most reminded him of love—had already been broken and sent into irretrievable exile. And so, in the name of an empire so godless that it worshiped itself, the soldiers had succeeded in striking at once two birds with each wrathful blow, for in the brittle aftermath of their awful brutality, her father's misplaced fury had gradually broken her mother's spirit forever.

"Are you listening to Ma Tee?"

Her grandmother's words jar the little girl from her sojourn into memory; jar her from recapitulation of the bitter things she has seen, heard, felt, and understood, yet did not understand. She is possessed by a sorrow that she does not comprehend.

"Uh, yes, ma'am," she sputters. "I . . . I am."

Reassured of her granddaughter's attention, Ma Tee continues.

"That Day changed everything, child. Oh yes, Lord, it did. Before, at least the men trusted us. Now it seems they blame us women for their pain. And for trying to be a comfort to them. But we saw how their memories of That Day were killing them, how much they were suffering, how ashamed they were, how hurt. So when the men had started to heal—at least in their bodies—the women got together to make over them, to let them know how much we love and appreciate them. Made a big feast, fixed ourselves up special. Rubbed henna on our fingers and our toes. Edged our eyelids black. Perfumed ourselves with stacte and myrrh, held fast our braided hair with decorative combs and crisping pins. We wore our finest tunics tinged with indigos, yellows, and reds. And talk about food! We fixed the men a meal that would have made any Passover proud. Served date honey and fine ground wheat flour cake. Loaves of barley bread stacked yea high. Lamb flavored with coriander and sour goat milk, with that sour-sweet pomegranate dipping sauce. Plates of stuffed vine leaves and yogurt sauce, salads of onion, parsley, and za'atar. Laid out melons, fresh dates, figs stewed with mulberries, pressed cakes of moist raisins. Pitchers full of sweet wines and pungent beers and cool spring water. And we women danced the dances of our people to the sound of bell, cymbal, timbrel, and lyre. Then we sang songs in their honor. The men ate and watched and listened and seemed to be loosening, seemed to be coming back to themselves. Then we stopped still and began to sing Moses' song of victory from the Book of Exodus:

> I will sing to the LORD, for the LORD has triumphed gloriously;
> horse and rider the LORD has thrown into the sea.
> The LORD is my strength and my might,
> and the LORD has become my salvation. . . .
> Your right hand, O LORD, glorious in power—
> your right hand, O LORD, shattered the enemy . . .

"We sang to let the men know that nothing had changed, that we still honored them the same as always. To let them know that our faith in them as bearers of God's strength for our people was undiminished and unchanged. To let them know we loved them. We sang loud and with feeling. As we sang, we looked into their faces to see the warmth of their appreciation. Their gratitude. Their pride. But what we saw was hard and blank, like that stone over there. What I remember most is that not one of them smiled. Not a one. Their jaws tightened and their eyes narrowed, and they just glared at us. And one by one they got up and walked away. Angry. At us. Like everything was the women's fault just for remembering. We heard them muttering as they stomped off, and saw them cutting looks over their shoulders that could have killed a camel. Finally we realized what had upset them so. They had taken our singing about triumph and might as ridicule, as ridiculing their power-lessness before the Romans. They just got up and walked away, down to their gathering place at the river. We watched their heavy swaying backs, bent so much that you could feel the sky get heavy as they walked, the sky weighing down on them, their eyes like slits, their jaws working wordlessly like cursing every hair on our heads. And there was nothing we could say that made a difference. Not a thing. The more we tried to comfort them, to lift them up, the more distant and sullen they became. That's when they left us, child. Old men. Young men. They never got over it. Their bodies stayed, but their souls and their spirits left us. They became distant, mean, protective of themselves. From us. From the reminders we have become of how they once saw themselves, from the witnesses we were to That Day, when they became less in their own eyes. Now it seems that every day since, one of us women has had the erwat dabar thrown into her face some kind of way."

Tears spill down her face. The little girl wipes the old woman's cheeks, leaving smudged and dusty streaks where the tears had run. "Don't cry, Ma Tee," she says through little tears of her own.

The old woman rubs her eyes and breathes deeply. "I'm alright. It's just that it hurts so bad, child. It hurts so bad." Her voice begins to crack, and she waits to regain her composure.

"They say that divorce has been a man's right since the time of Moses. But before That Day we hardly had any divorces in our village. The only time you ever heard about divorce and erwat dabar was when something went really wrong. Like when Bilhah got up one morning vowing never again to sleep with Ya'aqov, telling anyone who cared to hear that she'd rather hug a cross-eyed antelope than for Ya'aqov to ever slobber on her again. Or the time Abihail left a plum-sized knot on Hotham's head with the flat side of his ax and tried to take a chunk out of his backside, too, after he made the mistake of calling her a headache and a pain in his hind parts right out in public so everyone could hear. When the women finally got the ax from her, she said, 'Well, at least now he knows what a headache really feels like.' Funny, she didn't seem upset at all, just disappointed that she hadn't got to teach Hotham the rest of the lesson. But that's all. Even though they could have, men back then just didn't have it in their hearts to use erwat dabar as a tool against us."

To the women's everlasting sorrow, however, the reluctance of the past remained in the past. In the new world of banished affections and fear-impoverished love, erwat dabar went from a sad admission of marital failure to a bludgeon used often and much. What began in fear, as a toothless threat to carve emotional space without calling it that, little by little became an implement of meanness and indescribable hurt. Men who thought themselves no longer worthy of the love of their wives, or who found that emotionality and shows of affection reminded them too much of the selves they'd once been, firmly wedged the erwat dabar between themselves and everything that stirred their hearts. In their anguished logic they reasoned that whenever intimacy became too close, by raising the erwat dabar and the distancing that defined it, they could introduce into their unions a new impermanence, a new insecurity, a calculated new remoteness that would shield them from their suffering and self-doubt. But when they found that even that distance was not enough to ease their shame, the meanness set in, a wall of meanness that no feeling could scale. From then, erwat dabar was no longer a shield to protect the men from emotion, but a dagger to kill it. And the damning charge of gibora even in imagined form was all the permission needed to use it.

"After that feast, your grandfather lost whatever feeling he had for me." She pauses to blink back tears. "He never did love me, but he was dutiful. Sometimes kindhearted. He never loved me, but still, in all the times before, he had never treated me bad. But after That Day and the feast we wish to God we never had, in those last years before he died he became the meanest man in the village. Couldn't stand that we saw him helpless and naked after all his life being the rock of the family. *Defeated* was the word he used. 'You think because I'm old and defeated that I ain't no more man?' Then he'd pitch an ugly fit, call me all kinds of names, and *SLAP!*" She pauses again, her lip beginning to tremble. "After a while he started using his fists."

"Why didn't my daddy do something?"

"Do what? That was his daddy. Anyway, he was too busy mistreating your mama to think about somebody not being mistreated."

"But you're his mama."

"Uh-huh. And your mama is somebody's mama, too."

They sit quietly, the old woman struggling to retain her composure, the little girl trying to understand the swirl of images and thoughts and feelings that assail her.

"What women can do, Ma Tee? I mean, to get men to stop from being so mean?"

"It's not all men, baby; just some. What about Mr. Ishmael? He's not mean. And his crazy old friend, Mr. Pop. He might be crazy, but he's never said a cross word to anyone. And there are others. Mr. Yusef. Well, he's gone now, but he stood up against all this meanness to women until the men ran him out the village. Some men aren't mean."

"But most men are mean, ain't they, Ma Tee?"

The old woman is silent.

"So what can women do, Ma Tee?"

Ma Tee gently squeezes the girl's narrow shoulders and looks into her face. The old woman's eyes blaze like a pair of black suns. She speaks as if arming for battle, as if her words are swords and shields and helmets.

"Just pray, child. Pray. And wait on the Lord. And always remember, it isn't God making these fools act like this, it's pure evil. And whatever happens"—she repeats it for emphasis—"whatever happens, you have to remember that you are God's child just like men. No man is better than you. Oh, men act like they're better, but they're not. Still, they have the power in this world and they're acting real ugly with it. So you're going to have to be careful how you live so one day you don't wake up to some erwat dabar or sepher keritut or a stout stick across your back. Yes, you're every bit a child of God as a man, but you have to be careful how you live if you're going to get along in this man's world."

She holds the child's fearful, wondering face. "You hear me? You have to be careful how you live."

The little girl listens like she has never listened before, but she cannot hear, not really. She cannot understand how life can be given and withheld with the same savage, loving hand; how it can be given and crushed underfoot at the same time. But fully understood or not, it is clear to her that this thing *careful* is something she had better learn.

When the little girl emerges from the dim loving quiet of her grandmother's hut, atop the coarse woolen tunic that is her usual attire is now draped a stale, heavy garment of carefulness. Ma Tee has tried her best to craft it to her size, yet it does not fit. Still, she will dutifully struggle to wear it, though its weight will sag her heart to its knees, and its reek of untold smothered spirits will choke her very breath.

Chapter

2

Despite the ongoing complaint of the men that her gibora spirit poisons the village air, Aridai, her father, has not yet bothered to break her of it, simply because hers is a presence he has seldom bothered to acknowledge, for with focus can come attachment, and with attachment, pain. In his studied practice of looking past her, looking over her, looking around and through her, she has warranted his notice only when she has acted in ways that did not augur well for her future as a husband's chattel. On those occasions Aridai counseled her with the shocking violence of the back of his hand. But that has been all. Nor has the village gossip raised her behavior to him as a matter for discussion, for it is an unwritten code among men that none should meddle in another man's home. Now, however, as the unwavering hand of time pulls her toward the age of betrothal, the other men feel it their bounden duty to inform Aridai that his honor is in serious question owing to the long-standing legacy of dishonor that has been wrought by the sad spectacle of his gibora-minded daughter running around acting mannish and mouthy.

So one evening, as they slowly drift together on the path from their fields to gather and talk at the river before returning home to their suppers, the men share knowing glances that this day is as good as any to inform her father, with great relish and alacrity, that the size of the mohar, the bride-price he can demand for his daughter to become another man's chattel, is fast diminishing. The men's tongues wag with feigned concern, but it is clear to all that her father's humiliation is their gleeful goal.

"Brother, don't you know how to keep the women in your house in they place?"

This is the ultimate indignity for a man in their world: to be seen as too weak to control his household. The shock that he, Aridai, should be the butt of such an accusation leaves him with neither retort nor reply. A bird could nest in his mouth. "Wha-a-a . . . ?" he sputters. "What you all talking about?"

The men are happy to answer. "That girl-child of yours. Your youngest."

"What's wrong with her?"

"Man, you better wake up and look outside them eyeballs. She's gib-ora. As gibora as the day is long and Romans is evil."

Every face wears a smirk that none tries to hide.

"Gibora? What you talking about? No girl-child of mine is gibora. You all know I don't take that off any female—woman or child! You all know that."

Aridai is on the defensive and the men know it. They lick their lips and the taunting begins in earnest.

"Well, all we know is that she's running around like she owns the world."

"Speak the truth, brother."

"The scripture says God made them male and female. But your girl is running around, jumping and talking out loud like she's a boy or something, like she's trying to go against the law of God."

"That's the sure-as-you're-born God's honest truth, Aridai. I don't allow my girl-children to play with her anymore. I'm afraid they'll get all messed up in their heads with all that gibora stuff, then I'd have to whip them, and I'd probably still end up getting little pitiful mohars for them anyway. And that's a headache I just don't need."

"The man ain't telling no lie. My son's not the marrying age yet, but if he was, you'd have to pay *him* a mohar bride-price to even think about putting up with that gibora-minded girl of yours, and a whole lot more

than them two broke-down cows and that jokable billy-goat you got."
The men's laughter is loud and raucous.

"That's right, Aridai. Brother, you shouldn't even think about nobody paying you a price for that bride. You're gonna have to give that girl away for free. And that's if you're lucky."

"And even then won't nobody take her!"

They hoot and holler and laugh until they cry.

Aridai storms off to the men's torturous laughter, too humiliated to answer. He rushes to the fringe of underbrush skirting the riverbank. He begins to forage furiously, fuming an anger that is red-eyed and vengeful, mortified enough that his honor has been brought into question, but even more that his name has been brought low by a girl-child, a girl-child who does not know her place. He is a laughingstock because of a girl-child. What could be more shameful than that? A man that cannot control his sons is bad enough. Still, that is explainable, understandable, forgivable; it does not present the same threat to a man's honor. After all, they are boys, and boys are supposed to be gibora-brave and assertive; boys are even expected to act up and act out sometime—that is, if they are to become real men. But a man unable to control his womenfolk—that is no man at all.

In full sight of the men he angrily tears at saplings and long-armed shrubs for a supple switch, a cutting, stinging, whelp-raising, scream-inducing switch. How dare a girl-child of his shame his name? He will cut the gibora clean out of her. With a branch slender and supple and long enough to *crack* like a whip and *slash* like a knife, he storms off.

His first stop is the rock outcropping in the midst of the fields. "Where is that little gibora-minded girl-child of mine?" he growls at the startled children at play there.

They stare back in timid silence, all but Izevel, who answers with barely disguised delight. "She's with Ma Tee. She said she was going to Ma Tee."

As he stomps off, Izevel turns to the other children with high-chinned smugness. "See. I told you. You all think she so brave and everything, but all she is, is some old gibora thing about to get her hiney tore up. I told you. Hummph."

There is fury in his burning breath. His hot angry feet seem to scorch every blade of grass they touch. Slow, lazy dogs scamper from his ire. Goats and chickens scatter in instinctual dodging. With each step he is angrier, held more tightly by a vengeance wide-eyed and stalking. He grips the switch until his knuckles ache, with every other step cutting the still, silent air with its *whiiish*ing sharpness.

Aridai is a study in sinewed rage when he finds her in the yard grinding wheat with her mother and Ma Tee. He is already upon them before they see him. The women flinch fearfully as the fierceness of his gait and the violent *sssst* of the switch announce that one of them is about to be the object of violence.

Her mother screams, certain that she is to be the target of his brutality now as ever. She runs into the thin darkness of their hut to cower among her pots and few household implements, hoping to spare herself the humiliation of yet another public beating. Aridai does not notice her flight. His angered eyes are fixed upon his daughter, the cutting vengeful gibora-flayer jumping in his hand.

Ma Tee sees the dangerous wildness in his eyes. She knows it well. It is the same wild rush that erupted in the face of his father when he raised his fists to her. An old chill walks her spine. "Boy, what do you think you're doing?" she screams.

"Get out my way, Mama!" he hisses through his clenched teeth.

His fury is torrential, high-crested. It covers him in waves angry and unrelenting, washing away every grain of reason, every spark of familial compassion. Rage disfigures his face. Dull angry sweat drips from his thick red-brown beard. Wrath-narrowed eyes peer from his freckled reddish face. His mouth is an angry knot of full twisted lips. He has lost his prayer cap in his rampage; his reddish hair stands nappy and defiant. Broad-lipped and wide-nosed, Aridai is of medium height and build, yet in his consuming anger he seems larger, thick with violence and power. He lunges for his daughter, cutting at her with the long switch. Ma Tee grabs her tunic front and slings her away as the switch cuts the air like a sword. *Whiiish.* It catches Ma Tee's left cheek. A sliver of blood trickles toward her chin. Her granddaughter screams at the blood and at her father's bloodletting fury. In his hurt and rage he is aware of neither.

"Come here, girl!" he bellows, flailing the switch again, this time cutting Ma Tee's arm. Still the old woman keeps herself between them.

"What did she do? What did she do?" Ma Tee screams. "Why do you want to beat this child like this?"

He drops his arm and looks at Ma Tee with such whorling wrath that her flesh crawls. His eyes so bulge with hatred it seems they will burst. His voice is coarse and hot with betrayal and hurt. Sweat and tears write dark ragged lines in the field dust that covers his face.

"I never had one son!" he shouts. A stifled sob lurches in his voice. "The scripture says that a man with sons is blessed, but not me. Both times a girl-child. But I didn't kill none of them, did I? Lots of men kill girl-children if they're born before a son. They think firstborn girls are bad luck, and they're probably right, too. Still, I didn't kill none of them. You all begged me to let them live, so I just went on along. Every time a girl-child, but I just went on along. Could have divorced that woman"—he gestures angrily toward the girl's mother cowering inside the hut—"and took me another wife to get me some sons. But no. I just went on along handling my business like a man. But not one son! Not one. The men started questioning my manhood, but I just went on handling my business. And little by little the other men started seeing me for the full-blown man that I am. Sons or no sons, I had my women in check and my household was run like a man is supposed to. The other men had to respect me. But after all these years of earning respect, I get to the river today and the men are laughing at me like I'm no man at all. Talking about how this girl-child here"—he gestures sharply with his switch—"been out dishonorizing my name, growing up all mouthy and gibora-minded like she's a man-child or something, like Eve didn't come from Adam. Now the men are looking at me like I'm some kind of fool who doesn't know how to be the rosh of my own household. I won't have it! I'll kill her first!"

The fury that seemed to nudge toward sorrow instead flares again. Sobbing and cursing, he claws at Ma Tee to get at his screaming daughter. The three circle in a frantic dance, their feet shuffling in low explosions of dust, him reaching, striking, cutting, Ma Tee flinching at each arc of the slicing switch, desperately spinning the cringing, terrified girl out of his reach like an endangered puppet.

"Stop it! Stop it!" she screams. "Stop it! Don't you beat this child!"

"She's mine!" Aridai half-bellows, half-sobs. "And I'll kill her before I'll let her disrespect my name."

Ma Tee whirls and parries as he snatches at the little girl. "Stop it!" she cries. "Stop it, I say!"

Whiiingg! She flinches hard as the swift sharpness of the switch again scars the air.

"No!" he sobs. "This child is gibora-minded and I'm going beat it out of her just as sure as you're born!"

Rage has become Aridai's sovereign, but resolution will conquer rage. At first his wrath terrified Ma Tee. But as its contours become clearer, its deadly promise demystified by what it did not do, her fear and shock turn into the hardened resolve that puts fear at bay.

"No, you are not!" Ma Tee's voice was suddenly firm. "You're not going to beat this little child. You cut her with that switch, and she's liable to be scarred up for life. No. You better just go somewhere and cool yourself down, cause you're not going to beat this child today."

Ma Tee is willing to protect the child from him with her life, but she knows that Aridai is right. Her granddaughter is too gibora, too free-spirited, her spirit too unshackled for her time and place. Ma Tee has always known it would come to this. She grabs a handful of Aridai's tunic front and presses her face toward his. "But you're right."

Aridai tries to pull away but Ma Tee does not let go. "Listen to me. You're right!"

This time he hears her. It seems that he is beginning to calm, though his chest still heaves and his face is still a reddish mask of fevered emotion.

"You're right," she says again, with less urgency this time, but no less firmly. She is panting from exertion and fear and determination. "This child is too gibora. She is."

The little girl cannot believe her ears.

As she feels his rage become less mountainous, Ma Tee points to the switch in her son's hand. "Give it to me."

Aridai lifts the sharp switch shoulder high as if to strike again. He is breathing heavily once more. "You must be out of your natural-born mind. She's mine and I'm going to whip her right. I'm not going to have gibora nowhere in my household disrespecting me."

"Give it to me," Ma Tee repeats, as sternly as before. "I'll take care of her." She moves her face closer and repeats the words slowly and insistently. "I will take care of her."

Aridai turns his face fully away, as if Ma Tee's words bear a stench. When he looks at her again his breathing is less furious. He stiffly holds out the slender branch.

"Alright." His voice is a venomous hiss. "Alright, Mama. You beat her."

He looks at the child with a rage that makes her cringe even more. "You beat her. But you better get her straight. Because I will kill her dead before I let some girl-child of mine go around dishonoring my name."

He begins to stomp off, but abruptly turns toward the darkened entrance to his hut. "Woman!" he calls. "Get out here and finish cooking my supper." Then he is gone.

Ma Tee wipes the dust and sweat from her eyes. The terrified child's gaze alternates between the path that might at any moment bring back her enraged father and the terrifying switch in her grandmother's hand. When he does not reappear, she turns to Ma Tee, fearful and wide-eyed. The old woman melts at the fear in her eyes. She tosses the branch into the crude clay oven and hugs the trembling child hard, then half-sits, half-flops in the dust, cradling her granddaughter in her lap.

"You know Ma Tee's not going to whip her baby," she says softly, her face pressed against her granddaughter's tear-sodden cheek.

The little girl suddenly pulls away. "You're bleeding, Ma Tee! You're bleeding!"

The old woman daubs with her head covering at the slivers of blood on her cheek and arms. They have already begun to scab.

"It's alright, child. It's alright." Ma Tee shakes her head ruefully. "It's just that he's gotten so mean and evil that I don't know him anymore. That's why Oholibamah won't come around. Can't stand to see the way he treats your mama and can't stand him."

For a moment they slump together in fearful relief. Then the receding terror rears its head again.

"What I do, Ma Tee?" Her whole body trembles. "Why he want to beat me, Ma Tee? Why? Did I do a erwat dabar or something? Why, Ma Tee? Why?"

Ma Tee does not answer. The two of them, old woman and woman-to-be, grandmother and terrified seed of her own seed, sit trembling in the dust, clinging to each other in fear and exhaustion and desperation and relief. Ma Tee's tears, at first only a heaving, a catching of her breath, become moans of anguish, moans of her own remembered pain, moans for the pain lying in wait for this tender young life that she loves so dearly. She pounds the dust with her fist and turns to her granddaughter.

"I told you about your gibora self."

She grabs the little girl and shakes hard. "I told you, didn't I? I told you to be careful. I told you to stop all this running around and smiling at everybody and acting like you're free. You are not free. You are a girl-child. You are to walk through this life, not run. You are to be quiet, to lower your gaze and speak when you're spoken to. You are not a bird. You cannot fly. Menfolks won't let you. If you try, they'll pluck all your pretty feathers and leave you flopping on the ground. You are a girl-child. You are to act like a turtle. You are to walk slow like a turtle. Be quiet like a turtle. Be thick-skinned like a turtle. If you're going to make it through this life with anything like peace, whenever men are around go back into your shell and stay there. And if you're lucky, whatever husband you end up with will leave you be."

Ma Tee shakes the little girl again, so hard the girl's head bobs. Tears and silver streams of mucus dot the child's tunic front.

"You are not a bird, you little gibora-minded thing, you. You are a girl-child. To men you're not a sun or a star with brightness of your own. To them you're nothing but a moon, a moon that depends on men for light. That's all any of us are to men, just turtles and moons. I've told you over and over: be careful how you live. Now you know why. These men will break you if you're not watchful, or spend every day trying. If you're careful, you might avoid it. If you're not, you'll get a whole lot more than your daddy just tried to give you."

Ma Tee rises and leads her granddaughter inside her own low-ceilinged hut standing just yards away. She eases onto the bed mat, then desperately cradles the child in her lap.

"Baby," her tone is soft again. Exhaustion makes her voice even softer.

"Ma Tee loves you just as you are, baby. I don't want to change anything about you. But you're going to have to change. You're going to have to be careful how you live." Ma Tee sighs. "You're going to have to be careful."

They cry and hug until the lessening sunlight calls them fearfully back to the grindstone and the wheat and the breadmaking that awaits them.

Chapter
3

That is how she grows to womanhood: carefully. Careful how she lives. Careful to defer, careful to self-deprecate, careful to put men's thoughts and interests above her own. Careful to do as she is told. Careful to appear to be less than she really is. Careful to learn the place assigned to her. Careful to stay in it.

Despite her carefulness, the savage raiment of self-reproach does not fit well; for all her attempts at stifling her own spirit, the vestment of all-the-time carefulness still hangs upon her like loose flesh unacquainted with bone. She does her best to wear it, to fully fit into it, but she just cannot understand why the world so imperiously calls her to be careful of her every breath. So it becomes for her a rote thing, this carefulness. Despite the slowing of her own steps, the clipping of her own wings, there remain spaces beneath the suffocating cloak of village life in which she still instinctively poises for flight. In spite of all her efforts of caution and self-abnegation, the garment of careful just does not fit; her spirit chafes at its seams.

She cannot confide her struggle to Ma Tee who, in her fear of the harm that can befall an uncareful girl-child, admonishes her now if even her eyes twinkle. And she certainly cannot whisper her doubts to her mother, the silent broken woman who avoids questions like death. For both, careful is a woman's sole garment of safety. Only to Mr. Ishmael can she confide her inner conflict. Mr. Ishmael, her friend and confidant, who loves her as she is. He has sadly watched the gradual stunting of her spirit, and has mourned the creeping demise of the brave little girl that he knew. She finds him, as always, humming psalms to the Lord, kneeling, hands deep in the earth like prayer, with Mr. Pop silently toiling nearby.

Mr. Ishmael looks up as she approaches. "My little friend-girl!"

Mr. Pop waves.

"Shalom, Mr. Pop," she calls out, easing into Mr. Ishmael's doting embrace.

"Where's my—?"

She kisses his cheek before his words can hit air. He creakily squats before her with his ever-present smile. She is not smiling.

"Mr. Ishmael—"

The pain he sees in her eyes causes his smile to straighten. Worry washes over him. He takes the little girl's hands in his own. He looks over at Mr. Pop, but his attention is fixed on the work of his hands.

"Mr. Ishmael, what's wrong with me?"

The old man could cry. It has come, the madness of the men, the madness that moves them to devalue women and women to devalue themselves. He had hoped against hope that it would spare her, but it is clear that this dread disease of the spirit has insinuated itself into her young heart, already causing her to cast aspersions on herself.

"There's nothing wrong with you, sweetie pie." He forces a smile. "What makes you think something is wrong with a sweet little friend-girl like you?"

The little girl does not smile. With her free hand she distractedly explores the white woolly beard. "Nobody likes me, Mr. Ishmael. Nobody."

"Now, that's not true, little friend-girl. I like you and so does Phinehas, and I'm sure a whole lot of other people do besides. Right, Phinehas?" Mr. Pop's silence indicates that he is not in earshot.

"But everybody else is always mean to me. Calling me gibora-girl and stuff. Even my daddy is mad at me. One day he almost whipped me real bad with a tree switch just for being me and playing and stuff. Even Ma Tee been telling me to act different."

"What does your mama say about it?"

"My mama don't say much no more. She's real scared of my daddy. And she gets scared if I ask her any questions, 'specially if my daddy's around."

She lets go his beard and looks at him through eyes broken with hurt. "Mr. Ishmael, what's wrong with me that makes everybody so mean to me?"

The old man frowns hard, as if to will his words into her heart. "There's nothing wrong with you," he repeats with a sigh. He is suddenly very tired. "Nothing. You're just *nephesh,* full of life, that's all. It's not you those folks are mad at. They're just mad because they want to keep things a certain way. Men nowadays have the sad idea that women and girls aren't supposed to be nephesh, to have as much life, as much spirit, as a man, because men need to feel in control of things. I guess a brave girl-child makes them afraid they might lose that control. They see you laughing and running and being brave and—I don't know—it just frightens them, I guess, that they might not be able to control you like they want when you grow into a woman. That's why men act so angry when they see a brave little girl-child like you. And the women . . ." He shrugs. ". . . I guess women are just going along to get along. But that doesn't mean all women. Some of them do stand up, but they pay a terrible price for it. Beatings, divorce . . ." His voice trails off.

"But why men have to be bossin' everybody, Mr. Ishmael?"

He shakes his great wool-framed head. "I don't really know. I guess they have to feel in control of something because the world seems so out of control for them. And it could have something to do with the scriptures, too. The scriptures do give men rights they don't give to women."

"Yeah, Mr. Ishmael? Like what?"

"Like divorce."

"Divorce." She ponders. "Divorce means a man can put a woman out her house, but women can't put men out. Right, Mr. Ishmael?"

"I guess that's right, sweetie pie."

She nods her small head knowingly. "Ma Tee told me that. But why, Mr. Ishmael? Why the scriptures say men can put women out but women can't put men out?"

"I don't know."

She looks away for a moment, then turns back to the old man. "But ain't the scriptures from God, Mr. Ishmael?"

"Yes. That's what our people have always believed."

"Well, if the scriptures is from God and they let men do things but not women, then don't that mean God likes men better? Huh, Mr. Ishmael?"

He is very tired. His heart weighs a ton. "No, sweetie. It doesn't mean that at all. It can't. Our God is fair and just and loves everybody—man, woman, and child."

He smiles a tired smile. "That means you, too, little friend-girl." He pinches her nose. "God loves you"—he scoops her into his arms—"and you know Mr. Ishmael loves you, too."

She laughs as the old man playfully engages her, not her usual convulsive giggles, but an empty, polite laugh congealed with worry and confusion. Mr. Ishmael feels the heaviness of her spirit and blows funny air noises on her to lighten it, but she is not cheered. He sets her down. Her hand is still in his. She turns her toe in the dark earth of the old man's garden.

"But what I'm gonna do, Mr. Ishmael, to stop everybody from being mad at me and stuff? I don't know how to be somebody else. What I'm gonna do?"

Mr. Ishmael again pulls her within hugging distance. "I don't know, sweetie pie. We just have to pray on it, I guess. When everything else fails, God is still in the prayer-answering business."

"But Mr. Ishmael, women be praying all the time, but men still be sending them out their houses and beating them and everything. Some of the girls say their mothers don't pray no more at all, except when their daddies be looking, cause their mothers say God don't seem to hear women's prayers no more."

The old man nods gravely. "I know. When my Elisheva was alive, God rest her soul, she used to tell me about that—about some of the women not praying anymore. It's a sure enough shame. But then she said that some of the women started praying in a different way. They started getting together to pray to another part of God. They started praying to a feminine divine, what they called the woman-side of God."

The little girl's eyes light up. Her sudden interest surprises Mr. Ishmael.

"Oh yeah," he goes on. Her response has reinvigorated him. "This went on a good little while, until a few years ago when the men found out about it and raised a terrible fit. Sure was shameful. Women didn't seem to bother with it much after that."

The little girl is captivated. "The woman-side of God, Mr. Ishmael? There's a God who's a woman?"

"No, sweetie, not another God." He chuckles. "They were talking about another aspect of God, another side of the one true God that our people have worshiped since the time of Abraham, hallelujah, amen."

"But how is that, Mr. Ishmael? That God has some kind of woman-side or sumpin, I mean? Ain't God an old man? An old man with a beard?"

He laughs. "An old man with a beard, like me?"

She shrugs. "I guess so. You do got a beard."

"Well," he says, bemused, "that is what some people think—that God is a man with a beard. That's what they say, but that doesn't mean it's true. To me, God is just God. Not man, woman, or child. Just God, the master and creator of everything and everybody, hallelujah, amen."

"Well," she says, her little face pinched with intensity, "if God's not a man or woman, then why women be praying to the woman-side of God? I mean, if God ain't a man or a woman and stuff."

"I don't know, sweetie pie. I guess they do it because the scriptures say everybody was made in God's image. Since women are made a little different from men . . ." He cups his big hands at arm's length like two huge breasts. A giggle, a small one, finally spills from her. Mr. Ishmael feels victorious. "Since women are different from men, not just built differently but, seems to me, act and think in some ways different from men, then there must be a side of God that women were made in the image of. My Elisheva never really explained it to me. She did say that some of the women used to pray to the woman-side of God because they thought that maybe that way God would hear the prayers that just didn't seem to be getting through, like changing men's hearts and healing their pain."

"Yeah, Mr. Ishmael? You think the woman-side of God would hear

women's prayers better than they be getting heard now?" she asks excitedly. "How? How you pray to her—I mean, to the woman-side of God?"

"Now calm down, sweetie pie. Calm down. That I don't know.
Women didn't talk to men about that; it would have gotten them nothing but trouble. But I did hear my Elisheva call out a name sometimes.
It was . . . seems like it was Hokmah. Yes, I think that's what they called
this woman-side of God: Hokmah. It's a woman's name that means
'wisdom.' My Elisheva said some of the scriptures of the Jews—the
folks that live up in Galilee and down south in Judea—she said some of
their scriptures, like the Book of Proverbs, talk about this Hokmah or
woman-side of God. She said some of the women used to get together
and pray and recite them. That's all I know. But go ask your Ma Tee.
She can tell you. She'll know."

The little girl draws aimless circles with her sandled foot as she tries
to make sense of it all. She speaks without looking up.

"Mr. Ishmael, Ma Tee says that all girls and women are is turtles and
moons." She kicks at a fast-moving ant. "But I don't want to be no turtle.
Or no moon, neither. I just want people to stop messing with me all the
time. I just want people to treat me like everybody else. Like there ain't
nothin wrong with me."

"Your Ma Tee is telling you the best she knows how, sweetie pie.
She's just trying to protect you, that's all. She thinks she is telling you
how to keep people from wanting to bother you and treat you differently. But go ask Ma Tee about this Hokmah, sweetie pie. Maybe finding out something about this Hokmah will be a helpful comfort to you."

"Alright," she says. "I'll ask her."

The old man hugs her again. She starts off, then turns back to him. "I
wish you was my daddy, Mr. Ishmael," she says, her whole face a wish.

Mr. Ishmael fights to hold his smile. He looks to Mr. Pop for support, but he is engrossed with muskmelons. "You already have a daddy,
little friend-girl. A good daddy."

"I know, Mr. Ishmael. But he don't like me like you do."

He beckons her back to his thick-armed embrace. His voice is husky.
"Now, sweetie pie, your daddy likes you. I'm sure he loves you. He's just
hurt and confused, that's all, like so many of the men."

"I know, Mr. Ishmael. But the Romans beat you, too. And you're not all hurt and mean."

"I'm hurt, sweetie pie." He pauses as jagged memories of swords and whips and bloodletting intrude upon him. "It just didn't make me mean, that's all. Not all men react the same."

"I guess so, Mr. Ishmael."

She gently eases out of his half-embrace. "Well, I gotta go now." She pecks his white-bearded cheek and is on her way. A few steps down the path she turns to face him again. "I still wish you was my daddy," she calls, then sets off for home.

"So do I," he whispers as he limply raises his hand to wave. "Lord have mercy, child. So do I."

He realizes that he is crying. "Phinehas, I sure do love that child," he says softly, expecting no response.

"Me, too," answers Mr. Pop, careful to hide the tears in his voice. He has heard every word.

Chapter

4

She usually followed the guidance of Mr. Ishmael gladly and without question, but not this time. Nor can she speak to Ma Tee of any of it; this she knows with certainty. For it is Ma Tee who has so diligently labored to secure the careful stifling garments around her, the slowing, quieting, shriveling village vestments, drawing them almost too tight for breath whenever they even hinted of loosing. In her subordination of her granddaughter's spirit to the demigod of stolid fearful carefulness, Ma Tee has been diligent and unrelentingly watchful. Whenever the little girl spoke her mind, Ma Tee shushed her and told her good girls (that is, careful girls) don't do that. When she skipped too freely or laughed too spiritedly, Ma Tee shook her till her teeth clicked. At every turn the words of Ma Tee and the expressive touch of her rough hands spoke to the little girl, took root deep within her, weighed upon her like stones, lovingly but relentlessly goaded and guided her. *Be careful how you live.* The vestment grew tighter and tighter, stifling and shriveling her, forcefully reshaping her, squeezing the very spirit from her. In the fierce wake of Ma Tee's desperate love, the girl's gibora *ruah,* that spirit of spunk and boldness that had so naturally been hers, slowly threw up its hands, defeated, bloodless, ready to die the death so vigorously willed to it by so many.

Indeed, it seemed that everything in her world conspired against her spirit. Even her sometime playmates lent their hands to break her, repeating the disdainful assessments offered by their fathers.

"Gibora girl! Gibora girl!" they taunted. Called her mannish and ugly. Called her not-gonna-get-you-no-husband-cause-my-daddy-say-you-don't-know-your-place-old-gibora-thing.

The torturous, confounding words of her peers, of everyone, thick and rancid, rained upon her every step like refuse. The ferocity of the onslaught so whelped and scarred her that instinctively she began, of her own anguished volition, to pull close the careful, cautious garments for relief from the whirlwind of torment, the whirlwind of ridicule and loneliness, the windstorm of self-doubt and self-reproach that engulfed her.

Still she suffered deeply. Suffered until her every breath and movement, in their brevity of range and grasp, finally announced in the urgent choreography of defeat that she, too, was displeased by that very thing that displeased her tormentors so; suffered until her vacant eyes announced that she, too, saw gibora as a demon presence come only to disturb the old village air and torture her very life; suffered until she finally understood the self she had been from birth as so unnatural in the trenchant sight of God that men and their small daughters rightfully cast their stones upon her like a hen that crowed when it should have laid. Her suffering and her struggle ended when the encroaching doubt in all its pernicious finality devoured her, and with a cry of resignation and relief she at long last reached for the shackles prepared for her before birth. And walked on feet weighted with graceless admonitions.

The long seasons of Ma Tee's tortured love took their purposed toll. Reduced the old woman, tired and worn, to permanent defeated recline, laid thin and listless upon the creaking husking straws of her bed mat. Yet even in her incorrigible wasting-all-day decline, the march of the memories she cannot suppress begrudge her full peace. Since her first blush of womanhood so long ago, peace has seldom been her guest. She is tired of the struggle to find it. So when she hears slovenly death's whispered promise of peace, she does not turn a deaf ear. "I am ready," she says. "I am ready."

With waning strength Ma Tee sets forth her few possessions, the accumulated trinkets of a sad, long life, in neat array and places them in a small wooden box: a cracked wooden comb, a finely spun yellow cotton scarf, colored stones, bits of broken jewelry, dried sprigs of fragrant herbs, a tiny pot of oil scented with thyme. She calls her beloved granddaughter to her side. Her breath is thin.

"Dear heart, you'll soon be the age of betrothal. You've grown to know your place, so any day now young men will be coming to ask your daddy for your hand . . ." She catches her breath. "Ma Tee tried my best, baby. I have tried. I've tried to teach you what you needed to know to get you ready. I've tried to do a good job, but only the Lord knows if I've succeeded." She again pauses for breath. "Is there anything you want to ask Ma Tee?"

Ever since her talk with Mr. Ishmael, her granddaughter has harbored the question she has not dared to ask before now.

"Yes, ma'am. There is." She swallows hard. "What is . . . what is Hokmah?"

The old woman's eyes widen with surprise. "Child, what do you know about Hokmah?"

"Nothing, really. I-I . . . ," she stutters. "Mr. Ishmael said I should ask you."

Ma Tee begins to fuss—"That Ishmael! . . ." But her words in that coarse awful voice of almost-death hold resignation more than recrimination. "Well, I guess you were bound to hear about it sometime. I'm surprised you don't remember."

Her bony hand pats the bed mat for her granddaughter to sit.

"A lot of the women got all worked up over this Hokmah, but it wasn't anything but something to get women's hopes up and cause them pain. That's some of what got your mama in such bad shape. She was already beginning to be bad off, but she didn't become completely scared-natured until your father found out about this Hokmah thing and went off on her like that was what made people's crops fail . . ."

She nods off for a moment, then slowly shakes her head to clear it. "Don't you remember when your mama used to take you to the river and all the women were there singing and everything?"

"Yes, ma'am, I do. Sort of. But I was little. I thought that was just singing and grown-woman talk."

"No, baby. It was a whole lot more than that. Women used to have secret gatherings there at the river, almost like Sabbath meetings, singing and praying like God is a woman with woman feelings. It was something."

Her eyes light for a moment, then darken again. "But then the men found out and, oh Lordy! did a whole lot of women suffer for it." She raises up slightly.

"Suffered for nothing. Suffered for something that doesn't make sense. Because if God does have a woman-side, then why don't women have any say-so in their own lives? If there is a woman-side to God, then why do men have all the power? Power over life and death even, like men are gods themselves."

She weakly shakes her head to clear it. "No, child. Leave that Hokmah stuff alone. Please. You've finally learned how to do right, so please just leave well enough alone. Just stay careful and you won't need any of that Hokmah stuff. Just stay careful, and leave well enough alone."

Her granddaughter answers slowly. It is clear she is not fully convinced. "I'll try, Ma Tee."

The old woman is suddenly half-sitting. Her bony arms and looping sinews are taut black ropes. "Don't try—do it! You don't want to end up broken down like your mama, do you? Do you want to end up like her, beaten down into nothing, walking around like a flinching ghost?"

The startled girl shakes her head.

"Then be careful and stay careful. Live careful. Do you hear me?"

She answers quickly and fearfully. "Yes, ma'am. I will. I will."

The taut ropes become shaking ebony cornstalks; the cornstalks give way, flopping Ma Tee back onto her bed mat.

"Come here, baby," the old woman says weakly. She reaches for her granddaughter's hand, straining to look at her without betraying that

her own eyes are nearly useless now. She points to the box and arrange-
ment of objects on the dirt floor. "These are for you."

"Why, Ma Tee?"

"Because Ma Tee is tired, baby. I don't know how much longer I have
in this world."

Her granddaughter is aghast. "No, Ma Tee. No! You're not going to
leave me. You'll get better. You will. You'll see."

Ma Tee smiles a thin, tired smile. "No, I won't. No. It's Ma Tee's
time. I want to go, baby. Ma Tee is tired. I'm tired. I have borne enough
blows to the heart for any two women."

One of her cornstalks raises a veined bony hand to the girl's brow.
"Don't cry, child. We have loved each other hard, haven't we?"

"Yes, Ma Tee. Hard." She buries her face in the old woman's breast.
"Hard," she says, and weeps until no more tears come.

Except to fetch food and water or to remove the unwanted wastes of
their living, she does not leave her grandmother's side for days, sitting
with her in the musty half-light of her hut, listening to the old woman's
life slowly leave her.

Her father looks in on them briefly each day, at dawn and at dusk.
Each time he asks, "How's she doing?" Each time he receives the same
response: "She's fading, Daddy." And each time he leaves them quickly.
Leaves them, the one whose seed he is and the one who is his seed. He
once knew another way, before his voice changed and the men claimed
him from his mother's arms, before his tenderness was beaten into
something he could no longer embrace or even touch. Now he knows
only one way to love them, and that is to leave. Leave them to the care
of their own spirits. Leave them so he might bear his sorrow alone.

In the delirium of her death throes, Ma Tee's fevered mind empties
through her mouth. Feverish words, snippets of things long forgotten.
Old ghosted scenes crying out memories. Hobbling, unanswered hopes.
Vivid happinesses. Tunes and songs and chants that call from childhood.

One rusted tune in particular falls from her lips softly, unthinkingly, at
first like the spittle of sleep, then louder, harder, brittle like almost brass.

Does not Hokmah call out? . . .
"To you, O people, I call,
and my cry is to all that live,
O simple ones, learn prudence;
acquire intelligence, you who lack it.
Hear, for I will speak noble things,
and from my lips will come what is right . . .
Take my instruction instead of silver,
and knowledge rather than choice gold;
for Hokmah is better than jewels,
and all that you may desire cannot compare with her."

The strength of this chant, which marches out of Ma Tee's delirium whereas the others only crawled, perks her granddaughter's ear. "What's that you're singing, Ma Tee?"

The old woman half-opens her eyes. "Huh? Oh nothing, child." She touches the heat of her own brow. "Whew. I'm so light-headed I'm just singing all out my head."

A faint excitement peeks through the thick translucence of her granddaughter's sorrow. "You said *Hokmah,* Ma Tee. Was that a Hokmah song? Was that a song about the woman-side of God?"

Ma Tee fades out, then back. "Huh? Oh. I'm just talking all out my head. Baby, you just forget about that Hokmah talk. Leave it alone. I'm just talking out my head, is all."

At length, recognition again lights Ma Tee's face, and she struggles to sit, supporting herself on those veined black weathered cornstalks. Her voice is raspy and strained like old wood creaking. She looks at her grandchild through half-closed eyes, her face flooded with sorrow.

"I did what I could. I did what I could to get you ready for it. For marriage. For this man's world. I worked hard to take that gibora out of you. Running around. Talking and laughing loud and acting carefree. And all those questions. Men don't like questions."

She halts to gulp the air, then speaks in a desperate torrent. "I loved your gibora spunk, I did. It did me and all the women good to see a girl-child with some fire. But I couldn't let you go on like that. I knew it wouldn't serve you well, so I helped to break it out of you. I did. It hurt me so bad always to be on you, always fussing, always complaining, always putting you down. But better me than some hard-fisted man."

She is sobbing in that weak, thin way on the cusp of black-holed death. The raspiness sounds like a stick lodged in her throat, like a distant ass braying beneath her every word and breath. "All that spunk and spirit you had."

She wheezes harder now, speaking with a rushed unnatural rhythm. "I wish you could . . . have conquered the world . . . but spirit . . . in a woman . . . won't do . . . anything . . . but . . . get you beaten . . . or put . . . outdoors just remember: this . . . is . . . a man's world . . . right or wrong got . . . nothing to do with it . . . if you want . . . to get along, go . . . along . . . don't talk back . . . and just do . . . what you're told . . ."

She chokes back a cry. Her face is a mask of unfathomable sadness. "I'm so sorry . . . I helped . . . to break you . . . dear . . . heart, but I . . . had to. I had to." She lies back, her life draining from her, and weeps.

Ma Tee died soon thereafter, on the very day her younger granddaughter, her favorite, turned twelve, the age at which tradition declared her ripe to become a husband's chattel. In death, Ma Tee's still silent face reflected the small solace that her prayers were answered: she was taken before having to see her sweet child given to what she herself had finally known marriage to be: a misery of erwat dabars, sepher kerituts, undeserved beatings, and lingering loneliness; held together, if at all, by the thread of a woman's deadened expectations and the extent of her capacity for suffering.

And so she was married.

First they were boys, fulminating, incorrigible in their incorrigibility, fumbling lustfully in their skins hued of olive, pecan, date, and night, perched on the cusp of pubescence, their attention fastened upon the careful young almost woman with cinnamon flesh, smelling her, tasting her, at least wishing it so, yearning to know what they now could but imagine. In their panting distance they hovered after her like lost and wanton birds, longing to be closer yet not knowing how. Beautiful, demure, deferential, full-breasted, for her young would-be possessors she was the ultimate goad to agitated disconcertion and heat-fueled madness. Running, jumping, wrestling, risking moderate injury, shedding small amounts of blood, all in hopes of her attention, they were loosed yelping dogs in undeniable heat, speaking dutifully of marriage, but dreaming fitfully of sex.

Then they were young men, with only their strategies and more nuanced inanities for difference. No longer did they fight for her attention, nor did they compete to better their rivals in full and open view. Now they plotted courtships, nagged their fathers for mohar brideprices of competitive heft, and vowed, each of them, to best the others in the relentless race to possess her as his bride.

"Boy, you wait and see," said one. "She's definitely gonna be my wife! Fine young lady like that doesn't want no unspectacular fellas like you."

"I hear you talking," said the other. "But let me ask you a question. How is she going to think about somebody else with me walking around?"

"That's easy," replied the first. "She won't be thinking about somebody else—just me. And that's especially if she sees you walking around!"

"Well," said another, "you all can forget about her. That includes those that are here and those that ain't and those that wish they were, cause compared to me, all of you is ugly. Not only am I the handsomest Samaritan since Abraham heard from God, but my daddy's gonna put together a mohar bride-price that her daddy won't be able to refuse even if he wants to."

"Shoot, handsome never had a nose like yours," said the other one. "Anyway, your daddy's so poor you'll be lucky to marry a she-goat."

"Fellas! Fellas! Might as well stop working yourselves up into a sweat," said another still, "cause I'm the one and only who'll be sporting her hand when the Passover rolls around—as her husband, all day and all night. And particularly at night. While you fellas are home wettin' the bed, I'll be home sweatin' the bed!"

They laughed and fought, fought and laughed, all the same in their boyish lust and expectation, none actually having known the pleasures of which they dreamed, propelled instead by the curse of fecund imaginations into frenzies that only sleep could still; all indistinguishable in the torture of their unrequited lust, hating that no matter what their machinations, all that was left to them was to wait with their poorly feigned patience and their clumsy fevered hands. Except one. Although he shared their games, their companionship, their youth, he shared neither their innocence nor their benign intentions. His name was Jalon. He would be Her First, the first of the husbands whose beds she would share.

Jalon had been raised with the same admonitions, the same strictures, the same leaf-thin latitude accorded all the village youths. The contours of his life had differed little from theirs—until That Day, when the screaming village women were stolen away forever. He was a mother's son, a sister's sibling, until both were torn from him in that tragic maelstrom of Roman depravity. At first the hard soldiers, callous and insensate from their constant campaigns of brutality, had taken him along as well, clinging to his mother, bawling, hysteric, his impotent little fists flailing the grim soldiers, with his broken father, Ocran, just yards away, straining to rise on vanquished elbow and defeated knee, spewing vomit and blood and helpless invective.

The boy's screaming tears, his flailing, his wailing at the very height of his lungs took their toll upon the departing soldiers, who suddenly and disgustedly flung him from the cart that held his tied and trussed and sobbing female kin; those among the abductors that harbored the taste for boys agreed that not even the delicate pleasure of his young flesh was worth the aggravation of a grief so manic and overwrought. Then, in a sudden shock of finality, they were gone, captors and captives, rumbling away in a shrieking haze of terror and dread and an enveloping agony of loss.

It was at this moment, as if through stark and jolting realization, that the bereft five-year-old hysteric and his broken and bleeding progenitor became Father and Son. This new relationship—it was no longer "family" or "household," but now "Father and Son"—was more than relational; it codified a profound commitment, gave name to the excruciating mission of a father cleaved to the remaining remnant of the family he had not saved, bestowed unassailable title upon the bond he desperately believed to be his last chance for redemption as a protector and as a man. But more than that, "Father and Son" meant that Ocran would protect his boy in every way, reasonable or not, and exalt him far beyond the sons of others. So his persistent refrain, in that voice of constant bravado and overdone masculinity, became "My boy this" and "My boy that"—in tones so laudatory that he seemed to refer to a creature at whose feet all should kneel—as he sought to prove to himself and everyone he knew, by his construction of a tireless and assiduous facade of a son who surpassed all others in every way and every thing, that he himself was more, much more, than the Romans' crushing evil had portrayed him to be. This, then, is how Jalon, Her First, grew to almost manhood and beyond: indulged by a father who sought to give his son all that he asked, in the mistaken belief that somehow that would transform him into all that his father wished him to be.

Even as Ocran invented the redemptive fiction of a perfect son and himself as his perfect mentor, the identity Ocran needed most to redeem was that of protector. His selfless and heroic restraint, like that of all the men on That Day, had surely helped to save the village from slaughter. But what counted most for Ocran was not what he did That Day, but what he had failed to do. It was against this failure and nothing else that Ocran now measured himself. He thought back to Jalon's *berith,* his circumcision on the eighth day following his birth. He remembered how he'd held Jalon still as the foreskin was cut. How he'd dribbled new harvest wine into the infant's mouth to ease the pain. How he'd dressed the stinging wound with the wine and olive oil, terebinth balm and cumin. And how he'd vowed, as he soothed his son's cries, forever to protect him from hurt and harm, never to let anyone or anything again cause him to suffer, or deny him the best fruits of life. Now he vowed one thing more: that he would leave to no one else the deliverance of the last of those entrusted to him, not even to his solitary God.

Despite Ocran's consuming quest for redemption, however, somehow he managed to maintain at least the basic elements of a life. He had sleepwalked through the shock and the pain, the self-flagellation and hate that filled the months after That Day, yet beyond there he did not go. He did not descend into the drunken recriminations of some, nor into the fixed-eye torpor of others, mutely staring for hours at a span into a blurred and distant reality. He simply continued on, his pain still in tow, but now with a living squarely focused outside himself; his movements, his breathing, most of his thoughts, too, remained fastened upon fulfilling his self-proclaimed role of hedge of protection.

After months of head-hung mourning and furious cleaving to his son, one morning Ocran awoke to the sound of his own voice. "I must get back to living," he said, and he realized immediately, without a pang or a clue, that he had reconstituted himself as no longer a mourner or a man that clings, but at last as a studied and sober protector. When his amazement passed that he had indeed prevailed over the horror to whose spiteful evisceration he had once all but surrendered, it occurred to him that although, or maybe because, the Divine Presence appeared to have been anything but present on That Day, the fact of his return from the emotional abyss into which he had plunged was real and actual proof that God was now firmly back in the blessing business. So he began to call on the divine hand again, as much out of careful self-interest as of faith, and assumed the outwardly pious, self-justifying posture that the village men valued so highly. He resumed the utterance of loud prayers and wordy, prolonged table blessings at every offered opportunity, wiped his eyes with great flourishes of emotion when the Sabbath scripture was read, invoked the name of God often and much and without regard for the obvious transparency of his religiosity, and repented his blasphemous underestimation of divine omnipotence by conceding that deliverance and protection were indeed the province of the Almighty alone; it was just that with regard to his coddled and overindulged son, Ocran was sure that God had ceded the power of deliverance to him.

Now that Ocran felt himself alive, felt himself fully a man again, it was time to take another wife. Not for love or solace, for contrary to the vigorous counsel bequeathed him by the community of men, he had ventured to open his heart wide to the wife that was stolen from him, sharing his deepest self with her, but every bit of the love he managed in their years together had been wrested from him forever when he watched her and their firstborn trundled away to captivity. His need now was only for a woman to be helper, housekeeper, and that peculiar and tangential source of comfort that came not from what she did, but simply because she was there. So with little celebration and with even less feeling, he married a younger woman, Yedaiyah—a scandalized refugee of the spate of erwat dabar—induced divorces that erupted like sudden and multitudinous sores in the immediate aftermath of That Day, a woman who was herself deeply in need of redemption—in a numb and bloodless ceremony with neither kissing nor touch, not even a smile. Though bare of affection, this union gave each what was needed: he, a cook, a cleaner, a strong body for his field, a warm body for his bed; she, a hearty provider, an imagined champion, and the security and respectability of a roof she could call her own.

Ocran was prepared to abide by this dry and emotionless balance, as was Yedaiyah, to live with her, sleep with her, grunt to her over supper the gossip that masqueraded as village "news," offering her inflectionless comment on the progress of crops and livestock and gruff instructions for the next day's work before retreating to the emotional safety of sleep. But these were the only things Ocran would share with her; she would be allowed no further part in his life—and no part at all in the life of his son. This he made clear on her very first day in her new home.

At their first meal together, fresh barley bread and hummus and black olives and fine wheat-flour cakes dripping in honey, all lovingly and painstakingly prepared, Yedaiyah softly admonished her new son to practice good manners—"like civilized folks," she said with a goodnatured laugh, meaning only that he should sit still, talk less, and eat more. Ocran suddenly dashed his bowl to the hard dirt floor and shouted at her as if she had transgressed the most sacred of boundaries.

"That's *my* boy!" he bellowed with such venomous and frightening force that from that moment Yedaiyah cringed to think of giving Jalon even a querulous look, much less a spoken admonition. When her new almost son defiantly chimed in, "You're not my mama!" she realized that this home would never be fully her own, and resigned herself to an existence of thankless servitude and abiding superfluousness. As Ocran grunted atop her that night, unmindful of her tears and hurt because his own pain had long ago moved him past the point of caring, Yedaiyah reconciled herself to be cook and cleaner and washer of clothes for this coddled and indulged five-year-old center of the universe, but never his mother, or even the object of his respect.

When in ensuing years Yedaiyah saw signs of a growing perversity in the boy whose character was being shaped without the guidance or even the solace of women—the too long glances at her breasts, the too often accidental rubbing against them, the boyish hands that seemed to find new ways to brush her buttocks no matter how she turned to avoid him—she watched in fearful silence and wondered what manner of monster Jalon might become.

. . .

The grown folk of the village viewed the new relational dispensation of Father and Son with a strained and curious chagrin. They all knew Ocran's pain; many had been touched by comparable, even deeper loss. Still for Jalon, or for any child for that matter, to be so indulged by a parent was to them a clear and present wonder, for since the time of Moses the only logic they had known was that a child should honor his father and his mother, and not the other way around. At the elbow of the river, shaded and cooled by stands of poplar and willow, the men shared their estimations of this strange new development.

"Ocran's about to mess that boy up."

"Sure enough is. Nothing that boy ever do is wrong."

"That sure ain't no way to raise up a boy."

"But what you gonna do with a boy that his daddy won't let have a mama?"

"You sure don't make him think he's got more right to the tree of life than everybody else."

"You know you're right. Always talking about 'My boy this' and 'My boy that.' I got a boy, too, but you don't see me touting his every move."

"That's because your boy don't be doing much moving to be touting about."

"You saying my boy is lazy?"

"He's sure not vigorous."

"My boy is just relaxed, is all."

"Yeah. When it comes to work."

"Now wait a minute. My boy is just as good a worker as anybody's."

"We're just kidding you on, is all. We know he's a worker. But so is Ocran's boy. And as boys go, he's alright."

"I guess so. But no thanks to his worshipful daddy."

"Aw, Ocran's not so bad. All he does is spoil the boy."

"Well, I suppose you're right. But when you think about it, if spoiling that boy is Ocran's goal in life, he hasn't been too successful, has he? Cause that boy don't seem too messed up at all."

The men nodded in solemn agreement and turned back to more vexing concerns. For although he was coddled and accommodated, spoiled and indulged, Jalon did seem like the other boys. Like all the others, he worked. Everyone old enough to walk worked. After all, crops did not plant themselves, nor did livestock give milk or shear their wool on request. Everyone worked. Small boys brought drinks to their laboring parents and pulled weeds and insects from young plants in their rows; small girls carded wool with tiny hands and spun it; and on not yet steady legs infants followed harvesters to glean for their leavings. In a world in which to work was to live, Jalon was like all the others.

Unlike the others, however, the primary reason for Jalon's labor was not to wrest the cabbage from its earth, the wheat from its stalk, the date from the palm, or even to heed the timeless call of his people's abiding tradition of toil, for it was clear that these things his father would never require of him in any meaningful way. Instead, he was obliged, in a covenant unspoken yet mutually understood, to labor with the others simply so that the man whose progeny he was might have the pleasure of extolling the virtues of his son, real and imagined, to every listening ear. Every man in the village grew tired to hear, "My boy is young, but he works like a man." To the point of real exasperation they were told, "Jalon is a real worker; he plowed that whole field today," whether he really had or not, whether or not the conversation even had to do with work. And "My boy don't only work hard, but he works smart, too" was said so often that it got on nerves that most folks never knew they had.

The women had their own estimation of Jalon. In their weekly gatherings to wash at the shallows of the river, they shared their gossip and their news, lamented the newest mistreatment by their men, whispered secret hopes for the just intervention of God in their loveless marriages, and conversed openly about the new village wonder of Father and Son.

"Ocran acts like that boy is made of jewels."

"Jewels? More like gold. Jewels made of gold."

"But if it's made of gold, then it's not jewels."

"Uh-huh. And Jalon's not either."

"Try to tell his daddy that."

"Not me. I'm not thinking about disputing a daddy that spells *son* s-U-n."

"Me neither. The commandment says, 'Thou shalt have no other gods before me.' But Ocran is about to make his boy a god all alone by himself. And I'm sure not about to criticize no god."

"Lord, girl. You sure are blasphemous."

"Well, he must be a god. Gets everything he wants, doesn't he?"

"It sure seems like it."

"That's what I mean. He must be a god, cause a god has worshipers, and Lord knows that Ocran worships the ground that boy walks on."

"Umm-uh. Ocran won't ever have to make another sacrifice at Mount Gerizim again, cause he makes offerings each and every day—to that boy of his."

"Yeah. The boy probably got an altar instead of a bed mat."

"And you can be sure it's not no sacrifice-my-son altar like Abraham made for Isaac, either. Cause if Ocran even thinks something might harm that boy, he goes snatching and hopping like a jackrabbit in hyena country."

"And the way he won't let anyone ever discipline the boy but him."

"Not even Yedaiyah."

"I don't know how she lives like that."

"Hummph. Like any of us is living a whole lot better."

"But can't even discipline her own child?"

"It's not her child. It's his. And he doesn't ever let her forget it, either."

"Well, if I couldn't discipline him, I sure wouldn't cook for him. Clean neither."

"Then you'd better use the time you save to find a new place to live. Cause your man would be shouting 'erwat dabar' so fast it would make your head swim."

"That's why Yedaiyah should keep doing exactly what she's doing. At least that way she's got a roof over her head."

"And when you get down to it, the boy doesn't seem that bad."

"But Yedaiyah still doesn't seem that happy."

"So what's happy? Best to settle for safe and a roof over your head. That's happy to me."

"I guess so. But I sure do miss the way things were before That Day."

"We all do. Them old cuss-ed Romans took more from us than they'll ever know."

"Still, Jalon's not a bad child, considering."

"Considering what?"

"Considering he hasn't had a woman to love him since the Romans took his mama."

There. They'd named it, his true difference. Yet it still eluded them, the meaning of that difference for his life, the profundity of its effect upon him. Just to name his void did not tell how it made him who he was, how deeply it determined the gaps in his feeling for himself, and for others, too. Simply to pronounce what he'd been denied did not describe how it circumscribed what he could give and could not give, what he could and could not be. That is why, as if in unison, men and women alike could so easily season their assessments of Jalon, the son pedestaled by his father, with the assertion that was benign and affectionate and almost rote: "For a spoiled child, he's not so bad." They looked for no signs of troubled youth and saw none, blinded as they were by what they could not know: that the place within him that should hold love or warmth or at least the intimation of empathy, instead held nothing at all. His was a soul stripped and stunted by a tragedy of two dimensions. The one, the scarcity and brevity of women's love and succor in his life. The other, the perverse and secret sensuality with which he tried to fill that void.

Like others of the men, Ocran spent the first growing season after That Day healing from his horrendous beating, which prevented him from spending significant time tending his fields. The little crop he managed to produce was barely enough to feed the boy and himself, much less enough to garner a trader's crop, and with no surplus there was no reason to travel for trade. For the several seasons that followed, although he was by then hale and well and his harvests hearty, Ocran was unwilling to leave the village for fear of encountering the marauding Roman soldiers who intimidated and abused sojourners on the mercantile routes and robbed them of their goods. By the trading season of the

boy's eighth year the rogue soldiers had moved on to ply their lawless-
ness elsewhere; on the Samaritan routes they had accosted neither
traders nor pilgrims for some time. With a bursting harvest in and laid
by, the men decided it was finally time to again mount a caravan to the
bustling trading town of Shechem that lay at the foot of the holy mount
of Gerizim, as had their fathers and their fathers before them for seasons unnumbered. The men's excitement filled the air as they drew lots
to determine who would travel and who would mind the village. Ocran
was among those who would go.

The men carefully packed their goods for barter, laughing, bantering
with a rare and unencumbered good cheer as they tied and loaded
carded wool, brightly colored blankets and mats woven by the women,
salted freshwater fish, dried beans of various sizes and types and colors
and tastes, strings of fresh dates, prize sheep and cattle fattened for sale.
They eagerly looked to the camaraderie of travel, smiled to think of the
effortless daily laughter to come, and chuckled to themselves in expectation of the glad and rowdy ritual of swapping tales and telling lies (in
their merriment there was little difference between the two). Those less
God-fearing pondered the titillating prospect of partaking of the
charms of women not their wives, or at least the opportunity to flirt with
them and fantasize. This freedom, both wholesome and not, was predi-
cated upon leaving their women and children at home. But as the men
packed the camels and oxen and lined up in the predawn light to inch
down the rutted road, they noticed a boy standing poised to join them.
At first they were baffled, for everyone knew that children were never
taken on a caravan. Then they realized it was Jalon, the spoiled ten-year-
old whose every wish was honored by his obsessed and fixated father.

"Hold on, Ocran. You're gonna have to leave that boy at home. You
don't see nobody else tagging their sons along to slow us down."

With many of his goods for trade already loaded and secured upon
his patient camels with their swaying necks, Ocran continued packing
provisions for the trip, the coarse brown barley loaves and pungent
goat's-milk cheese and the goat-hide drinking skins filled to roundness
with spring water and diluted wine, and of course the boy's implements
of play and extra blankets to warm him. Ocran replied in a flat tone.

"In the scriptures the Hebrews took their sons with them into the wilderness. No reason I can't do the same."

"Yeah, but we're not living in Moses' time. And anyway, the Hebrews weren't going to no trading market; they were looking for somewhere to live."

"Well, I'm not going to nitpick the scriptures with you. My boy wants to go, so I'm letting him go. Anyway, how am I going to be sure that the Romans won't come trouncing in here while I'm away and take my boy like they did his mama and my girl? No. I ain't leaving my boy for anyone else to take care of, not even God."

"See, now you getting ready to blaspheme."

"I'm not saying that God can't protect him; it's just that I can't never tell when God will decide to. So I'm not taking any chances. The boy is going with me, where I can make sure no rogue or Roman can get near him."

The men muttered to themselves. Several in turn stepped forward to answer him, but they all thought better of it and turned away in disgust, for they knew Ocran's fixation.

As the first hint of light broke the hills behind them, the travelers said good-bye to their families, kneeled to pray for traveling mercies, mounted their camels and donkeys and ox-drawn carts, and pulled off into the slate-gray dawn.

Outside the village they passed the makeshift camp of the discarded ragamuffin women silently peering at them from threadbare tents thrown together from scraps of cloth and old blankets. Each man cast a small package to the ground culled from the goods they carried along.

"For the women," Ocran explained. "So God will bless us in our trading for being so generous."

To Jalon it seemed that real generosity would have been to rescue the women from their plight. But this thought occurred to him for only a moment before the excitement of the departure set his mind to other things. He was on his way to see the sights of Shechem; he had never been more thrilled. The coddled and overindulged boy who would be Her First could not have known that in Shechem he would experience more, much more, than he could ever dream or wish.

Chapter
6

Shechem was like all the trading towns of Samaria. Narrow alley-ways yawning, grudgingly yielding to man and beast, the one leading, driving, or astride the other; narrow lanes dusty from the heat, dotted with clumps of dung, winding tight between gray rows of cramped, squat dwellings of stacked stone standing mute and observant and so close that each seemed to share its shadowed walls with its neighbor. Most rose a single story, more than a few twice that. Stray goats and dogs and the occasional cow wandered the muddy roads and pathways leading to the dung-seasoned trading yards with their cloth-draped booths, their split-rail corrals, their lean-to mangers and low, crooked stalls. And Shechem was like other trading towns in one thing more: the scandalous pleasures of fleshly companionship it offered to those with goods to spare and too few scruples to say no.

Knotted with their lowing livestock and creaking carts, their mouths agape at the sights and the smells, Ocran and the others trudged the ribbon of livestock droppings and puddles of urine and dust and some-times mud. And suddenly they were before them, smiling Jezebels of various shades and sizes, posed in their doorways robed in gauzy array, beckoning, inviting, calling with their painted eyes, their tattooed hands and ankles, their hennaed hair scandalously uncovered and piled high atop their wagging heads; their jangling bracelets of turquoise, car-

nelian, shaped silver, and polished bronze; their belled and embroi-
dered shawls sloped on the curve of their hips and hung low from the
crooks of their arms. Calling, smiling, flirting, seducing, they offered
their charms for produce or for the shekels they preferred.

The men stared in unabashed wonder. These were far different from
the women they knew. These neither asked for marriage nor would
they accept it, and seemed to care little for men's opinions or respect.
They sought only coins for their purses, grain for their bread, spices for
their tables, skins of wine to drink. They called to the gawking farmers
turned traders, inciting some to smile stupidly and stare, others to actually drool and rub their thighs, contemplating ways to eke from their
meager goods the price of a woman who pleased men for a living.

Although they smiled and gestured, charmed and laughed, in truth
these were women who were angry with men. Angry for their domination at the hands of men, at the hallowed words of scripture men
invoked to justify it. Angry at the war men waged against the fullest
flowering of women, against their right to dream, against their right to
live as children of no less a God than the one men called He and Him.

It was not only their anger that kept these women from marriage.
More than anything, it was that they refused to be any man's chattel. So
they chose for their lives the path that allowed them not only to remain
unattached to men but also to exact their vengeance upon them and
still have men willingly supply their daily bread: they left their loved
ones behind, settled to forever live on the outskirts of propriety, and
committed themselves wholly to the commerce whose currency was
their own devalued flesh.

There were women who plied their trade for other reasons. Some
were forced into it by deep and desperate poverty. Some fled into it
from dishonored relations bent on avenging some tenet of family
honor thought to have been sullied. Some were disowned into it by the
unrelenting disgrace of a publicly known rape, voiding as it did their
value to those charged with negotiating their worth on the unforgiving
market for maiden brides. But none of this pertained to these beckoning women at Shechem. These were moved to their craft by neither
fear nor failure. The painted lives they lived were of their own open

choosing: they sold their bodies that they might own themselves. What seemed to be the barter of flesh for shekels was to them the bartering of their flesh for the prize of their own freedom. Freedom and power. Freedom from arranged marriages. Freedom from erwat dabars. Freedom to decide how to live and with whom to live. And the power to refuse without apology anyone who tried either to abridge that freedom or to enter the sanctity of their lives without explicit invitation.

The women's anger, their jealous guarding of their tenuous and costly freedom all showed in the way they treated the expectant men who sought their favors. They never addressed them by name (they seldom knew their names, anyway), never referred to them as "men" or "guests" or even "clients." "Crows" was their only appellation, uttered with voices full of derision and disdain.

"Just look at them," the women laughed. "They're all one shade of dark or another, and they'll put their beaks on anything. If that's not a crow, I don't know what is."

"And if they spot something good they'll all come flocking, hoping to get in a peck. That's crows alright."

And that is how they handled men, as cawing nuisances to be bartered a taste then shooed away. But the women paid a terrific price for dismissing men in the same way that men dismissed them. For if to them the men were crows, to men the women were meat, carcasses imbued with breath and animation, tawdry lumps of flesh without sense or feelings. Devalued, occasionally beaten, mere meat to those who sought their favors, these were the lives they chose. It was their work. So in their beckoning doorways they called out in tones that dripped enticement, and promised pleasures that made men tingle.

"Come here, sweetness. I'll give you love your daddy never dreamed of."

"Let Big Mama hold you close, honey darling. I guarantee you won't feel no pain."

"You can lay your head on my bosom anytime, Mr. Man. Or anywhere else you want to."

Never had Jalon heard words like these, so rife with closeness, so thick with what seemed to him tenderness and warmth. The sound of their sayings brought to mind the affection he'd watched between mothers and their sons with wonder and, yes, a measure of want; the soft words, the smiling eyes, the reassuring touch. It was the same warmth he felt whenever a gesture, or a saying, or a particular turn of movement brought to mind his long-ago mother, though whatever love she had given him was as long gone in memory as it was in deed. Her touch, the shape of her words, the pitch and lilt of her voice had faded with each rise of the sun until every reminiscence was now indistinct, like something imagined or even dreamed. But the words of these women, the feelings they conjured in him, their beckoning laps and ample bosoms—these were real.

The others heard the enticements the women dangled as offers to trade in the heated coin of pleasure. Jalon heard them differently, not as trade or transactions but as promises of warmth and affection. This was new to him; he could recall no woman promising him anything before. He was transfixed, beguiled by this new feeling of anticipation and assurance, of expecting touch and wanting it, the promise of holding another and himself being held.

The women saw the young boy's gaze fix hard upon them, intense as any man's, as he passed with the slow creaking caravan. With great amusement they called to him, "Little boy, little boy," enjoying the embarrassment and shock they brought to his face. Jalon heard them, felt them, saw their glistening mouths as they spoke, grew wide-eyed and sweaty and absolutely enthralled.

The caravan snaked past the women through the bawling livestock and the moiling men and the overloaded carts and the closely guarded piles of waiting goods, and finally pulled into the crowded trading grounds. Yet in his beating heart and his fired loins, Jalon remained in the dusty, overripe alleyway with the painted, jangling, calling, enticing women who, he just knew, had all that he needed, but could not yet name.

For the rest of his time at Shechem, Jalon thought of the women. While he assisted his father, sorting and lifting, weighing and bundling, he thought of them. Cross-legged in the fire-lit camp pretending interest in the tales the men hatched, he thought of them. Even when the men's contentiousness flared into fighting, when names were called and blows exchanged and his father snatched him from the tumult like an unfired pot about to be broken, still he thought of them and tried to understand the waves of feeling that covered him.

After several days of barter and drink and laughter and the energetic spinning of yarns told and enacted with mock solemnity and outrage, the farmers began their slow and deliberate journey home. To avoid the pickpockets and thieves who thought it their life's work to relieve others of their goods and their shekels, the men departed by a different route. Jalon was sorely disappointed to miss a last sight of the beckoning women and their sparkling display. Still he thought of them, calling with their painted eyes and their supple mouths. On narrow roads through groves of juniper, oak, cypress, and pine, he thought of them. In valleys lush with mint, wild mustard, coriander, and dill, he imagined that the feral smells wafting his way belonged to them and none other. And when his village finally appeared with its familiarity and friends, thoughts of them—the women—lingered hard upon him. Even in his home again, firmly ensconced in his old rhythm and routine, he thought of them still. Throughout the seasons, in the fields, at the Sabbath prayers, in his hot fitful sleep, he thought of the jangling women and their promises of warmth and touch and closeness and love. He not only thought of them, he dreamed of them as well. And when his father's wife passed close to him, and especially when at night he heard his father's rhythmic grunts and her faint fleeting moans in syncopated response, he lusted for them, too.

For days and nights and haunted weeks he thought of them. Then, with the drift of the seasons his ardor began to wane, and it seemed he might be free of them. Whatever fantasies did arise invariably fixed upon the ample form of his father's wife, whose buttocks he grabbed at often, daring her to tell. But when the crops again were high and the time for trading near, his thoughts of them again grew daily, the prating women at Shechem, and the sweat beading his brow was not from field work alone. He thought of them and dreamed and lusted and imagined he would burst without them.

When it seemed that he could not wait another day to stand before them, to hear their laughter and feel the warmth of their flesh, the announcement went out. It was time again for the caravan to assemble.

The men chuckled at Jalon's excitement, unaware of its real cause. They laughed all the more because they knew there would be no trip for him; it was Ocran's turn to stay behind. Others had goods to trade, and someone had to stay behind to keep things up.

When Jalon heard that he was not to accompany the caravan, he rushed to Ocran in a spitting panic. "We're not going to Shechem, Daddy?" he cried.

"Not this year, son."

"But I wanna go, Daddy. I wanna go."

Ocran half pleaded and half explained. "We have to give someone else a turn at it, son. Fair is fair."

"I don't care about fair! I want to go, Daddy! I want to go!"

"You sure? You know it's a considerable trip."

"I don't care. I wanna go!"

Ocran's face took a determined look. "Alright, son. Alright."

On the day of departure the travelers and traders assembled in the predawn found that their number was higher by two than they'd planned.

"Where you going, Ocran?" the men asked almost in unison.

Ocran replied without the least hint of shame. "The boy wanted to go, so I decided to go."

Binyamin spoke from an oxcart piled high with goods and produce in a voice pitched with exasperation. "But I have all your stuff already packed up with mine. You said you wanted me to trade for you, now you're changing your mind?"

"Nothing's changed. Except now me and the boy is going, is all."

The men angrily shook their heads and returned to securing their goods and herding their livestock. They were not going to let anything spoil their trip, especially not this obstinate and overindulgent father who seemed never to hear reason unless it came from his own mouth.

With its lurching camels and stiffly walking men, the caravan again wound its way down the verdant hills, past terraced slopes, through valley floors with their orchards of dates and almonds and apples and pears. Despite the ceaseless banter of the men with their clumsily coded jokes and surprisingly scandalous confessions, the days crawled like weeks for the boy astride the loping camel or skipping behind the carts and the swaying livestock. Then, after an eternity of waiting, they were again at Shechem with its crowds, its commerce, its riches, its unrepeatable pleasures.

Jalon's eyes grew wide and his brow beaded with heated anticipation. He craned his neck, straining to catch sight of the smiling, calling, gyrating objects of his desire. More long strides of the camels, more creaking spinning of wheels, a turn down one alley, a bend up the next, a crooked expanse, a curving way, and there were the painted women, breathtaking in their shamelessness. Jalon's heart jumped as the women laughed and called and posed invitingly in their entryways. He drank in everything about them. The crooked rows of teeth, the tongues licking and flitting, the toes writing enticingly in the dust at their doors, the hands beckoning to whatever eye met their own.

When he'd first encountered the women, to them he had been "Little boy, little boy!" Although since then he had thought of them, dreamed of them, lusted after them, their estimation of him as a child named a distance he still did not know how to bridge. But now as he passed, the women responded to him differently. Maybe they saw that his previous wonder had given way to lust. Or perhaps it was the certainty of his desire as he stared at them, unblinking and unafraid. Whatever the reason, they called to him differently now. "Little man! You, little man!" they said, and he knew he could dream no longer.

The caravan arrived in late morning and proceeded directly to the trading grounds. While his father and the others bartered and dickered and drank sweetened tea and barley beer, Jalon slipped away to find them, the painted women with their heated promises of touching and warmth and the answer to his every want. Past the tethered lambs and goats and oxen and cows, the stalls laden with fruits, ripe and dried, exotic and everyday. Past the baskets overflowing with onions, endive, muskmelon, and leeks, tables piled high with flax cloth and linen and cotton and fine wool. He wound through the tight alleys and the bustling crowds and the dust and the dung and finally found himself at their door, filled with a trepidation that was both delicious and daunting.

Several men squatted outside, their blank expressions betraying nothing of the lust with which they awaited the call to enter. At intervals long yet not overlong a grinning sweating man emerged and another rose quickly to take his place. The boy impatiently watched the shadows grow and tried to imagine the world inside. Then all the men had entered and left and he stood alone at the beckoning door, attempting to look blank like those before him, yet betrayed by the heated anticipation that clung to his face, the flaring of his nostrils, his watered, panting eyes. Before he could regain his composure there she stood, a woman youngish and plump, a faint glisten of perspiration upon a brow the color of boiled lentils, the fringes of her dark coiled hair wet and flat against her forehead and fleshy cheeks. Draped upon her was a low-necked garment of a finer cloth than Jalon had seen before. A practiced beguilement inched her face, which was full and plump and painted and only slightly amused.

"Well, whose little boy is this?" she said with a mocking tone.

"I ain't no little boy," Jalon replied sharply. "I'm almost a man."

She called through the door. "Ladies, come look what we got here. A little crow. An almost-a-man crow." A brace of raucous laughter stung his cheeks.

She turned back to him, still unsmiling. "Is there something you want?"

"Yes, ma'am."

"Well, what, Mr. Almost-A-Man?"

"That," he replied, pointing to her finely clad body with a downward sweeping gesture.

"And what is 'that,' you fresh little thing?" She spat the words through lips puckered with disdain.

"What all them other men be wanting." He did not blink or look away.

She laughed a derisive laugh. "Boy, go on home and find your mama."

"I don't have a mama. I got a daddy."

"Well, I don't care where you go or who you go to. Just get on away from my door."

She made a dismissive gesture and turned to go inside. When she heard no movement from the boy, she pivoted, hands splayed on her hips.

"Didn't I tell you to get?"

Still Jalon did not move. He stared back with his unblinking stare.

The woman stuck her plump finger in his face. "Boy, you act like you got a right to what you want just cause you want it."

He shrugged dismissively with his stare of entitlement.

His insolence angered her. Still, she found something appealing in his naive arrogance. The others the women called crows were work for them, but this one, she thought, this one could be sport: a young boy a woman could control, one a woman could dominate as men tried to dominate them; even with his childish insolence, this was too good to turn away. They—the women—could enjoy him and teach him to please them. This might be a welcome change.

More than that, they would make him need them, they would see to that. They had their shekels, their freedom, a greater measure of control over their lives than most women in their world, but in their hearts they knew they were not needed. Beyond the sweating and grappling and lust-induced professions of love, they were necessary to no one—and they knew it. Each had paid the same awful price for the freedom she now flaunted, having left kith and kin far, far behind. For if their families were to learn of the choices they'd made, a father, a brother, even some distant male relation would be bound to murder them where they stood—publicly and ceremoniously and with the avid support of every onlooker—as punishment for the capital crime of bringing disrepute to family and village. Thus with no families or friends, only client crows to gauge their humanity, these women needed someone to need them. More than that, they had so long made certain to pad themselves with moss and drink the daily infusion of fennel seeds that kept their wombs closed and staved off conception, and if they did conceive, to use the potions of harsh herbs that dispatched the tiny hearts in their wombs before they began to beat, that each knew it was unlikely that her polluted and overused body would ever bear a child who would value and need her. This eager, wide-eyed boy might give them the chance to experience some of what they'd missed.

But it was not the scowling woman's yearning that Jalon sensed. What he'd felt first was her impatience and her anger, and those were the feelings he fastened to. He knew nothing of her need or anyone else's—in his world it was only what he felt that counted—but impatience and anger he knew well, for those were the emotions that had greeted him whenever he pressed the grown folks in his village to grant him his way. After their many rebuffs and his tearful retreats to the comfort of his father's coddling, Jalon had evolved a demeanor of contrived affability that overcame their anger and often persuaded them to give in to his wishes. It was this practiced persona of boyish charm and glowing self-effacement that he presented to the frowning woman holding the key to his smoldering desire. He averted his gaze, dropped his head in feigned and sudden decorum, and half-whispered in his most practiced tones of innocence, "I don't mean no harm. I just want to be close to you pretty ladies is all."

Two other painted women had emerged by then, brazen and profane and increasingly interested. The one was tall and slim and angular, with smooth amber skin. Her thick hair was plaited and pulled into a headful of neat twisting braids. Flat features reposed upon a flat and shining face in which was inserted a huge smiling mouth that seemed almost to cover it.

The other woman was big. Not plump like the first, but fat, a big, big-boned woman with breasts like big sleeping dogs in a sack, and an enormous kindly face.

The fat one eyed him up and down, smiling, her fat mouth revealing teeth surprisingly white and even. "Ooowee! Don't he talk sweet."

The slim one pursed her enormous mouth and said in a faintly orgasmic tone, "He don't only talk sweet, but he kinda looks sweet, too."

"Umm," said the fat one. "A sweet-talking, sweet-looking almost-a-man little crow. I've got so used to those big crows grunting and nodding their heads at us like we're some kind of cattle that I forgot what a sweet one sounds like."

The slim one flashed a smile that revealed even more teeth. "Well, I think we should give him some," she giggled.

"Hummph. He's so young he probably wouldn't know what to do with it," said the dour plump one who, despite secretly sharing the sentiments of the others, was not yet ready to change her tone.

"That's alright," said the fat one. "As long as he has some sweetness, Big Mama can teach him the rest."

Jalon grinned with great self-satisfaction. He eagerly stretched out his dirty palm to reveal a single shekel he had removed from his father's money pouch, which he'd held on to even when his father had cursed and glared at the other traders accusingly.

"I got some money," he said excitedly.

"You keep your shekel, sweetness. Just keep on being sweet, and do what Big Mama says, and everything will be alright. Just come on in and let Big Mama show you what to do."

She waved the others away, ignoring the resentful sucking of their teeth as she led Jalon inside. "You girls go on about your business. I'll take care of this little crow."

Enclosing Jalon's slender hand in her own, she said to him in a tone that was at the same time good-natured and conspiratorial, "You take care of Big Mama, and Big Mama will take care of you."

The next hours passed for Jalon in a blur of raw and shameless sensuality.

"Take off your clothes," said the big woman with the same imperious tone she used with the men who paid her. "Let's get rid of those fleas."

All traders had fleas, she laughed, and she'd already washed from herself the last of those the sweating, grunting farmers had left with her that day. Pesky mementos from pesky crows.

Big Mama laughed aloud at how eagerly Jalon complied, like he was used to bathing, when as far as she knew farmers washed only when they were too dirty to stand themselves, or when there were ritual purity issues at stake. Dirt, she knew, did not bother farmers. They lived in it every day except the Sabbath and whichever holy days the demands of their work allowed them to observe. So she found pleasing Jalon's eagerness to please her.

She poured pitchers of lukewarm water over Jalon and scrubbed hard his back, his slim arms, his bony legs. She scrubbed his pubic hair and the hair of his head as if they were the same, so firmly that he winced and yelped despite his best attempts to be stoic. Yet there was a tenderness in the way she touched him, and a vaguely maternal air. She'd once had a son of her own, conceived, she was sure, during the week she hadn't taken time to replenish her bowl of fennel, and the harsh herbs she'd taken subsequently had failed to vacate her womb. Of course she couldn't identify the father; she'd accommodated maybe dozens in that span. But for her that was no cause for bother. She was not going to raise the child at any rate; the midwife would find it a home and be glad to. Rather, it was the inconvenience that bothered her. For weeks, even months before the child was due, pregnancy would make work uncomfortable for her, and the last weeks of her bigness would render her wares distasteful to all but the most perverse of her client crows. Then for weeks afterward, the combination of the time needed for healing and the mandatory period of uncleanness prescribed by the scriptures that was observed by most of the hypocritical crows—forty days for a boy-child, eighty for a girl—meant a significant hiatus in business for her. The issue of her womb was nothing but a nuisance Big Mama heartily looked forward to being rid of.

As soon as the child drew its first breaths, she banished it to the midwife's care without holding it or even gazing upon it, admonishing the midwife to an immediate protective silence. Big Mama wanted no honey-sweet pronouncements—"Isn't he cute?" or "Aww, she's a pretty little thing"—to haunt her moments; she would countenance no thoughts of the child's future, where it might go, what it might become. So she breathed through her mouth to avoid smelling the baby's scent and refused to see its face lest its tiny brown features invade her already troubled dreams; the last thing Big Mama wanted was to think of the life issuing from her as real. However, as she lay panting with relief and exhaustion, the midwife, thinking she was safely out of her hearing, announced to the curious women gathered outside that Big Mama had borne a son. "A beautiful one," she said, despite the nastiness of the mother. "As brown and beautiful as the crust of fresh-baked bread. And the heifer doesn't even want him."

From that moment to this, Big Mama had never asked after her son; never let on that she knew. Had he lived? Was he healthy, was he whole? She'd never asked, but every day she wondered.

In her dreams she loved him, held him, bathed him, the same way she bathed this almost-a-man-but-more-like-a-boy hunched beneath the lukewarm stream from the upraised pitcher at the end of her arm. He was just a crow, she reminded herself, but she would not shoo him off like the others. His feathers she would stroke, if only for once to know what that was like.

When she had washed him and dried him and covered him with the fine woolen blanket a grateful client crow had given her just that day, she cast aside the mat she used to conduct business, and set aright the low scrolled couch leaning against a wall. She spread upon it blankets dyed the red of safflower, the orange of henna, the yellow of saffron. Upon them she arranged pillows of crimson, indigo, and green. Then she pushed Jalon down upon them.

As Big Mama gently eased her girth beside Jalon, caressing and swaddling him in the folds of her flesh, her emotions ran so high and in such jumbled confusion that she thought she might weep. Instead the well of pent-up feelings spilled on Jalon through her fingers, her hands, through the much touched breasts that had never suckled, through her rolling, clinching thighs and her full and wetted lips. She made her feelings real in the only way she knew, through a fervent, devoted, unrelenting rehearsal of the most sensual arts of her craft. Several times the boy was sure he had died and gone to heaven, so intense was the pleasure she gave him, only to be brought back to life with undulations of her tongue and thigh that rolled his eyes in his head and set his trembling mouth to moaning.

Jalon and the painted woman who sold herself for a living joined fast in their cult of hungering need, though neither knew enough of intimacy to touch even the corners of their own emptiness; he had never learned, and in the daily blur of beards and hands and frenzied limbs, she had long forgotten. So despite the longing that oozed from their every fevered pore, in their crazed and furtive couplings it was not the depth of their needs that was served, but the heights of their lusting. Afterward, panting in the flaming shades of dusk licking through the narrow slitted windows, reposed upon blankets of henna, safflower, and saffron, satiated beyond anything he'd ever imagined, Jalon clung to the beating bosom of this woman who was more to him than a pleasurable experience. She was Big Mama, the only mama whose arms held him close.

When Jalon returned to the traders' camp, the sun was already down. He knew his protective father would be crazed with worry, pacing the camp and cursing the others for letting his vaunted son slip away. Jalon warily approached the fire of his father's caravan, one of many scattered about the open field skirting the trading grounds, and began to prepare his spurious explanation and his assumed look of contrition. Scanning the men seated on their haunches, he met the eyes of his father. Jalon had just begun to arrange his face to lie when his father said with obvious delight, "Hey, son! Enjoy yourself?"

The response so surprised Jalon that despite his deceptive intentions, in his befuddlement he could speak only the truth. "Y-y-yes sir, Daddy," he replied. He puzzled for a moment, then said, "You not mad I been gone?"

"No, son, not mad at all."

This was strange behavior indeed.

"Why not?" asked the boy.

"Cause I knew where you were. I saw the way you looked at those women back there. That and the nervous way you were acting made it clear to any man with eyes that you had going back there kicking around in your mind. So I had Bilshan here keep an eye on you, and when you went off he followed, just to make sure nobody did nothing to you. He stayed until you got inside alright and came back and told me where you were. Then he went back and waited. You know I'm not going to take any chances of something happening to my boy."

A grinning figure moved into the ring of firelight. "You were in there for a right long time," said Bilshan in a tone that pleaded to know more.

"You not mad?" Jalon repeated, ignoring him.

"Mad? No, son, I'm not mad. Every man's got to learn sometime how a woman is supposed to treat him. And I hope you learned something."

The boy nodded and grinned. "Sure did, Daddy. And I liked her, too."

"Liked her? No, not 'liked her.' Not 'her' son, *it*. Liked it, what she did for you. Wasn't her you liked. She's not somebody to be liking; she's just another woman pleasing a man. She's just doing what she's supposed to. Just next time don't be taking my shekels; ask me. Anytime you want to go to those women just ask me, and I'll take you myself so I can make sure they learn you right."

The next day Jalon returned to Big Mama with his father in tow. He excitedly followed her to her room while his father disappeared behind another set of secretive curtains, his rough hands already groping the narrow buttocks of the slim painted woman with the flat brown face and the smiling mouth that covered half of it. That day passed in a blur of lusting passion. Jalon returned the next day as well, this time with Bilshan, who was thrilled at the prospect of experiencing for himself what Ocran had raved about. Jalon twitched and moaned and sweated through the afternoon and all the night. Happy and sated, but with an already growing sense of melancholy, he reluctantly arose before dawn, his eyes tearing and wet with leaving, and departed with Bilshan to rejoin the weary caravan for the journey home.

In the year away from Big Mama Jalon's blood remained heated. As before, his thoughts were aflame with yearning, but now they burned with specificity: not for gyrating painted women, but for Big Mama alone. And he not only thought of her, dreamed of her, he smelled her, too, felt her, felt her hands upon him, felt her mouth, heard her jangling promises and thrilled to her whispered commands. It was as if Big Mama had turned something loose in him, set him fully ablaze and raised in him a conflagration of longing that knew no relenting.

Secretly leering when the village women passed his way, rubbing against the wife of his father, his frantic hands touching himself—that is how he made it through the months, through the planting, though the plowing, through his lusting days and unbearable nights, until the time of Shechem should come again.

The next trading season again found Jalon in Big Mama's arms. He so loved the moments with her that now he all but lived for them. Yet even in his happiness he heard his father's words. Despite his bliss, he was dutifully reminded that it was not the woman he called Big Mama that moved him so, but the world of pleasure beneath her garment. His tender thoughts of her, the hard, expectant beating of his heart each time he saw her anew, the whispered thrill of her words as they lay glistening with sweat upon blankets of henna, saffron, and safflower—these he worked hard to attribute not to a conscious and generous sharing of her deepest self, but to the routine wonders she worked through her flesh with no more of herself invested than that; rote and practiced wonders that Jalon believed to be not only his due, but the due of every man who sought them. He felt the sour taste of these conflicting emotions and was aware of a vague emptiness without being able to name it.

For her part, Big Mama had also come to look forward to his visits, and their time together presented a problem for her as well. She overlooked the fact that when Jalon was in Shechem she garnered far fewer shekels because of her summary dismissal of all the blank-faced crows awaiting her when he appeared. But he was taller now, his limbs beginning to thicken, his voice deepening, his face sprouting the first hairs of incipient manhood. She looked at him and felt a mixture of pride and satisfaction that both surprised and saddened her. Try as she might, Big Mama just could not reduce him to a simple thing of pleasure. That was the problem. She knew she should be laughing his name—or better yet, painting a hilarious caricature of him to her housemates as she had so many others, regaling the women with vivid recountings of awestruck clumsiness and youthful ineptitude, of how she so easily drove him to stuttering distraction and panting helplessness. Instead she said nothing and shared her deepest self with the boy that was almost a man.

Instead she imagined him a son though she spread wide her rolling thighs as to a lover. Instead she claimed him in her heart although he was neither son nor lover nor anything she could rightfully covet.

As they lay clutched in desperate embrace, locked in their frantic cult of need, Jalon said offhandedly, "My daddy says it's time for me to get married. I got to choose me a wife."

Big Mama twitched and stiffened a little, but said nothing.

"Yeah. He says it's time," he casually repeated. "Says I got to get started as soon as we get back."

They lay in momentary silence. Then Big Mama asked, "Well, do you want to get married?"

"I guess so," Jalon said, oblivious to the seriousness of her tone.

"Well," she said, drawing away slightly so she could see his face. "Why?"

"Why?" He chuckled at what seemed to him a nonsensical question. "So I can get loving every day, that's why. Whenever I want it. And have somebody to do what I need done." He chuckled some more.

"Well, Big Mama don't know nothing about somebody serving you or anybody else. But I do know about loving. And you think you gonna get loving like this every day?"

"Yeah. I guess so. Loving is loving, isn't it?"

"Boy, you got a lot to learn."

"I'm not no boy. I'm—"

"I know. You're almost a man. But you're not a man yet."

"Well, you been treating me like a man, ain't you?"

"I have, have I?"

"You sure have," he said triumphantly.

"Then why don't you want to marry Big Mama?"

Of course the thought of marrying this child was absurd to her, but she needed to know if she was needed. All she'd ever wanted of him, of any of them, all those cawing crows and strangers with their eyes shining at her door, was to feel needed. She loved her small measure of freedom, and she was freer than most women. And yet the price she'd paid was too much loneliness, and it now seemed more days than not that she would trade all her independence for the smallest lasting attachment, for even the least bit of real and enduring closeness. So she awaited his answer as if it mattered deeply. Because it did.

"Well, a man can't marry a . . . a . . ."

"A what? A paid-for woman?"

"Well . . . yeah. I guess."

"That's why you wouldn't want to marry Big Mama? Cause I'm a paid-for woman?"

"Well, yeah. No. I mean, if it was up to me . . . if it wasn't for my daddy . . . I mean, he'd never . . . you know . . ."

She smiled to herself. He wanted to be with her. That was the same as being needed. He could go wherever he wanted now, she never had to see his face again, as long as she knew he needed her. That was enough to hold on to. She could think of him, speak of his need for her to every listening ear, hold it as her dearest consolation when the loneliness became too much. "That boy is just crazy about Big Mama," she could say. "Says he wants to be with me all the time. Every time he comes around I can't move for him trying to be close to Big Mama . . ."

She pulled him to her big bosom. "It's alright, Mr. Almost-A-Man. Big Mama understands. Anyway, I hear that in your village they'll throw that erwat dabar at a woman in an eye blink. That's not the way Big Mama wants to live. No sir. I like my freedom and my space. I like to be able to tell a crow when to leave, where to go, and how to get there, if you know what I mean."

Her big body jiggled with laughter. "But listen to Big Mama good. There's one thing you're going to learn in life: every woman living with a man is a paid-for woman. All them so-called respectable married women are just like us: sleeping with a man so he can buy her what she needs. The difference is in what my kind of paid-for women gives back."

Big Mama gestured around her house of commerce. "We only give our bodies. Oh, we let men think they're getting more, but they're not. We don't even give them our real names, much less let them in on what makes us, us. But married women don't just give men their bodies, they give them their freedom, their souls, everything."

She suddenly became somber. "And for what? So they can wear out their wombs dropping a new baby every year, with most of the little things dying before the next one is born, and that's if the women don't die themselves birthing them. And then on top of it all being treated like she's done something wrong if she doesn't have a boy? They give up their whole selves for that? So they can be used up and sent out to pasture when their bodies break down, like a lame ox or a sheep with the mange?"

Big Mama realized she was crying and she was not sure why. Her tears embarrassed her. She had not let anyone see her cry since she'd left behind her sad-faced mother and her wine-maddened father and claimed her liberty when she was little more than a child herself. Even when it appeared she would die from thirst, alone on the deserted roads, even when the traders who found her took their turns atop her as the price for a few mouthfuls of water—even then she had not cried. Maybe that was why she cried now, for all the times she should have and did not.

She had wept for only a short while before she let out a sob, sharp but final, then lit into a smile, like all her pain had been miraculously exhaled. "It's alright, Mr. Almost-A-Man. You go ahead like your daddy say and marry you one of them country girls, so you can be just like all the rest of these men walking around thinking they're gods."

He looked at her with a mixture of puzzlement and relief. "I don't know about all of that, Big Mama. All I know is women got they place and men got theirs and that's the way it is. And that I got to get married. That's all I know. But I'm gonna come back and see you when I can, Big Mama. I am."

She held him in an embrace so rife with emotion that it threatened to overwhelm her. Then she playfully slapped his thigh.

"Well, Mr. Almost-A-Man, I'm not looking to marry no little crow like you, anyway. You go ahead and get you one of those good little country girls to cook your food and jump when you sneeze. You know there's no way in the world Big Mama is ever going to do that. You just make sure you come back and see Big Mama when you can."

She threw her log of a leg over his and pushed him onto his back. "But before you go, Mr. Almost-A-Man, we better let Big Mama give you something to make sure you come back."

When Jalon left Shechem a few days thereafter, his head pulsed and spun like he'd lain in the very arms of God. The hairs stood on his neck and he winced sharply when he thought of Big Mama and the magic she'd worked with her body in farewell. Still, this time leaving was not as hard as before, because now he had cause for excitement at home.

Chapter

7

In this, the season of nuptials, the village buzzed with its annual pageant of arranged and routinized betrothals, its yearly rituals of sober and prolonged negotiations between the anxious fathers of marriage-aged daughters, eager to avoid the disgraceful burden of spinsters squatting childless and unattached in their huts, and the blustery fathers of marriageable sons, each careful to seek full value for the bride-price he would pay. The men haggled with mouths filled with figs and goat curd, gestured over bowls of black olives and goat cheese and steaming pots of thick sweetened tea. They sat earnest and cross-legged in their yards beneath the poplars and firs and bending palms; they crouched in shaded corners of their choosing staring away eavesdroppers and anxious listening sons; and argued in waving animation beneath the sycamores and watchful willows at their refuge at the river's bend, alternately buoyed and chastened by advocates and arbiters and scripture-quoters and friends. Their haggling was civilized, inherently civil, though always loud and intense, for while every man sought to gain standing from the proper betrothal of his child, each sought all the more to avoid the dishonor of fruitless negotiations attached to his family name.

The thorny bougainvillea continued to bloom their rainbow of hues. The gnarled-armed orchards still hung heavy with fruits in their seasons. And Ma Tee's tortured love left a sad and haunting wake with seasons of its own that differed only in their regularity; moment-to-moment seasons sprouting sad-eyed fruits of caution, careful fruits that hung down and weighed upon the granddaughter she loved. Ma Tee's desperate years of remolding the now almost woman with cinnamon skin had succeeded in teaching her to hope little and dream even less, to breathe her breaths from only the thinnest air, and to admonish herself with *Careful! Careful!* as if it was a rote recitation from the very heart of scripture.

So the girl whose heart once leaped with the joy of life now lay as earthbound as any turtle or snail or bird without wings. She no longer wore Ma Tee's mantle of carefulness; she did not need to. Now it wore her. Its shape was her shape, its folds were her folds, its slopes and curves indistinguishable from her own, as if imprinted upon the very texture of her soul. The brave and carefree girl who had excited the bullying passions of so many was now a demure and excessively deferential young woman who even herself could not remember the bold and bubbling child she had once been.

Although she was timid now, the fathers of the village had not forgotten her childhood sin of spunk. No matter how careful, no matter how deferential she was at present, to them she still was "that gibora girl" who had committed the unforgivable sin of disgracing her daddy in the full sight of his peers.

Yet their sons, fully possessed by the heat of their fevered loins, cared little about their fathers' complaints. They saw only her erect bearing, the fullness of the hips and breasts that gave her tunic its shape, the strong calves that showed themselves as she raised her feet to walk, the face perfect in its shape and symmetry: high-boned, heart-shaped, graced by almond eyes beneath dark languid lids, set off and punctuated by full oval lips the color of ripe grapes. The passivity of her manner made her even more desirable, and all the youths yearned to have her, to touch her softly at night, to reach for her in the coming light of dawn, to lift high her tunic in the midst of the day when the bean plants were high and no one could see, or when the noonday meal called to them in a voice far fainter than the alluring softness of her skin.

Winning her hand became the goal of all the excited young men who, in truth, sought more to own the bragging rights that each knew would come with her possession than to marry for duty or social substance or even personal suitability. But more than any of the others, Jalon knew the ecstatic heights that could be wrought by the curve of a woman's hips, the moist meeting of her thighs, the soft peak of her breasts. His desire was an informed desire, a desire born of experience, not of dreaming; thus his yearning to possess her was more real and more determined than that of any two of the other young men combined.

That she was the focus of such frenzied attention from the young and hopeful potential husbands was not lost upon the other marriage-aged girls, who could not decide whether to admire or despise her. Ever since her spirit was reined in, they'd had no cause to give her quiescent presence any more thought than they would a shadow. It was true that Izevel, their leader in all things social, had herself never warmed to her, but as her spirit had become increasingly quiet, Izevel, who by then no longer viewed her as a competitor for the attention of the others, had no further reason to torment her. However, as it became clear that she and not Izevel was the prize sought most by the young men this season (for in every betrothal season there emerged a favorite), Izevel's dormant resentment became once again what it had been: a seething anger that flirted with hatred. More than that, Jalon, the arrogant spoiled youth whose father thought he walked upon water, was the object of Izevel's ardent hopes, for she believed what Jalon believed about himself—that his arrogance was appropriate because he really was a superior being sent to grace the lives of them all. And so Izevel planted daggers wherever she went, acted ugly in a myriad of ways, and did all she could to disrupt the life of the one she saw as her rival for the young man who, if the truth be told, was desired by no one but Izevel herself.

That his daughter was the most sought after of them all was of great moment for Aridai. In fact, there was no question in his mind that this was the crowning event of his life. Of course he had married off his other daughter, Oholibamah, but her betrothal was routine and uneventful and inspired no particular attention. And he had never forgotten that on account of this last daughter, the men had once made him the object of their fun. Having persevered and redeemed himself by his determination to reshape her, Aridai now had something the other men coveted. He thought it was justice indeed that those who had derided him now had to request his consideration, now had to stand outside his hut and call for his favor.

How Aridai loved the attention. Every father of every marriage-aged son came to sit solemnly before him. He dickered with them with pompous formality and listened to the bride-prices they offered with the newly found decorum of a man who has recently discovered a fresh source of self-regard. As his visitors coughed to stifle their yawns, their eyes glazing with disinterest, he extolled the transformed virtues of his daughter as one boasts of a prize cow.

"Yes sir. Taught her myself. As soon as I saw the first little bit of sass in her"—he was careful to avoid the use of *gibora,* the very thought of which could only hurt his bargaining position—"I took over her upbringing and whipped her right into shape. But she's not broken, mind you. Don't worry, you wouldn't be getting a broken girl for your boy. No sir. My daughter's not broken, she's just bent."

Aridai laughed hard at his own humor, as if it was not a joke he had told every day for several weeks.

"So, you see, she's got the best kind of upbringing a young girl can get: trained by a man how to serve a man. Yes sir, me and my mama, God bless her sweet soul, turned her into the first-class girl-child she is today. Hard worker, obedient. Good cook, too."

Aridai had the countenance and bearing of a man who couldn't be more self-satisfied if he had found the tablets of Moses intact and unbroken.

In spite of Aridai's bluster and bragging, in spite of his acting like his daughter was worthy of the world's highest bride-price, in spite of the best bartering and cajoling of the other fathers in their attempts to satisfy the randy wishes of their sons, Ocran, the doting father of Jalon, was determined that it would be his son who claimed her.

So, like the others, Ocran also made his way to the hut of Aridai, starting his negotiations low and inching higher. Unlike the other fathers, however, Ocran's offers went beyond what he could really afford, so set was he that his son should have the bride that he wanted, the bride most sought by all, whose possession would be yet another demonstration that the son he had sired was more special than the sons of others. That is why when the bride-prices that were proffered spiraled beyond what he could possibly match, in desperation Ocran made a concession so generous that Aridai could only smile with sly acceptance, while offering the stern and nonnegotiable addendum that their agreement must remain a secret that only the two of them would share.

Thus it was that flush with victory, Ocran, the father of the one who would be Her First, happily walked the path to his own nahala, kicking stones with the giddiness of a child who has outfoxed the world. But it was not that he himself was so enthused about this girl. In fact, he'd tried hard to talk Jalon out of pursuing her.

"Why you so hard bent on courting that girl, son?" he had asked. "Go get one of the other girls. One that was raised up right. The last thing you want is a gibora wife dishonorizing your name. Besides, so many of the other young fellas are begging their daddies to ask for her that by now her price got to be more than she's worth."

Jalon was not about to be denied. "Maybe she was gibora before, Daddy, but she's not anymore, because Mr. Aridai and her grandmama beat it all out of her. I heard you say so yourself. Now she's a good, quiet, obedient girl. Just watch the way she acts at market. Hardly raises her head. Don't even look you in the eye hardly, and none of the fellas ever heard her say not one sassy word to nobody."

Ocran was not ready to give in yet. "What I said is it doesn't look like she has any gibora left. *Doesn't look like.* But that don't mean she don't. You just can't take chances with this kind of thing, son. Gibora is like a disease. It might seem like it gets better, but you never know if it's going to hit again. So you need to just go on and marry one of those other girls. Girls that been raised right without any questionableness about them. You know those girls are going to be obedient wives cause they've always been obedient. It's a sure enough aggravation always having to argue and fight to keep your wife in line, so you got to make sure you get a good one."

"I hear you, Daddy, but that's the wife I want. Simple as that."

"Why do you have it in your head that you got to have that girl?"

Jalon grinned and repeated his fellow youths' oft-repeated description of her. "'Cause she's fine, fine, fine as new harvest wine."

Ocran threw up his hands in disgust. "Fine? Good-looking and fine don't mean a thing. After a couple years of field work and three, four babies, she's going to look worn out just like the rest of these women. Worn out, fat, tired, and sagging, just like the rest."

For the young man whose very flesh jumped at the thought of Big Mama's corpulence, the idea of added weight and sagging flesh was not a worrisome prospect.

"When I say she's fine, I mean beautiful fine. She's built up all nice, and got pretty skin and everything."

"'Built up nice.' I'm telling you, son, in a couple of years 'built up nice' won't even be a memory. What you need is a wife that's built for work first and everything else second."

He looked Jalon in the eye. "Hear me, son. She's going to be your first wife, but that don't mean she's got to be your last. For your first wife you need a woman with good, wide hips that can give you some sons without her going and dying on you. You don't want a skinny woman, cause when the babies come, skinny women can die on you too quick. No. You need you a good stout woman, a good, obedient wife with some meat on her bones that can give you some sons and be a good worker herself. That's how a man can get ahead. After you get you some sons and you want to go get somebody else, that's when you can worry about 'fine' and 'built up nice,' and all that other stuff. But for now, get yourself a good, stout, hardworking girl. That's what I say."

All Jalon knew of the female body was the size and girth of Big Mama. This had so colored his expectations that he imagined that beneath every woman's garment was the same.

"But Daddy, she does have good hips. Big hips."

"Big hips? I don't see no big hips. I see a girl that could use some more meat on her bones."

"But she does, Daddy. You can see her swaying when she walks. I don't like skinny women neither."

"Well, at least you got that part right," Ocran said. "Nobody wants a bone but a dog."

They shared a momentary laugh. Still Jalon was not through arguing his case. It was his way to relent only when he was given what he asked for.

"And she seems like a real hard worker, too. Every time you see her she's doing something, carrying something to market or from market or helping her mama with the grinding or the weaving or something."

"Alright. Alright. Maybe she would make a good wife for you. But I don't think I'm going to be able to beat out the bride-prices the other fathers are offering. Most of them have a bunch of workers on their nahalas—you know, big broods of sons and daughters—so they can raise a bigger crop than us. We only got the crop that you and me and that woman I'm married to can raise."

Jalon did not give a care about the sacrifices a winning bride-price would cost his father; he cared only for what he himself coveted. So he turned on his practiced charm in earnest and did not count the cost.

"Come on, Daddy. Good-looking as she is, she's bound to give you some good-looking grandsons. And all the fellas want her. If I'm the one who gets to marry her, then everybody will know that my daddy outdid the other men. All of them. And everybody will know that your boy outdid all the other fellas, too."

It was his last point that struck home.

"Well, son, suit yourself. If you just got to have her, I'll go see what her daddy is asking for. Really can't be much though, considering she was born with that gibora in her. While I'm at it, I'll see what kind of dowry he's talking about giving."

Then he wagged his finger in Jalon's face. "But let me tell you now, if you marry her and she starts up that gibora mess, don't come crying to me."

"I won't, Daddy." Jalon grinned. "I'm going to control my wife."

"And you'd better, too." With this Ocran seemed to relax. "As long as you're talking sense, the least I can do is go see her daddy. Who knows, we might just be able to work something out."

Chapter
8

After weeks of haggling, Ocran found himself hauling a bride-price he could not afford to the hut of a man he did not like for a daughter-in-law he did not really want. What he did want, however, was the boon she could be for his own reputation and the source of vanity and conjugal pleasure she could be for his son. So he'd swallowed his pride and wrangled and cajoled with every bit of craftiness he could muster.

Thus, it was with a mixture of great pride and great ambivalence that Ocran carried to Aridai a carefully selected sheep, one goat, and a large dappled cow, all swaying and sauntering before a cart piled with goods and produce. Ocran loosely tethered his beasts at the edge of the yard, shouted a civil greeting, patiently waited to be invited inside, and sat to finalize, with shared bread and strong drink, the secret agreement with Aridai that only a man of desperation would proffer and only a man with few scruples would accept.

After numerous toasts, the two men plunged into a meal spiced with wine-sodden joviality and insincere words of mutual appreciation, peppered with prickly eruptions of one-upmanship, as the wine caused each to speak ever more expansively of what he believed to be the notable merits of his child.

When Ocran had eaten and drunk enough to honor his host's hospitality and satisfy his own appetites, he bid Aridai shalom and shakily departed, leaving behind the livestock and the neat stacks of goods that constituted the payment he had brought in fulfillment of his word. Then he staggered home, his empty cart the source of some anxiety, comforted only by his sanguine expectation of what this marriage would mean for both himself and his son.

After the departure of his drunken guest, Aridai strode around like a cock newly loosed into the world of hens, announcing to his household, as if to a crowd of admirers, the news of the husband whose bed his remaining daughter would share until death—or erwat dabar—should part them.

"Ocran must think real highly of me," he crowed, his eyes closed to savor the moment, "because he gave me a mohar bride-price a whole lot higher than I ever thought you'd bring."

He did a triumphant little dance. "And you should be grateful, too, girl, because gibora as you used to be, you were on the way to being an old maid as sure as you're born. But look at you now. The pick and the prize of them all."

He rattled off the spoils that the promise of her hand had brought: the ephahs of grain, the baskets of produce, the three head of livestock, the lengths of cotton and wool. His chest fairly burst with pride.

"Pretty good for a man without a son, eh? I bet nobody's laughing at me now, are they?"

Then the smile left and his eyes narrowed. He jabbed a finger a finger's length from his daughter's eye.

"Listen to me good. I don't want to hear any mess from you. When that boy comes for you, you go. You understand? Go and serve him. And don't come back. And don't displease him, neither. And you better not disgrace me."

His eyes were so fierce she cringed.

"You understand me?"

"Yes, sir. I understand."

"Make sure you do, cause if you mess around and dishonor me I will. . . . You just better not." He gritted his teeth and spat on the ground.

. . .

She stumbled from the hut in a welter of dismay. It was not that she had not known that marriage was afoot for her; of course she had. She'd heard the village talk, felt the young men staring and wishing, seen the stiff, unsmiling fathers trudge every dusk to her yard to call out her father's name. But no one had said a word to her. Not her mother, not the fastidious Mr. Ishmael, not even the fussing village "aunties," the elderly women who dispensed unsolicited guidance to every girl-child that crossed their paths as if the words from their mouths were the very thoughts of God. No one had sat her down to speak of marital realities, of bride-prices and dowries, of courtships and betrothals, of wedding nights and mornings after. Without the nearness of their words, everything had seemed so far away. Now the finality of it all was upon her without anyone having asked her thoughts or gauged her feelings. No one had asked, Are you ready? Hopeful maybe? Do you have any fears? No one inquired if she knew how it would be when she'd been pronounced one with his flesh and the unyielding darkness proclaimed it was time for her to prove it. Or if she had the least clue how to touch and be touched in her first connubial nocturne, how she should breathe, when she should whisper rather than speak.

As she puzzled tearfully at the frightful unfolding of her life, her feet led her along their own path and apparently of their own accord, for her growing disquiet left little room for awareness of anything else. After wandering the hard paths through the rock-strewn meadows, through the fields of barley and beans and lentils and emmer, she became aware that her stride had brought her to a tiny grove of poplars standing anomalously at the grassy brow of an overgrown gully. She slowly walked among the trees, her attention only partially there, finding her way to a scooped-out hollow in a limestone outcropping that held forth in the shaded midst of the grove.

She sat and rested, hoping for a sign or a realization that would make sense of the turn her life had taken. But in truth, she expected no more than the sensations of which she was already aware: the rising foreboding, the joyless beating of her heart, the saltiness of her tears. Several times she thought she heard her name in a whisper, stilled herself to listen, then dismissed it as the lazy rustling of the leaves. Another whispering sound, but she dismissed that, too, and decided it was just her wishing.

When she arose, her feet again decided her route. The rocky path forked and she veered without a thought of where she was or where she was bound. After wandering the path that her legs had charted she was surprised to see before her Mr. Ishmael's neat nahala and realized that had been her destination all along. She was glad to be there, for it held for her the warmest of sights: the smiling Mr. Ishmael and the taciturn Mr. Pop, each of whom loved her in his own particular way.

With the tail of her head covering she wiped away her tears and breathed in what she imagined to be bravery and stepped into the clearing with a quickly conjured composure.

"Shalom, Mr. Ishmael. Shalom, Mr. Pop."

Both slowly arose in gentlemanly deference, patting the dust from their hands and smiling.

Mr. Ishmael greeted her with unaccustomed awkwardness, his big hands fidgeting with his tunic. He was used to opening his arms wide to her, but he did not seem to know how to respond to the young woman she'd become; social propriety now restrained him from requesting familial hugs and pecking kisses. Rubbing his beard and the back of his neck, he shifted his weight as she threaded through the neat furrows, according her the respectful distance that was due a young woman from even a moderately respectful man. Then he saw the sadness in her eyes and longed to hold her as would a father.

"Shalom, Miss Friend-Girl," Mr. Ishmael said, peering at her intently.

"Yeah. Shalom," said Mr. Pop. His face was as expressionless as usual, but she felt a smile from him nonetheless. He turned back to his work and left the art of conversing to his friend.

"To what do we owe this surprise pleasure, young lady?" asked Mr. Ishmael.

Her tears began to flow again. Mr. Ishmael gestured toward a large rock off to the side of his garden. They sat in a thick silence, the frightened soon-to-be bride and the pensive old man awaiting her words.

When she finally spoke it was as if she was announcing her own impending death.

"Mr. Ishmael, my daddy has married me off."

The old man looked into the distance, careful not to betray a response, careful not to let on how deeply her sorrow cut him.

"Really?"

"Yes, sir. And I don't know him at all except to see him, always staring with those eyes looking like he wants to grab somebody. That, and once I heard my daddy say him and his daddy think they're better than everybody else. But that's all I know. Oh, and his daddy is paying a real high bride-price for me. I guess I should feel honored. At least that's what my daddy says. But I don't want to marry him. He makes me feel funny, with those looking eyes and that sneer on his face. But I can't tell my daddy, because there's no telling what he'd do if he thought I was dishonoring his plans. I guess I just have to go on and marry him."

Mr. Ishmael painted the brightest colors he could. "Well, the scriptures do say that everybody should get married, little friend-girl."

"I know, Mr. Ishmael. But I don't know what to do. I mean . . ." She thought for a moment. "I mean . . . I don't know how to be a wife . . . I know I have to cook and clean and do field work, but the other stuff . . . you know. How to do what he wants and . . . you know . . ."

"I think I understand. And your mama's still not talking much, huh?"

"No, sir."

"And with Ma Tee gone . . ." His face suddenly lit up. "I know. Why don't you go see one of the aunties? See Ritzpah. I know she's mouthy and gruff, but my Elisheva always said she had a good heart."

He was smiling now. "Talk to Ritzpah. I'm sure she can help."

"I don't know, Mr. Ishmael. I never talked to Miss Ritzpah before. I never talked to any of the elder ladies, except for their fussing at me and stuff. You think she'd really talk to me?"

"I'm sure she would. The aunties mean well. They're just old and bitter after years of mean men, then being widowed and the Romans and all. They fuss because they care and the young generation doesn't seem to appreciate all the wise wisdom they have to share. But if you go to Ritzpah with your problem, I know she'll be glad to give you all the advice you need."

A few more moments of silence and she asked him sharply, "I have to get married, don't I, Mr. Ishmael?"

"I'm afraid so."

She clasped her hands in despair and fought back the tears. "I don't want to be married. I wish I could just run away."

"Aww, don't be like that. It's not that bad. Anyway, what would I do if I couldn't hear you calling 'Shalom, Mr. Ishmael' with that sweet voice of yours?"

She tried to force a laugh, but what emerged was a torrent of tears. The old man laid her head on his shoulder and stroked her face. "Don't you ever think you're alone in this world. Ever. I care about you. Me and Phinehas both. And Ma Tee is always with you."

"I try to talk to Ma Tee," she sobbed, "but she never talks back. I want to ask her advice on things, or just hear a nice word. But she never speaks to me."

"She hears you. Just keep talking and listening, and if you listen hard enough you'll hear her. I promise you that. But for now, go see Ritzpah, alright?"

That night she dreamed of Ma Tee for the first time. The old woman was clad in fine and shining raiment. Her face shone, too. Ma Tee was smiling and gesturing and saying something of which only the last word was clear: ". . . always." In the dream she asked for Ma Tee's help again and again, and each time she received the same answer, unintelligible except for one word: ". . . always." She awoke warmed by the sight of her smiling grandmother, yet perplexed, too, because she had asked Ma Tee for guidance and she had received from her nothing but a word that could refer to anything.

Late the next morning, the young woman scooped the kernels of wheat from her lap, set aside her grindstone, and slipped away from her work for the short walk to the hut of the old auntie. Ritzpah's dwelling sat on the small nahala of her son, alongside his hut, smaller yet tidier, except for the abandoned loom that leaned outside her door and shards of clay pots that lay scattered about.

Miss Ritzpah was a stout woman with a narrow face the color of copper whose delicate features were now cast in a perpetual scowl of etched frown lines and furrows. Her rumpled tunic bulged and strained over her broad old-woman bosom, and her wide old-woman hips and buttocks gave her the ongoing impression of bending even when she was standing erect. Her head covering had the askew hang of one past the point of concern for her own appearance. It covered half her wrinkled face and most of one eye, leaving the rest of her head and short gray mane exposed. Her hands were callused and gnarled, yet surprisingly small and constantly moving. She gestured a salutation without looking up from her spinning. Her young guest bowed in greeting. The old woman sat cross-legged upon a frayed brown woolen rug that in spots betrayed flecks of color indicating that it might once have had a ceremonial use, perhaps as a birthing mat or some such. She did not return the greeting. Instead she asked, "What's wrong with your mother?"

Her head was still bowed. "Why doesn't she talk to anyone anymore? She never comes to the river when the other women are there. And why doesn't she talk to you? Must not, if you're here with me."

"I-I-I . . ."

"Stop your stuttering, child, and answer me."

"I . . . I don't know. I guess she's just scared."

"That's it? Scared? Hummph. A whole lot of us women are scared. That doesn't mean you got to lose your mind and disappear from everybody's company."

The old woman's eyes were not cruel, nor was there the self-conscious gleam that usually accompanies intentional insult. Rather, because she was both self-absorbed and plainspoken, she paid no thought to the effect of her words on the feelings of others. But once she had voiced her complaint her countenance seemed to change, which was a welcome relief to the young bride-to-be. Still, Miss Ritzpah did not smile, her gaze remaining fixed upon her spindle.

"Well, we women saw her going downhill. A lot of the women went downhill after That Day. But she went faster than most; farther, too. We saw how she was. The knots and bruises. Every day more quiet, and

always looking like her mind was somewhere in the distance somewhere, anywhere but where she was. And seeing that hurt silence
draped all over her, we all wondered if she was teaching you, preparing
you to be a woman and to be somebody's wife."

"No, ma'am, my mama never told me anything. I used to ask her
questions, but questions just made her scared and she'd shoo me away.
Never really said anything. Now my daddy has betrothed me off to that
boy Jalon whose daddy treats him like God's gift to earth, and I don't
know what I'm supposed to do. That's why I came to see you."

"I know. You didn't never come talk to me before. So I didn't think
you were here to tell me Moses was a prophet."

For the first time the old woman smiled, but the smile quickly
ceased. They sat in silence as Miss Ritzpah fingered her spindle and
woolen thread.

Finally the young woman broke the quiet. "So what do I do, Miss
Ritzpah?"

The old woman dropped the spindle into her massive lap. "Well, I'm
glad you came to me instead of that Huldah, always talking about the
woman-side of God or Hokmah or whatever you call it, and how
women have to look out for themselves. Old as she is, she should know
to stick to midwifing and birthing babies, and leave the God-talk to
Abba Samuel."

Miss Ritzpah made a dismissive gesture. "Women don't need all that
Hokmah talk. All they need is to remember that the main thing a
woman has to do is please her man. Don't worry about him pleasing
you. You just please him."

Her young guest's expression was quizzical. "I don't understand,
Miss Ritzpah."

"You don't understand what?"

"I mean, well, I don't mean any harm, Miss Ritzpah, but I don't
understand why a woman should forget about herself and just look to
please her husband. We have feelings, too."

"Hasn't your mama taught you anything, child? It's in the scriptures
that a woman is supposed to please a man. And nobody but a fool and a
heathen is going to question God. Which one are you?"

"I don't mean any harm, Miss Ritzpah, but how do we know it's in the scriptures? I mean, all we know about the scriptures is what men tell us."

The old woman's jaw dropped. Her face was frozen in disgust and unbelief. Her young visitor felt a heightened uneasiness. The last thing she wanted was to anger the razor-tongued old woman. She spoke carefully, quietly.

"All I mean is, do women ever get a chance to be happy?"

Miss Ritzpah shook her head like she had seen the ghost of Pharaoh. "Girl, do you realize how gibora you sound?"

"I'm sorry, Miss Ritzpah. I don't mean any harm. I was just asking you . . ."

"I hear what you're asking, and I don't like it. Sounds like blaspheming to me. After the whippings your daddy put on you, and all the time Ma Tee spent trying to teach you right, I thought you would've had enough of all that gibora. But you haven't, I see. So let me tell you: just stop this crazy talk right now. You better do right, unless you want the rest of your life to be one big mess. Do you hear me?"

The young bride-to-be was close to tears now. "I didn't mean any harm, Miss Ritzpah. I was just wondering out loud."

"Well, don't wonder. Not about that, not about anything. You understand me?"

"Yes, ma'am."

Her tearful assent calmed Miss Ritzpah a bit. Her tone became more instructive, though petulance still suffused her every word.

"Now what did I tell you?"

The young woman answered quickly. "That I have to make sure I please my husband and don't put my mind on anything else."

"Now you're talking sense."

"But that's what I came here to know, Miss Ritzpah. How do I please him?"

"You really don't know? Well, how does your mother please your father?"

"She doesn't please him at all, to hear him tell it. He never acts like he's pleased."

"Well, she must do something right to get by at least."

"She just does what he tells her and what she thinks he wants."

"Then do that."

"But Miss Ritzpah, there must be more to it than that."

"No. There's not. It's really that simple. If a woman wants peace, she has to try to please her man. If you can do that, you'll be fine. If you don't, you won't."

"What about the rest of me? Isn't there more to being married than that?"

Miss Ritzpah's patience was almost gone. "I'm going to tell you one more time and then I'm though with it."

Now she spoke with pedantic condescension. "If a woman wants peace, she has to try to please her man. If you can do that, you'll be fine. If you don't, you won't."

She lifted the spindle from her lap. "Now go on home and get yourself ready to be married. And don't ask any more of those gibora questions either, if you know what's good for you. Shalom."

The flustered young woman backed out of the hut, bowing and nodding. "Shalom, Miss Ritzpah. Shalom. Thank you."

The old woman dismissed her with an irksome wave.

"Little fool," she mumbled. "That's a child bound for trouble."

Chapter

9

She awoke earlier than usual and was immediately aware of a knot in her stomach that was accompanied by an overwhelming feeling of dread: this was her wedding day. She lay stunned and perfectly still, as if perhaps the world would forget her if she did not move at all.

She heard her father snoring on his bed mat, and her mother moving with small, furtive motions, trying not to wake him. Despite her mother's careful silence, Aridai awoke with an abrupt snort and sat straight up, energized by both the promise of the day and his anxiety for everything to go well.

"Wake up, girl. You're getting married today. Act like you've got some business about yourself."

As the bride-to-be hurried to her feet, Aridai turned to her mother. "Woman, start getting your girl-child ready. I don't want no problems today. She's the one getting married, but today is my day. Now go get me my new tunic and make sure that girl-child of yours is wedding presentable."

Her wedding litter was draped with panels of brightly colored fabric and garlands of lilies and chamomile and narcissus. The litter rested on the shoulders of young groomsmen who gladly lent their muscle because it enabled them to parade their strength before the young maidens who merrily followed the cortege. The procession proceeded, as was the custom, from the bride's nahala to the nahala of her betrothed. Aridai walked before the litter loudly leading the wedding hymns, caring little for the words, seeking nothing as much as to draw the attention of the onlookers to himself. When the wedding party arrived, the young women sang and clapped and swayed together, while the young men stood around trying to look aloof and interested at the same time. In exaggerated merriment Aridai called to Ocran, who emerged from his hut with the groom, and the two fathers danced together briefly in forced camaraderie.

The bride was arrayed in a finery of embroidery and color. At the harsh instructions of her father, which in actuality had begun in earnest weeks before, her mother had come temporarily to life and prepared the presentation of her daughter, though not as her father directed but as she, her mother, wished. She adorned her in a linen wedding tunic dyed a deep yellow. Wound about her a mantle of bright red. Affixed tiny bells to her veil and the borders of her wedding shawl. Perfumed her body with oil scented with thyme. Transformed her hands and the soles of her feet into palettes of decorative henna. Set upon her head the wedding crown of jewels and gold, and made thick her hands and wrists with the bracelets and rings that were passed on and shared by each succeeding generation of village brides. And in a gesture so unaccustomed and so touching that it moved the almost bride to tears, her mother tenderly combed her hair to hang loose and uncovered as the proud and traditional public sign of the intact virginity of this, the last of her daughters.

"Comb it all the way out," Aridai said when he came to inspect her, obviously pleased with her appearance but unwilling to say so. "I don't want no questions or no suspicions."

At the wedding Aridai made an extra show of handing out ears of roasted corn, a tradition that also announced the wedding of a virgin bride.

Still, it was the groom that was the center of the wedding attention, as was the tradition as well. Jalon wore a striped yellow-brown tunic of the finest linen, tied with a mantle of yellow. The kaffiyeh that covered

his head and shoulders was of a striped fine cotton, and his neatly knotted sash was made of silk that Ocran had brought from Shechem. Hired
musicians trailed behind the groom, their drums and flutes and lyres
alive with songs of celebration. Jalon smiled and waved with such a victorious flourish that one would have thought he was Joshua newly
arrived from Jericho.

The villagers assembled in the yard, the women ritually separated
from the men by a chest-high, richly carved cedar partition brought
from the synagogue. The young men and the fresh-faced boys who
clustered about stood a small distance behind their male elders. The
young men shuffled and shared nervous humor, kicking at the dust in
the freshly swept yard, trying not to betray their envy at having been
bested in their quests to possess the soon-to-be bride, instead whispering sly speculations about the young women giggling behind the ranks
of their buzzing mothers.

The young women loosely flanked the scowling Izevel, who was
their de facto leader simply because her fearsome temper was the most
outstanding personality trait that had as yet been displayed by any of
them. In true and predictable form, Izevel did not hide her displeasure
at the attention directed at the bride, whom she had decided was again
her rival in life.

"That old gibora thing thinks she's so much," Izevel huffed.

"Well, she does look pretty, doesn't she?" replied one of the dreamy-
eyed girls.

"Pretty? She looks like a hag in a sack."

"Oh, come on, Izevel. If she's so ugly, why were all the boys trying to
court her?"

"They weren't all after her," Izevel said defensively. "They were trying to court me, too."

"You? Who?"

Izevel peevishly pointed to the groom. "I could have had him if I
wanted. I saw Jalon looking at me at market every time I turned
around."

"Izevel, that's just how Jalon looks. He looks at every girl that way.
Old jackal."

Izevel's anger was mounting. "Well, I don't think he's a jackal. And if I wanted him I could have him."

"Oh, really? So why is he marrying her and you're standing here with us?" The girls erupted in laughter.

Izevel glowered so angrily that it instantly burned the smiles from the young women's faces and induced an abrupt silence in them all.

"Just look at her," Izevel hissed. "That old gibora lucky-to-get-her-a-husband old thing. About as dumb as a rock and twice as ugly." She rolled her eyes, wagged her head, and made a grotesque face.

The girls snickered uneasily until the older women silenced them with frowns and cutting eyes. For once, the girls did not mind being hushed, for none wanted to further chance becoming the subject of Izevel's murderous tongue.

Except for the attention it focused on him, Jalon had little interest in ceremony or scriptures or vows. His thoughts were of the marital bed that awaited.

His stride was proud and cocky as he made his way through the crowd to the wedding canopy of palm fronds and cedar branches. When his eyes fell upon his veiled and bejeweled bride, he grinned, winked, and began to lick his lips.

As they waited for the ritual to begin, Aridai strutted before the canopy, his neck inclined so steep in self-importance that his Adam's apple protruded like he had swallowed a pomegranate whole.

The crowd's murmuring took on a new urgency as two solemn-looking men approached, preceding a much older man dressed in a tunic of white linen. The object of the two men's attention, whom they attended with great solicitude, was the village elder Abba Samuel, the rosh of ha-knesset, the village council. Abba Samuel was old and thin, but only slightly stooped, and walked with the step of a much younger man. Wisps of crinkled gray hair stretched across an otherwise bald head that was covered by an ever-present frayed and sweat-stained woven prayer cap. A white kaffiyeh was draped over his head and shoulders. It seemed that all the wisdom of his people was chiseled into the deep brown of his face.

The crowd hushed and quieted when Abba Samuel stepped with his dignity before the soon-to-be newlyweds.

"*Shemayeh, Yishrael!*" he said of a sudden in a surprisingly resonant voice. "Hear O Israel! The Lord your God, the Lord is One!"

The crowd bowed their heads and said, "*Ahad!* One!"

"Amen," said Abba Samuel.

"Amen," said the people.

Abba Samuel uttered a prayer infused with words of scripture. Then one of the solemn attendants handed him a scroll from which he offered the wedding sentences for the groom to repeat.

". . . you shall be my wife according to the law of Moses," the groom recited. "And if you are taken captive I will redeem you and take you back as my wife."

As was the tradition, the bride was asked nothing. Her bewilderment was hidden by her wedding veil.

After the last sentence had been read and repeated, Abba Samuel turned to the gathered men and asked, "Tell me, my brothers. Would a sane man mistreat his own flesh?"

With one voice they answered, "No sir, Abba."

Then Abba Samuel quoted from Genesis that two are to become one flesh. He concluded with what he called "logic straight from the mind of God": "If you mistreat your wife, you are mistreating your own flesh; you are acting the part of a madman. Does God want us to be madmen?"

"No sir, Abba," the men answered.

Abba Samuel squinted at the crowd to see if his words had touched anyone's heart. He saw the women's heads bob ever so slightly in agreement, careful not to offend the sensibilities of their husbands. From the men's glazed eyes it was clear that the meaning of his words had fallen on deaf and unyielding ears. They had learned to tolerate Abba Samuel's occasional homilies against divorce, to hear them without hearing them. After all, man of God or not, Abba Samuel was old and obviously out of touch with the realities of life. And the boredom beneath Jalon's lustful look revealed his response to be no different, if indeed his rampant fantasies of the night to come allowed him to hear Abba Samuel at all. The old man blinked back his disappointment and resolved that his meaning yet would be heard.

"What God has brought together, let no man put asunder," he challenged with a peeved and somber gravity.

The indictment of the men and their epidemic of erwat dabars was undeniable and exceedingly clear. What is more, it was buttressed by the authority of scripture; this they could not dismiss as the complaint of an old and out-of-touch man. They could not help but hang their heads before Abba Samuel's withering gaze. An awkward silence followed. Even the children stood hushed and still, so thick was the blanket of chastisement and chastened quiet.

Finally Abba Samuel sensed that his point had been made; the hung heads of the men seemed to betray that he had at least caused some of them to think. His eyes reflected a slight satisfaction, and the stern expression began to ease. With a wave he pronounced the ceremony complete and the marriage inviolate. Then, with unfolding bemusement he pointed to the wedding feast that Ocran had provided.

"And speaking of putting asunder," said Abba Samuel with dignified humor, "I'm sure God wouldn't mind us putting asunder the food and drink this man has laid out. Go on, children. Eat, drink, and be merry in God."

The guests feasted on lamb stew and roasted goat and honey-dipped breads and crisp, fried cakes of chickpea flour and sesame oil. They slaked their thirsts with three types of beer, with smooth thick beverages of yogurt and honey, and a good deal of wine.

The men danced with one another in the tradition of their people, and the women, doing the same, laughed as they seldom could, their tunics swirling about them as they spun from sister to sister, woman to friend. The young men jumped and whirled with muscularity, casting quick glances to see if they had the secret attention of their female counterparts, while the younger boys and girls danced in their separate groups with little self-consciousness to spoil their fun. The bride's father staggered about, drunk and happy; her mother stood silently at the edge of the festivities as if wishing to disappear; her father-in-law trafficked among the guests in boastful deportment; the women chattered advice and admonitions her way at the same time; Izevel stared daggers at her as the other girls stood sheepishly by; her new husband was forcefully insisting that she abandon the entire scene so he could begin to taste his conjugal entitlements; and the new bride stood in the midst of them all, wondering if she was losing her mind.

And so she was married.

In the predawn dark of the first day of her new life, she lay sore and bruised in the hut Ocran had built for his son and his new wife with the same stone walls and roof of dried reeds held fast with the same mortar of mixed mud and clay as all the huts in the village. She stared at the stone walls, smelled the still-drying mortar, felt her new husband spooned against her, his sweaty hands on her sore breasts, his sex twitching even in sleep, and thought back through her day. Much of it was a blur—the rituals of preparation, the wedding march, the ceremony, the festivities that followed. Still there was a fluidity to it, a flow, no matter how overwhelming. But her wedding night she remembered only in snatches and pulls. Pulled from the arms of her well-wishers. Pulled into new quarters without a hint of welcome. Pulled from the ceremonial garment her tired mother had spent a week of ill-lit nights preparing. Pulled onto her knees before him. Her face pulled against the throbbing in his groin. Pulled to her feet and onto the waiting bed mat. Legs pulled apart like kindling. He pulled away when he had finished and pulled from her grasp when she reached to him for comfort.

With Jalon's breath upon her neck, she silently enumerated the nocturnal affronts and humiliations. When she stood naked and vulnerable and he sputtered, "I didn't think you would be so skinny," that was one. When he thrust into her mouth and ignored her gagging, that was another. When he discounted her tears as he forced himself between her tense and quivering thighs, that was one also. When he pulled away the moment he was done with her, that was yet another. When he responded with cold indifference as she reached for some small reassurance, that was one, too. It seemed her hopes, her halting dreams, and in a real sense, her self-worth, too, had been snatched and pulled away before the dawn of their first morning together by the empty, grasping man-child with whom she had been sentenced to share her life. That is how her marriage began.

She thought she'd been prepared for the emptiness of marriage. She really had not expected much. She was sure that the sad smiles of the women, their vacant eyes and continuous complaints had prepared her. Her mother's fearful deference to her father, the way he ignored her presence when she spoke or entered a room, Ma Tee's admonition to accept defeat before battle had begun—she had been certain that it all had prepared her well. She'd had no illusions that a pedestal awaited her, but she never dreamed it would be like this, that her life would begin to ooze away the very first night. How could she know that the lifelong emptiness would begin at once, that he would simply climb off her, the saliva stringing from his mouth, snoring before she could even repeat his name, and that she would be "woman," only "woman" from the first moment of their first dawn together?

At the first flicker of day she eased from his sleeping grasp, slipped on what was left of her wedding garment, and arose to survey the breads and fruits and cheeses and fresh dates that had been laid aside for their first meal together. He drew his arms to his chest and pulled the blanket close about him. He did not stir immediately. He finally awoke grinning as she sliced the last of the fruit. Without a word, he reached for her. She pulled away.

"Don't. I'm sore."

"Come on. It won't hurt."

"The food is here waiting."

"That's why I have to work me up an appetite."

He pulled her again and took great pleasure in her pain, which made him thrust even harder, as if each cry from her was testimony to his prowess and power.

Her days lurched from one indignity to another. She strove to please her new husband, but she found that nothing she did was enough. In courtship she was a prize, her hand sought for bragging rights and sanctioned satiation of lustful desires. But bragging rights soon have no meaning, and she'd come to him a virgin ill prepared to meet his well-schooled lust. Although her virginity accorded her the right to live (the scriptures would have had her stoned if Jalon had found that she'd lain with another), in truth he did not care if she was a virgin or not. And any wife could cook, clean, wash, and plow. What Jalon wanted was practiced pleasuring. So she could do nothing right.

> Why's my food so hot? / Why's my food always cold?
> Why do you run your mouth so much? / Why don't you have anything to say?
> Why're you always in my face? / Where in the world have you been?
> Girl, you sure are skinny. / Move your big behind out my way.
> Go comb your nappy head. / Why are you always messing with your hair?
> The other fellas' women keep them satisfied. / What's wrong with you?

Nothing right. And she tried. His meals always on time. The hut neatly kept. His tunic laid out before light. She tried so hard to please him. Did the work of a man from can't-see in the morning to can't-see at night. Planted crops. Pulled roots. Dug potatoes. Fed goats.

And then there was the "woman's work." Carried water. Spun cloth. Washed clothes. Ground wheat.

And then there was the night work, when she was reduced to a thing, an object to be acted upon without even the respite for her menstrual blood that the scriptures commanded. Their time in bed was for her a time of unrelenting revulsion. She associated spanking with anger, not with titillation as did he, and biting with pain, not with pleasure or play. Nor could she shape her mouth to form the salty words he told her to speak to him, or to take into her mouth what he tried every day to force into it. It was all she could do not to turn away from him in screaming disgust. It was not that she did not want to please him. It was just that what so aroused him, sickened her. She did not want to tie him, or spank him with a stick, or lap milk from his body like a dog, or perform the other distasteful acts his seasons with Big Mama had taught him to expect. Still he tried, and sometimes half-succeeded, but just as often he stomped off in anger because she wrenched away from his demands and cringed.

Other than the things she could not bring herself to do, she tried everything she could to be pleasing. Splashed her skin with water scented with lemongrass oil. Dressed her hair with lilacs and anemone. Kept the holes mended in her everyday tunic. Slept close to him in the posture of a dutiful wife in spite of his repugnant and uncaring demeanor. Said "Good morning" to the grunts that passed as his greetings and "Good night" to them, too. Did everything she could, but Jalon just was not to be pleased. He didn't care that her every move had his comfort in mind; that, he thought, was what a wife was supposed to do. All Jalon knew was that he was not feeling what he wanted or thought that he should.

After weeks of cajoling his new wife, trying to manipulate her into his carnal bidding by criticizing and berating her; after nights of continual frustration, of turning from her stricken with dissatisfaction so thick he could choke on it, Jalon finally realized that what he really wanted was more than a woman's body, more even than a woman who knew how to use her body. What he desired, what he needed, what he craved was rolling heft and an enveloping bosom to make him feel safe and loved. And not just loved, but loved like a son. He didn't care about manhood; he had time to grow into a man. And if he knew nothing else, he knew what it was to be the son of a man. What he knew of but little, and wanted most of all, was to feel himself the beloved son of a loving woman. The safety, the security, the enveloping cocoon of happiness— since the theft of his mother, these he had known only when he lay in Big Mama's arms. So his discontent with the women who shared his home became so thick and harsh and immutable that he could see her as nothing but a source of eternal offense to whom he owed neither kindness nor consideration.

Thus the tone and the tempo of their lives were determined by Jalon's whims and wants. Her days were uniformly stolid with the unchanging sameness of the dry and dusty landscape. On occasion there were rain showers, and then there was the excitement of variety and newness. When it rained briefly and with little conviction, the earth was wetted, but only as a tease of the refreshing change that could be, for in reality it retained the sandy sameness that characterized most of its days. Even when the rainfall was not strong, if it lingered it could transform the parched dirt into a soothing alchemy of moisture and earth that was at once refreshing and luxuriant, salving new hurts and sometimes old ones. Or in the rare case of a deluge, the truest rarity in her dry and stony land, there were puddles and torrents and gullies come to life, a landscape born anew with the soaring exhilaration of hope and fertile portents. But always the heat and the dryness returned, the barren gullies and parched dry earth, the same scrappling sameness as always as if the grand gesture had never been, and then she was left with the same old dust, the same old dryness, the same stifling heat, the sameness of her life. Up before light to relieve his lust and fix his morning meal. Stooped low in the fields throughout the day wresting a crop from the earth, her toil interrupted only to serve his midday meal and lie with him before returning to the soil and the heat. Then home to cook, spin, and grind in the waning evening light, and finally to lie in the dark beneath his callous and grunting form trying her best to ignore his complaints, which were sometimes shouted, sometimes hissed.

If she did not do a thing exactly as he would (or as he thought he would), speak or explain with the same words and pacing of response as he, he leaped upon that as proof of her unworthiness. And although he'd never called her by name, now even "woman" was too endearing for his tongue. "Stupid" became his main term of address, with "ugly" and "skinny" not far behind. He reserved "heifer" for the occasions when he really wanted to denigrate her, implying as it did that she was a creature valued only for her flesh and nothing more.

Through it all she did not even have the joyous expectation of motherhood to season her despair. From the very first his coldness and insensitivity had frightened her into secretly visiting the midwife Huldah for advice on how to keep from conceiving. Huldah asked the nature of her distress, but the anxious young woman remembered Ritzpah's admonition and without answering paid Huldah with two turnips and a faint smile. How could she confide in a woman who at every turn questioned men's right to rule, when the scope of her truest fear was much more narrow: the new outrages Jalon might inflict upon her when she was heavy with child or weakened from birthing and even more vulnerable to his cruelty.

Without asking again, Huldah silently poured a large measure of fennel seeds from a wide bowl into a length of cloth, then added to it several handfuls of the thick green moss that grew at the base of the trees at the river. She wrapped the cloth into a bundle and handed it to her guest.

"Every day drink a tea of fennel. Use the moss to protect yourself at night, just to be sure." Huldah handed her the bundle, then touched her arm and looked into her eyes. "I'm here for you if you need me. Don't let the gossip keep you from my door."

"I won't," she said. But she knew it already had. And though she felt Huldah's sincerity, and part of her longed to drink in her strength, she thought it better to hurry from the midwife's door. She had enough problems without being associated with an old troublemaker who was tolerated only because she was good at birthing babies not her own.

As harvest time drew near, Jalon took to drinking great amounts of wine and forcing himself upon her with that sense of entitlement that accompanies drunkenness. She was particularly careful not to resist him when he was inebriated because, loosed as he was from the little restraint he had, his treatment of her could be particularly rough. In these moments of passivity something strange began to happen. As Jalon snatched and pulled at her, Ma Tee began to appear as a presence she could see not only in her dreaming but in her waking, too. Ma Tee beckoned to her and spirited her away. Together they journeyed from the hut that smelled of wine and sex and self-centered meanness masquerading as desire, to places so beautiful they made Shechem look like a hovel. To jeweled temples and flower-filled meadows and verdant valleys that stretched forever. Ma Tee took her to enclaves of strong and loving men, of well-clad, smiling children, of women secure and satisfied, happiness writ large across their glowing faces. She guided her to all these places and more, and they traversed them together as long as Jalon slobbered atop her. It was only the happy worlds revealed in those journeys with Ma Tee that kept the suffering bride from descending into the beckoning grasp of madness.

Just when it seemed she could bear no more, she began to sense a change in Jalon, a lightness, what seemed to her a possible harbinger of something good. His demeanor became almost pleasant, he smiled to himself often and even talked to her more, and about more than carnality. He began to speak of their life together, that it was his belief that a husband and wife should do anything for each other. She thought he was leading to a new sexual offensive, but even that part of their lives became more restrained, and he now approached her less often, and now without force.

She did not know what to make of his new persona, but she thought to attribute it to the pride that accompanied the harvesting of his first crop as a man. Whatever its cause, however, it was such a welcome change in her world that she was not as skeptical as she might have been, for Jalon spoke of trust, of adventure, of together sharing new things in their new life, and, for the first time, called her his wife.

"A man's got to show his wife new things," he told her, "new things in life so things don't get moldy and old so quick that you wake up one day and wonder where the young parts of you went."

For the first time in their life together, she began to venture a sense of hope, though small and halting, but hope nonetheless. And now she smiled more, too, and sometimes sang in the fields. At home and even in the midst of their labors she fussed and made over Jalon, wiped his brow or brushed the dust from his head and wispy beard, now that she did not fear that small shows of kindness and concern would ignite his juices and cause her to feel like prey. His smile in response to her small demonstrations of affection at times looked to

her like slyness, as if lurking behind it was something other than gratitude and growing fondness, but she chose to ascribe her discomfort
to her unfamiliarity with this side of him. To her joy and amazement,
in those weeks their life together began to take a tone of untroubled
ease and a semblance of peaceful constancy. Still, even with this she
was more than surprised when Jalon told her that it was his intention
to take her to Shechem.

"There's a lot a man can experience with his wife in Shechem."

"But women don't ever go on the trading caravan, do they?"

"Well, they said that boys weren't supposed to go either, but I went.
I guess when there's something folks don't do, they don't do it until
they finally go on and do it. I want to take my wife to Shechem, so that's
what I'm going to do."

Still, it was more complicated than that. Women and travel, that was
a bother. But a woman and a trading caravan? Not only would she be a
nuisance, but surely her presence would do dangerous things to everyone's luck. So in the end, Jalon gave his trading goods to the safekeeping
of the others, and he and his bride set off to Shechem apart from the
men, which quieted their complaints and their fears.

As they traveled the parched and dusty roads together, Jalon was
more animated than she'd seen him before. He regaled her with
descriptions of the narrow roads and winding alleys of Shechem, its
two-story dwellings like huts stacked one atop the other. She smelled
the smells of its streets and markets, the pungent odors of its livestock
grounds, the stench of its open sewers. And she marveled at his tales of
the women who each, he said, dressed every day like a queen of Egypt
or an empress of Persia.

"How do they dress so fine?" she asked.

"The men give them gifts to thank them for acting like a woman is
supposed to act."

She sensed again in him what seemed to be that slyness, and there
again arose in her a sudden chill of suspicion. But he'd been so good to
her, taking her along even in the face of the men's opposition, and his
manner now seemed to her so earnest, almost charming, that she convinced herself to lay her doubts aside.

"How is that?" she asked. "I mean, how do they say a woman is supposed to act?"

"Well, I can't rightly say . . ." This was indeed a new thing, Jalon admitting uncertainty about anything, which disarmed her even more. ". . . because they're town women, and they know a whole lot more than us country folks. But I'm sure it's nothing bad," he added with even more of his studied affability, "cause if it was, you can believe that those town fellas wouldn't appreciate it and give them all those gifts. Right?"

Before she could answer, however, he spoke with great and smiling innocence. "But town folks are more sophisticated than us country folks. So let's go ask some of the town women what they know about how a woman is supposed to act."

When they finally entered Shechem, Jalon was so giddy with excitement that he dismounted and led his donkey. His wide-eyed wife gazed from side to side at the strange dwellings standing tall and straight like cedars. She stared with amazement at the gaudy, half-dressed women flicking their tongues and blowing kisses at the men as they passed. Unlike the other men, Jalon did not seem interested in the spectacle of the women; he barely seemed to acknowledge them. Instead, he seemed to look for something specific. She watched the movement of his back and felt pride at his casual worldliness. She was impressed and grateful that he'd had the presence of mind to plot their trip on routes that were free of bandits. And then he'd spiced her nights with his tales of big-town living. But there was more than that. She'd felt him rub against her as they snuggled for warmth beneath the stars, yet he hadn't once torn at her clothing. Didn't that mean that things were different? And now she was at Shechem, something no other woman of her village had experienced. He'd even defied the other men so she might be with him. She felt a measure of security for the first time since Ma Tee left her.

Jalon's soft command woke her from her daydream. "Let's stop here," he said, halting before one of the stone dwellings. In the doorway of the dwelling stood a fat smiling woman in a rich, flowing garment, weighted down with gaudy jewelry that hugged her fat wrists, circled the folds of her neck, lay flat against the mounds of her bosom. "Well, if it ain't Mr. Almost-A-Man, come back to see Big Mama!" she squealed.

The young woman dismounted and leaned against the donkey in confusion. This big, bejeweled woman of Shechem was shamelessly addressing her husband—her husband—with unbridled familiarity. Jalon stretched wide his arms and said in a low growl, a voice she'd never heard before, "Looka here, looka here. It's Big Mama, with her big sweet self."

Jalon buried himself in the fat woman's bosom and they hugged in a way that did not appear to be quite decent. After what seemed to her like full minutes of swaying embrace, Jalon suddenly turned in afterthought and pointed to the openmouthed young woman.

"Big Mama, I got someone for you to meet." He pointed. "This . . . this is . . . my wife."

The big woman looked from Jalon to his bride. "Your wife?"

Big Mama did not hide her consternation. Jalon continued with affected nonchalance. "Yes, ma'am. I'm married. I told you I was getting married."

The big woman said nothing. Just stared with a stunned look that was fast unfurling into a frown.

That this Big Mama disapproved of her presence was clear, but she thought it was because Big Mama was a city woman and she was a stranger, and a country girl at that. So she decided to placate the big woman with friendliness and respectful familiarity.

"Hello, Big Mama," she said, smiling with a warmth she did not really feel.

Big Mama stared a moment more, than turned to Jalon, trembling with anger. "What you bring her here for? You trying to play with me?"

In the face of the big woman's ire, Jalon could no longer maintain his cool facade. "No, ma'am, Big Mama. I thought maybe you could teach her something. She's only a girl. She doesn't know anything about being a woman. I need you to teach her how to treat her man."

Jalon winked when he said it, and Big Mama felt a bead of sweat trickle between her big breasts.

"Well, I guess she is just a girl."

The young woman thought she sensed a stir of warmth from Big Mama, although her own cheeks stung with embarrassment. She strained to maintain her smile.

"Well, bring her in, bring your donkeys around back, and make yourselves to home. Then let's see what we can learn her." She returned Jalon's wink.

With a grudging smile Big Mama led her to a room in the back of the dwelling and gestured toward the low scrolled couch that filled most of it.

"The other girls that live here are gone to work the crows at a religious get-together in Sebaste for a few days. This room belongs to one of them. You can rest here. Won't nobody bother you cause everybody knows that no one comes into this house without being invited. In the meantime, me and Mr. Almost-A-Man, I mean, er, your husband, we going upstairs to talk a little while."

Jalon returned from securing their mounts. Big Mama said to him, "You come upstairs so Big Mama can talk to you."

"Yes, ma'am," he said, grinning. "Let's you and me talk."

She wanted to call to Jalon as he mounted the stairs, to call him back to her, but she was too confused to speak. She did not want to distrust him unnecessarily; maybe it was just her unfamiliarity with town ways that was the cause of her discomfort. So she nodded instead and offered a weak smile.

Jalon and Big Mama disappeared upstairs and she was left alone to study her surroundings. A pitcher of fine ceramic fired with rose-colored designs sat in a ceramic basin. Several double-wicked oil lamps lit the room, which was vaguely smoky from the lamp oil and burning pots of spicy incense. She lay back on the soft pillows of the low couch to ponder the new and quickly unfolding events and almost immediately drifted into a deep sleep.

When she awoke it was hours later. Dusk had overrun the room. The oil lamps cast long overlapping shadows from their spacings about her. She heard low voices but saw no one. She rose and took short, tentative steps about the strange room, then into another, calling softly. When there came no response, she listened again and realized that the voices were those of Jalon and Big Mama above her. She began to mount the stairs, paused halfway and called again. When there came no answer, she took the last few stone stairs, which led her into a large room with several empty couches. The room itself was dark, but through a doorway to its left a lamp glowed faintly. From the room drifted the laughing voices of Big Mama and Jalon. She heard pieces of their conversation, and sounds that were usually heard after a satisfying meal.

The young woman pushed aside the curtain and entered the room.

They were reposed upon a couch that was larger and higher than the one from which she'd just risen. Jalon lay with his head in Big Mama's lap, one hand loosely across his chest, the other caressing her big knee and thigh. Big Mama half-wore a thin robe rather than the rich tunic that had draped her when she'd seen her last. It was very loosely pulled around her, falling away from her cleavage and much of her thighs. Jalon lay under a blanket that covered only his midsection; his chest and his legs from midthigh lay shamelessly exposed. His tunic was flung in a corner atop a stack of pillows. Both Big Mama and Jalon emanated the strong smell of new and hard-earned sweat.

She must have let out a startled gasp, because they looked at her at the same moment. Neither made an effort to move or cover themselves. Their eyes lighted, not from shame or even welcome, but from something else, something she did not recognize.

The big woman spoke first. Embarrassment had long ago left her emotional vocabulary. She smiled with the nonchalance of one who was simply doing what she pleased with what she considered to be rightfully hers.

"Don't stand there like you on the other side of the chilly Jordan," she said. "Come in here and join us."

Jalon did not try to disguise his excitement. "Yeah, girl. Come on over here. Big Mama said she's going to teach you and me about big town–type loving."

She did not move immediately. She did not want to seem like she did not trust Jalon; of late things had gone so well that she did not want to cause a problem between them now. She knew that she had not been a pleasing wife, not in the ways that he wanted, and maybe this was her chance to learn. But this . . . something about this did not feel right. Still, he seemed so different, so concerned for her. What if this really would be good for them?

"Come on, now. Sit on down with me and Big Mama," he said again, patting the couch and grinning.

She moved toward them, but slowly, looking from one to the other, finally primly alighting at the edge of the couch cradling her knees. Jalon began to rub her back.

"Big Mama's going to teach us," he announced grandly, his smile even broader now.

"Alright," she said without moving.

"That's right, baby," said Big Mama. She also began to rub the young woman's back, then her thigh. Now both their hands were upon her. She tried to smile, but she was too uneasy.

"Come on," said Jalon. "Take off that tunic and get yourself comfortable. So Big Mama can show us what we ought to know."

A part of her was straining to go along, trying hard to preserve the newly comfortable terrain of her marriage, but a larger part of her said no. She thought she heard Ma Tee whisper *Be careful* with more urgency than she ever had in life, and she found herself mouthing the words herself, as if Ma Tee was speaking to her and through her.

She pulled away and stood to face Jalon. "I'm sorry. This doesn't feel right. I want to go, Jalon. Please."

Jalon did not move. The smile left his face. "Now wait a minute. Big Mama is fixing to do us a favor."

"I don't know Big Mama," she said. "And why do I have to take off my clothes to learn something?"

Jalon flashed a smile that was breathtaking in its transparency. "We can't teach you about loving with your clothes on, now can we?"

"We? I thought Big Mama was teaching us. Seems like you and your friend here have been cooking up something to trick me into."

"No, sweetheart," said Big Mama, reaching for her again. "We just thought we all could enjoy each other and learn ourselves something in the bargain."

"We could learn something?" she said as she pushed away the fat woman's hand. She turned to Jalon. "You know this isn't right. I'm your wife. It's supposed to be me and you, one flesh before God, hallelujah, amen, like Abba Samuel said. This is wrong, you and this old woman lying here half-naked. It's wrong and it's ugly, and God does not like ugly."

The big woman raised up, her eyes flashing. "Who you calling old, you skinny little stick of backcountry kindling? I'll . . ."

Jalon jumped to his feet. "Hold on, Big Mama. She came with me. I'll talk sense to her." He reached for his wife's arm and squeezed it hard.

"Listen, woman. Ain't nothing ugly but your skinny little no-loving self. I'll tell you what's ugly: the way you can't do anything right anymore, especially when it comes to pleasing your man. You know why I stopped putting my hands on you? Cause I got tired of you whining and squirming and acting like you don't have the first clue to being a full-blooded woman."

He pointed to Big Mama, who was fuming and heaving, her fat fists balled and pressed at her hips. "This here is a real woman. She got meat on her bones and she knows how to treat a man with it. You need somebody to teach you *something*, and Big Mama's forgotten more about loving than you even thought about learning. So you just sit yourself down and do what your husband says. You can start by taking off that tunic."

Jalon grabbed at her garment.

She struggled to free herself. "No! I want to go!"

Jalon drew back to strike her, but Big Mama caught his arm.

"Now wait a minute," she said. "I don't care what she's did. Big Mama don't allow no woman-beating in here. By nobody." She glared at Jalon until he loosed the young woman's arm, but his anger was not cooled.

"I'm your husband, and I'm telling you what I expect you to do."

She began to cry. "But I can't. I can't do this. It's not right."

She touched his elbow. "Please. Let's leave here and go on and camp somewhere for the night."

Jalon jerked away. "We're not going anywhere. This is where we're staying. Here. With Big Mama."

"No. I don't want to stay here."

"Well, go ahead then. I'm staying here. If you leave, you're leaving alone."

"But where am I going to go? I don't know anybody in this big town."

"I know. That's why you need to calm down and sit down."

"But you don't just mean stay. You mean stay and do what you want."

"What's wrong with that? I'm your husband."

"You're my husband and I want to please you. But I can't do this. I won't."

"Listen, heifer, didn't Eve come from Adam? That's why men are over women. And that's why women are supposed to obey men. That's scriptural."

She knew nothing of the scriptures, so she could not rebut him. All she could do was shake her head as vigorously as she could. "No. No."

Jalon raised his shoulders then let them drop. "Alright. Suit yourself. But I'm staying here." He took Big Mama's hand.

"But . . ."

Jalon interrupted her. "But nothing. Either sit yourself down like an obedient wife or go on out of here and see what happens to a woman that don't respect her husband. And don't touch none of the provisions we brought, neither." He turned his back with an air of stark finality.

Her eyes filled with tears. She looked from one to the other, then turned to leave. Big Mama spoke up when the young woman reached the stairs. The big woman looked stricken.

"Now, wait. You can't let this country girl go out into town without knowing anything or anybody and without a shekel to her name."

"That's her choice. She said she don't want to stay."

"What she means is that she don't want to do what you got planned for her. Don't she have a right to say no?"

"Not to her husband she don't."

"I don't care. Don't no woman want to be alone in a strange place. Let her stay. She can use that same room downstairs."

"Well, I ain't sleeping with her. I'm sick of her."

"That's just fine, Mr. Almost-A-Man. You gonna sleep right up here with Big Mama. Your wife," she said with a sniff, "can sleep downstairs."

It was light when she awoke to unmuted voices and the sounds of heated carrying-on above her head, the same sounds to which she had fallen asleep in the late watches of the night. She lay clutching Ma Tee's little box of trinkets and broken mementos, reclining in the room of a stranger on a couch that smelled of too many bodies and too little myrrh, tossed and tormented by the sounds of her husband dishonoring her. The awful day before she'd fled from his nastiness into the teeming streets and tried to slip unnoticed into the crowd of staring farmers and vagabonds and beggars and thieves, each seeming more threatening than the last. Each glance she met, no matter how fleeting, reminded her that in these overflowing alleys she was a woman unprotected, a woman who knew no one and had no destination. She'd thought to look for the caravan from her village, but what was she to tell them? That her husband lay in the arms of another woman, big and profane and without the least acquaintance with modesty, whom he preferred nonetheless to the wife with whom he slept every day? And even if they were to suck their teeth and shake their heads with disgust, she knew that none would interfere in the marital affairs of another man.

So she'd returned in quiet humiliation. Big Mama's voice bellowed down to her the moment she stepped inside.

"Who's that?" the big woman said threateningly. "Don't nobody come in here without being invited."

She did not answer; the veil of her humiliation was too thick for speech. The big woman stomped threateningly down the stairs.

"Oh. It's you," said Big Mama in a tone that was almost empathic. "Ain't nothing to be ashamed of. You not the first who lost her man to Big Mama. But don't worry, I'll give him back. I know he's your husband, but you just remember that when he's in Shechem he belongs to me. He's welcome to see Big Mama whenever he gets ready, and I'm going to welcome him just like he's my own . . . like he's my own."

The big woman tossed her head. "There's fruit and goat cheese on the table and a pitcher of date wine under it. You welcome to it."

Big Mama turned and remounted the stairs. "We'll be down soon," she said over her shoulder.

For the rest of the day she saw neither Jalon nor Big Mama. They remained sequestered in their passion. When they were hungry they nibbled on the small fare that lay strewn among her jewelry and jars of perfumed oil, and they used her chamber pot when the need for comfort arose.

Although she did not see them, she heard them, at times loud and profane and as shamelessly uninhibited as animals, at other times tender and loving, sharing words of affection as soft as butter. She was mortified by their debauchery, but it was the sounds of caring and affection that struck her worse. All that she had known of Jalon was his mountain of complaints and his dissatisfaction with everything she did. Yet he not only sounded satisfied with Big Mama's every act, but with everything about Big Mama. He laughed at Big Mama's jokes, listened to her thoughts, whispered words so sweet they might have been made of honey, complimented her every breath and movement. And the big woman reciprocated with a rush of affection so deep and needful that it seemed that her goal was to consume Jalon. As his young wife lay on the scrolled pillowed couch beneath them, Jalon professed his undying love for Big Mama and reveled in his undying lust.

. . .

"Get up, woman." It was Jalon calling through the dawn-lit motes of morning. In truth his wife had risen long ago to prepare for the journey home, so anxious was she to be gone from this site of humiliation and hurt. Though she had spent an almost sleepless night, she was not fatigued; she simply was ready. Ready to leave and waiting to do so.

For the last two nights and the mornings that followed there had been happiness and laughter at the top of the stairs. Now as they prepared to leave, there was only the awkward shuffle, the stifled sob, the thick and only slightly broken silence that exuded from the young man and the big woman in their palpable sadness. Finally, there were words.

"I got to go, Big Mama."

"I know. Just let Big Mama hold you. Just a little while. Before you go."

Then again, "I got to go, Big Mama."

Now the sound of movement.

"You know Big Mama is going to miss you, you little crow."

"I'm going to miss it, too, Big Mama, being with a real woman who knows how to treat a man for real. And who got some meat on her bones. But I'll be back, and next time I'll stay more than a couple of days."

"How you gonna do that? What about that girl downstairs you're married to?"

"What about her?"

Except for Jalon's occasional barked command to her or to the donkeys, their journey home was silent. His face held a scowl that was broken only by sleep or by the small distractions of eating and drinking. He rode ahead, keeping his distance from her. He remained aloof when they made camp at dusk, sitting with his indifferent back squared against her, and sleeping that way, too.

They were within a half-day's journey of home when she finally broke the silence.

"Why are you treating me like this? You act like I did something bad to you."

Wielding the tongue he'd been sharpening all the way from Shechem, Jalon flung his words without looking at her.

"It's not what you did; it's what you didn't do. You ain't satisfied me once since we got married. But when you get a chance to do something about it, all of a sudden you're ready to leave."

He slowed his mount to make sure she heard him. "I'm sick of your whining and all when I'm just trying to get me some marital satisfaction like God says I'm entitled to. If it wasn't for your daddy, I would have left your little skinny uncooperative self in Shechem and let you see how far your whining will get you."

"I didn't do anything. What you asked me to do is wrong."

"Don't tell me nothing about what's wrong. It's wrong not to satisfy your husband, that's wrong. It's wrong to walk around all skinny without no meat on your bones. Skinny and disobedient. That's wrong."

"I try everything I can, and still I can't do anything right for you."

"That's for sure. You haven't done a thing right since I married you. Can't cook, don't know how to treat a man, ain't hardly no help in the fields at all. Can't do nothing right."

"I've been the best wife I could. You never—"

"Just shut your mouth. I don't want to hear another word from you."

"But—"

"Shut up, I said! I'm through listening to your whining. Just shut your mouth."

He spurred his beast ahead and reclaimed his angry distance.

Neighbors waved and offered distracted half-smiles as she and Jalon wound their way through the fields toward the familiar sight of their own hut, riding in tandem in their tense and oppressive silence. At last they sauntered their donkeys into their yard. Silently dismounting, they began to loose the few bundles from the backs of the beasts. She had filled her arms and started for the hut, shooing away the nosying goats, when Jalon caught her arm.

"Where you think you're going?"

She looked at him quizzically. "Inside. To start supper."

He shook his head and pulled her away. "Don't you touch nothing."

"What do you mean?"

"I mean you don't live here no more. I'm divorcing you. The scriptures give me the right and I'm using it."

"Why? But what did I do? I tried to be a good wife."

"What did you do? Girl, you sound right pitiful."

"But—"

"But nothing. What you did back there with Big Mama was an erwat dabar if there ever was one. Disobeying your husband. Storming out into the street all by yourself. Sleeping downstairs and leaving your husband alone."

"But you put me out. And you weren't alone. You were with that fat old woman."

He broke at her as if to strike her. "Don't you disrespect Big Mama. She's more woman than you ever thought about, you little skinny thing."

"But I—"

"But nothing. I need a woman to satisfy me. I need a woman who'll let me lie on her bosom; who'll rub my head and stroke my face and rock me like her baby-child. I need a woman to give me what my mama never got a chance to."

"But I'm not your mama."

"I know you're not. That's why I'm divorcing you right now. I want a mama, a woman who will rock me like a baby and rock me like a man, both. You don't do neither one. So you can just get on away from here. I don't want to spend another night with you, you scrawny little thing."

She thought of her father's fierce admonition, and desperation began to set in.

"I'll do better. I will. I can learn. Just give me a chance. Please."

Her helplessness appealed to him, made him feel all the more important and all the more in control. Yet it was not nearly enough, for what he really wanted was to return to Big Mama, and this time for good.

"I don't care how much you beg. I'm through. I don't want nothing else to do with you."

"But where will I go?"

"That's your problem. You should have thought of that when you were disobeying your husband and cringing around in bed like you were scared you might break. Now go!"

Through her ordeal at Shechem she had been too stunned to cry, to really cry. But now she wept. She was on the verge of begging, and she would have had she thought it would do any good. Instead she shrugged in tearful resignation. What else could she do? She dropped her head and spoke in a voice suddenly drained of emotion.

"If that's the way you want it, I guess there's nothing I can do."

"At least you got something right," he said with a sneer.

"Well, if you'll just collect my ketubah, I'll go."

He gave her a look that was one part surprise, one part cruel triumph. "Your ketubah? Your daddy didn't tell you? You don't have no dowry."

"What do you mean? There's supposed to be a dowry for a bride to fall back on if she needs to."

"Not for you. How do you think my daddy outbid all the others? Cause he saved your daddy the price of a dowry. My daddy told your daddy that if he would accept our bride-price, he wouldn't ask a dowry for you. They kept it quiet so Abba Samuel wouldn't find out and raise a stink about it."

Jalon laughed as if he was thoroughly amused.

"So there's no dowry for me to give you. You came here with nothing, you didn't do nothing, so you're leaving with nothing."

"But how am I going to live?" she sobbed, the specter of the dispossessed women encamped helter-skelter outside the village suddenly looming before her.

"You got that little box of your grandmother's old worthless stuff," he laughed. "And you can keep that sack of old bread you're holding. Go on," he said, "take it. It's stale anyway."

Chapter

12

The air is thick with wine and sweat and the lingering weight of sadness. She rises in the dim light of the creeping morning and yawns loudly as she dons her everyday tunic. She does not worry that she will wake the snoring figure beside her, for his nightly drunkenness shields his sleep from any sounds she might make, from even the words she ventures to speak. She frowns at the hovering stench of stale wine and rotted fish on both his unwashed body and the garments he has again passed out in.

Slipping on her sandals, carelessly pulling a frayed scarf over her head, she stoops through the doorway of the hut, picks up a large clay jar, deftly balances it on her head, and sets out for the well at the far end of the village to fetch the day's water.

She returns with the full vessel and carefully sets it down. She spills none of it. Without pausing she lifts a small clay jug, steps outside again, and chases down a shy goat. Kneeling in the dust, she reaches beneath it and, after a succession of swift spurts, picks up the half-full jug and goes back inside. With a hollowed gourd she ladles water into a shallow clay bowl. After washing her face and hands, she slices a cucumber and a small hunk of goat cheese and neatly places it all in another bowl next to the jug. The sun is peeking over the horizon now.

"Man," she calls to him. "Man. It's time to get up."

He is Her Second. "Man" is not his name, but what she calls him, what everyone has called him since his solitary arrival from Galilee, as the fullest measure of what he offered of himself and of what they knew him to be: only that he was a man, that he was alive, though barely, and that he did not care—for anything. He'd stumbled into the courtyard with eyes like a corpse and a body so angular and emaciated that he looked like a stunted cedar draped in an oversized tunic, a tunic so filthy that every woman that saw him—and some of the men, too— longed to burn it. His dark hair was nappy and matted with dirt, and his thin, bearded face with raven's eyes and almond skin was almost stately in its impassivity. When the men greeted him, his eyes did not light in recognition nor did his blank expression change. His only acknowledgment was to blink slowly and nod more slowly still. When asked his name he parted his parched lips, painfully and haltingly, and exhaled a breath sour with sorrow so great that those around him felt the urge to weep without knowing why.

"A man," he said in a voice that rasped with thirst and old grief. "That's all. Just a man."

His accent betrayed his origins as a Galilean and a Jew, a traditional and age-old enemy of Samaritans everywhere. This moved one of the men to hiss, with more bark than bite, "He got some nerve, a Galilean coming down here. Send him home with some knots on his head and I bet he'll be more careful where he goes next time," to which the other men murmured swift assent. Yet even in the face of such open menace, the man's countenance remained stolid and unmoved.

Despite their threatening words, however—the result of years of strident religious propaganda and idle campfire mutterings of contentions whose meaning they had long ago forgotten—the men's true response to him was not hostile at all. Instead it contained a shared sorrow, so deep was the sadness that oozed from his every pore. And that is why he, a Galilean and a Jew, was accepted into her village without the traditional gauntlet of difficulty when his ancestry would have otherwise made him unwelcome. Yet he asked for nothing, and his lifeless eyes gave the distinct impression that he did not care if he tasted food or drink again. Still the men bade him to follow so they might feed him and guide him to the river where he could wash and take his rest. He would have followed, too, if at his first step he had not collapsed at their feet from hunger and exhaustion and thirst and a prolonged and long-standing uncaring if he lived or died.

When he finally awoke it was two days later, under the sycamores and willows at the bend of the river, where he lay beneath a makeshift tent like the one that had sheltered Yoram. His filthy tunic was gone and in its place he now wore a garment that was clean but threadbare. The layers of desert dirt that had covered him had been washed from his hands and face, and from the morsels in his beard it was clear that someone had fed him during his insensate sleep. The realization that he had been the recipient of these kindnesses caused a sharp pang of remembrance to wash over him. He squeezed his eyes shut, shivering with emotion.

When his memory was at last dispatched, he pushed up on his elbows and looked at the men at the river's edge, not forty paces before him, talking and laughing and hoisting skins of wine. He raised himself from his improvised bed of stacked palm fronds covered by a coarse woolen blanket. The men turned to him and stared as he approached on faltering legs, his reddened eyes pleading, his shaking hand word-lessly extended before him. After a moment of pause, one of the startled men passed him a wineskin.

"It's straight wine, not diluted," said its owner, "so be careful you don't drink too fast. Don't want you falling out again and all."

The man ignored the admonition and drank with deep and unquiet desperation, pausing only when his imperious lungs demanded that he breathe. Wordlessly he turned back to the makeshift tent, the half-full vessel still in hand, his pain slowly dulling from the drink. Of course he had tasted wine before the drought destroyed his life, but then as a staple, not as an inebriant. His people had frowned on drunkenness, and so had he. This was a new sensation—his sorrow blunted by the sweetness of wine—but one so welcome that he resolved right then that he would never again be far from it.

The wineskin's owner opened his mouth to ask for it back, but the man's sadness suddenly overcame him and instead he dropped his head, stared into the gurgling river, and uttered a thanksgiving to the Lord of Hosts that whatever had murdered the spirit of this stranger had not befallen him.

"Uhh. Woke up drinking," one of the men whispered, giving voice to the silent thoughts of the others. "Lord only knows what that man been through."

From then the men of the village accepted him as their drinking partner but nothing else, because he asked for nothing more and offered even less. They were relieved he did not share the source of his suffering with them, for they had enough pain of their own.

When he'd regained his strength, which was a miracle in itself in that his only staples were his daily wine and what little fish he managed to snare when he was not impaired with drink, the stranger remained there at the river, living beneath the makeshift tent, silently sharing the men's company and desperately attempting to drown his sorrowful memories in whatever fermented drink he could pour through his lips. No matter how much he imbibed, however, his memories still managed to invade his stupors. At those times he shivered and sometimes wept, but only silently, for he did not want to violate the inhabitants of his memories by mingling his cries of anguish with his recollections of their laughter. When he did weep he wept bitterly, and more bitterly still when he recalled the man he'd once been and the life he'd once had.

For long ago, long before he became Her Second, he was an admirable man, ebullient and respected, with a name and a nahala and a family of his own—a wife who was his committed helpmate and the children of their thankful hearts: a plump and robust girl, who was their firstborn, and two lively sons who still toddled more than walked. His wife he loved so deeply that the men of his distant village ridiculed him as a dreamy fool or at best a naive master of folly for violating their social protocol of at least giving the appearance of emotional reticence. Despite the derision he sensed in their bemusement, still he fawned over his wife and doted on his children—his daughter included—such that it seemed to him that it all was a sacred act of prayer, which in some ways it was, owing to his unshakable belief, in defiance of social convention, that his wife and children were not his chattel property but a trust and a blessing from God.

Together he and his spouse, with enthusiastic but minimal help from their little brood, wrested a sustenance from the nahala of which he was so proud that lay upon a gentle sloping plain in the midst of the fertile Galilean hills and on which their well-kept hut stood amid the ringing laughter of children. His wife, energetic and meticulous, flitted from grindstone to fields to the tending of their young ones, then back to her hoe or a swinging sickle, always bearing a smile or a laugh or a good-humored admonition. He in turn was easygoing and solid, a hard and diligent worker and very much proud to be. Moreover, he took whatever time he could to instruct his children in the ways of their God and even to participate in their most nonsensical amusements and play—another set of social novelties that caused the men to shake their heads in amusement. Still his world was satisfying and steady and as predictable as a life dependent on the land and subject to the caprices of conquerors was allowed to be.

Then one day he and his fellow farmers noticed that their crops were beginning to yellow, yet the portent of rainfall was nowhere in sight. They began to pray daily to the God of Israel for the heavens to open and pour down upon them, but the air remained arid and the skies clear. They commenced to pray for rain at their rising and again at their lying down but the sky, if it heard them, did not respond. They thought then to haul water for irrigation from the village well, for in all the generations of their village the well had never gone dry, but they found that their efforts did not even begin to quench the thirst of the parched ground. So they began to pray at noon in the midst of their fields, hoping that hearing their pleas from there God might better comprehend the depth of their anguish. With desperate spontaneity they even began to make collective supplications at the end of the day wherever the farmers chanced to meet. As the ground became more parched, they spent their entire Sabbaths in tearful and huddled entreaty, and in all their conversations were even more careful than usual to pay proper reverence to God.

When their crops began to wilt in earnest and their desperation increased, the farmers proffered an array of biblical sacrifices and offerings and, with heads bent in fear and veneration, fasted for days at a time. Yet the sun continued its relentless vigil upon the now flagging and withering crops on which every life in their world depended. Soon the wheat was all but straw and the planted rows mostly dust, and the heavens still refused to speak. The promised time of harvest had come and gone, and the only thing to be reaped was a crop of despair and the prospect of privations so great they could destroy them all.

Thankfully the desperation the villagers felt was not yet matched by the hunger they feared, because the last of the previous year's harvest still lay in the shallow slanted sheds behind each hut that served as storehouses. And there was still the poultry and the livestock, the goats, the sheep, the few oxen and cows. Although the sheep were for shearing, the oxen for plowing, and the cows kept for their milk, the meat of each could be eaten if slaughtered according to the guidelines of scripture. So the animals were butchered before they became sickly or lost too much meat from their bones. Yet even as the people dined on their stews of ox and goat and mutton, they knew that these provisions would not last long, even when guarded with the most judicious restraint. So the villagers carefully rationed their salted meats, their dried beans and dates and figs, and especially the wheat for their bread, the staple on which they built their lives, praying and hoping for the best.

In their home he and his wife served even smaller portions than most of their neighbors. When their children asked for more, he distracted their hunger with laughing games of the type that did not require much physical exertion, so as not to arouse further their mounting pangs. He attempted to augment their meager fare by hunting small game, but it seemed that every farmer for miles was determined to do the same, with the result that the forests and underbrush were soon hunted so bare that his spear could find no target and the snares he set remained undisturbed. His prayers were wracked with desperation and his nights with fearful dreams. He and his wife and even the children spent their days foraging the brush for stray hen's eggs and edible roots. Their storehouse was not yet empty, but there was little left. And it still had not rained.

It was then, when it seemed that things could get no worse, that a contingent of Roman soldiers burst in with yet another of their despised visits, seeking supplies from the locals to support their endless marches of subjugation. When the officer in command made the usual unnecessarily formal announcement of their intent to confiscate village goods, in addition to their usual protest the angry villagers now offered an even more compelling argument.

"But we're here starving. We don't even have enough for ourselves."

The leader of the soldiers seemed perplexed. "What do you mean you're starving? Why?"

"A blind man could see we got a drought here. We didn't have a bit of a harvest to bring in, and now we're running out of food."

The soldier still seemed confused. "No food? How is this? Didn't you receive any of the grain that the emperor shared from the imperial storehouse?"

Now the villagers were confused. "Grain? We didn't get no grain."

"No? The governor released vast stores of grain to your priests in Jerusalem with instructions to distribute it to your people, even to you out in this hinterland."

"No sir! We never got a speck."

"Well, you should have. But that's your problem. I suggest you discuss it with those priests of yours. After all, they are your priests. But in the meantime, we'll still have to take what you have. An army cannot be expected to fight on an empty stomach, now can it?"

The soldiers took edibles from every hut, even food from cooking pots, departing without even a backward glance. Fortunately, the inhabitants of this village, like most living beneath the Romans' heel, had learned to bury a portion of their harvests where it would not be found by Roman hands. These were the emergency rations that in the end could spell the difference between life and slow death by starvation and, thus, were to be used in only the direst of circumstances. With everything else now gone, the villagers had no choice but to reluctantly retrieve these caches, knowing that beyond them lurked the hulking specter of death. As the villagers silently stared at their remaining provisions and agonized over how to stretch them so their families would not become buzzards' prey, their anger and their anguish ran so deep that it was all they could do to keep from cursing God.

The days of drought continued to pile up, and his wife carefully and fearfully made their meals even smaller now. Though just a fraction of their predrought repasts, the portions were still enough for the entire family to maintain their strength. He began to notice, however, that although the children retained much of their exuberance and his own body still felt strong, his wife now seemed always to be tired. And although they all were losing weight, she was much thinner by far. He mentioned his concern to her, but she waved him away with a tired smile and pronounced herself as fit as he. Still she continued dropping weight at so alarming a rate that even the children began to worry. Finally the growing weakness she had managed to hide could no longer be overlooked when she began to find it hard to stand.

Soon he had to kneel to feed her as she lay upon their bed mat, lethargic and bony. It was then that he learned what had emaciated her so, for early one morning while feeding her he momentarily arose, leaving her bowl at her side, only to turn to see her straining to scrape her own food back into the pot from which it had come.

When he asked her why she'd starved herself, she explained that she had not really meant to, but when it became clear that their five mouths would deplete the food faster than they'd supposed, she thought she would simply skip every other meal to conserve what little they had. Still the food was dwindling too fast, so she began to eat every other day. Then she noticed her little boys' ribs beginning to show and she lost the will to eat altogether. When through his tears he asked how long she had denied herself, she told him it had been weeks at least.

"Why didn't you tell me?" he sobbed. "I could have eaten less, too. I could have done something."

Breathless from the strain of talking, she whispered, "I know. But we need you to keep your strength. In this world as long as the man can keep going, a family has a chance. I couldn't hunt for game or slay hyenas if they gathered at our door or negotiate with the men to make sure our family isn't overlooked in anything. But you can. We need you strong. Promise me you'll do your best to stay strong for the children."

"But what about you? How can we make it without you? Whatever made you think that a woman is less important than a man?"

He cried and hugged her hard, as if he could return her strength by the beating of his heart alone, but she was too weak now even to hug him back. He knew then that without a miracle from God she was going to die, for the increasingly smaller portions of their fast-diminishing provisions could not stop the deadly descent upon which her health had too long been embarked.

From then he spent every moment with her that he could, but her demise came much sooner than expected: one day she simply did not awake with him to mark the dread of yet another blazing dawn. He lay his head upon her flaccid breast and wept as if he would never stop, his wailing children each clutching a part of her, an arm or a leg, all of them encased in grief as thick as amber.

For her burial he was forced, weeping all the way, to drag her body to the site on their bed mat because now he was too weak to carry her. When he found that the soil was baked too hard to dig a grave, he had no choice but to place her lifeless form atop the parched and dusty ground on a spot he cleared of rocks and debris, covering her with nothing more than heavy stones, a blanket of dust, and the bitter tears of her children.

His grandmother had always told him that death makes its appearance in threes, and so many times he had seen her proved right that a part of him was sure that there was more grief to come. It was not long before his grandmother's maxim began to ring true, for his two sons soon became fevered and listless, worn down by hunger and a debilitating sense of loss. His daughter, though ashen and tired, seemed to fare better than her brothers owing both to being older and larger and to her former plump robustness, but she was weakening as well. Their food was down to almost nothing now, and he struggled with a consuming guilt when he ate even the merest morsel because he knew it would be one less bite for his children. Yet he also knew that his selfless wife was right, that without him the children would have even less chance to survive. So he forced himself to choke down at least one tasteless mouthful every day, sobbing with every swallow.

Soon even their most disciplined consumption whittled their store of nourishment to the point that meals consisted of handfuls of grain mashed in water to form a kind of mush, which they now dared to eat no more than once a day. To save their strength they spent most of their time in their hut, except when the sad father left to fetch water from the nearby village well which, remarkably, still brought forth, although jars and waterskins had to be let down much lower now to be filled.

Despite his best efforts, however, despite his every sacrifice and prayer, the deprivation and the hunger and the grief took their toll. The boys' bellies swelled up and bloated and their navels poked out like thumbs. Whatever of their hair that had not fallen out lay lifeless upon their little brown heads with the telltale golden orange of malnutrition. And in all of this there was nothing he could do but watch his sons' inexorable decline. By night their sobs and labored breathing tortured his writhing sleep. By day their sunken eyes and listless limbs haunted his every breath.

Miraculously, his daughter did not show the same effects. She, too, was now thin and moving slowly, but apparently one handful a day somehow was enough to keep her going. So she spent her time and her slightly greater strength comforting her fevered brothers, bathing their faces when their father could stand no more of their suffering and staggered outside to beg God to have mercy on his dying seed.

Then one afternoon as he prayed beside them, his younger son let out a gasp and began to make gurgling noises. By the setting of the sun the boy was a corpse. It was several weeks before his brother joined him, but his end was not so peaceful. He moaned loudly in painful delirium. In his last hours he was completely oblivious to the screams of his father for God to grant his son the merciful refuge of death.

He buried both sons as he had their mother: beneath a dismal coat of rocks and tears with his daughter by his side. When the last was laid to rest, with leaden steps he returned with his daughter to their hut, shook his fist at the cruel meagerness of the last of their grain, which did not even half fill one small clay bowl now, and lay at his daughter's side, resigned that they would soon die together.

Weakened by their hunger, fatigued by their grief, the two slept most of the next several days. Even with the little they ate, their food was all but gone. As their lives ticked away he spoke to the girl of her mother's love for her, and of his own, and assured her that soon they would all rest together, nestled with her mother and her brothers. They hugged hard and confessed to each other the immortality of their familial love. She drifted to sleep in his arms, and they shared vivid dreams of verdant pastures and orchards overrun with smiling fruit.

The next morning, weak and feverish, he was awakened by what seemed to be strong, hearty voices. This confused him, because the rest of the surviving villagers were like him, too weak to cause a tumult. Then someone was calling from outside his hut.

"Shalom! Anyone in there? Shalo-o-o-m!"

At first, his fatigue and the thickness of his grief did not let him answer. Then his daughter stirred and he remembered that he yet had reason to live.

"Y-y-yes. Shalom," he said in a hoarse and haggard whisper. "Come in." Two men entered.

"Shalom, brother." They stared at his sleeping daughter. "Is she . . . alright?"

He could tell by their accents that they were from the south in Judea, maybe even from Jerusalem. "She's alive," he rasped, "but she's fading."

"Can you stand, brother?" one of the men asked.

He struggled to rise, but his head started to swim and he dizzily lay back upon the mat.

"That's alright. You just rest there. We got some things for you, but we can bring them in if it's alright with you."

"Things?" he asked dizzily. "What things?"

"Food and things."

"Food? Where'd you . . . ?"

"Caesar. Gave a bunch of grain to the priests in Jerusalem to give to the hungry folks."

His memory was weak, but something whirred in it. "I heard. But why'd it take so long to get to us? I lost my wife, my boys, and my daughter is . . ." He started to cry.

One of the visitors touched him softly. "We're sorry, brother, but that's the priests for you. Romans gave them a whole storehouse of grain to give to the folks that was starving. But the priests didn't pass out but a little, and kept the rest for themselves and their cronies. Then the drought got so bad that I guess the priests got worried that so many folks would die that there wouldn't be anyone left to make the pilgrimages and pay the tithes and offerings. Cause if there's one thing a priest cares about, it's tithes and offerings. So I guess they finally realized that to keep a good thing going they better go ahead and give the grain out."

"The priests are men of God," he wheezed. "They wouldn't—"

"I know, brother. I know. I didn't want to believe it neither. I always believed like the scripture says: 'Touch not the head of my anointed.' And not touching them meant not bad-mouthing them, too. But if the truth is bad, that's not giving them the bad-mouth—that's just telling the truth. And the truth is that not every priest is anointed by God. Some are just looking for status and shekels."

"How can you say that?" He closed his eyes to stop his head from spinning.

"I know how you feel because I didn't want to believe it neither. But it's true. Priests nowadays don't want to serve; they want to be served. Remember what the scripture says about the sons of Eli, how they were priests but all they cared about was women and shekels? It's sad, but that's the way too many of the priests are today."

The men stepped outside and brought several sacks into the hut and placed them in a corner. Without comment they opened one of the sacks and measured out grain and commenced to grinding and fetching water and kneading dough. They had already started a fire in the oven in the yard, so the bread did not take long. Then the men placed the food before the starving denizens of the hut without taking any for themselves. It was the first solid food he and his daughter had eaten in weeks. They both pinched off it and ate slowly.

"You're not going to stay and have some?" he rasped.

"No sir, brother. We got to keep moving. There's a whole lot more folks that need help, too."

"Who are you?" he asked weakly as they stooped through the

entrance to leave. "I mean, you're Jews, too, but you don't seem to have much use for the priests."

"We're just folks trying to be good servants of God, is all. And no, brother. We're not against priests just cause they're priests. But the priests these days seem to have forgot that they're supposed to serve the people and not the other way around. Seems like the only thing priests care about now is shekels—dressing fine and wearing gold jewelry and living in the biggest houses and riding the finest chariots. Act like they got a right to live in all that luxury. But they're living off the little people who pay for it all and don't really get anything in return. The prophet Ezekiel says, 'You shepherds of Israel who have been feeding yourselves! Should not shepherds feed the sheep? You eat the fat, you clothe yourselves with the wool, you slaughter the fatlings, but you do not feed the sheep.' That's what they were like then and that's what they're like now."

"I never heard anyone talk like this," he wheezed.

"We follow a man called John the Baptizer out in the wilderness parts. He is a preaching somebody! We get out to hear him whenever we can. He's not for no foolishness, neither. Teaches straight from scripture and doesn't ask anyone for anything; he takes his living from whatever the Lord gives him. By his own word he says that he's not the Messiah, though. He's just trying to get something started for the Messiah to come to. That's his way. And that's what we are: brothers of the Way. The Way of the Lord."

"Thank you." He touched the hand of each man.

"Just thank God, brother. Just thank God. And pray that the Messiah comes, and comes soon, to get us out this mess we're in."

"Amen," said the other men.

After the kindness of the strangers from Judea, the harvest of fresh corpses atop hard ground abated. The villagers began to regain their strength from the gift of grain, even if the sun was still unbroken save for the respite of night. Though he was bowed by the unrelenting weight of his grief, his legs were steadier and he no longer half-slept most of the day and night, his daughter's head nestled in the crook of his arm. The light began to return to the little girl's eyes and her mouth once again hosted torrents of questions. The two of them grew stronger on the grain the Romans periodically released, which the priests now grudgingly distributed to the hungering people. Finally the rains came with a deluge that even Noah would have loved, and the farmers began to replant their fields and rebuild their sunbaked lives.

Yet even as life trekked slowly to normalcy, his grief and loss blanketed him like a shroud. He stumbled through his days with halfhearted interest, and was sometimes felled by spasms of grief that attacked him with the slightest provocation. Despite the painful toll his sorrow took upon him, however, it never completely engulfed him because through it all God had allowed him still to have the daughter of his heart; his mourning was tempered by the abiding joy of having her at his side. The totality of the love he'd once shared with his entire family he now gave to her alone. It was his love for his busy, chattering daughter that kept him from finally wasting away.

She became the center of what little universe he had left. He taught himself to mend the rends in her tunic and to prepare her favorite dishes—a salad of pomegranate, cucumbers, and mint, and crispy patties made of leeks. He learned to plait her hair and to keep it free of lice, and she, in turn, picked the nits from his beard. He held her close and rocked her as her mother had, softly chanting psalms to lull her to sleep. He kissed away her tears, taught her minor intricacies of the farming of wheat, and constructed dolls for her of clay, sticks, and bits of cloth. There remained in him a flowing undercurrent of heartache that could without warning jolt him, leaving him panting and exhausted, but the innocent joy of his daughter and his diligence to raise her happy and well left little time to focus upon those that had been taken from him. In time his underlying grief slowly abated until he no longer had to feign joy. Then his laughter again came from deep within.

From their love and commitment to each other a satisfying new texture was added to the fabric of their lives, and father and daughter became inseparable in all things. When it was time for field work he did not leave her with the others in the daily care of older children or kindly elders. Instead he cheerfully took her to labor with him amid the rows and the rising stalks to banter away the hours of toil, he in the work, she engaged in that playful childish busy-ness that passed for labor. Most nights found her curled beside him while he regaled her with humorous recountings of her infancy, of misadventures from his own childhood and, on occasion, sensitive accounts of his courtship of her mother. On the Sabbath father and daughter walked hand in hand to synagogue and were the decided object of the men's laughter when they were seen skipping down the path as she guided him in the game of her most recent invention. In this way a new life arose for them from the dust and rubble and pain of the drought.

Then one afternoon, as the sun approached its zenith on the horizon, a large contingent of Roman soldiers rode into their village. With the blast of a trumpet the soldiers called the villagers to assemble. When he entered the dusty courtyard where the Romans awaited, his daughter at his side, he noticed that the soldiers did not have their usual swagger. Most held the usual range of expressions, from hateful menace to bored indifference, but in the rear ranks some of them wore sickly looks, while others seemed almost too weak to remain in their saddles. At the far rear of the column was an ox cart in which several soldiers lay completely motionless save for loud and labored breathing. He noticed boils and raised red welts upon their skin, which he knew were not the wounds of battle but the marks of some disease. He pulled his daughter closer and whispered. "Be careful," he said. "Don't touch nothing. The soldiers, their horses, nothing."

When the anxious farmers had fully gathered, the commander of the column announced their intent. The villagers could relax, he proclaimed, because the soldiers were not in need of provisions and therefore would not confiscate their goods. At any rate, he assured them, this was a practice that the Roman army undertook only when it was absolutely necessary. Instead, the soldiers were there to arrest the brigand chief Barabbas for the capital crime of rebellion against the Roman empire.

For many months Barabbas and his band of Galilean insurgents had waged guerrilla warfare against the Roman colonizers in the name of malkuth delaha, the sole sovereignty of God. Moses was moved by this belief when he led his people from the hegemony of Pharaoh. Gideon the Judge proclaimed it aloud in response to his people's attempts to make him king: "Only one shall rule over you, that is God alone." It was this belief that empowered the farmer Judas Maccabeus to vanquish the seasoned Greek invaders when they tried to force Israel to worship other gods. This unshakable belief in malkuth delaha had animated and inspired fighters for Hebrew freedom since Hebrews crossed the Red Sea. And it still did. Although they were smaller and far fewer than in years past, freedom-fighting bands still reared their heads in Israel. Villagers throughout the land supported them as they could, with provisions and information and warnings and, occasionally, a place to lay their heads, but most villagers were no more than innocent bystanders, quietly supporting the insurgents from the shadows.

The denizens of his village admitted nervously that they were aware of the activities of Barabbas but explained that none of them had ever participated and none knew where he was now. This was only partly true because a number of the men were secret supporters of Barabbas and had even visited his camp in the Galilean hills. But apparently the men's silence and the other villagers' fearful deference convinced the Roman commander of their lack of complicity. This was evidenced by the fact that the soldiers did not put all the villagers to the sword or impale each of them on crosses.

The assembled throng stood in the courtyard beneath the high afternoon sun under the merciless eyes of the soldiers while their huts were searched. They were not allowed to sit.

It was late in the afternoon when the soldiers finally completed their sweep. As everyone expected, no trace was found of Barabbas, no caches of weapons or evidence of subversive activity of any kind. Surprisingly, the soldiers kept their word and confiscated nothing from the village, although some of the villagers returned to their huts to find half-eaten bread on their floors and pots that had clearly been picked in. Apparently, no soldier had eaten from his pots, but one had urinated on the floor of his hut and spat upon the bed mat of his daughter, which he did not realize until she lay down that evening and felt the glob upon her skin.

Several days after the Romans' visit, he awoke to the sound of his daughter vomiting. He brewed for her a tea of mint and bay laurel and her nausea seemed to wane. The next morning it was back, this time accompanied by a blazing fever. Propelled by the terrible prospect of yet another unbearable loss, in his panic he pushed and pulled to his hut both midwives with their life-giving hands and elders known to be authors of particularly fruitful prayers, all hurried by him with such urgency that they stumbled and half-ran along the path. The midwives, who were also the *roheim,* the village healers, administered to the girl the traditional medicinal cures, while the elders prayed until their feet swelled and their limbs went to sleep. Still her fever raged and the pain in her legs and her belly continued unabated. The healers studied her stool, smelled her urine and tasted it, questioned her father to ascertain if he had sensed the recent presence of demons or had lately trans-gressed the Ten Commandments of God, but they were finally stumped as to the source and the nature of her illness.

"Never seen anything like this," they said in a puzzlement of alarm. "Must be yet another evil Roman illness, probably the one those sol-diers had. Lord. If they're not stealing our sustenance or striking us down with their swords, they're killing us with the evil residues of their ungodly presence."

Through the night the elders and the midwives continued their prayers and infusions of healing teas and herbs, but by morning his daughter's body was covered with the raised red marks he had seen on the faces and arms of the sick soldiers, and her writhing body was bathed in sweat.

"Guess it *was* demons," said one of the elders, shaking his head as he looked up from his prayers and saw the rampant discolorations on her skin. "Demons with pale skin who think they're God."

With his wife and boys his appeals to the mercy of God had been shrill and intense, but still within the realm of prayer. Now, with the prospect of the loss of the last object of his love and his last link to the passions of life amid so much death and so abject a suffering, his entreaties became terror-filled pleading more than they could be called prayers. He begged, he bargained with God, he cajoled. He offered as evidence of his faith the cogent reminder that in spite of his losses he had never cursed the heavenly hand. Every contestation he could conceive was proffered as barter for the deliverance of his child. He promised to perform with a new zeal the three daily prayers and each of the pilgrimages replete with their prescribed offerings, and pledged to dedicate every waking moment, and his dreams as well, to the unstinting service of the Lord of Hosts in return for this one dispensation of mercy. He even offered his own life in her stead, anything, everything if she would just be allowed to live.

"You have taken away all my others," he cried, his upturned face swollen and drenched with tears. "Please don't take away the last drop of my life. Please. Please don't."

Despite his prayers, his pleading, his promises; despite the unstinting supplications of the elders and the best ministrations of the midwives with their multiplicity of treatments and cures, in three days the girl was dead.

It was then, as his daughter lay lifeless in his arms, that the part of himself he had struggled to keep alive for her sake abruptly died, and his wails and weeping, which had increased as her condition worsened, instantly ceased. In fact, everything about him that evinced that he was a live and sentient being came to an end, except the trembling of his flesh and his shallow, labored breathing.

When the weeping midwives finally lifted her stiff little body from his grasp, he did not speak or even move. When they carried her away to be washed and buried before sundown as the scriptures prescribed, he neither answered their tearful pleas for him to join the procession nor even heard them. He sat that way until the next dawn, not moving, not speaking, barely taking breath. It was a woman wailing in the distance for the fevered death of her own child that finally penetrated his grief and roused him, though he was still thick-lidded and his jaw remained slack.

Arising with the uncertainty of one pushed to the very bounds of his sanity, he looked blankly about him, then slowly began to pile the hut's few possessions in a heap: wooden bowls, bed mats, several woolen blankets—everything but a solitary doll. With the few smoking embers left in the day-old cooking fire he set the mass ablaze. Stumbling from the hut as the flames licked through the roof of dried reeds and mud, he lurched forward on faltering feet. He did not look back as the fire crackled and burned and sent thick black smoke into the air, for he had already set out to die a solitary death in the wilderness, and there was nothing behind him he needed for that.

Chapter

13

His gait was sometimes halting, sometimes more steady, but always with the same destination: a site to host his death. With no food or drink and no cloak to withstand the cold desert nights, at the outset of this his last journey he expected the setting of his demise to be near, but he found that the desert was farther away than he'd supposed. He continued to stumble upon streams and edible vegetation—mandrakes and dwarf chicory and mallow—that he consumed out of instinct, without sense or thought that it would prolong the life he sought to end. And although the nights were cold, to his biting disappointment he found that they were not as cold as he had supposed, so he shivered with discomfort, but the cold did him no further harm.

In his search for death he trudged up rocky hills, faltered over their crests, and slid and stumbled down each stony incline. He circumvented the few settlements he encountered and avoided contact with the occasional shepherds and herdsmen and fellow travelers he chanced upon, for he was resolved that his was to be a solitary death.

Soon the vegetation became sparser and brooks and streams farther between, narrower and more shallow, and the dark thick soil gradually became sandy and the sun-bleached color of camels, and he knew he had reached the desert. The same sun that had burned the life from his bloodline glared relentlessly upon him, and his lips began to parch and split, his skin blistered and burned, and every step became an effort of agonized proportions. His tongue swelled like a gourd inside his mouth, his eyes commenced to fail, and the remainder of his strength began to succumb to the days of deprivation and scorching heat and the nights of shivering exposure. Soon he was staggering about and reeling. He tried to reach the meager shade of a forlorn and almost leafless acacia tree, but one step more and he fell heavily to one knee in the burning sand, then crumpled onto his back. He closed his eyes, thankful that his life was ending.

He awoke beneath a blue-black night sky sown with a profusion of stars. His first thought was that he was dead, but the pain throbbing in his temples and the painful blistering of his lips told him he was not. Glancing about, he discovered that he lay beside a large black rectangular tent with its sides rolled up unevenly and tied fast, from which the laughter of men and women drifted out on spikes of flickering light. A broad man with a dark, neatly trimmed beard that framed a face of uncommonly light complexion emerged from the tent swathed from head to foot in garments so rich they were almost foreign in flavor: a handsome purple linen tunic worn beneath a luxuriant, richly brocaded robe striped with lush yellows and reds and indigos. On his head was a turban of finest cotton. The man was of medium height with a round protruding belly. He possessed a booming voice with a pronounced liturgical lilt to its phrasing. Around his thick neck swung a number of amulets and talismans of various sizes and degrees of luster, and his wrists and fingers were filled with bracelets and rings with large colorful stones. Upon his feet were brocaded slippers instead of sandals. His rich robe was belted at the waist with a jeweled dagger thrust in it, and he smelled of camels and wine and other scents that were strange and elusive as to their origin. He walked a few paces from the tent, a smiling half-clad young woman hanging onto him, raised his robe and urinated in the sand, still talking loudly to his compatriots in the tent with a mixture of authority and condescension.

Looking about in the moonlight, he glimpsed the whites of the half-opened eyes of the man stretched out on the small rug upon which he himself had placed him. Turning on his heel, the well-clad man was suddenly standing over his prostrate guest shouting, "Come back to life!" while he looked out the corner of his eye to make sure he'd caught the attention of the others. Assured that their eyes were firmly upon him, he yelled "Aiyeeii!" and danced about, stomping and spitting and flailing the air at some presence that was apparent only to himself.

"Begone, you demon of death! Let him go! Turn that man loose!" he boomed. He appeared to grab some unembodied force from the ether and engaged in furious battle with it until he threw the invisible being to the ground and stomped upon it.

"There, you demon!" he said, his arms raised in victory. "My powers are too great for you!"

He looked down upon the man on whose behalf he had waged this spurious battle, then stretched out his hand, shouting, "Parshandatha the healer, the great man of God, commands you. Awaken from the dead!"

Then Parshandatha clapped his hands with such wildly exaggerated ceremony that the recumbent man flinched, thinking now it was he that was under attack. The half-clothed girl saw him cringe.

"He moved!" she squealed. "The dead man moved!"

Parshandatha made several other ceremonious gestures that seemed to be for nothing as much as for the edification of the fawning girl beside him and the women and men who had spilled out of the tent at his first exaggerated command.

"Arise now!" he said to the prone man. "Parshandatha the chosen of God commands you!"

The man pushed himself up, slowly and obediently, to lean weakly on his ashen elbows. He did not want to anger this strange man.

"It's a miracle!" cried a richly clad onlooker. He was one of two sly and jaded "ministers," cunning and crafty operatives who were every bit as devious as Parshandatha. It was their job to convince everyone in earshot that Parshandatha was not the charlatan that any lucid observer would immediately see him to be, but instead a true healer whose cures were based not on illusion, sleight of hand, or the exaggerations and outright lies that was their real origin, but on nothing less than pious faith and divine powers directly given him by God. These "ministers" had carried the unconscious man themselves, all the while claiming to the others that he was dead, careful not to let them see that he was not. The others in their party included several young women, fawning and beautiful and so taken with the self-avowed healer that they would do anything for him, and several newly garnered patrons invited to travel with Parshandatha to witness his "miracles" in hopes he could solidify their material support for his "healing ministry."

"The great man of God has done it again!" proclaimed the other finely clad minister. "Another miracle! Truly Parshandatha the healer is a man of God!"

The gushing women draped themselves upon Parshandatha. The men patted their approval upon his back and shoulders and beamed. Parshandatha raised his jeweled hand to demur in dramatically feigned humility.

"It is not I who is great, but God alone. I am but a holy instrument of divine healing." He glanced piously at his hearers, then looked down upon the parched man with an expression of exaggerated benevolence.

"My son, I am Parshandatha, possessor of the powers of divine healing, and humble servant of God. This day I have been the divine instrument of your sojourn back from the darkest depths of death. While crossing the desert on the way to yet another venue at which I might work the healing wonders of God, we found you lying in the sand with the vultures casting lots for your flesh. I lifted your body with my own hands"—here he wiped an imaginary tear—"and with my faithful ministers carried you to this very place so I could use my holy powers to bring you back to life that all might know that my powers are truly divine. God has told me to heal you, and by the divine power within me I have returned you to the ranks of the living."

Then Parshandatha turned to the astonished, adoring faces and said with pious solemnity, "Now I pray that you would leave me to talk to this man of the secret things of God of which he has been the beneficiary this day."

When the others had returned to the tent talking excitedly among themselves, the voice of the bejeweled healer immediately steeled and the lines of his broad face hardened.

"So you're awake now," he said, the ceremonial affectations gone from his voice. "Good. Let me tell you how things are going to be. You're the first man I've encountered who had absolutely nothing to take, so I decided to take you. We know I didn't bring you back to life, but I did save you from certain death. And so it is, let us say, only scriptural that in return for saving you that I should expect a just and goodly recompense." Parshandatha's laughter rang in the black desert night. "After all, you were dead, remember?"

The prone man's throat felt as if sand had been poured into it, and a terrible pounding still danced in his head. He closed his eyes and did not answer.

A sudden and intense cruelty arose in Parshandatha's moonlit face. He fingered his jeweled dagger, and with a scowl kicked the prostrate man hard. "You were dead, weren't you?" he growled.

Despite the force of the blow the sad man lay motionless, his eyes shut. What the blow could not accomplish, however, Parshandatha's angry, penetrating gaze did. It bored into him with such intensity that he instantly opened his eyes, looked directly into the raging face of the sham healer, and nodded in wordless agreement.

"Good. I see that you know what to say. I found you without a shekel to your name, so as recompense for saving your life you will give your testimony at our miracle healing services for everyone to hear how you were plucked from the jaws of death by the power that God has given Parshandatha the great. And you will give that testimony—or you'll find yourself dead for real."

Then Parshandatha's fury seemed suddenly to relax and his voice once again bore its pronounced liturgical affectation. "Now, my son, you must regain your strength so you can travel. The girl will bring to you dates, a precious piece of salt, and a skin of water. Drink from it slowly so you do not get sick. Sip it, eat the dates, and lick the salt and you'll be ready, of a fashion at least, to travel by morning."

The sunbaked supposed-to-be-dead man lay outside the tent, under the stars, his head throbbing, his stomach in knots, listening to the laughter and sounds of overdone piety drifting from the tent, feeling cheated of the death he had traveled so far to earn. He was suddenly overcome by a shackling impassivity that stripped him of his will and every spark of protest and defiance, leaving him with all but the smallest sense of resistance to the baffling forces that engulfed him. He had journeyed from agony to defeat, he thought with sad and impotent outrage, and still he could not accomplish his own demise.

The next morning the pompous healer watched as his operatives and his willing sycophants dismantled the large dusty tent, bundling it and the decorative wool rugs that served as its floor. Upon the backs of the donkeys that were kept for that purpose alone they loaded their stores of "recompense," which the anxious supplicants at Parshandatha's miracle healing services thought they were presenting to God, not Parshandatha, in hopes that their offerings of shekels or goods might change the trajectory of God's will for their lives. Parshandatha's party loaded leather sacks filled with jewelry, a jangling bag of coins, jugs of oil and wine, sweets and cheeses and vegetables and dried meat, and their few other belongings: changes of clothes and the like. The supposed-to-be-dead man ate the morning bread they handed to him like a cow chewing its cud, out of habit alone and nothing more. When he was told to mount a tethered camel, however, he did not move, defiantly sitting as motionless as a rock. Parshandatha called to him in pretended affability. Then, as if to offer a comforting embrace, Parshandatha drew near, cursing him quietly so only he could hear. Furtively drawing his dagger so the others could not see its gleaming blade, Parshandatha threatened to slit him from gullet to belly, yet the sorrowed man remained still and impassive, sure that this time the end really was near, and welcoming it.

Because his recalcitrant guest had not spoken since he found him, it dawned upon Parshandatha that he might be addle-brained and mute rather than stubborn. Deciding that this was the case, Parshandatha sheathed his weapon and ordered his operatives to hoist the silent man atop a ruminating camel. All the sad-faced man could do was hang his head. His yearning for death was just as great as it had been, but after this latest defeat there was no resistance left in him. He rode with the

others silently, the beast on which he sat tied to the tail of the one loping before it.

In his stolid and unbroken passivity, the supposed-to-be-dead man
immediately fell into the routines of his captor hosts. He rode when
they rode, ate when they ate, drank when they drank, slept when they
slept; they inside the large rectangular tent with its floor of overlapping
carpets of different colors and designs, he outside alone beneath the
winking stars. This pattern continued for days as they journeyed
toward the venues at which Parshandatha staged the spectacles of
miracles and healings from which he made his considerable living. As
the group inched through the scorching desert to the sound of the
sham healer's pompous orations, vegetation began to reappear and a
distant patchwork of browns and greens emerged, increasingly visible
on the approaching hills. Another day atop the jerking camels and the
group suddenly halted, their faces full of pious greed and excitement. In
the valley below lay a settlement of the black tents and lean-tos of a
clan of seminomads. Though loosely configured, the dwellings were a
goodly number, and the large contingent of camels tied among them
testified that there was prosperity enough to warrant a visit from the
healing caravan.

The pattern of their grandiose entry and dramatic performance at
this village was the same as the others that followed. Parshandatha's
ministers entered the settlement before him, singing his praises and
heralding his coming with shouted proclamations. "Parshandatha is
coming! Parshandatha, the great worker of miracles! Parshandatha, the
great servant of God who heals every malady of spirit, mind, and body!
Parshandatha, who speaks the word of prophecy to remove all impedi-
ments to prosperity, who will remove the curse of financial need and
unfulfilled wants!"

Each of the ministers then testified to the miracle cures he claimed
to have witnessed personally. Then they fanned out among the unsuspecting inhabitants to inquire of their illnesses and complaints, which
they were sure to note carefully and remember. After their fact-finding
was completed, the guileful operatives announced that shortly they
would return with the greatest healer since the days of Elijah and his

disciple Elisha. And accompanying Parshandatha, they proclaimed with spine-tingling exuberance, would be living proof of the divine powers he possessed: a forlorn and ragged man that he had found lifeless in the desert and raised from the dead.

Upon their return to Parshandatha, who was encamped a short distance away, the operatives carefully described the most promising prospects they'd identified in the village and recited for him the particular ailments of each.

With much fanfare and ceremony, Parshandatha entered the village swathed in a turban and robe of matching pure white, his talismans and amulets sparkling in the sun as he perched pious and smiling upon a camel adorned with a brightly colored saddle and matching bridle with rows of tiny hanging bells tinkling at the camel's every move. With a great flourish he kneeled the beast, dismounted, then with decorous tones gestured a dramatic benediction to the curious crowd.

"Who is the first to wish a miracle?" Parshandatha asked. He scanned the throng to identify the promising prospects that had been described to him. He noticed several attractive young women and made a quick mental note; he would see if he could lure one of them to his temporary camp for a private "healing." Then, before anyone could answer, Parshandatha summoned forth what he called the greatest evidence of the divine potency of his powers: the sad-faced man the sham healer claimed had once been dead but who was now so obviously alive.

The supposed-to-be-dead man slowly emerged from the rear of the retinue. The residuum of his blistered skin and parched lips gave added and striking credence to Parshandatha's claims. The crowd fell back, stunned, murmuring in awe. Then with a flourish Parshandatha pointed to a prospect he recognized from his ministers' descriptions and called the trembling soul forward. Dramatically pinching the thumb and forefinger of his left hand to his brow, his other hand upon the bowed head of the anxious supplicant, Parshandatha announced the supplicant's ailment as if at that very moment God had spoken it to him. With great drama Parshandatha uttered the same sounds and made the same gestures he'd affected at the supposed-to-be-dead man's resurrection days before, then declared the villager's condition cured, decisively and without qualification and for all time to come. Parshandatha's ministers raised their voices in spurious, guileful praise. The others of his entourage by now were crying, lifting their hands, and shouting, "Thank you, Lord! Thank you! The spirit of God is surely in this place!"

All his sycophants ran around as if Parshandatha had truly unleashed the presence of God upon them. "Thank you, Lord! Thank you!" they shouted. "Thank you for the man of God who rightly reveals your healing truth in our midst."

They cried and leaned on one another as if they were so overcome they might faint, fanning one another with the loose ends of their flowing sashes.

At this point the amazed crowd was ripe for Parshandatha's shameless plucking. "Arise, my child," he said, his voice choked with contrived emotion. "You are healed forever." His retinue began shouting again. "It's a miracle! A miracle, I tell you!"

Eager villagers came forward, anxious to be healed. Parshandatha "blessed" each as he had the first. When all the trusting supplicants had been "healed," Parshandatha raised his hand. All eyes were upon him.

"All that is left to seal the healing forever," he declared, "is for you"—that is, the grateful, crying recipients of his manipulative machinations—"to make a thank offering to God by rewarding the vessel of God's healing. Sow a seed of faith that you may be blessed by God."

The vessel in question, of course, was Parshandatha himself. At this point he employed the strategy that was so successful that he never strayed from it: he always rejected the first gift offered to him as much too small to properly honor God for sending so great a miracle worker to them as Parshandatha.

"After all God has done for you, and you can't praise God with a self-sacrificial offering today?"

He went on to explain that the Almighty wanted their appreciation for divine blessings to take the form of handfuls of shekels or armfuls of foodstuffs or more, else, Parshandatha lamented, the healing surely would not last on account of the subject's unforgivable stinginess.

Those who had just received what they believed to be a miraculous cure were always afraid to risk their new lease on life by refusing his request. As an added incentive, Parshandatha announced that he would make special daily supplications to God for all those who gave particularly large offerings.

After dutifully filling the offering sacks and baskets held by Parshandatha's operatives, those rejoicing in the cures of themselves or their loved ones always extended the customary hospitality by inviting the caravan to recline and eat and drink to their satisfaction. Parshandatha never refused their invitations; he ate and drank to excess, no matter how scant his hosts' stores of food and drink, though he was always sure to gather his entourage to leave as soon as he had eaten his fill, for he wanted to be long gone when the rush of emotion and self-convincing belief wore off and those he had deceived realized that the pains and infirmities they thought were healed, in reality still plagued them as much as they ever had.

This was the pattern of Parshandatha's miracle healing forays, the only real miracle of which was the willingness of so many to hand the fruits of their own labor to a strange man wearing brocaded slippers.

The supposed-to-be-dead man continued his role in Parshandatha's traveling travesty at the many settlements at which they took advantage of the people's gullibility and trust; his only task was to show himself as a living being and nothing else. So beaten was he in spirit and so absorbed in his own pain, that he did as he was told without the least thought or hesitation. He continued in this way for weeks, numb and obedient and unquestioning, until something outside of him pierced the husk of his unfeeling.

At one of the villages victimized by Parshandatha, a recipient of his meaningless cures was a small girl who clearly was very ill. In the emotional aftermath of Parshandatha's sham healing of the girl, her tearful parents rejoiced aloud that they could now dispense with the herbs and prayers and the dedicated efforts of the village healers that had seemed to be bringing the little girl back to health, but much too slowly for the comfort of her frightened parents. Parshandatha heard their joyous proclamations, but he continued smiling beatifically despite knowing that cessation of the others' authentic healing efforts would probably result in the little girl's death.

It was this unconscionable thing, the prospect of harm done to a child for no other reason than to satisfy a bogus man of God's faithless greed, that finally was more than even the sad-faced supposed-to-be-dead man who had lost his every will could bear. He looked at the helpless little girl, turned and slipped away to leave behind forever the cynical Parshandatha and his shameless exploitation of the fears and hopes and crucial needs of trusting, unsuspecting souls. He thought by walking away he could simply wash his hands and be done with it. But suddenly he saw his own daughter with her smiling, cherubic face as if she were actually there before him, and he knew he had to turn back.

Parshandatha was holding forth with his usual extravagant deceit. He had not noticed the absence of the living, breathing supposed example of his miraculous powers. The supposed-to-be-dead man made his way back through the rapt crowd and stood before Parshandatha. For the first time he spoke in the presence of the shocked and chagrined charlatan.

"I was never dead," he said in a flat, halting tone. The crowd froze in suspended belief, every jaw dropping in shock. Then he said it again, more loudly this time. "I wasn't never dead. This man didn't heal me. And he can't heal you, neither."

An undulation of outrage swept over the many who watched. Those who had begun making offerings angrily took them back, asking, "Is it true? Tell us. Is it true?"

Parshandatha's shock immobilized him for only a moment. He regained his composure, then burst into action. "This ungrateful cur is lying!" he bellowed and struck his accuser with such murderous force that he crumpled senseless to the ground. The villagers fell silent. Then Eliahba, an elder of that village, broke the quiet. "That's not the way a holy man is supposed to act," Eliahba said, his eyes narrowing with indignation.

"Maybe he's not really a holy man," said another. Then turning to Parshandatha the man asked, "Are you a holy man?"

Parshandatha was worried. He knew he had to stem this tide of disaffection or he could be in deadly trouble. "Yes. Yes. I am a holy man. God talks to me. God is the source of my powers."

"If you're so holy, then why did you hit that man?" Eliahba asked.

Parshandatha was really worried now. "A-a-a demon was . . . was in him. Yes, a demon made him tell lies on a holy man of God. I struck the man to free him of the demon inside him."

Eliahba's tone was sterner now. "But he said you didn't heal him and that you aren't no healer. Are you? You better tell us the truth now."

"Yes, I am a healer. That man has a demon. You can't believe him. I have healed folks all over this land. From Arad to Jericho to Cana and all kinds of folks in between. I am a man of God. I am telling the truth. This man has a demon."

A frowning man pushed his way to the front of the crowd with a look of recognition and immediate appall. "That was you who did the bogus healings on those folks at Cana? I heard about that. Folks died because of you, telling them they were healed when you knew they weren't. Sick folks getting worse by the day, but because of you they were blaming themselves. 'The holy man says I'm sick because my faith is weak. I have to strengthen my faith so I can get better.'"

The man turned to the crowd. "They said there was this old man there. He had been sickly for a while. But after this charlatan here came the old man swore he was healed. He wouldn't take it easy anymore like he had been, and he wouldn't take care of himself. All his people—his children, his grandchildren—begged him to take his time just to see if he really was healed, but he kept on pushing himself back out into the fields. He said, 'I must be healed. That's a man of God. He wouldn't tell me I was healed if I wasn't.' He got so weak he could hardly walk, but he just kept on going, saying, 'The man said I'm healed, so I must be healed.' That old man worked himself to death right in his field, all the time saying, 'I must be healed. The man of God said I'm healed.'"

The frowning man turned back to Parshandatha. "That old man's blood is on your hands, you lying blasphemer."

Another stepped forward. "I heard about that. That was this man here? I heard he's got a string of babies, too, from north to south."

"I thought something didn't look right with these young women traveling along with you," said Eliahba. "If you're so holy, why do you have these young women fawning around you? How you going to be so holy with women hanging on you?"

Another man raised his voice bitterly. "I caught him winking at my daughter when he was laying hands on her. I thought he was just putting her at ease, but I see now that he ain't nothing but an old lecher."

The sick little girl's crestfallen parents were crying with disappointment and rage. "You would have let our child die. How can you lie and blaspheme and prey on poor folks in the name of the Lord?"

The villagers were really enraged now and getting angrier by the minute. Parshandatha knew he was in trouble. He looked at the angry faces and suddenly broke into a run, but his brocaded slippers were not made for haste. The crowd easily caught him and set their fists upon him, beating him bloody. He shouted, "Stop! I am a man of God! You cannot assault a man of God!"

The men were waling on him with their fisted hands; the women beat him with sticks. "What's stopping us? You're not any more a holy man than you're a Roman."

"Don't touch me!" Parshandatha yelled through the blows. "I am a man of God! If you disrespect me, you disrespect God!"

After enduring a terrific beating Parshandatha finally escaped from the furious crowd at a running gait, his slippers gone, his immaculate robe torn and stained with rivulets of his own blood, his amulets and talismans strewn in the dirt, his camels and entourage running close behind.

"But I am a man of God! You must have faith!" he screamed through his swollen lips as rocks and clumps of dung stung his back. "I will heal you! I will!"

"If you ever come around here again, you're the one that's going to need a healing!"

Jeering youths chased the bogus holy man and his routed entourage with stones and shepherd's staffs, while the rest of the villagers gathered about their unconscious benefactor, bathing his brow and force-feeding him infusions of potent herbs, praying that he would not die before hearing their heartfelt words of thanks.

By the next day he was awake and lucid and ready for solid food. The villagers took turns bringing him delicacies and drink with words of great gratitude, and each in turn asked him to remain in their midst, as befitting a loving brother who had so admirably demonstrated his goodwill, and at the expense of his own well-being, too. For several days he did stay, out of his same unfeigned passivity and indifference more than from succumbing to the open arms of their hospitality. But when the father of the sickly daughter whose precarious plight had caused the supposed-to-be-dead man to break his silence offered him his oldest daughter in marriage, it was clear that he could not remain another day. At the least, he should have been flattered by this honor. Instead the gesture triggered in him a barrage of memories so unbearable that he was overwhelmed by a sickening sadness. He vomited bitterly, suddenly and without warning, spewing the delicacies and kindnesses he had just enjoyed upon the appalled man and his horrified daughter. Aghast at this newest turn of his suffering, he stumbled from the village gagging, as if the source of his pain and torturous sense of loss had at just that moment crawled back into his entrails.

From there the scorpions and the brambles and the open fields and rocky hills were his only companions and his only locales of repose in a journey that was as solitary and directionless as the one that had brought him there. On occasion he allowed himself to enter the dusty confines of a village and tiptoe among its tiny huts like a ghost, driven by the small part of him that still longed for human succor. But then he would witness some act of kindness, or worse, see a woman's contented smile or laughing children running beneath the trees, and he was jolted back into his anguish, and that part of him that wanted to feel nothing at all would again set his feet to flight.

So mostly he slept beneath terebinths and great spreading oaks, in ceilinged groves of tamarisks as quiet and undisturbed as temples, or along lapping streams overhung by swaying willows and poplars and sycamores. He slaked his thirst at the streams and narrow gurgling brooks, and assuaged his hunger with wild almonds and pistachios. He moved without direction or conviction, except that he should go forward and never look back, hoping each step would take him farther from the horrors of home, only to find that those very horrors had taken inextricable residence in the deepest parts of himself.

This was the tone and tenor, the blood and gristle of his existence from dawn to dawn and sunset to sunset, until the day he stumbled filthy and grief-ridden and too hungry and broken to stand, into the village environs of the careful young woman with cinnamon flesh who had found to her own mortification that she had not been careful enough.

Thus he found himself still alive in yet another village that would not let him die. He finally had to acknowledge that his was a failure almost breathtaking in its irony. When it was life that he coveted he was unable to keep even one of his loved ones from death; but now that he sought death, after days and weeks of murderous travel over much hard ground he still had as much life in him as when he'd started. It occurred to him then that perhaps failure in the one was his just and fitting punishment for his unforgivable failure in the other.

The shock of this unwelcome thought gave his world a crisp and startling clarity: that the fate of the flame of his life was not to burn brightly, casting its light about him, as he once had believed. Instead it was destined to smolder within his singular breast as the excruciating penalty for himself having been saved when he had not saved his others. Freed in this way from the pretense that there was anything he could do to ease his pain or to escape it for even an instant, he surrendered to defeat and right there abandoned the search for a site for his death, assuming a posture of resigned and sedentary sorrow, and developed so strong and so immediate a craving for the solace of fermented drink that the entire village thought that besides his pain, a taste for wine was the one thing he had brought with him. It was for this reason that despite the bitter air of sorrow that enveloped him, and in spite of his hated origins as a Jew from Galilee, he was welcomed by the broken-hearted men of the village into their circle of sadness and self-loathing, so gratified were they for the presence of one among them who was even more broken than they.

Chapter

14

"But she's my sister," Oholibamah half argued, half begged. She was speaking to her husband, who had about him an unmistakable air of perturbed indifference. His given name was Mattityahu, but everyone had called him Sonny Boy since he was a child. That nickname was first hung upon him when his father, seeking to assign him a chore or admonish him for some childish infraction, momentarily forgot the name he had given him, which was understandable in that it was one among many in a brood so large that its size seemed meant to engender forgetfulness. Mattityahu's siblings so teased him over this new term of personal address that it eventually took root and became as much his own as his sad, crooked smile.

In the several years since Oholibamah left home to marry, she and her sister had not been close, for their father believed that after a daughter left her father's mastery for the mastery of a husband, a bride's only rightful place was in the home—her own home and no other. In truth, it was Oholibamah's decision to keep so complete a distance because of the hateful air her father breathed upon his household. Despite her time away, Oholibamah had retained an older sister's sense of responsibility for the sibling she'd left behind.

"She's my sister, Sonny," she said as she served his supper of stewed lentils, goat cheese, and dates. "I can't leave her out there in that camp full of thrown-away women."

Sonny Boy spoke without looking up. "I know who she is. But that don't make her my responsibility. I'm not her daddy."

"You know what a hard man my daddy is. The only thing he cares about is how things look. And as far as he's concerned, she's made him lose face and disgraced him beyond forgiveness. She's lucky he only disowned her. He could have killed her."

"That still don't make her my problem. We have these babies to worry about, and we hardly got enough for them."

"But you saw her, stumbling around lost and blank-eyed without a shekel or a crust of bread, standing numb and wet-eyed with all those pitiful women beat down by that old devilish erwat dabar—"

"Watch your mouth, woman," Sonny Boy said testily. "That's a biblical law you're bad-mouthing. God said it and Moses told it and don't nobody have the right to question it. Anyway, she should have thought about what was going to happen to her when she did whatever she did to get herself put out."

"How do we know she did anything?"

"Don't be silly. A man wouldn't put her out for nothing."

Oholibamah did not react. She knew to challenge the motives of men at that moment would not serve her purpose well.

"She's my blood, Sonny."

"I can't help that. A man's responsibility is to his own household, not to some woman who can't keep her man."

"But who can she turn to if not her own sister?"

There was no one else. After her dispossession at the hands of the spoiled, lascivious boy who pretended to be a man, the rejected young woman thought to turn to Mr. Ishmael and Mr. Pop. She knew they would welcome her, but she thought she should spare them the scandal of the presence on their nahala of a young woman not their kin, although they almost certainly would have yielded her the hut and slept outdoors themselves. It would not have mattered that they were old men, or even that they slept every night beneath the stars. According to village propriety it still would have caused a scandal, one she knew would have moved her embarrassed father to avenge his sullied honor for sure.

Her only hope for relief lay in Oholibamah, who was as careful and powerless as she. Oholibamah's powerlessness was evident in that while she offered concern for her sister, she could not offer her a roof, for Sonny Boy had long thought it his duty to deny his wife's every request. His long litany of noes, none ever successfully repealed by her, had reduced Oholibamah to a quietude of vanquishment that sometimes approached that of her mother. In fact, so accustomed was Oholibamah to refusal that she passed it on to her sister without reflection. "No use of me even asking him," she said. "Sonny won't let you stay."

Still, her sister's desperation stung Oholibamah deeply. To her own surprise, she found herself raising the issue to Sonny Boy again, the first time she had ever resurrected a request that he had put to rest. Surprisingly, however, he did not fault Oholibamah for asking; he simply did not think it was his responsibility to care for her failed sibling and said so. She then implored him with tears, but Sonny Boy would not budge. In the end Oholibamah was left with nothing but to pick her way through the ranks of the ragged hung-head women and their hollow-eyed children gathered on the cusp of village life, to kneel at the feet of her dejected sister and beg her forgiveness for failing her.

It was the fragile fabric of her sister's life and not her own that lay so tattered. Nonetheless, in the depths of her nights Oholibamah cried, too. Not for herself, but for the sad sights she saw in the camp: a score of women, most past the peak of their youthfulness, with few possessions among them and even fewer moments of peace; fearful of their futures, bitter at their pasts, numbed in their present by a plight they'd never dreamed would be their own. In their midst dwelled her dispossessed sister, depressed, alone, forsaken, and hungry, lacking even a threadbare tent, her meals the barest gleanings from the fields and handouts of others. With this picture so fretfully impressed upon her, each night Oholibamah cried herself into a fitful sleep, and each day arose to marvel at her own unforgivable timidity.

Finally it was enough. With a burst of forcefulness that surprised no one more than herself, Oholibamah again raised to Sonny Boy her desire to take in her sister, but in truth it was not a request, because she had purposed in her soul that this time she would not be denied. She hoped she would not have to resort to stronger means than talk, but she was sure beyond every doubt that she would if she had to, so clear was she of what had to be.

She sat Sonny Boy down, then sat before him. With unblinking eyes and hands that did not tremble, she told Sonny Boy in the clearest of terms that the nausea that had of late diminished her effectiveness in the day—and her receptivity to him in the privacy of their nights—was not the result of illness, but from constant and debilitating worry for her sister's plight. She further explained that she could not imagine a change in her performance in either regard as long as her sister remained rootless. At the time she spoke these words Sonny Boy had already begun to miss the full complement of her work, both in the fields and in the marital bed. The unhappy prospect of even more unrequited nights made Sonny Boy more readily agreeable than Oholibamah had ever expected. Nonetheless, Sonny Boy was careful to give the appearance of deliberating upon her request in order to make it clear, at least in his own mind, that he was still in charge. Yet in the end Sonny Boy responded in the only way that the profound purposing of Oholibamah's heart would allow: he agreed that her dispossessed sister could stay under their roof. Grudgingly, but he agreed. Still, he wanted it understood that what he offered was temporary.

"Make sure you tell her not to get too comfortable, cause she can't stay here long."

Then he reached for Oholibamah, but she was already out the door.

Chapter

15

She was thankful for the corner of her sister's hut where she could lay her head. But this did not allay the great insecurity of knowing that she was only a whim away from homelessness again. So she did whatever she was asked as if she had been told, then made certain to do even more. Expanding with bursts of action when there was work, then shrinking again when there was none, she assisted Oholibamah in all that she could and attended to Sonny Boy's every casual request. Never offering idle conversation, she spoke to Sonny Boy only when she was spoken to, except when demurely greeting him in the morning and demurely wishing him rest at night.

Despite the grudging nature of his welcome, however, Sonny Boy found himself pleased by her agreeable manner. But more than pleased, he was titillated. By night he was excited by the nearness of her when he reached for Oholibamah in conjugal embrace, and by day he was enticed by the tempting curves of her tunic when she stooped before the cooking fire or bent low in the fields at work.

She was aware of his new warmth and thought it was simply a brother-in-law's affection, but Sonny Boy did not see her as a sister of any kind. Far from simply tolerating her, he found himself fastening his full attention upon her as the unremitting object of a surprising new desire. This development was not welcomed by Sonny Boy, for it was nothing he had planned or even wanted, and it left him confused and chagrined. For although it was true that he routinely denied Oholibamah's every request, his refusals in no way reflected a lack of affection for her. Rather, they were his way of asserting the ongoing control he believed a real man should have. The reality was that if Sonny Boy had known how to articulate his deepest feelings, he would have told anyone who listened that he loved his wife more than his own life. The one thing Sonny Boy did know, though these words were never to escape from his mouth either, was that he was contented with his life as it was. That is why the last thing he wanted or needed was the complication of another woman invading his thoughts, and especially not a woman of his kin in his own home.

Oholibamah knew of Sonny Boy's passion for her sister almost as soon as he did. She tried not to see, but the look in Sonny Boy's eyes when her sister was near, as if he was beholding the sunrise for the first time or had just tasted something exceedingly good to eat, became so obvious that she could not help but notice. Despite her love for her sister, Oholibamah began to fear for the stability of her home and her own place in it. That is the reason Oholibamah offered not a word of opposition or even asked why when Sonny Boy awoke one morning declaring that rather than going straight to the fields as usual, instead he was on his way to secure a husband for her sister, and on that very day if he could.

What moved Sonny Boy to such urgency was a sigh. The night before the morning he arose a newly insistent matchmaker, he had just lifted Oholibamah's sleeping garment and climbed quietly atop her when he heard her sister sigh in her sleep. This excited him so that while he lay in the arms of his wife he could think of nothing but her castaway sister. What made him seek a husband for her with as much haste as he could muster was when she sighed a second time and he'd begun to fantasize that the panting body beneath him was hers. His chagrin turned to real terror when his body arched and, nearing the peak of his passion, at the very moment he always called out the name of his wife, he almost called the name of her sister. He lay awake the rest of the night, frightened to breathlessness by the calamity that had almost befallen him, desperately awaiting the rising of the sun so he could go forth to rid his home of this threat to his life as it was.

"Where you going to get her this husband?" Oholibamah asked Sonny Boy, not in challenge but to gauge his chance of success.

"Down to the river," he said. "Where else?"

"You talking about the men always hanging around there when they should be working?"

"That's not a nice way to talk about people."

"Sonny, you know those men are just as no-account as the day is long. And they drink, too. Seems like all they do is drink. Can hardly feed themselves, much less a family. How can you hardworking men put up with such sorriness?"

"Don't nobody like it, 'Bamah. But they're still neighbors."

Oholibamah was too busy fussing to hear his reply. "The only time you see any of them raise a hand to work—other than playing at fishing—is when they run out of drink and go off to work somebody's field just long enough to get another skin of wine. Or a jug of that smelly barley beer."

"Alright. Alright. I hear you. But nobody else I know of is looking for a wife, especially one without a dowry that another man has already got tired of. Beggars can't be choosers, you know."

He set out as soon as it was light. When he reached the bend in the river, there were men already there. Some had slept in the threadbare tents and tipping lean-tos that dotted the riverside; others were already perched upon their daily thrones of water-smoothed stones beneath the overhanging trees. Several had tied the hems of their tunics into their sashes or stripped to their undergarments and waded into the river on naked legs to cast their nets. Shards of discarded clay jars littered the banks of the river, and the discarded bony frames of many roasted fish lay strewn amid the blackened remnants of cooking fires lit helter-skelter upon rock and soil.

Sonny Boy greeted each man by name. Some were already glassy-eyed with drink. He went from face to face taking inventory of who was married, who was not, and who was otherwise ineligible for his purposes. Again and again he discounted the object of his scrutiny as an already married man, or a known bully, or someone who was not a prospect for family provider because he was barely feeding himself, or one who was so sickly and weak from too much drink and too little food that it seemed a sure bet that any wife he married would soon be a widow.

Sonny Boy shook his head in despair. He knew this was the only place he might find an eligible husband, other than the never-married young men of the village whose strident fathers would never betroth their (supposedly) virgin sons to a woman who not only was not a virgin but had also committed the cardinal sin of getting in and out of marriage so quickly that it sullied her family name.

"Lord. What do I do now?" Sonny Boy muttered at the dawning realization that apparently there was no man available to marry the sister-in-law whose heated presence threatened the very fabric of his household.

Then he noticed an unsmiling, slightly stooped figure trudging upriver, his casting net on one arm, his wineskin slung on the other: the sad-eyed Galilean who drank much, talked exceedingly little, and answered to a description rather than a name. Sonny Boy studied him keenly, for although it was true that he was intent on marrying off his homeless houseguest, his growing tenderness toward her would not let him betroth her to just anyone. In his scrutiny he could find little to commend this man. No family, no wealth, he was not even the recipient of regular gestures of respect. But he'd built a hut of discarded wood on the river a little farther upstream. And to Sonny Boy's knowledge the pleasureless man had never shown any evidence of bad temper or the telltale signs of suppressed meanness lying in wait for defenseless prey. In fact, despite the thick air of sadness that trailed his every step, there was something vaguely likable about him, something endearing and almost gentle. And he was known to be kind, even loving, toward the small creatures that crossed his path. He had been seen binding broken wings, removing sharp rocks and briers from the paws of limping dogs, and was the object of fishermen's fun because he was careful always to throw back the little fish when a few of them on the fire would have quieted his growling stomach. And he was particularly affable, sometimes with eyes that were strangely teary, to the little brown boys who seemed to go out of their way just to smile at him, call out "Shalom, Mr. Man!" and see him wave in return.

He's not that bad, Sonny Boy thought. *Beggars can't be choosers.* And surely the unfortunate posture of his castaway in-law, whom he wanted gone from his home at the earliest possible moment, was as close to a beggar's stance as one could get.

"Man!" he called, beckoning to him and removing the skin of wine from his shoulder in one motion. The sad-eyed man dropped his nets on the bank of the river, right above the waterline, and silently ambled over to Sonny Boy.

"Shalom, Man," said Sonny Boy. "Have a drink?"

He nodded without looking up.

"I was just looking around at the fellas and I realized that you're one of the only full-grown men in the whole village without a wife. Did you know that, Man?"

He shook his head. With his own full wineskin still on his shoulder, he took Sonny Boy's vessel and raised it to his lips.

Sonny Boy answered his own question. "Well, it's true. And that ain't good. Folks in this village don't trust a man without a woman. They think something's wrong with him, like something's not natural in him or else he's getting ready to steal something and he don't want nobody to slow him down when he's trying to run. See, that's how folks think around here." He paused for effect. "That's why it's time to get you a wife."

At that, the one called Man flinched, but Sonny Boy did not notice. "You need a wife. And just by coincidence on purpose"—he chuckled at his own small humor—"don't you know that my woman got a sister right now that needs a good man like you."

Suddenly the other spoke without looking up. "I don't want a wife." His voice was soft and rasping from lack of use. Words from him were so unexpected that Sonny Boy blinked with surprise.

"But a man needs him a wife, and some children, too," said Sonny Boy, quickly regaining his composure.

The brief silence that ensued seemed much longer to each of them. The sad man still had not lifted his gaze from the sandy soil beneath his hard feet, which he now moved self-consciously, shifting his weight from leg to leg. Finally he said quietly, in almost a mumble, "Don't want no wife. No children, neither."

"But how you going to know? You don't have no family. How you know what you're missing?"

At this the sad man cringed. Choking back a sob, he turned away and slowly walked to his nets, his head hung so low it looked like he would tip forward.

"Man. What I do, Man?" called Sonny Boy. "I'm just trying to get you a wife."

His face pinched, shoulders heaving slightly, the tormented figure spread his nets on the shore and said nothing.

"Man, I'm telling you. You need to get married. Single, and a Galilean, too—if you want to stay around here, you got to get you a wife like everyone else." Sonny Boy's tone was vaguely threatening, but it did not register on Man, who focused his attention on the gaps in the net's meshwork.

"But it ain't like you don't know her. She already cooked and did for you."

At this the joyless man looked at Sonny Boy for the first time.

"Oh yeah," Sonny Boy said with forced joviality. "That first time you walked in and passed out for two, three days, who do you think fed you and looked after you and sewed my old piece of tunic so you could have something decent to wear? It was her. My sister-in-law. She was the one."

An avalanche of emotions swept over the tormented man. He remembered the warm feeling when he'd awakened beneath the makeshift tent at the river, newly washed and fed and dressed, feeling almost safe. That was the first comfort he'd known since the sun had turned his fields to traitors and his loved ones to dust. While still in his stupor, a part of him had been aware of tender hands attending him. He'd smiled in his stupefaction at the pleasing fragrance of thyme and female presence. When he awoke he thought it all had been a dream. Realizing now that it had not been imagined, that the pleasing touch and the fragrance and the presence were all real and were now his for the asking, a panic broke over him and he drew back in terror, for the last thing he wanted was for his heart to feel.

Fully unaware of the sorrowed man's struggle, Sonny Boy continued with the mistaken belief that the words he shared were welcome.

"That's right. She took real good care of you. Did it once; she could do it from now on. She'd make sure you eat good, not just fish and wine. And keep your hut up. She don't have a dowry, though, but she's a hard worker. And obedient, too."

Feeling a sudden vulnerability that filled him with terror, the one known as Man doffed his tunic. Holding his nets, he quickly waded into the licking river clad only in his undergarments. The wineskins he'd dropped on the shore. A pack of prepubescent boys who made a daily pastime of spying on the men, whose every word and movement they found immensely interesting and entertaining, suddenly hooted from their hiding place in the brush at the sight of naked underclothing, and tore back toward the village convulsed with laughter. But Sonny Boy heard nothing except his own pleas and arguments, which he now pressed with even greater insistence, while the object of his appeals silently wended his way downstream, casting his net before him until he had worked himself out of earshot. His quarry gone, Sonny Boy shook his head in disappointment and started for his fields.

Chapter
16

Between forays to the riverbank for wine to dull the ache that
Sonny Boy had raised within him, the sad fisherman on his way
to drunkenness halfheartedly cast his net for the rest of the morning,
then dragged his meager catch ashore and lay in the shade of the willows
for several hours of besotted sleep, the river breezes whispering in his
ear. When he awoke he started his way upstream, pausing every so often
to raise the wineskin to his lips. When he reached the men's gathering
spot at the river's bend, he stepped out of the water and eased himself
down upon the large smooth rocks in the midst of the others who fished
part-time and drank full-time, and joined them in their guzzling and
dozing. He had just drifted into another dream-ravaged sleep when he
heard the voice of Sonny Boy, who had gone to his fields when he left
him and had even begun to work, but who found that he could not stay
there because of the disturbing presence of his alluring houseguest.

Sonny Boy had returned to the river. When he saw the sad-eyed
drunkard who had so unceremoniously rejected his offer, he began to
loud-talk him.

"I told Man he need to get married," he said loudly. "I told him that's
what he need to do if he want to stay in this village with some comfort-
ableness. But I might as well been talking to a hummingbird for all the
good it did."

He turned to the others in their various degrees of recline and said, "He need to get married. To somebody. Ain't that right?"

"Yes, sir. We're a marrying village around here," slurred one to the nods of the others.

In fact, all the men agreed, even though some were too drunk to fully understand what they were agreeing with. The discussion became a test of wills for all of them, the few who were sober and the many who were not, and soon they were more concerned with winning their way than with parsing the social necessity of marriage.

"Sonny Boy's right, Man. Bad a shape as you're in, you need somebody to at least cook and do for you."

"And wash that filthy tunic you ain't changed since you got it."

"And go get your wine for you."

"And give you some loving. And some sons."

"Especially some loving. It's not natural for a man to go without loving. After a hard day in the fields ain't nothing like a little—"

"You telling Man that loving is more important than sons?"

"I'm saying you can't have one without the other. And if you do it right you're gonna . . ."

"Here he go again, talking about loving like don't nobody know but him. Talks about it so much you wonder if he gets any."

"I know you're not questioning how much man I am in my own house."

"I'm just saying that them that can, do. Them that can't, talk."

"See. There you go signifying again."

Sonny Boy threw up his hands in exasperation. "Fellas! We're talking about Man, not trying to see who can sound like the biggest fool. What we're saying is Man need to get married. You all need to put that wine down for a minute and start talking to him like you got some sense."

After perhaps the tenth turn of the argument in which the men, shamed now by Sonny Boy into a semblance of sobriety, were so intensely engaged, the one called Man finally acceded with a sigh. The deciding factor was his fear of feeling. To continue to refuse in the face of the men's spirited jibes and exclamations he would have to assert himself, and that would necessitate mustering a strong emotion, marshaling the force of a countervailing opinion, and then what would stem the ensuing flow of feeling? In the end he did not give in because he saw the wisdom of the men's claims, but simply to allay the mounting agitation of his own heart.

Thrilled with the prospect of relief from his fevered nights, Sonny Boy brought his drunken compatriot home that very evening, for he was determined to finalize the arrangements as quickly as he could. Oholibamah was in the yard tending the smoking oven when they approached.

"This is Man," Sonny Boy said matter-of-factly. "He's going to be your sister's new husband."

Oholibamah stared at the bedraggled figure swaying with his impassive face, awash in the sour smell of wine and fish. She was motionless except for her eyes with their judgmental squint.

"Don't forget your manners, woman," Sonny Boy scolded. "Go get the man some dinner. And call your sister."

Following the table blessing the meal was silent save for the sounds of eating. The four sat on the dirt floor of the hut upon rush mats, dipping their hands or flat loaves of barley bread into the fare that Oholibamah had set before them: a pot of hot lentil stew, a bowl of ground chickpea sauce with little triangles of baked dough stuffed with pungent herbs, a small array of dates and figs, and one boiled egg. The children hunched in an unlit corner giggling, eating from wooden bowls they balanced upon their knees, their faces and tunics smeared with the drippings of stew.

Conversations customarily commenced after a few mouthfuls of each delicacy had been sampled, at which point guests complimented both the savor of the meal (no matter how it tasted really) and the hospitality of their hosts. But Sonny Boy was so anxious to get the betrothal started that he could not wait for the traditional niceties. To his wife's silent consternation, he spoke up before the last dish had been tasted.

"He want to marry you. Ain't that right, Man?"

His drunken guest was silent.

"Tell her, Man. Ain't that right?"

The sad man reluctantly nodded through his wine-sodden daze. He thought of his wife shriveled in death to the size of a child and breathed a sudden sob. He caught it in his throat, before it became the full cry it needed to be, but still the sound contained such sadness that both women flinched as if they had been struck. The rush of emotion was ignored by Sonny Boy, who thought it to be nothing more than a drunken belch.

In the awkward silence the young woman being offered as if she had not a feeling or a thought shuddered. *Not already,* she thought. Why were they—it was clear it was *they* because Oholibamah registered no protest to the pronouncement, not even with her eyes—why were they suddenly so intent on ridding themselves of her that they'd pass her to a drunk with eyes so empty it seemed you could throw stones in them and he wouldn't blink?

"He got a hut on the river," said Sonny Boy. "He's a fisherman. Nice fella . . . How soon you be ready?"

"Huh? I . . . I . . . don't know."

"What you mean, you don't know?"

She leaned to Sonny Boy and whispered, "But he's a drunk, Sonny. And I don't even know him. Please."

Sonny Boy fastened upon her face, upon the vulnerability of it, and a great twinge of passion arose in him. He was suddenly aware of how much he'd love to caress her, his hands touching her face, cupping her breasts like the most delicate of all things. But rather than moving him to tenderness, his passion instead became a flash of anger at his powerlessness to have her for himself.

"Know him?" he said aloud. "What that got to do with marriage? You know you need a roof over your head. You know you can't stay here forever. If you want to know something, know that. Now get yourself together and marry this man."

Exactly two days later, with solemn words and pronouncements, a scowling and displeased Abba Samuel consecrated the saddest union he had ever witnessed. Sonny Boy had left his fields as soon as the sun began to set and fetched him and hurried him to the lean-to on the river where Oholibamah and her sister and the silent groom awaited.

The intendeds stood stiffly in the leaf-strewn clearing before the leaning wooden structure that would be their marital home. The smell of rotted fish mingled with the wafting scent of honeysuckle and pine. The bride's parents were not present. After her dispossession by Jalon, her embarrassed father had disowned her to the hearing of everyone who'd listen, which meant that her mother, whose fear of her husband would never let her contravene his decisions, in effect had disowned her also. In fact, there were no celebrants to wish them well except Abba Samuel, Oholibamah, and Sonny Boy, each of them so taken aback by the emotional wreckage so glaringly evident in the hapless couple shivering before them that they barely stifled their wonder that so much sadness could reside in so small a space.

The couple stood apart an arm's length or more, both staring at the ground, unbelieving, uncomprehending. The face of each was a study in despair and resignation.

The bride closed her eyes and saw herself reeling on the edge of a precipice. The groom hung his head and wondered when life would tire of torturing him.

Abba Samuel was aware of a dull ache in his stomach. His usually resonant voice was barely a whisper as he recited the holy words of troth.

"What's your name, son? I need a name to call you."

Man was silent and still.

"Alright," said Abba Samuel in a daze of sadness and appall. "Alright. I pronounce you . . . man and wife."

He turned and walked away from the hung-head newlyweds as fast as he could.

And so she was married.

Chapter

17

When first she saw him, the one she knew only as Man, he lay unconscious beneath the makeshift tent at the river. She'd felt only disgust for his cowed and beaten demeanor, his slovenly appearance, the distasteful odor that emanated from his body. Yet as he stood beside her repeating the wedding sentences in a voice so soft it seemed he might only have been exhaling, even in his drunkenness she felt from him a surprising gentleness, which was all the more unexpected given his palpable reluctance to be there. It was the way he handled his disinclination that touched her. She noticed his ample mouth quiver, subtly yet clearly, and the smallest tear swelling his eye, yet still he continued as if the unwelcome nuptials were the fruit of his own unfettered volition. That is, he did not frown, not even slightly, or sigh loudly, or respond to the ritual questions of Abba Samuel with even a tinge of outward reluctance. It was as if he was in his way more concerned for her feelings than for his own.

It was this small selfless kindness that made bearable for her what otherwise verged on the unbearable. In fact, it was something so altogether new for her that even in the midst of her angst she became aware of a curious twinge of gratitude warming her. When at the end of the ceremony Abba Samuel ritually placed Man's hand upon hers, she felt an unmistakable tenderness in the lightness of his touch.

That is why, alone with him now in his shack, after the witnesses to their union had fled as soon as the final syllable of the marital oath was uttered as if they feared that the couple's profound melancholy would invade their own unprotected hearts, to her great surprise her only impulse was to please him. Of course, her reaction was in large part the consequence of having been found unpleasing on her first wedding night, a night so infused with meanness and uncaring that even the thought of it caused her pulse to quicken. But what moved her more than that painful memory was the kindness she felt from this sorrowed man even as he shied from speaking to her or even glancing her way: his wordless civility, the gentleness of his gesticulation, the benign language of his eyes and facial expressions.

Her warm feeling for him was made warmer still by his response to her poorly concealed disappointment at the sorry state of his shack. She mustered as much calculated nonchalance as she could—she did not want to be found unpleasing—but from the tightness about her eyes it was clear to Man that the undisturbed filth of his shack and its reeking stench appalled and disheartened her. For like everything about her new husband, the shack itself was in shocking disarray. Not more than fifteen paces from corner to corner, its uneven walls were permanently swayed, with glints of sunlight blinking through gaps in the leaning poplar planks and stripped crooked saplings where the dried mortar of black mud and river clay had fallen away. Its uneven dirt floor was dotted with a dozen or more fish heads lying blank-eyed atop fine-tooth skeletons strewn among a scramble of last year's dried and crumpled leaves. Companies of ants freely ranged over uneaten heels of bread and decaying fruit thrown carelessly upon the rotting boxwood stump that passed as a table. Clay jars caked with the sour residue of spoiled wine lay in a pile, broken and discarded. The whole construction groaned softly in the breeze gusting off the river. Stinking of rotted fish, the soured sweetish smell of fermented drink lingering even in the yard, her new home was a hovel by any measure she knew.

Man noticed her surveying the mess, and saw the flush of disappointment in her face. He dropped his head and without looking her way uttered his first words as her spouse, mumbled but heartfelt. "I'm sorry . . . ," he said, grunting as his words trailed off, stooping to scoop up debris and the fetid remains of fish.

She turned to him in pleasant surprise at this small expression of caring, the likes of which she'd no longer dreamed to expect of a man.

"It's alright . . . I'll get it," she said in a tone of such gratitude and affection that Man rushed outside, kicking at the dust, blinking hard and spitting, straining to keep at bay the waves of emotion threatening to overcome him.

His new bride was stunned at his abrupt turn. Ironically, with this sudden eruption of discomfort she realized that until that moment the anxiety and fear with which she had approached their first night had from his first gentleness to her gradually dissipated to the point that now her defenses were barely raised. She concluded that this was not a good thing. She thought to be on her guard and was convinced that she should, but she simply could not muster alarm; it was true that Man had rushed away for some unfathomable reason, but he had not been unkind. She resolved to quiet the fear trying to take hold of her so that when her new husband returned she might offer him warmth without reserve. Humming softly, she untied the bundle containing the few belongings she brought to her new life: a hunk of goat cheese and several loaves of barley bread from Oholibamah, a boxwood comb with several missing tines, one change of clothing, a threadbare woolen shawl, and the treasured wooden box of odds and ends that Ma Tee had left her. Then she began to tidy the disarray of her new home, feeling remarkably calm even with her great mix of emotions. Still she was careful to disturb only the rotting food and nothing else; not the threadbare cushion carelessly cast into a corner, not the curious little doll he'd constructed from clay and twigs and cloth that now sat upon a small altar of sticks, and certainly not the wineskins and unbroken clay jars carelessly strewn at the head of the bed mat. She would be careful to fit into his life as seamlessly and unobtrusively as she could.

Chapter

18

Man returned late in the night, full of wine and nervous trepidation. He found his new wife asleep on his bed mat, the debris gone and the dirt floor swept with a leafy branch, and a supper of goat cheese and bread awaiting him. His hunger quieted by drink, he ignored the food and quietly crawled onto the bed mat beside her, out of nothing even approaching desire, but simply because he did not want her to feel any more rejection than she already had. He did his best not to touch her, but his drunkenness made his movements awkward and he woke her nonetheless.

She lay silent and still, hardly breathing, expecting to feel lustful hands upon her, to be wrested into submission, her legs parted, her garments flung away. Her new husband seemed kind enough, but unkind treatment was all she knew to expect of wedding nights. Instead, to her surprise he lay as still as she, though the sameness in the cadence of his breathing betrayed that he was yet awake. Her own breath quickened, her body grew rigid in anticipation, but still he made no movement toward her. Then she began to wonder why he had not touched her. Was he testing, waiting to see what he could expect of her, what kind of wife she would be, whether she would please or disappoint him? Or could his reticence simply be consideration for a sleeping wife? At any rate, to be safe she yawned to let him know that she was awake, for she did not want to take the chance that morning would find his heart hardened against a bride he thought had feigned sleep to avoid her wifely duty. But even with her stirring, the rhythmic rise and fall of his breast remained his only movement. In desperation she faked a cough, but she did it with such force that she began to gag. Man turned to her. "You alright?"

She nodded in the dark, then managed a weak "Uh-huh" as she struggled to catch her breath. Then they were still and silent again.

Man's expression of concern touched her deeply. Since the death of Ma Tee she had heard few words of care. In fact, aside from Mr. Ishmael and the taciturn Mr. Pop, as far as she knew no man had ever shown her concern. More touching still was the thought that her new husband's expression of caring meant that despite the deprivation of her new surroundings, at least there she might be treated like a person rather than a thing. She was so grateful for this happy prospect, for she was not accustomed to happy prospects, that she responded to Man in a way that she had responded to no one but Ma Tee: she reached for him in a spontaneous and gushing show of affection. As she touched him she noticed that he immediately stiffened. Because reticence seemed to be his approach to all things, she did not consider that he might be rejecting her. *He's just nervous,* she thought, attributing his response to the newness of things. Encouraged by what seemed to her an attractive shyness, she lightly kissed his forehead, then his dry, unpursed lips.

He felt the soft curve of her breast upon him, her warm fragrant breath on his cheek, and suddenly the unrequited seasons of passion for the wife he could not save rushed in upon him. He'd barely turned away from his new bride's embrace when the grief he'd held at such feeble bay again erupted in a sweetish spew of vomit that dripped from his beard, ran down his tunic, splattered the freshly swept floor.

Thinking his nausea was the result of too much drink and too little food, not even imagining that it had to do with her, she quickly rose to help him. He was on his knees, doubled over and still retching. She rubbed the nape of his neck to soothe his discomfort but he stood, pushing her away, and stumbled from the shack upon unsteady legs to make his way to the whispering river. He splashed his face, retched

again at the water's edge, then collapsed in the cool mud in great panting sobs. When he had cried himself out, he pushed to his feet and
slowly returned to the shack. He paused at the doorway for a moment,
then stooped through it and paused again, his eyes downcast. She
looked up from the bed mat, cross-legged and confused.

"You alright?" she said.

He answered without looking at her. "Uh-huh."

"I . . ." She started to speak, then stopped when he moved toward her.
She expected a word or a touch, but Man said nothing. Instead, he reached
past her for one of the two skins of wine that lay beside the bed mat. He
retrieved it and turned to leave.

As he stooped through the doorway she called to him. "Man?" He
stopped. His back was to her. "Did I do something wrong?"

He moved the ragged curtain aside.

"Where . . . where are you going?"

He hesitated for a moment, as if to speak, then let the drab cloth
swing behind him and hurried to the river to drink himself into a
numbing stupor.

In the shack she sat perfectly still, her gaze alternating between the
splatter of regurgitation congealing at her feet and the empty spot
made by her husband's departure. She cast her eyes about her at the
freshly swept dirt floor, the creaking mat of woven rushes thrown and
crumpled in a corner, the stump she had cleared of dust and rotted
debris, and shards of clay vessels stained the color of fermented grapes.
Alone in her new deprivation she could do no other than think that
she had failed yet another man. She was overwhelmed with such disquiet that she thought she, too, would become sick. Then little by little
she calmed, for when she allowed herself to reflect it became clear that
the spike of emotion that sickened Man was not her fault. He had
come to her broken; sad and broken and ashen with grief. Yet there
was something more about him, a gentleness, an unnamed goodness
that touched her so deeply that she wanted to hold him, to lay his
grief-ravaged head in the hollow of her lap and hum to him the songs of
comfort, as Ma Tee had for her.

Yet Man's sorrow did not just remain his own; it invaded her spirit, too, for she had to admit to herself that despite her best efforts she was a consort in yet another failed wedding night. Still, she felt no need to withdraw from him, because somehow she knew he was doing the best he could. As she reflected further she recognized in his flight from her equal measures of desperation and kindness, for although his departure could not have been more abrupt, he had left without recrimination or the merest word of indictment. Right then, she resolved three things: that she would be kind to him in return, that she would do all that she could to honor his grief, whatever its source, and that she would be careful.

Chapter

19

He was awakened by the rain upon his face. It was a light rain, so brief that it seemed its only purpose was to wake him. He stirred and splashed himself with river water, shaking his head to clear it. Squatting on his haunches in the early morning light, he fixed his thoughts upon the previous night, recounted its pain and confusion, and sighed deeply. He squatted this way for a long time. Eventually he stretched his legs and walked slowly to the shack. He stood outside and made several false starts to enter. Finally he lifted the curtain and his new wife looked up. She was fully dressed. She had already been to the well to retrieve their water for the day.

"Oh," she said. "Good morning. Shalom."

"Shalom," he said, his eyes downcast.

"I was getting some breakfast. The rest of the cheese and bread. Have some?"

He entered wordlessly and picked up the clay doll from its altar of twigs. He fingered it briefly, mouthed a string of inaudible words that seemed to be a prayer, set it back down, then pulled a dusty mat from its corner and squatted upon it. She placed the bowl of food upon the box-wood stump and eased herself down. They ate in silence, their eyes alternating between the bowl and the backs of their hands, until finally she departed to take her place in the fields beside her sister and Man retreated to the safe solitude of his nets and the river.

This was their unchanging pattern for the next weeks: his stupors at the river at night, his mouthing words at the clay doll before their silent shared breakfasts at dawn, then off to their separate venues of toil. At dusk he returned for another meal in silence, then left again before it was time to retire. In his unvarying routine he was dutiful in his leaving, dutiful in his return, and dutiful in his avoidance of their marital bed. He knew he could never give even the smallest part of himself to her, so he gave her what he could: a pattern of behavior that he knew was less than satisfying, but that nonetheless she could depend upon.

What did change, however, is that little by little she began to venture to him a thought here, an observation there, a bit of village news, comments about the weather. She began this slowly and haltingly, gradually and delicately recasting their wordless balance.

First she ventured by asking about food. "Had enough? How was it?"

From there she began to compliment him for the fish he brought her which, though they were never very large in size or in number, she nonetheless broiled on a spit or stewed in spices and lentils or with the potatoes and cucumbers she brought home from Oholibamah's fields. She advanced to speaking of her days in the fields with her sister, how much they had planted or picked together, the outrageous stories with which her sister regaled her, the youthful antics of her nephew and nieces.

Gradually the range of his responses to her grew as well, slowly expanding from his thick unbroken silences, to an occasional grudging nod of recognition, to audible grunts of acknowledgment, to muted replies that were at times even accompanied by the fragment of a smile, and finally to brief, truncated answers.

Eventually she became comfortable enough to talk about things that meant more to her, things she felt, her musings, her dreams. To these he nodded and grunted and sometimes even offered the semblance of a reply—"yeah" and "oh" and sometimes "really"—which prompted her to think, *We're getting closer.* So she went further, became more personal and playful. She was careful not to ask of his past, for she feared that would cause more anguish, maybe even a recurrence of the nausea that had despoiled their first night together. The one thing she did ask was his name, for she longed for him to share at least that much of himself. She knew to be careful, so she couched her question with gentle teasing.

"Man? I can see you're a man. That's not a name, that's a description." To which he half-smiled with that sunken sadness in his eyes, but never did he answer.

Yet she felt no sense of strain with the silent man who shared her life. She noticed his efforts to consider her comfort even in the midst of whatever it was that tortured him. And although there never passed a day for him without the solace of strong drink, he was never unkind to her, and there was seldom a day that he did not bring for her cooking pot at least one fish for their supper to complement whatever she brought from her days in the fields sowing, planting, plowing furrows, and pulling weeds with Oholibamah while Sonny Boy sullenly labored nearby, always facing away from her, no matter where she stood.

She began to anticipate their time together with growing contentment. They had not consummated their union, had not embraced or even kissed. Still she felt a developing closeness. She grew to comfort in the routine of their cohabitation, and for the first time in her life came to know a relaxed sense of security at home. With the debacle of their wedding night now far behind and nothing having since occurred to raise it again, she began to feel in this contentment a rising affection.

As their weeks together became months, those things about him that were disdained by others—and which she herself had once disdained as well—became for her a source of endearment. Beneath his silences she perceived a depth of feeling and thought she'd experienced only with Ma Tee and Mr. Ishmael. Where others saw drunkenness, she saw the desperate salving of painful wounds. Where others saw self-absorption, she saw the self-protection of a sensitive soul. What they dismissed as silence, she now knew to be his tortured response to the unspeakable.

What is more, she was reassured by the rising trajectory of his kindnesses. The way he always was sure to clean his catch to save her the effort. The care he took not to offend the cleanliness and order she brought to the shack. His small attempts to improve his appearance and hygiene by taking occasional baths of immersion in the river, even at times cleansing his breath of the smell of wine with sprigs of mint. It was true that he did not give her much, that he did not say much, but he accepted her as she was. No hard eyes of judgment, no tests of submissiveness to determine her worthiness. This was the freest she had ever felt.

Little by little she commenced, and little by little he allowed her, to attend to him and in small ways to care for him, to sweeten his goat's milk with honey, to pick bits of straw and fallen leaves from his hair. After their evening meal, when he'd left for yet another solitary night at the river, she took her spindle and loom in hand to fashion a new tunic to replace the now-tattered one he had worn since she had bathed and clothed his unconscious form after his collapse on his first day in the village. Every night she spun and wove on a discarded loom she had painstakingly restored, until sleep called her from it. Her heart skipped and she smiled broadly when she imagined the gratitude that would bloom in Man's face when she was done. Yet when he returned one morning from another night of wine-sodden river sleep to find the newly finished garment laid out for him, he refused to wear it. This hurt her deeply, but she was careful not to let it show. She just folded the garment tenderly and placed it atop the rush mats piled in the corner. Then one evening she noticed the tunic was gone and she was crushed to think he would so easily discard a gift that had come from her heart. But the next dawn he appeared wearing it without fanfare or mention.

In this way the sad man and the careful woman developed a working balance in which the one never transgressed the boundaries of the other. She could talk, even to chattiness, as long as she was careful that her words did not prick the feelings that tortured him. At times she went so far as to touch him as she spoke, but no more than a nudge to a forearm or an elbow, carefully enough done so as not in any way to be misconstrued as an attempt at intimacy.

In this peaceful equipoise he began to relax his defenses, even silently to enjoy her. Most nights he still slept at the river, but now from time to time he allowed himself to fall asleep in the shack. At first he would not stay there for succeeding nights, for the sight of her on successive mornings, her face still and soft, her voice whispery with sleep, was too much for him to bear.

In time, however, he became used to her, or convinced himself it was so, and gradually quit his nights at the river. He did not give up his stupors, however, for he needed some way to keep his grief at bay. Every night he thought of the dead woman who'd loved him and the children he had lost, and every night he mourned them anew, and again in the mornings, and especially when this new presence in his life evoked them for him with her heartrending smile. Each time her laughter rang, or he heard the kindness and compassion in her voice, he felt his heart beginning to hunger, the rise of feelings that were first as sweet as clover then as bitter as bile, and he would suddenly reach out for nothingness and drink himself into it. Afterward, he tossed in his drunken sleep, plagued and tormented in the hungering dark by a thing his wife could not fathom.

"I can help you. I can. I can," he cried in his sleep, sobbing until he forced himself to wake. Then he would reach for the little clay doll and lie awake until dawn.

Only at these times could she touch him more than fleetingly without him recoiling. She gently mopped his brow, quelling the storm within him as best she could. But he always regained his distance in the morning, disclaiming in the day all that his heart had felt in the night.

And so went their life together. The careful woman and the grieving man had been married for more than a year now and still they had not consummated their union. Despite the denial with which they both clothed it, however, an earnest desire for the arms of the other began to bedevil them. She attempted to cope with it by repressing the throbbing beneath her garments, or by touching herself in secret. For his part, he dealt with it as he dealt with all things: by withdrawing into the safety of his drink, then retreating from her presence when even that was not enough.

That was in daylight. It was different in the night. In the night each took unspoken comfort in the closeness of their bodies, in the other's rhythmic breathing, the exaggerated yawns, the conspicuous coughing and clearing of throats, the yearning figure tossing beside them.

Longing lived beneath the surface of all they did, beneath their every breath, their every gesture and look, their every phrase and movement. It filled their eyes and nostrils and tripped them underfoot. Sometimes it allowed them to sleep and sometimes it did not. Each night they wrestled hard with their desire, heard its whispered call and felt its siren breath, but never did they respond to it or even betray it as something that their hearts dared to feel.

This cycle continued, the call of their passion and their turning from it, but their barriers were weakening. Man did not reciprocate her shows of affection or her endearing gestures, but despite his every intention not to, he slowly began to look forward to seeing her at the end of each day, to hearing her voice, to finding her baking in the yard or preparing the fare she'd brought home. On the days his luck occurred early he returned with his catch just past midday to await her, dozing and nodding beneath the poplars that ringed the shack, always awakening filled with a strange excitement moments before she appeared at the turn in the path, as if his burgeoning desire attuned him to her presence beyond even the measure of his senses.

On one such day he awaited her, telling himself as always that what he so eagerly looked forward to was his supper and nothing more. He waited and dozed, then dozed some more. He awoke to see from the position of the sun that she should be returning soon. He dozed a bit more to find when he awoke this time that although the sun was now well below the crests of the trees she still had not returned. This had never happened before. He began to worry. Then a cold fear seized him that now she, too, was lost to him. He tried to rise to go in search of her, but his fear of what he might find paralyzed his limbs, for the calamities of his life had taught him to expect nothing but the worst. He could not even rise when his bladder commanded; he found himself in a pool of his own urine overcome by a fear that cut so deep he wished he was dead. He thought to pray, but he knew his prayers had never allayed death. In fact, he suspected that his supplications actually called death forth, that his appeals to God uniformly brought demise upon those for whom he so desperately sought deliverance. Afraid to pray, dispossessed of courage, devoid of every hope, all he could do was wait in a choking terror of uncertainty. He sat for what seemed an eternity, until he thought his dread would never end. Then he heard footfalls and raised his head to see her approaching. She looked down at him, saw the streaks where tears had stained his dusty cheeks. She saw his wetted tunic, the wild look in his reddened eyes, the terror that still roiled them, and she thought her heart would break.

"I'm sorry," she said. "I'm so sorry. Mr. Ishmael was under the weather so when I left Oholibamah's I went by to make a stew for him and Mr. Pop. I'm sorry. I'm sorry I worried you. I am."

Man said nothing. He reached for his wineskin, but this time he did not go to the river. Instead he remained in the yard, guzzling his drink until it streamed down his chin and onto his wetted tunic. When she was out of earshot he sobbed quietly into his hands, offering tearful thanks for her return and cursing it in the same breath.

At supper she served him nervously, laden with anxiety, fearing she had displeased him just when things seemed to be going well. He said nothing and ate little. Although he had not spent a night at the river for some time, surely he would this night, she thought with a tinge of sadness. To her surprise, when he pushed his bowl away and rose to his feet he did not leave. Before their meal he had cleansed himself and his spoiled tunic and draped himself in the old threadbare one that she had washed and mended and folded in the corner, but he removed it now, quietly and deliberately, eased himself down onto the bed mat and lay with his hands folded across his chest, clad only in his underclothing with a blanket to cover him. She saw him undress from the corner of her eye, but she did not notice the longing gaze he fixed upon her as she cleared away the remnants of food and covered the cooking pot and swept the crumbs and droppings outside. Then she quenched the wick of the lone lamp, stripped to her undergarments as well, and slid onto the mat beside him. She did not look at him; she was much too nervous for that. But in her mind she could still see the terror in his eyes, his stricken demeanor when she returned. More than that, lying beside him she began to sense his desire. Beneath his fear was a yearning for her so deep that it took her breath away. She longed for him, too, and had since his first kindnesses on their first night. She yearned to touch him, his face, his lips, to lay his head upon her breast, to caress him and hold him close.

They lay together, side by side, half-clad, their hearts beating more wildly than they thought they could. She was able to hold back no longer. She touched Man and held her breath. He did not stiffen. She touched him again. He did not recoil. She kissed him, no more than a peck, and she heard him sigh. Then she turned his face to hers and kissed him hard. He kissed her back. The river breeze blew through the cracks in the coarse walls. It carried honeysuckle and the clean smell of evergreen. She felt tears on his cheeks, his chest beginning to heave, but she did not stop and he did not either. The breeze was blowing, a gentle wind, and she heard the cloth at the door rustle softly. Then she felt his arms around her and great waves of passion seemed to wash over her. She smelled honeysuckle and the clean smell of pines and the river and the strong scent of his hair and his skin. He raised himself atop her and kissed her hard. She yielded to him and they loved for all the life that was in them, all the love, all the mountains of feeling, the rivers of want and the oceans of need, for all of heaven they had not known and all of hell they had. The wind blew cool across their damp bodies and they gave themselves one to the other with such desperate passion that time and space ceased. They were one now, panting and laughing and crying for all the seasons of their pain and loneliness and unrequited need. In their one flesh they were no longer a broken man and a fearful woman; they were lovers now as lovers should be, loving as if their lives depended upon it, and their spirits and souls, too: fiercely, freely, transcending even the one perfect self they had become.

Afterward each slept with a restfulness they had not known since the happiest seasons of their long-ago lives. Ma Tee appeared in her sleep. The old woman was smiling and gesturing and speaking with graceful animation, but still only one word was discernible: ". . . always." In the dream, again and again Ma Tee spoke to her with loving urgency, but she could hear only one word: ". . . always."

When she awoke it was not only Ma Tee's visitation that warmed her; she was still filled with the passion that her night had awakened. Yet when she reached for Man she found that he was gone. This was a new development because it was usually left to her to awaken him from the aftermath of yet another night of stupor. It did not trouble her, however, because after their night of requited love she felt that everything between them was new.

He's acting more responsible now, she thought, ascribing this development to the fresh step in their union, as she donned her tunic and went smiling to the well with the water jug upon her head.

Throughout the day she labored beside Oholibamah with a presence so dreamy that at first her sister thought she was ill. Through the hours of their toil she sang and smiled to herself, and moaned softly and happily when she thought of her fevered night. She heard little of what Oholibamah said to her and answered her sister's questions as to the change in her with only a smile. When perspiration beaded her brow, she thought of Man's sweat mingling with her own. When the afternoon breeze brushed her face, she thought of his breath against her cheek. When she straightened up from bending to the earth, she thought of the way her back arched at the height of her rapture. She continually smiled and sometimes laughed aloud as she moved forth in her work with a mind that clearly was elsewhere.

Even Sonny Boy, who always did his best to ignore her, saw the change in her demeanor. "What she grinning so much about?" he asked Oholibamah, who shrugged and said nothing, though she was sure she knew.

The end of the working day could not come quickly enough for the blithesome woman. By the time the sun had descended halfway to the horizon, she could wait no more. "I'm going home," she chirped.

"You go ahead. This field will still be here tomorrow," said Oholibamah. Then Oholibamah hugged her and whispered, "You seem so happy. I'm glad to see you happy."

She kissed Oholibamah and wiped the dust from her hands and shook it from her tunic. Hurrying along the path toward home, she waved energetic greetings to her bemused neighbors as she passed. The sky was clear and almost cloudless and birds glided overhead and chattered in the poplars and firs lining the path. She noticed a plume of smoke rising beyond the distant trees. It was feathery and light and at first raised no concern in her; it could be a reluctant stump set ablaze or the smoke-curing of newly slaughtered meat. The smoke grew suddenly thick and dark, then darker still. As she rounded the path she realized that the plume was rising from the direction of her shack. She gasped and, lifting her tunic, began to run, her heart pumping wildly. Several times she fell in her headlong rush and rose without noticing, flinging herself forward in terror-filled abandon. Now through the trees she could see leaping tongues of orange. At last she burst into the clearing to find her shack fully engulfed in flames.

"Man!" she called. He must be here, she thought. Surely by now he would have seen the flames and rushed back, unless . . .

"Man!" she screamed and rushed at the shack to reach him, but the searing heat and acrid smoke held her back.

By this time a handful of men had dropped their nets and scrambled downstream. "You alright?" they shouted above the roaring flames. Then, "Where's Man?"

"He's inside!" she cried.

The burning frame of the shack collapsed with a crash. There was no movement in evidence save the furiously dancing flames. The men squinted against the heat and gravely looked one to the other. One slowly turned to her. "If he's in there . . . ," he said, "I mean, if he's in there . . . he's gone."

"Oh God, please! No!" she shrieked. She tried to run into the leaping flames but the men caught her. She pulled away and fell to her knees. Then something caught her eye that in her blind terror she had missed. Laid neatly beneath a tree at the clearing's edge was Ma Tee's treasured box of trinkets atop the neatly folded tunic she had made for Man. Lying beside it was the little altar upon which his clay doll had slept. Her heart was suddenly seized by a new pain. Man was not dead. He had left her.

Chapter

20

She no longer spoke every day. Sometimes a word here and there to Oholibamah in the sweltering fields—and only in the fields because that is where she saw her and nowhere else—but to no other. Not to Mr. Ishmael, nor to his friend Phinehas, not even to the dispossessed women like herself whom the erwat dabar had relegated to the scorned encampment of tattered tents and tumbling lean-tos that was the sorry lot of rejected women, and to which she herself now so sadly returned each day.

Despite Oholibamah's strongest pleas, Sonny Boy was adamant that her sister could not live with them; his fear of his own desire would not let him welcome her into his home again. When Oholibamah asked Mr. Ishmael to shelter her sister, he replied, "Yes, of course my little friend-girl is welcome," just as Oholibamah knew he would, but her careful sister still feared that her presence would provoke a scandal, and at any rate she was too ashamed and dejected to face him.

Her unbroken misery from finding herself again in the settlement of castaways, this on the heels of the loss of her new love and the roof she had come to call her own, leached the lyric from her soul and the speech from her tongue. Her life was a solitary cocoon of cheerless days and wordless nights. She eschewed even the hint of joy, embracing her misery, unwilling to seek for something more for fear she might find less than she already had. So despite her every effort, Oholibamah could not hearten her. Her avoidance of Mr. Ishmael denied him the opportunity even to try. Abba Samuel demurred to come to her without invitation, her father had long since repudiated her as his kin, and her mother's fear ran too deep to reach beyond his judgments. So she lived her solitariness in a fog of fearful confusion, withdrawn inside herself with no idea of her place in the world and too broken and weary even to wonder of it.

It was not only the loss of the man she had finally come to love and her shivering lonely nights with the desperate, defeated women that drained her of spirit, but other tribulations as well. For as if awakening from a dream in brief but portentous intervals, unaware of where she was and wondering how she got there, clothed in her shattered confidence she found herself again thrown into the scalding cauldron of marriage simply because she was too numb to refuse; that is, since the departure of Man she'd endured the mistreatment of two spouses more. Despite the pain these new husbands each visited upon her in their turn, she experienced a small grace with each, that while they were well practiced in uncaring, both lacked polish in the actual arts of meanness. And because neither had even the smallest interest in her person beyond her cooking and the sensual pleasure they so conscientiously derived from her, the indignities she endured from them were not as bad as they might have been. In their absence they were little more than ciphers to her now, having shared so little of themselves that she had all but forgotten their names, had forgotten even the subtleties of smell, sound, and touch that usually mark the remembrance of things past. There was nothing notable for her about either man, and nothing memorable about them but their insults.

When she'd found herself wed to them, she'd hoped that each would give her rest, but their dismissal of her right to live unwearied denied her even that. So when each had tired of her poorly feigned passion and moved on to their third and fifth wives, respectively, and even before they had pronounced her unwelcome beneath the shelter of their roofs, she'd found herself groping through her hours enshrouded in a depression so deep she could imagine nothing else for her life but more of the same.

In her overwhelming despair, the memory of her days with Ma Tee were no longer vivid, and she could not recall the name of God. That is why Nahshon could so easily woo her. He was Her Fifth, the fifth man whose chattel she was.

Chapter

21

Nahshon had long admired her comeliness, but for him that was not lure enough. Not that he had ever esteemed women more deeply than their skins; indeed, their skins, particularly their coloring, were of great importance to him. But what was absolutely essential for Nahshon was that a woman be too needy, too diminished in spirit to withstand him. He had bled his last wife at every turn until there was nothing left of her but a grave. He was now in search of another. That is why he fastened upon the hung-head young woman who was so beaten down that she seemed oblivious to everything except the effort it took to place one foot before the other.

He had seen her throughout her years, in her sojourn from spunk to carefulness; through the gauntlet of marriage and dispossession, repudiation and erwat dabars, emerging from her trials as the solemn wraith that now shuffled past his field every dawn and every dusk. He had watched her progressively weaken through her struggles without a male relation to defend her. In these last months he had seen her clothing slowly tatter and her sandals come undone. He watched her head hang a bit more every day, watched her jaw go slack and her gaze dissolve into the distant look of defeat. Now that she was totally despondent, her hope murdered by despair, bereft of champions, bereft of everything except the clothes she wore, now she was ripe for his attentions.

. . .

Nahshon stood in the corner of his field that fronted where the path fell away over the little rise so she could not see him until she was upon him. He was hunched in pretended concentration over calf-high rows of bean plants when he heard her footsteps. He turned as if he was startled, then dramatically bowed at the waist and offered his widest smile. She showed no reaction at all.

"Uh, beg your pardon, ma'am. Shalom. If seeing me surprised you like seeing you surprised me, then you must be pretty surprised." He grinned.

She shrugged.

"But I guess I'm sort of glad that somebody . . . I mean, life gets so lonesome sometimes . . . I mean, don't things get lonesome sometimes?"

Her eyes were twin pools of disinterest. He wondered if she saw through his genial facade.

"I mean, uh, it sure is nice to talk to a kindhearted woman sometimes. Sure does make a man's life worth living."

He fumbled in the awkward silence and again stooped to feign study of his greening crop. When he looked up she was already on her way.

"It was nice talking to you, Miss Lady," he called to her. "I sure hope we might be talking again sometimes. I sure do hope so. Shalom."

For the next several afternoons he awaited her at the same spot at the same time. She met his attempts to converse with the same silence he'd endured at their first meeting. With each encounter, however, she acknowledged him a little bit more: first a flicker of recognition, then the slightest nod, to fleeting glances directed toward the sound of his words. These were just polite courtesies, however; although the small part remaining of her that still felt such things sensed his interest, she had no use for it. The attention of men had only caused her pain; there was no reason to expect anything different from him.

She'd seen Nahshon many times in the village, strutting, talking more loudly than he ought, no matter the occasion always clad in a tunic of finer cloth than anyone else's. She'd heard the things that were said of him. They did not paint a flattering picture. He was said to be greedy, mean-spirited, a terrible braggart, and an exploiter of his neighbors' misfortunes. It was the commonly held opinion that Nahshon cared nothing for his village compatriots except to insult and belittle them and flaunt his wealth before them; that he went to synagogue only for show and then slept soundly through Sabbath service from beginning to end. One report of him was particularly troubling, that although his last wife had slashed her own wrists, it was his abominable mistreatment that had driven her to it.

Because of the things she'd heard of Nahshon and the depleted state of her own emotions, she responded to him with the barest civilities. This surprised and chagrined him. He had expected her to be wary of his advances, but he was unprepared for the great distance she lodged between them.

After a week of daily attempts to elicit more than a few brief words from her, he decided to take another tack. Just before the time she usually passed on her return to the dismal encampment of the women, he placed at the spot of their daily meetings a large and resplendent bouquet of spring flowers. Then he hid in a spray of bramble bushes on the other side of the path just down from the rise. As she approached the place where he usually awaited, she steeled herself to endure yet another of his attempts to engage her. To her surprise he was not there. In his place was a splash of bright color. It took a few moments for her to realize that what she saw were flowers. She stooped to examine them and marveled at the red lilies, the crown daisies, the blooming chamomile neatly piled on the path, and it dawned on her that they might be for her. Then it further occurred to her that because they lay at exactly that spot at which Nahshon usually met her, they could only be from him. She looked about but Nahshon was crouched low and hidden. She felt a strange sensation in her cheeks and the corners of her mouth and she realized that she was smiling. Her realization of this made her smile all the more. How long had it been since she had felt joy? Then she caught herself and shut the door of her feeling, and her face became impassive again. She stood and started off down the path, leaving the flowers where they lay and with them the flickering of joy they had momentarily lighted. Nahshon watched as she disappeared up the path, her countenance stolid and unyielding again, but he was not disappointed. He had made her smile.

He purposely did not return for several days. When he did, he left for her a gathering of white lilies. Seeing no one, she stopped to touch the blossoms and admire them as she had the others. When she departed the flowers still lay where he had placed them, but this time she carried one stem with her. Several days later he left a bouquet of wild roses and saffron blossoms and at first she left those behind, too, but they were her favorites and she returned and gathered them in her arms. Her smile this time was more enduring. Nahshon took great pleasure to see her defenses crumbling, knowing that now she was in his reach.

The next day she was surprised to find Nahshon again waiting to greet her.

"Shalom," he said with a wide smile.

"Shalom," she said, friendly but hesitant.

She politely thanked him for the gifts and engaged in brief conversation. Nahshon did most of the talking, about himself, how much he missed the presence of a woman in his home, the things he cared to do for a wife. But what is more, in his effort to give the impression of sincere interest, he asked questions. This was new to her; she did not remember being asked about her feelings since she was a child, and then only by Ma Tee and Mr. Ishmael. That is why, although his questions were neither deep nor far-reaching, she could offer him no answers. Moreover, Nahshon did not betray impatience or berate her when she searched for words and found none, although she thought she saw veins begin to bulge in his forehead and his neck. On the whole he seemed pleasant enough, and the interest he expressed in her person was a new and pleasing development. She had not forgotten the distinctly unfavorable village estimation of him, however, and at any rate she was not ready to chance openness to anyone. So when there appeared a lull in the conversation, she offered a last nicety and politely took her leave.

Soon after resuming her journey she realized that her steps were suddenly lighter. She cautioned herself to stem the tide of her interest in the smiling, gift-laden man at the rise in the path.

Watching her disappear over the horizon, Nahshon was satisfied. He smiled to himself and thought of how he would approach her next.

For a brief span there were no gifts to greet her and no Nahshon. But several days later a muskmelon and two pomegranates lay for her on the path. A few days after that, she found a bag of almonds and ripe apricots tied with an indigo-colored woolen string. The effect of these gifts was a gradual burgeoning of her spirit and the unfolding and reanimation of emotions that had been in exile since the one called Man abandoned her. In her nights alone, she thought long about the meaning of the generosities and finally concluded that they were acts of kindness, not calculation. Other than Ma Tee on her deathbed, no one had ever given her gifts. Despite the distaste he'd first raised in her, and despite the objections she made to herself against him, she began to feel the stirrings of thankfulness for the change that his largesse was causing in her. She had begun to reclaim a measure of her own self-worth and was commencing to look to her days with a sense of cheerful anticipation. That is why when she encountered her calculating benefactor at the path after this latest round of gifts, she felt not aversion but genuine warmth and a large measure of gratitude. She was inclined to converse with him now. He greeted her with a smile. In his hand was a single wild rose. There was a soft breeze. It felt good on her face after her day of toil.

"Shalom. Begging your pardon, Miss Lady," he said with a face full of smiling. "I hope I ain't been too forward with my gift-giving and all."

She stood about ten paces from him. Her eyes did not meet his. "Shalom," she answered. "No . . . Thank you. It was kind of you."

"Well, to tell the truth, I been admiring you for a long time so . . . well, I know it's not the most proper thing to, uh, to talk to a unattached lady out here on the path all by her lonesome self. And Lord knows I wouldn't want to bring scandalizing on your name. But I knew that if I was to talk to you at synagogue or at market or such, folks' jealousy would eat 'em up and they couldn't wait till I walked away so they could bad-talk me."

"You think so?"

"I know it."

"Why do folks talk about you so badly? There must be something to it."

"No ma'am. I've done good for myself and folks is jealous, that's all. You can give and give, and the more you give the less folks appreciate it. You see the kind of man I am. I'm a giving man. But folks don't appreciate that. They're mad if you give and mad if you don't. A giving man can't win for losing." He offered his best imitation of hurt feelings and sad-faced resignation.

"See, I'm a gentleman. My mama raised up a gentleman. I'm just looking for a woman I can be good to is all." His face seemed to light up. "If you think that what folks say won't make you look at me cross-eyed, would it offend a woman like you if a gentleman like me took the time to speak to you in a more proper way tomorrow after synagogue meeting? That be if Abba Samuel isn't so long-winded that afterwards nobody wants to do nothing but go home and sleep."

"He can be long-winded sometimes." She was surprised to find that she was laughing.

"But it don't matter to me if he is. I'd call it a honor and a blessing, hallelujah, amen, to speak a sociable word to you anytime you say." He handed her the rose.

"That's right gentlemanly of you—"

"Nahshon. My name is Nahshon."

"Yes. I know your name."

"Probably from folks bad-talking me."

"Well . . ."

"You can't believe everything you hear. Sometimes you got to go with what you see. Have I been gentlemanly to you?"

"I suppose you have . . ."

"Then can I court you tomorrow?"

"Court me?"

"I got proper intentions. My mama raised a gentleman. Can I . . . tomorrow?" He smiled, clasping his hands in mock prayer. She noticed his gold rings.

She was taken by his courtliness, disarmed by his respectful manner, flattered that he, the richest man in the village, would show interest in her.

"Court me? You mean like . . ."

"Yes, ma'am."

"Well . . ." She smiled to herself. The right of choice, the power to decide for herself was new. She was surprised at how pleasing it felt. "I suppose synagogue would be proper," she said, trying to sound as if she was used to making decisions for her life.

"Yes, ma'am? That's great. I'll be considerable proud to court you."

She lay awake that night excited and confused. Nahshon had been so nice, so giving and generous. And he was such a gentleman, asking her permission, offering her a choice—almost like she was a man. In all her unions she had never been courted. They'd wooed her father, or come to her unwillingly, or simply offered her a place to live in return for her labor and conjugal comforts. She did not know what it was to have her permission asked. Nahshon seemed wonderful, yet she could not forget that folks had such bad things to say about him. She decided to bide her time and give him the benefit of the doubt. It was to be the worst mistake she had made yet.

Chapter

22

Nahshon was possessed of a beautiful coloring of deep berry brown, almost black, and features that so recalled the profiles of Nubians that he could almost have been one of them. Yet he thought his appearance was the biggest curse of his life. His mother's twisted and bitter view of the world inculcated this in him, for he wore the coloring and features of his father, who had invoked the erwat dabar upon her when Nahshon was yet in her womb, married another, then promptly died from a raging fever, leaving no inheritance for his son and no sustenance for the boy's mother.

For the rest of her life she railed long and hard against the father of her son. "That low-down black dog!" she wailed on days of particular hardship, in fact on all occasions when something went wrong. More than that, in her color-coded view of the world she evolved the strange notion that since the rich conquering Romans had pale skin, then pale must be the color of natural privilege and power and, therefore, was infinitely preferable to the darker complexions of her own people. By her tortured logic, brown and all its shades and permutations collectively comprised the color of defeat and the inalienable badge of the inferior.

These unfortunate notions were internalized by her son, who grew in his years hating himself and his people for what he held as the tragic color of their subjugation. This hatred showed itself in all that young

Nahshon did. He was pleasant to no one but his mother. He half-spoke to his elders, and if he could not think of a biting criticism or an insulting or hurtful thing to say to his peers, he said nothing to them at all. When the other youths challenged his affronts, he attempted to bluff and bully them. If they did not back down he retreated into timid silence, fearfully refusing to repeat the insult even when openly challenged to do so.

His fellow villagers grew to detest the ugliness of his deeds and the surliness of his demeanor, though Nahshon was convinced that what they scorned most was not his actions but his appearance. This could not have been farther from the truth. Nahshon was of a dark hue, the legacy of the northward migration of his people from Egypt and Ethiopia and points south even of there (for Samaria—and Judea and Galilee, too, for that matter—were only a few days' walk from the soil of Africa), but in this regard there was little difference between Nahshon and those he lived among. Unfortunately, this fact offered him no consolation. He became so insufferable and his hatreds lodged so deeply within him that he was routinely described as "that ugly Nahshon," for which he never forgave his fellow villagers. He felt isolated and ill favored among them; he saw everyone as his adversary and believed each one he passed silently pronounced him unlovely. In childhood his peers teased him unmercifully owing, again, to the ugliness they felt emanating from him rather than an outer unattractiveness; in their youth they simply were not equipped to articulate what they sensed, so they attributed the feelings he excited in them to what they could see. Nahshon's lips were no more prominent than theirs, but that did not matter; they called him liver-lips and fish-mouth nonetheless. And although the deep brown of his skin was only shades darker than most, and some of his peers were actually darker than he, still they called him *laylah-ish,* "night man," and in a mean turn of humor, *shemmish-or,* "sunshine."

After suffering for years the slights and rejections of his peers and neighbors, Nahshon came to the conclusion that the best defense he could mount against their torments was to reject them before they rejected him. He directed this sentiment toward everyone, regardless of gender or age. But toward women in particular he harbored a hatred that came from an even deeper place. It emanated from the inviolate space shared by a mother and a son.

Because of Nahshon's resemblance to his father, particularly with regard to the color she so reviled, his mother could never stand to look at him. Hers was an ambivalent love: she tried her best to love him as a son but found she could not love him as he was. She felt warmth for him in his absence, felt concern for him and worry, too, but she could express none of these things in his presence. She did not greet him with a morning kiss, or a nightly one, or with a hug at any time. When they spoke she would not look into his face because she knew it would cause the bile to rise in her throat. The times he ran to her for comfort from the teasing and the torment, she did not dispute the taunts that hurt him so, for these were the same thoughts she held herself. She could not bring herself to care about or even to acknowledge his tears, or to stroke his needful face so contorted with sadness and hurt. She could offer no other comfort than to say with sad resignation, "It's not your fault; can't everyone be good-looking," with her tight smile and her face turned away, unable even once to pronounce him beautiful, not even in her prayers. In his deepest self Nahshon knew that her's was a love he could not trust. And if he could not trust his mother, he could trust no one.

Nahshon's mother was fortunate to have a brother who allowed them to live in a hut on a rocky corner of his nahala. As a dispossessed wife who never received another invitation to marry, she owned no property of her own, so Nahshon worked the land of others. A stocky boy, from the first he worked harder than any of his peers to compensate for the inferiority he believed resided in his skin, for he was determined to distinguish himself by amassing possessions and wealth as conspicuous marks of his worth. This he did with a dedication that most of his neighbors exhibited only in their commitment to the welfare of their children and in their respective quests to see God. Nahshon was the first in the fields in the morning and the last to quit at dusk.

Working from can't-see in the morning until can't-see at night, and with no land rent to pay at home, he slowly began to accumulate a small stake of shekels and goods he took in barter. He was a shrewd trader and soon assumed the role of moneylender, first to his peers, then increasingly to his elders. The rates he charged were higher than was honorable or even moral, but his mother would not intervene, although the villagers pointedly asked her to; she just did not feel that the brownness of their skin warranted her special consideration. And Nahshon had convinced himself that he cared nothing for the disapprobation of his fellow villagers. Rather, he seemed to revel in their disdain, counting it as envy, as an unmistakable sign that he had the upper hand. When harvests were sparser than expected, Nahshon was there with his usurious rates. When his borrowers found themselves unable to repay him, Nahshon showed himself to be other than a man of mercy by summarily annexing their lands to his own. He took great pride in the desperation of their appeals and savored their postures of despair when he rejected them.

Nahshon's mother died before his first betrothal. In fact, she was the reason he had not married before then, although his peers had already begun families of their own: because no marriage-age young woman available to Nahshon had a complexion light enough to suit her. As she lay in the last grasp of death, he asked her, his palpitating heart full of hunger and need, "Mama, do you love me?"

"I just wisht," she said in a voice that revealed not a hint of emotion, as if she was simply relaying information to which they both had long been privy, ". . . I just wisht you didn't look so much like your daddy."

On the occasion of her death there was no one to mourn her or even to attend her burial except Abba Samuel, whose duty it was, Ritzpah and the other village aunties, who counted it their duty as well, and Nahshon's uncle, who, in truth, had been no more close to his sister and her son than the rest of the distant villagers.

Nahshon was inconsolable. He cried himself into nervous exhaustion and sank into a deep torpor. For twenty-seven days he ventured no farther than the yard of his nahala. He ate only what was at hand and whatever sustenance was brought to him by Ritzpah and the other old women, which they did not out of affection or even concern for him, but because that was the way things were done and they did not want to be seen as derelict in the duties that afforded them such satisfying self-righteousness.

Nahshon emerged from his doleful crucible of mourning faced with the crushing reality that even on her deathbed, the woman whose womb had borne him could not bear to look into his face. He became so stricken by this realization that he narrowly escaped the beckoning refuge of madness only by recasting her on the stage of his memory. She was no longer an ambivalent mother whose bitter love never came close to bridging her emotional distance from him and who made no effort to protect her son from the taunts of those who despised him. She became instead a presence that had been so loving and warm that in this new lexicon of remembrance she was akin to an angel to whom no other woman could compare. In a matter of days he had fully emancipated her from his stinging resentment and sense of betrayal at her grudging love and placed her firmly upon a pedestal that none could approach.

After several years of dedicated avarice, Nahshon accumulated significant property from the misfortunes of his brethren. He eventually extended his holdings into the largest nahala for many miles. He married several times to women he considered trophies, attractive but dim-witted women whose acceptance of him he thought put the lie to the notion that he was ugly. The wives collectively bore him eight children, of whom only four lived beyond their first day of life, all of them sons. But Nahshon did not take pride in his healthy brood; rather, they excited unbridled anger in him instead, for Nahshon blamed his wives for the unspeakable crime of bearing sons who looked too much like him.

The first wife he beat from his nahala with the erwat dabar and his fists. The second died after too many births too close together, the result of Nahshon's refusal to be denied his pleasure even when it was clear that her well-being was at stake. The spirit of the third wife he crushed so badly that finally she despaired to live even one more day. Looking with happy anticipation to the first peace she had known since she married Nahshon, she took a sharpened knife to the coursing veins in her wrists and watched her blood seep into the ground. Nahshon was left with his cowering sons who trailed behind him like beaten hounds, upon whom he unleashed terrible curses at the least provocation, and his never-ending quest for more spirits to conquer and goods to possess. That is what fueled his interest in the downtrodden object of his current pursuit: he saw in her an attractive possession with the mark of distinction in her skin that he so greatly prized.

Chapter

23

The next day Nahshon was already seated at synagogue when she arrived with an expectant air, in the company of several blank-eyed women from the encampment. This was the earliest Nahshon had ever been seen at Sabbath services; he always came late to demonstrate his disdain for his neighbors and to make the grand entrance he thought himself entitled to. But he made sure to be early this day in order to claim a seat in the front rank of the men so his every move would be conspicuous.

After the service the worshipers stood about, talking leisurely and softly laughing, enjoying the respite from toil that the Sabbath afforded them. Nahshon wound his way through the milling throng with great drama—"Excuse me. Oh, excuse me if you please"—and made a big show of presenting her the impressive gift of a decorative jar of expensive balsam oil. She was so enamored of his attention that she did not notice how exaggerated his courtliness was; she was oblivious to how much of his demeanor was bravado. He wore his most expensive linen tunic from Shechem with a silk sash loosely tied with a contrived insouciance. He conversed with great animation to draw everyone's attention to himself conversing with her. He was especially diligent to make obvious the interest she expressed to him in return by inclining his ear to her with a look of great concern for her every word. Both were afflicted with a selective blindness. He saw only her skin and what it meant for him, not her tattered tunic or the disdain with which men and some women, too, treated her as a denizen of the camp of the dispossessed. She saw only the reminders of his wealth and the excessive attention he lavished upon her, not the contemptuous looks his presence elicited from everyone he encountered. And both were oblivious to the way their neighbors shook their heads, sucked their teeth, and muttered "Lord help" as they passed.

In the succeeding weeks he openly courted her at synagogue and on market days, plying her with gifts at their every meeting: sugared figs, a fine woven shawl from Shechem, little baskets of foodstuffs to take with her to the camp. These attentions were not for her sake, however, but as always to showcase his wealth and to present himself as something other than the insecure man of avarice that everyone knew him to be. Also, he loved the thrill of the pursuit, the challenge of persuading her of his goodness and winning her hand. "One day soon I'm gonna take you out of that raggedy camp," he proclaimed loudly and often, to the knowing disdain of everyone near enough to hear. Their budding relationship was the foremost topic of village gossip, particularly of Izevel and the village auntie Ritzpah.

"Lord have mercy. Miss Ritzpah, can you believe those two together? That and a kindhearted Roman and I will have seen everything."

"Looks to me like they deserve each other."

"Yeah. One can't keep a husband, the other can't keep a wife."

Oholibamah saw the same spectacle as everyone else. But she had also seen the years of her sister's pain and deprivation. She did not approve of the source of her new happiness, but she was thrilled to see her treated with care. So Oholibamah said nothing. She did not speak when her elated sister chattered happily to her in the fields. She looked away from the nauseating display of Nahshon at synagogue posturing and preening and grinning at the object of his attention as if she were something good to eat. She bit her tongue when her sister showed Nahshon's latest gifts, and bit harder still when again and again each word of Nahshon's flatteries was repeated to her. Oholibamah withstood it all without flinching or letting her feelings be known for the simple reason that she eventually expected her sister to see Nahshon for the hateful man that he was. Everyone else did. But it had become increasingly clear that each week her sister was becoming more enamored of him and that now she eagerly awaited his proposal—a proposal that no one doubted she would accept without qualification. Oholibamah could keep silence no longer. She enlisted Sonny Boy to help her speak sense to her sister.

"I want to talk to you about Nahshon," Oholibamah said.

"What about him?"

"That man's a wolf in wolf's clothing."

"Oh, folks just say all those things about him cause they're jealous that he has so much."

"He has so much because he don't share," Sonny Boy said. "He takes people's land and even then he don't share what he got. Anybody else have a good harvest, a good year with their flocks, they throw a feast to share it. Not him. It's not honorable to let yourself have so much more than your neighbors who are working just as hard. It's like gloating or rubbing it in or making like you something special in the eyesight of God, like you got a right to a bigger branch of the tree of life than everybody else."

"Well, he says that he has so much because the Lord has smiled on him for trying to do right."

"Trying to do right? You might as well say he has stole from his own people. Lending to folks and charging them all kinds of interest when they're down and can't do no better—is that trying to do right? Uh-uh. It ain't scriptural and it ain't right."

"He said you would say that. He told me you'd be jealous. You Oholibamah, because I'm going to marry the richest man in the village. And you Sonny Boy, because he's done so much better than you. He told me just what you'd say, and lo and behold, he was right."

"J-jealous? Ain't nobody jealous of that plug ugly—"

"Did he tell you about his last wife?" Oholibamah interrupted.

"Yeah. Did he tell you about that?"

"That she died?"

"That she killed her own self."

"Yes. He told me."

"Did he tell you how he drove her to it?"

"He told me that's what folks think, cause at the end she was crazy and beside herself, telling folks he did all kinds of things he never did. He said her craziness had her talking all out of her head."

"Did he tell you she made up those knots and bruises on her face and arms, too?"

"He . . . he didn't tell me anything about that."

"I didn't think he would," Sonny Boy said with an air of smugness.

"But crazy people can do all kinds of things. She probably bruised herself up running 'round acting crazy. If she was crazy enough to kill herself she was crazy enough to run into something and hurt her head."

"Why are you so bent on marrying a man that nobody has any use for?" Oholibamah said, full of exasperation.

"They don't like him because they don't know him, is all. And they're jealous."

"Folks don't like him because he's so low-down," said Sonny Boy. "That's why they don't like him."

"Well, I like him. He's good to me. He's offering to give me nice things. All my life I never had anything. Got nothing now. Look at me, living out in that shameful camp. Four men have left me and what have I got to show for it? If you and Sonny Boy didn't let me work your fields, I don't even know how I'd eat. People accuse Nahshon of all kinds of things, but I haven't seen any sign of it. All I see is a gentleman who respects me and wants to give me nice things."

"Some gentleman."

"He is a gentleman. He's even going to pay a bride-price for me, but he's going to give it directly to me. A big bride-price, too. Who ever paid a bride-price for me?"

"And I just bet he'll be glad to hold your bride-price for safekeeping," said Sonny Boy.

"Maybe. He is good at handling things."

"Something about that doesn't sound right," said Oholibamah. "Isn't Daddy supposed to get any bride-price?"

"He says I haven't lived under Daddy's roof for so long that the bride-price rightfully should be mine, you know, in case something happened to him."

Sonny Boy threw up his hands. "Great God in heaven."

"You know Daddy disowned me after Jalon. I'm just glad that I'm finally going to have something of my own with a man who respects and cares for me."

"I'm telling you that man don't respect nothing but shekels and goods for barter," said Sonny Boy.

"I believe you're wrong."

"Cause that's what you want to believe."

"I'm going to marry him, Oholibamah."

"I was afraid you would say that. Well, don't expect me to come. I can't stand to see a lamb led to slaughter."

Chapter
24

Because of the perversity of Nahshon's spirit there was only one villager who even came close to calling him friend: Kenaz, who had endured Nahshon's boorishness since childhood. Any affection Kenaz might have held for Nahshon had been squelched long ago by Nahshon's ceaseless insults. What bonded these two now was the supply of wine that flowed from Nahshon's own winepress. Although Nahshon loved the fruit of the vine almost to excess he never cared to drink alone, for that reminded him of the social isolation he worked so hard to ignore. He was so glad to have a companion to drink with and bear his ramblings that he made it a point to unseal a new jug of wine whenever Kenaz visited, although with a requisite scowl to hide his pleasure, of course.

On one such visit, after a few jugs had passed between them, Kenaz's tongue was sufficiently loosened and his courage sufficiently bolstered for him to venture a challenge to Nahshon, who always took offense if he was given anything less than total acceptance of even his most outlandish claims.

"Why you want to marry that woman? If she's not damaged goods, she's sure used goods."

"I don't care about none of that stuff. What I care even if she had fifty men? That's a fine-looking woman, no matter how many men she's had. And she's light-skinned-ded, too. Always wanted me a light-skinned-ded woman. Going to give me sons look like Romans."

"You always talking about Romans. Romans ain't nothing but thieves and demons."

"Yeah? Then why they got all that power unless God gave it to them? Seems to me that they're the chosen people, not us. Got more power than anybody on earth. And smarter, too. I'd marry me a Roman woman in an eye blink if I could. Now tell me, why would any man want to be a Samaritan if he could be a Roman?"

"Well, I wouldn't. Don't want no pale Roman woman either. Romans don't know Jehovah God, hallelujah, amen."

"They don't have to. They're rich. That's why I'm going to marry that light-skinned-ded woman and have me some sons that look like Romans, so they can pass for Romans and get some of that Roman money."

"Why you keep talking about how light-skinned she is? She's not that light-skinned. Whole lot of women more light-skinned than her."

"But there's not a whole lot of women as helpless for a man as she is. She got nothing. Daddy even disowned her. That's a woman a man can do anything he wants with and won't nobody give him a problem— especially not her. Where she going to go? And she's light-skinned-ded, too? Man, that sounds like dying and going to heaven to me."

"Well, I ain't never going to have use for no Romans. And I don't care what you say, she's not all that light-skinned, neither."

"Well, she's more light-skinned-ded than me."

"Shoot, man, everybody's more light-skinned than you."

"See. Now you're signifying."

"No, I wasn't. I was just—"

"Just get your poor-mouth self off my land is all."

"But I—"

"But nothing. I'm rich. You're supposed to respect me. Get off my land and don't come back until you're ready to treat me like the rich man I am."

"Every time I disagree with you, you kick me off your place."

"And you always bring your poor self right back. Cause you like being around rich folks. Now get off my land."

"Alright, I'm going."

"Looka here. You coming to the wedding, ain't you?"

"Everybody'll be at this wedding. Wouldn't nobody miss this: you feeding somebody who's not your kin."

"Folks going to see something at this wedding. They're always talking about me. Now I'm going to give them something to talk about. Be the biggest wedding this village ever had. Bigger than my last one even."

"Well, don't forget that nobody got any use for a show-off."

"Not going to be no showing off. Just going to show folks how God has blessed me, that's all. And make them wish they had some of what I got."

Chapter
25

The festivities were held at Nahshon's nahala, as was customary. His was more elaborate in configuration than the homesteads of most, but in actuality it was no more luxurious. It contained a number of stone huts in a loose ring: two huts for his tenant workers, a separate one for his sons, and the hut Nahshon built for himself. Nahshon's dwelling was slightly larger than the others, but that was the only difference. He did not have an edifice like others of his means, with several rooms, some even boasting second stories. Nahshon preferred using his shekels to add to the preponderance of his lands—and to adorn himself in the finest jewelry and most luxurious garments—rather than on his personal living space. That was his peculiar conceit. But he spared no expense for the feast.

Feasts were important. A time to share the largesse of the Lord, to extend joyful hospitality to neighbors, they were also venues for carefree socializing and sharing the blessing of community. But Nahshon cared nothing for these things. The purpose of the wedding feast for him was to celebrate himself and the goods he had accumulated—and, of course, to excite the envy of his peers. And what a feast it was. There was more food and drink than anyone had ever seen, and more picturesque, too. Tables piled high with salads of mint, rue, green onion, coriander, green fleabane, carmint, coleroot, celery, lettuce, and thyme.

Artichokes and boiled mustard greens. Chard cooked with lentils and beans. Roast lamb with hot mint sauce and chicken with mustard and honey or roasted with onions and sumach. Dried apples mixed with toasted sesame and dried pears boiled in wine and drenched with honey. The tables were decorated with sprays of roses and pots of smoking incense, and huge stone jars were filled with the best wine in anyone's memory, into which a steady succession of cups and pitchers was dipped throughout the festivities. Nahshon strode about touting the cost of the wine, the cost of transporting it from Shechem, the cost of his bride's wedding attire imported from Caesarea, the number of lambs and chickens he'd had slaughtered and dressed, the measures of wheat and spices and vegetables and the number of days of preparation that had gone into the proceedings. And Oholibamah was in atten-dance after all—at the last minute Sonny Boy had persuaded her—but she shook her head constantly, wiping tears during the wedding cere-mony and during the feast, too, her misgivings so deeply etched into her face that she looked like she was in mourning.

The men grumbled at Nahshon's puffed-up airs and braggadocio, but that did not stop them from consuming as much food and drink as they could. They believed they deserved at least that much compensa-tion for having to endure his obnoxious character. Some had sought an even greater compensation: they instructed their wives to bring lengths of cloth in which they might carry home enough food for the next day's supper and maybe the day after that.

"A man who got this much food, he should share with his neighbors. Doesn't the scripture say 'love your neighbor as yourself'? Well, I'm Nahshon's neighbor and I'm going to let him love me with some of this here food I'm taking home with me."

"Sounds scriptural to me. Just wish I had a big old jug or at least a couple of wineskins to take some of this good wine. But the way those fellas from the river are drinking, there won't be enough left to sop a piece of bread with."

Nahshon strutted about the yard puffed up with his sneering pride, playing the role of potentate more than host, bragging openly to every ear about the coloration of his bride.

"See, I got me a light-skinned-ded wife. She's light. And she don't have no old flat nose, neither. She's going to give me some sons look like Romans."

He barked orders at his hired workers and his sons as if there was no difference between them. "Boy, go dip more of that wine for folks to drink." Never sure to which of them he had spoken, all Nahshon's sons fearfully jumped to do his bidding.

His happy bride sat with the women under a canopy of palm fronds accented with lilies, basking in the glow of the moment, drinking in the newness of the life set before her: the extensive lands with the dwelling that was now her home, the large quantities of foodstuffs and supplies stored in neat stone sheds, the presses that produced more olive oil and wine than in any village for miles. More than that, she had consumed the finest foods she'd ever tasted and was attired in the finest tunic she had ever seen, even finer than the finery of Big Mama.

The women stood and sat about her, engaged in light banter, the conversations they did not want their men to hear quietly spoken behind their hands. From time to time they erupted into constrained laughter. Despite the occasion, however, the women were not festive; there was a somberness about them, a carryover from the laments they had shared among themselves in the days leading to the wedding.

"Poor thing. She's got no idea what she's in for."

"She thought those other ones were bad, but now she's going to find out what bad is."

"You can call him bad if you want to, but I say he's the devil."

"No need to insult the devil."

"Well, the devil is a deceiver and that one sure has deceived her. Look at her smiling at him like he's normal. You can almost see his mind planning meanness."

"Why didn't somebody talk sense to her?"

"Oholibamah tried, but she wouldn't hear a word. If she wouldn't listen to her own sister, you know she wouldn't listen to any of us."

"What about her mama?"

"What's she going to say? Aridai disowned the girl, so that means she did, too. Anyway, these days she doesn't seem to know where she is hardly. She's gotten too pitiful for words."

. . .

When the sun dipped behind the verdant hills, the last of the wedding guests drifted away: those moving slowly because they had eaten more than usual, the hard drinkers doing their best until the very last moment not to leave a drop of wine undrunk, and those unfortunates who had imbibed themselves into stupors early and missed the festivities and food. As she watched them depart into the gloaming, she began to think of the night to come, and an old foreboding crept over her. Of all her previous such nights not one of them had been even vaguely satisfying. But, she thought, never before had she been given gifts. And never before had she been courted. These hopeful thoughts progressively raised her spirits until she began to look to this night as the welcome culmination of the pleasant courtship that had so lifted her days and warmed her shivering nights.

Chapter
26

The newlyweds lay not upon the customary bed mat, but upon a scrolled couch of fine brocaded pillows like the one she had thrashed upon in Shechem. The small room was lit by two double-wicked clay lamps that flickered from waist-high carved wooden stands. Ma Tee's bequeath to her shared a stand with one of the lamps. Nahshon had placed the box there for her.

"What's that?" he'd asked as she laid out her few belongings after the wedding guests had departed.

"The only thing I have left of Ma Tee," she'd answered.

"That's important," he said, smiling and nodding. "Let's put it where it won't get broke."

The quivering light of the lamps shadowed their movements on the coarse stone walls like large-winged birds. It caught the glisten of perspiration on her cheeks and her brow; her face seemed to glow beneath him. Nahshon rested upon one elbow, studying the prize that lay in his arms, wide-eyed, almost unable to believe she was there. He breathed in the smell of her hair, the perfume of her body. He marveled at the texture and tone of her skin, its color and tint, the meaning it held for him and that he imagined it held for others. His heart beat wildly from pride and desire.

Their first night was wonderful. It was so different to share her wedding night with a man who was happy to be with her. She shivered under Nahshon's hungry gaze and thrilled to the intensity of his desire. He could not take his eyes off her. In the lamplight he stared long, his eyes devouring every part of her. He gazed at her as she slipped from her wedding garment. Gazed into her face in the throes of lovemaking. He gazed at her as he lay at her side, kissed her lips and stroked her hair, and marveled that he who thought himself much less than beautiful should share his bed with such a vision as she. His new bride signified for him all that he hoped to have and all that he hoped to be.

Let's see who's ugly now, he thought, barely containing a sneer as he supposed that every man he knew envied him and longed to be him. *Let's see what they say when we have sons looking like Romans.*

She could not name the feeling that came from him, but it warmed her. He touched her softly, carefully, like a vessel of fine glass. His caress was gentle. His kiss was awkward but tender. Of all her men, only one had kissed her and then only for a night. But in the span between dusk and dawn Nahshon kissed her many times, her face, her neck, even her eyelids. He was glad to be with her. She thrilled to the feeling.

In their succeeding days he came to her again and again in the nights and anew in the mornings. "Good-looking as you are, we're sure going to have us some good-looking sons," he said with a wide smile as she lay in his arms. "I wish my mama coulda seen you."

For the first time she felt truly desired. And cherished. For the first time she did not dread the night and shrink from the dawn. For the first time, in those early weeks with Nahshon, she felt no drudgery in her days. For the first time she could imagine a future that did not break her heart. She was now a participant in life, not its prisoner. So with only the smallest tinge of disquiet she decided to put away her fennel and her clusters of moss. She was ready for the child that for four full unions she had feared to bear. "Nahshon wants sons," she said, "so I'll give him sons."

She had seen the midwife Huldah many times since the day she secretly sought her guidance, but her fear that Huldah's reputation for flouting social protocol and tradition would taint her as well had kept her from the old woman since their initial encounter, except for the occasional "Shalom" and neighborly wave of her hand. But now she sought out Huldah, and for a new reason: to seek her counsel for conceiving and bearing a healthy child—preferably a son.

She found the midwife in the little garden next to her hut tending her herbs and medicinal plants.

"Shalom, Miss Huldah," she said with a bright smile.

The old woman nodded. "Look who's here. What brings you around now? All you been through, I thought you would have found your way to my door before now."

"I-I—"

"I know. Ritzpah and the others probably told you that you should stay away from Huldah the troublemaker. But I guess you got into enough trouble on your own, didn't you?"

Huldah's words stung. "I've had some hard times, but I believe they're over now. I finally married a man who treats me right."

"Oh? I thought you married Nahshon."

"I did. And I don't care what anybody says. He treats me right."

"Well, suit yourself. So to what do I owe the honor of this visit?"

"You told me to use the fennel and the clusters of moss and they worked. Four husbands and I've never gotten pregnant. But things are different now. Now I'm ready to have children."

"So what do you want from me?"

"Miss Huldah, what can I do to make sure I give Nahshon a child—a son? Cause that's what he wants, a son."

"They all want sons, but only God can decide if it's a boy or a girl. All I can do is help you make sure that your husband's seed falls on fertile ground."

The old woman went into the hut and emerged with a cylindrical clay amulet on a cord of braided wool. "It's for fertility. So you can be fruitful. See that writing on it? It's from the scriptures. It says 'Be fruitful and multiply.' Wear it around your neck when you pray. And especially when you're with your husband in that way. And make sure you think godly thoughts." Then the old woman handed her a forked root the length of her hand. "Mandrake root," she said. "Every day cut a little piece and make a tea from it."

She thanked Huldah and hung the amulet around her neck. The mandrake root was firmly in hand. "Nahshon keeps all the shekels, but I'll bring you a measure of wheat tomorrow."

"Just have you a healthy child and that'll be thanks enough."

As she turned to leave, Huldah caught her arm.

"Remember this," the old woman said, "and don't ever forget: if you're woman enough to have a child, then you're too grown to be treated like one, hallelujah, amen."

As often as he could Nahshon strutted with his prize through the village. After synagogue he called her aloud for no apparent reason—"You are one pretty woman"—and other times loudly pointed her out to the other men.

"Something, ain't she? Light-skinned-ded, nose kind of straight, fills out her tunic real good. She's something, ain't she? And wait till you see our sons. Going to look like Romans."

Nahshon spent every moment of their days looking forward to their nights. But he did not always wait until night. Sometimes he led her to the hut and let their field work go so they could devote themselves instead to conceiving the first of the sons that would look like her. And in no uncertain terms he instructed the sons of his likeness to make no demands of his bride at any time so she would be free every moment for his every call and pleasure.

Then, as the weeks turned into months, the newness of her began to wear away, and with it his charm and his kindness. The gifts that had come at every turn abruptly ended. There were no more compliments or kind words or long looks of admiration. His hands no longer offered tenderness or touched her soft with romance. There were no kisses or caresses and he did not let his eyes meet hers. He still reached for her in the mornings, but roughly now and only to satisfy himself. In the day he was thankless for all that she did, barking his imperious orders to her, belittling her before the hired workers and his sons. In their nights she was invisible except to his lustful touch. Their once pleasurable couplings were no longer intimate; they were now abbreviated and without passion, with little hint on his part of any feeling that ran deeper than her skin. With their interactions now reduced to little more than routine and habit, she had finally become for him what in truth he had married her to be: a cleaner and a cook for himself and the cowering boys of his likeness, and a fertile womb to bear other sons that did not look like him.

When she realized that her new life was beginning to slip from her, she denied that there was anything seriously wrong. "It's only temporary," she assured herself. "He's worn out from work. Or tired by the neighbors' jealousy. Or just feeling unwell. It'll pass and we'll be happy again."

She took it upon herself to make things as right as they had been. Every day she renewed her efforts to please him. She tried to anticipate his wants as well as his needs, and offered herself to him with all the eager sweetness she could muster. Eventually it seemed that her every breath was breathed and her every movement made to please him. But every day he seemed more ill-tempered and spiteful, more disagreeable and malign, the loving companion he had been having left with the newness of their union.

Chapter

27

In the span of a few months Nahshon passed from infatuation to indifference to annoyance to something akin to hatred. He was beset by the paradox of exulting in her beauty and despising her for it. His old insecurity had finally bled through the novelty of her, and he was sure now that she thought him ugly, too.

Whereas before he'd banished his sons from making demands upon her, forcing them to fend for themselves—eating with the hired workers or consuming vegetables and dried dates from the nahala's storehouse as hunger got the best of them—now he pushed them upon her.

"You're my wife so they're your sons, too. So go cook and do for them. Whatever they need done, you do. Don't make me tell you again." This in addition to the field work he now required of her as if she, too, was a worker in his employ.

She found herself reeling from this sudden turn. No matter how hardworking and dutiful she was, his treatment seemed to grow worse daily. In addition to almost a full day in the fields, he required her to prepare his sons' meals in the separate hut to which he'd exiled them. And then there was his every call and need to be served: cooking, caring for the fine clothing he flaunted at every opportunity, and the unnecessary chores he ordered her to perform for no reason at all. And of course there was his nightly pleasure. But no matter what she did, there was no word too harsh for him to utter to her and no mood too unpleasant for him to subject her to. After a particularly painful confrontation, the cause of which she had no idea but which left her humiliated and hurt nonetheless, she tearfully asked, "Why are you treating me this way?"

"What way?" he huffed.

"You used to treat me differently. Flowers, gifts . . . and you were kind. You were kind to me. Why are you treating me like this now?"

"I'm just treating you like a woman, is all. What makes you think you're so special? Because you're light-skinned-ded? Well, you're not special. You're a woman, and ain't no woman special. The only thing special about you is that you're my wife. Keep running your mouth and you won't even be that."

It was then, possessed and puffed up by the power of his own words, that he began his quest to break her in earnest. From there the trajectory of his abuse rose steadily until he assaulted her senses with impunity. Browbeat her. Berated her in public. Wielded humiliation like a club at home, in the fields, in the marketplace, even at synagogue. But that was not the worst of it. What came next was what Ma Tee had so fervently prayed for her to escape.

One morning Nahshon awakened angry, cursing at the memory of some slight, real or imagined. She had already gone to the well and was readying his morning meal when he bellowed, "Hurry up, woman, and fix my breakfast."

He glared at her, spewing hot invective beneath his breath. His anger was palpable. It was clear that he was building to another abusive tirade. There was taut tension in the air; her hands trembled as she rushed to appease him. Then Nahshon yelled, "I said hurry up!" at the same moment that she lifted his bowl to place before him. Startled by his vehemence, she dropped the bowl, spilling its contents at his feet.

"You crazy?" he screamed. "Throwing my food on the floor."

"No. It was a mistake," she pleaded.

"No it wasn't. I saw you. You meant to do it."

"No, I—"

It came out of nowhere. His fisted hand crashed against her jaw. She fell to the floor, sprawled and dazed. The side of her face throbbed and there was the taste of blood in her mouth. He stood over her with a look of triumphant menace.

"Now get up and do it right this time. I don't raise these crops for you to waste them. Get up and fix my food. And stop that crying."

She went through that day fearful and stunned, wondering what she had done to cause this awful shift in Nahshon and how she might make him pleased with her again. She carefully tended her chores in the fields with the hired workers and the four boys with their eyes darting like birds until the sun neared the horizon, then hurried home to ensure that Nahshon's evening meal would be ready for him when he was ready for it. She was careful to act as if nothing had happened, as if he had not struck her with the force of an enemy. She betrayed no upset or hurt, but she flinched whenever he came near and kept him in view from the corner of her eye, stunned to feel suddenly so threatened in her marital home. In the days that followed, her bedazed quality receded, but her bewilderment did not, nor did her fear. She became extra careful in all that she said, all that she did, all that she thought.

In the next weeks Nahshon became more imperious and demanding. He isolated her from anyone who might remind her of her worth, even forbade her to interact with Oholibamah. But he did not strike her.

At harvesttime with its air of closure and accomplishment the cloud of meanness that had settled over Nahshon seemed to lift, and his treatment of her appeared to lose its mean-spirited edge. Still she did not rest in her efforts to be careful, nor was she comfortable or secure in her days or even in her nights, because she could feel his anger and meanness beneath the surface of his every word and deed.

The next time Nahshon struck her was after the harvest was in and put up. He and Kenaz had guzzled wine all day in celebration. Stumbling drunk, he led Kenaz out to the press where she had spent her day extracting oil from the bushels of olives the workers gathered from his groves. Her back was to him as they approached. Nahshon barked an imperious instruction to her. Immediately she stepped back from the pressing wheel to comply, but she never could have moved quickly enough, for Nahshon's real concern was to impress upon Kenaz the degree of control he exerted over her. Barely a moment had elapsed when he drunkenly hissed, "Do as I tell you, woman."

Grabbing her scarf and hair in one hand, he spun her around and slapped her several times, so hard her teeth jarred. In the midst of his blows she saw a faint smile curl his lips and a look like triumph cross his face, and she knew that he assaulted her not out of anger but for the feeling of power it gave him. For even though he prized her beauty, he was willing to destroy it if destruction would attest to his command over her. In his assertion of power he acted out all the aggression he feared to release upon his peers and that he was afraid even to imagine against the Romans, the very thought of whom excited in him an intimidating melange of fear and awe. In fact, he was the only man in the village who did not consciously harbor enmity toward the Romans. That is why beating her was so gratifying: when he struck her it made him feel like the conqueror he knew the Romans to be. But he also struck her for another reason that had just as much to do with her and just as little: because he wanted no one around him, especially in his own household, to feel good about themselves when he himself was so full of self-loathing. And then there was a final reason: he sought to punish her because he could not help but believe that she thought him ugly, too.

From then his abuse lurched and spiraled until it seemed that every day he beat her. He struck her if she talked too quietly. He struck her if she spoke up. He struck her if his food was too spicy or if what she prepared was something other than that for which he had a taste. At the smallest provocation he beat her. If she took an unpleasing step or breathed an unencumbered breath, he beat her. He seemed to seek reasons for displeasure; if one could not be found, he fabricated it. His abuse had no rhyme, no rhythm. The thing that set him off seemed to change from day to day, and sometimes the thing that sat well with him in the morning sent his fists flying in the afternoon.

The uncertainty and unpredictability of her existence kept her in a state of anxious tension. She developed a nervous twitch. She kept a headache and her hair began to fall out. Smiling again became foreign to her. The brief flowering of her happiness completely withered away. All she knew, all she could think, was to be careful, as careful as she could. And even that was not enough. So she sought desperately to understand his moods, closely listening to the tone of his voice, straining to discern the meaning beneath his movements, his gestures, even the angle at which he held his head and the frequency and manner in which he cleared his throat. She walked on tiptoe whenever he was near and made herself as invisible and unobtrusive as circumstances allowed.

So this is what it's like for Mama, she thought bitterly and fearfully as she picked at her supper opposite him, silent, her head bowed, and wondered what would become of her.

Little by little her face became decorated with the evidence of his abuse. She tried to hide her shame by feigning illness on synagogue days and appearing at market only when she absolutely had to. On the occasions when she could not avoid venturing in public, she wore her head covering drawn tightly forward to hide as much of her face as possible, but the swelling and discolorations were still evident to those who cared to look. When she encountered the women at the market (she avoided their place at the river by doing her wash in well water she hauled home herself), she bowed her head and hurried by, but she could not conceal her misery.

The women gathered at the river for the sole purpose of engaging in their weekly washing; at least that is what the men thought. In actuality that juncture of rocks, overhanging trees, and eddying waters was a space that was almost sacred in its meaning to the women; it was for them a temple comprised of the river, the rocks they squatted upon to wash the dirt from their bundles, and their own thirsting spirits and souls; a space consecrated by their tears and shared travails, in which the women communed, commiserated, advised, and affirmed one another. It was there they shared their concern for the battered bride of Nahshon.

"Lord. Have you seen her face? Poor thing."

"Been a long time since we've seen a black eye, thank the Lord."

"I'm sure her lip was busted."

"Seems like she was limping, too."

"That must be the meanest man God created."

"You know good and well that there's others just as mean."

"I know. Maybe his ugly just makes him seem meaner."

"He does have plenty of that."

"But I don't think he beat any of his other wives this early on."

"And not that bad, either."

"He must be getting worse, if that can be."

"Getting uglier, if you ask me."

"Just be thankful it's not one of us."

"Yes Lord, cause it could be one of us tomorrow."

"Cause you know it sure was some of us yesterday."

"Every day I curse the Romans and That Day with every curse I can name."

"And still nothing ever changes."

Kneeling on the river-smoothed stones, squatting in the lapping shallows, they sucked their teeth and shook their heads in silent lament. Then one started to hum, and they all joined in. With the rushing of the river and the birds and the gentle breeze and their humming, even the air seemed holy. One woman began to pray aloud, and the others did the same, each in her own voice.

Chapter
28

Their coupling was totally without feeling now except for his raging determination to sow the seed for the first of the many sons he hoped for. He climbed atop her with great roughness, without regard for her satisfaction or even her comfort, often drunk, grunting his hot breath in her ear, swearing and berating her.

"Woman, when's your belly going to start getting big? It better be soon. And it better be a son. Don't you bring me no girl."

Every night she fingered the amulet from Huldah, brewed tea from a bit of mandrake root, and prayed to be with child. She was convinced that her only chance for happiness, or at least a respite from Nahshon's mistreatment, was to bear him the son he hungered for. Then one day she realized that she had missed her monthly, but she knew that was no sure sign. A few mornings more and she awakened to soreness in her breasts, and she became hopeful. When soon thereafter she roused to retching nausea, she knew that she had finally conceived. It was her plan to wait until another monthly course had passed before telling him so she could be sure of it; the last thing she wanted was to excite Nahshon's anger with a false alarm. When she was certain, she would tell him with quiet pride over a meal of his favorite dishes. But in the end she was denied even that. She wound up blurting it out just a few days later when Nahshon raised his hand to strike her for yet another imagined infraction. "Don't," she cried. "I'm carrying your child."

At once the anger left him. He looked at her in shock. Then he let out a shout of triumph, called for the sons of his likeness, and immediately left for the village with them leading an oxcart carrying several large jars of wine from his vineyard to celebrate and brag and trumpet his news to the other men.

"I'm going to have me another son. That's right. And pretty as his mama is, the boy is bound to look just like a Roman."

The welcome news conjured a changed Nahshon. Suddenly he was kind again, courteous, as considerate as he had been mean. He no longer required her to work in the fields or to toil over the oil press or to perform her other strenuous chores. She spent her time weaving and cooking and looking after the lighter tasks. And no longer did he beat her. Instead he took pains daily to inquire of her comfort.

"How you feeling today?" he asked every morning. "And how's my son?"

Overnight he went from sullenness to garrulousness. He spent their time together excitedly speaking of his plans for his new son.

"We're going to name him Pontius, just like the governor. Or maybe Caesar. You can't get no more Roman than that. I'm going to take him to Caesarea every chance I get, maybe even to Sepphoris, too, so he can see how Romans live, how they act and dress and do things."

Since the advent of his displeasure Nahshon had refused to purchase clothing for her and even took from her and hid away the garments he had bought, despite himself wearing luxurious apparel daily. But now he sent for expensive tunics from Shechem to adorn her, fancy sandals for her feet, jewels for her hands, her wrists, even her hair. He paraded her in the full bloom of her pregnancy at synagogue and on market days, too, arrayed in her costly new garments, pointing out her new jewelry and bragging about its cost. There seemed to be no middle ground for Nahshon. Either he ground her underfoot or stood her high upon a pedestal. The truth of it was that he was unable to engage the full breadth of her humanity—her strengths, her flaws, her feelings, her needs—because that would accord her an intrinsic worth and a creditable existence apart from himself, which in his self-loathing and self-doubt he could conceive only as being complicit in his own denigration. But as his trophy she was something he had won and now owned. The gifts, the exaggerated courtliness, particularly in public, were all calculated to place his trophy wife upon display. This had finally become transparent to her. That is why his new civility troubled her so: because she knew it was conditional and transitory. Still she could not help but enjoy the welcome respite from his meanness.

As her belly grew, so did his excitement. At night he laid his head upon her stomach and caressed it as if it held the most important of all treasures. He spent his days with a constant eye for her comfort. But what should have been her happiest time of anticipation was instead laced with fear and uncertainty. She'd been able to confide her growing anxiety to no one since Nahshon had forbidden her interactions with those who might cause her to question him. As she ruminated on her dilemma Huldah came to mind. Yes, she could justify visiting with Huldah the midwife and healer, on whose skills even the men of the village grudgingly relied.

The two women sat in Huldah's hut drinking a tea of chicory and honey.

"It'll keep you from binding and bloating," the midwife said. They sat in silence until Huldah asked, "So what's bothering you? A blind man could see something's bothering you."

Her guest sighed. "I should have listened to you, Huldah. Nahshon is just as mean as they say."

"Yes. You should have. I didn't get this old being stupid, especially about menfolks. But regret is not going to change it. Anyway, that's old news now. There's something more bothering you."

"Well, I was just thinking, what if I have a girl? Nahshon takes for granted that I'm carrying his son. I guess he thinks he's too much man for me not to have a son. But he's made so much over this child being a boy, a boy who'll look exactly the way he wants him to . . . I mean, he's talked himself up and the other men down so much that he's bound to have a fit if this baby is not a son."

"No, I guess he wouldn't like it too much."

"And just how am I supposed to have a son who looks like a Roman? I don't want to displease Nahshon, but who wants a son looking like those hateful Romans?"

"Shouldn't nobody want that."

"And what if it's a girl?"

"What if it is a girl? Aren't girls God's creatures, too? It sure is hateful the way men act like a girl-child is some kind of curse, especially if she's the firstborn."

"But what can I do, Huldah? I can't talk to Nahshon about it. He'll have a fit if I even hint that it might be a girl."

"I guess he would. Well, answer me this: if it's a girl child, are you willing to fight to protect her?"

"Protect her?"

"Protect her. I've seen men get pretty mean when a woman's firstborn is a girl-child. Especially if they were fool enough to brag about having a boy before the baby was even born, like they're some kind of prophet or something. That's why if it's a girl you might have to protect her. And yourself, too. You willing to do that?"

"You mean fight Nahshon? I don't know if I could. . ."

"Then you better pray, cause a good prayer is stronger than a whole army; just ask old Pharaoh. But don't just pray. Make sure you pray to Hokmah, the woman-side of God, cause Hokmah hears women's prayers. Pray that Hokmah will protect your baby, boy or girl."

"Huldah, I know you mean well, but I don't know anything about Hokmah. And if this Hokmah is so much in the prayer-answering business, then why do men have all the power? I'll pray, but I don't think it'll be to Hokmah."

"That's just because you've never been taught. When you were just a little child the men stopped the Hokmah gatherings we women had at the river. There was a drought and the men said it was because praying to Hokmah insulted God. We tried to tell them that Hokmah is just a different aspect of the same God. But some of the women got beaten and all of them were scared. Some were so afraid that they turned against Hokmah. Your Ma Tee was one of them. Women don't talk much about Hokmah anymore, except for a few of us in secret. But Hokmah is real, a real part of God, a real part of God's compassion and power, hallelujah, amen."

"Huldah, I have enough problems without something new for Nahshon to be angry about. No. I'm going to pray to the same God that men pray to. Maybe that God can change Nahshon's heart."

That night when the hut was filled with Nahshon's snoring she arose, quietly and surreptitiously, and slipped outside. A profusion of stars lighted the blue-black sky like a sudden scattering of burning embers.

"Lord," she whispered, "you have never answered my prayers before. Still I've never, ever blasphemed or taken your name in vain. I'm just asking you to answer this one prayer and nothing more: please let me have a son. Just this once, please hear me. Even if he's not light-skinned, let it be a boy, dear God. Else I don't know what that man will do."

Her womb grew full with the life flowering within it. The mother-to-be examined the changes in herself daily and each time was amazed at the roundness of her belly, the tenderness of her breasts, the spreading of her hips, the new way she walked, the new straightness of her spine, the radiant glow that shone from her skin. Her spirit soared when the baby moved or she envisioned it in her arms. She could almost hear its laughter and its precious needful cries; she could almost feel its newborn softness and its hungering mouth at her breast. But whenever Nahshon rhapsodized about his coming son she was beset by despondency and fear. The more he bragged, the more frightened she became. She wanted to tell him to rein in his expectations; to tell him that all babies are beautiful, that girls can love their fathers in a way that even sons cannot. A daughter could make him proud too, she would tell him; important men would send their sons seeking him, seeking his approval to court his beautiful girl. She wanted most to remind him that only God knew what lived inside her womb, so he should wait until a son lay in her arms to announce him. Yet she knew that Nahshon was so taken with his own visions of grandeur that nothing could change his course now; too much of what passed as manhood for him was tied to the birth of a son.

Chapter

29

Nahshon was in his vineyard with the hired workers cutting back and pruning when his oldest boy rushed to him.

"She says it's time, sir."

"Time? Alright. Alright." Nahshon was breathless with excitement. "Go get old Huldah and tell her to be quick. I don't want nothing to happen to my boy. Now go."

Huldah arrived to find her pacing the hut with one hand on the small of her back, the other on her stomach. The midwife instructed the boy where to place the birthing stool and the thick woolen mat she'd brought rolled under her arm. Upon the mat she placed the herbs and teas and amulets and other implements she pulled from an old cotton bag decorated with green appliqués—the color of life. Huldah examined the expectant mother, brewed a tea from crushed colchicum seeds to calm her fears and help with the pain. She soothed her and comforted her and prayed with her. Then it was time.

The soon-to-be mother sat upon the birth stool pushing and straining. The contractions were coming more often now. Huldah kneeled behind her giving orders and encouragement.

"Alright. Bear down now. One more time. Push! Push!"

She grimaced and strained. Sweat ran down her face. The taste of the colchicum seeds was sharp in her mouth.

"There," Huldah said. "It's coming. It's coming!"

She pushed with all her strength. A cry escaped from her so full of pain and determination that she did not recognize her own voice. Huldah cried out, "You did it. You did it." The new mother heard the baby's cry. She laughed from joy and relief, then fainted away from the strain.

She awoke on the woolen birth mat with Huldah dribbling into her mouth a strong-smelling tea of coriander seeds. The midwife had placed a wet cloth on her forehead.

"What did I have?" she asked.

"You had a girl."

"Where is she?"

The midwife was silent.

"Where is she?"

"Nahshon took her."

She felt a stab of terror. "Took her where?"

"I'm sorry."

"Huldah?"

"I tried to stop him but he took her from me."

"Oh God. No!"

"I know. I know, dear child. I'm so sorry. But you're still young. The birthing went well. You can have more children."

"No! No!" She thrashed about, hysterical, inconsolable. "Please! No! My baby!"

Nahshon heard her screams at the far edge of the olive grove, but he did not stop digging.

When Nahshon returned, his limp wife lay in Huldah's lap in the fitful throes of a fitful half-sleep, exhausted by grief more than the strain of delivery.

"What's wrong with her?" he asked. "She sick?"

"She's sick of you. And so am I."

"Don't nobody care what you think, old woman. And mind your tongue. Remember, you don't have a man to protect you."

"I got God to protect me."

"What God cares about you?"

"God cares about right, and you're not right. None of you men playing God over women is right."

"How do you know what's right except a man tells you? If you think—"

The grief-stricken mother awoke sobbing.

"Why?" she screamed at Nahshon. "Why?"

"I told you not to bring me no girl-child, didn't I?" Nahshon raged.

"But how could I—"

"You wanted a girl. Just to make me look bad. I know you did."

She was shaking and sobbing. "But why?" she cried.

"Why? You knew that all this time I been telling all the men how I'm going to have me a son. And then you bring me a girl just to make me look bad."

"How could I make her anything but what the Lord created—"

"Aww, you women got a way to fix things up. I know that Huldah could've given you something. You just didn't want to have no boy, that's all. Just to make me look bad."

"But she was your daughter, too. How could you?"

"I don't want no girls and I'm not going to have none. Why you think only my boys lived?"

"No, Nahshon. You didn't—"

"I sure enough did. I told their mamas like I told you, not to bring no girl-child into my house. Anyway, what you making such a fuss about? It was only a girl."

From there her days were an unbroken continuum of grief for the child she had not held or suckled, the actual yield of her womb in all its unequaled majesty, quiescent dormancy, and unlimited reserve, conceived in her flesh, yes, but created alive and whole by her dreams and hopes, and her travails, too; the handful of jerking flesh and not yet hardened bone, soft and quivering in its absolute wonderment at a world that suddenly was not a womb; the tiny body fully formed yet not as fully as it would be, the microcosm of the future self and all the selves that would spring from it if allowed its full complement of days; so new and precious in that miraculous wholeness that she had not defecated, had not taken even as many breaths as she had fingers and toes; purposely ceased now and ended with unerring malice in flagrant repudiation of the God of Abraham and any other god ever thought to have given life and sustained it. And she, the mother, every evening cradling the small box of the legacies of her ancestor, mourned with her every tremulous breath the part of her taken forever, the best part of her, she thought, that part of her she loved when she loved no other, that she loved even without seeing or knowing if it was of Adam or of Eve. An implacable brokenness filled her, but emptied her, too, into an abyss of self-renunciation so roiling and so profound that she wanted nothing more at any moment than to cease to exist. She would have died by her own grieving hand, succinct, irreversible, and final, but she was so utterly vanquished by the act of he whose child it also was that she felt too worthless even for that.

She continued with the motions of living, but in truth she was no more than the husk of the life that once wore her skin. At first her unresponsiveness did not bother Nahshon; she did as she was told and did not protest when he had his way with her, not even when in callous abandon he came to her before she was fully healed. Nahshon had not brutalized her since he killed their child because she was so blank and unresponsive that there would have been little satisfaction in it. But he'd finally tired of her silence and her blank uncomprehending stare. More than that, now he saw the paucity of her response to him, her uncaring if he spoke or did not, if he touched her or did not, as a real and manifest denial of his power to control her movements, even her smallest moods, as real as if she had cursed him to his face.

"I'll fix her," he said. "She's going to respect me even if I have to kill her."

That night they had just sat down to supper when Nahshon asked with that heraldic air of menace, "It's about time for you to start getting big again, ain't it?"

Opposite him at the table she was vaguely aware of him talking, but it did not occur to her to answer. Nahshon heard her silence differently now; he heard not the quiescence of defeat but the declaimed and proclaimed language of impudence and overt challenge. He hesitated for a moment, then furiously leaned her way and slapped her hard. She did not respond or look at him. He slapped her again, still seated, harder this time, but still she did not look at him. In her listlessness and languor she did not care what Nahshon said or did or thought or felt; she did not even care what she herself felt.

"I'm tired of you walking round like you're dead," he said. "Won't eat, won't talk. It's like living with a dead woman. Look at me! Answer me!"

She said nothing. His rage ranged beyond his fists now. He looked for something with which to strike her and saw the box of Ma Tee's legacies. With a snort he jumped to his feet and grabbed it from its resting place on the lamp stand.

"You won't answer me? Well, let's see what you say when I burn up your little box of junk. Shouldn't have brought this junk in here no way."

Now she looked at him.

"I bet I got your attention now, don't I?"

She tried to speak but she could not. This enraged Nahshon all the more.

"Oh, so you're just going to try me, huh? Let's see what you say now."

He rushed outside to the oven lying low and mute and hot, and threw the box into the glowing coals. It flared into flame with a sudden flurry of gray smoke. She heard it crackle and smelled its sudden smoke, and she felt a sensation like something within her had burst into flame, too; like something had broken loose, given way, and suddenly she could think and feel and even taste the sorrow and the hurt, the soaring anger and searing grief that her all-enveloping numbness had kept in abeyance.

Enmity welled up in her like she'd never known. Her eyes were angry slits. Her nostrils flared and her chest heaved with rage. Nahshon reentered the hut with more taunts poised on his tongue, but the glare of hatred that confronted him stopped him in his tracks. He found himself shivering. His lips trembled. He instinctively took a backward step.

There was much less bluster to him now. "Go ahead . . . and . . . and . . . finish up this dinner," he stammered, hiding his sudden fear as he quietly backed out of the hut.

From then there was something different about her. Nahshon felt it. She did not flinch now when he gestured, or tense when he cleared his throat. She no longer jumped to obey; she moved at a pace that betrayed no urgency to please him. He watched her, perplexed and unsure of his power. He had not struck her since the day he burned Ma Tee's box of legacies; he'd convinced himself that it was simply that he had not cared to. But every day she seemed to fear him less. He felt the heat of her hatred now every time she was near. When he mounted her at night she no longer felt passive and afraid to his touch, just impatient for him to be done. He missed that passivity devoid of all rage and overt challenge, and its illusion of power that he wore with the necessity of a tunic and the baseless pride of a crown. In a real sense she actually was absent now, so far was she from caring what he said or did. Lying beneath him or working beside him, she seemed hardly to acknowledge him at all.

In truth, she had begun to feel again. She relived the beatings and the pain and the abject terror she'd endured in her own home, and did so not only when Nahshon was near—his presence raised in her a searing outrage more than hurt—but also at the oddest occasions: while combing her hair or feeding the goats or drawing water at the well. But it was lying still at night, caressing the breasts that had never suckled and laying hands upon the stomach that was no longer protuberant and full, that she thought of the child she had carried but never held, cast now into a hole that was not even a grave, alone and astonished at the quickness and brevity of its sojourn from womb to world to naked earth without ceremony or marker, and the aggrieved mother despised Nahshon all the more. Hearing his breath beside her when her child drew no breath, feeling him turn and move when her daughter lay cold and still, at times she was possessed of such hatred that it was all she could do to contain it.

Barnes & Noble Bookseller
5405 Touhy Ave
Skokie, IL 60077
(847) 329-0460
12-24-03 S02552 R007

GIFT
Living Water   RIGHT
0060000880

GIFT RECEIPT

Thank you for Shopping at
Barnes & Noble Booksellers
#90720 - 12-24-03 03:02P LORI

Full refund issued for new and unread books and unopened music within 30 days with a receipt from any Barnes & Noble store.

Store Credit issued for new and unread books and unopened music after 30 days or without a sales receipt. Credit issued at <u>lowest sale price</u>.

We gladly accept returns of new and unread books and unopened music from bn.com with a bn.com receipt for store credit at the bn.com price.

Full refund issued for new and unread books and unopened music within 30 days with a receipt from any Barnes & Noble store.

Store Credit issued for new and unread books and unopened music after 30 days or without a sales receipt. Credit issued at <u>lowest sale price</u>.

We gladly accept returns of new and unread books and unopened music from bn.com with a bn.com receipt for store credit at the bn.com price.

Full refund issued for new and unread books and unopened music within 30 days with a receipt from any Barnes & Noble store.

Store Credit issued for new and unread books and unopened music after 30 days or without a sales receipt. Credit issued at <u>lowest sale price</u>.

For all her seething, she felt something more than hatred and hurt. Since her death, Ma Tee had appeared in her granddaughter's dreams speaking words that she could never fully make out. But what was indistinct in her dreams suddenly became clear in her waking when she no longer cared if she ever pleased another soul in this world. It was then, as if wafting on the ether, that she heard the fullness of Ma Tee's message to her: ". . . always. Love yourself always."

"I will," she said. She felt something like iron forming within her, something of stone, not a stony hardness but a genuine unbreakability, a strength more ineffable and sure than anything she'd ever known.

Chapter
30

Nahshon thought long and hard about how to address the change in her. He could try to charm her until she was again disarmed and pliant—but that might seem like weakness, like he needed her to feel differently about him; more than anything, Nahshon did not want to seem weak. Besides, any affirmation, no matter how small, might strengthen her, make her feel good about herself, and that was not the way to bring anyone under control. "Or," he said, "I could beat her," but somehow a simple beating did not seem to be a large enough gesture to answer her long weeks of sullenness. No, a more dramatic action was needed to answer that. He settled on a plan that he knew would not only break her spirit anew but, he was certain, would also help him to recover the standing he'd lost, such as it was, after the embarrassment of a daughter when he had guaranteed a son.

The next Sabbath Nahshon insisted that he accompany her to market, after which they would attend synagogue services together. "Come on, now. A woman should worship with her husband. That's in the scriptures."

She had avoided the synagogue and the market, too, since the first of Nahshon's assaults left its mark upon her. She thought it strange that he would insist that she go with him now—he had never insisted before—but she looked forward to socializing with the village women, particularly the prospect of seeing Oholibamah, especially now that her cuts and bruises had faded.

"Come on," he said excitedly. "Let's get there early this time. So we can get the best goods, I mean."

"Alright, Nahshon," she said. She donned her yellow linen tunic, a gift from Nahshon in the early days of her pregnancy, then slipped a knife into a small pouch she hung from her sash.

Nahshon had become the instant object of ridicule when the men learned of the birth of his daughter. They so detested him and were so happy to see him humiliated that they made light of a situation in which, in truth, they really saw no humor.

"So where's that new boy of yours? Gone to Rome?"

In the weeks of the men's insults and his wife's insolence and detachment, Nahshon had begun to question his own swagger, begun to feel again the true measure of weakness and want and the absolute terror of rejection that he'd kept in such dubious and unsecret suspension. She noticed that Nahshon seemed edgy as they walked, but his spirits were high. She attributed his jauntiness to his new purple linen tunic, with its elaborate embroidery and rich pomegranate appliqué, which he wore with the exaggerated air of a king.

When they approached the marketplace his gait abruptly changed. He passed through the crowd with his sneer and his most arrogant strut. He could still see the derision in the men's eyes, the smirks that reappeared the moment they saw him, but that was about to change. He greeted everyone he encountered, even villagers he had never condescended to greet before, slowly waving his hand in acknowledgment so everyone might see the fine sweep of his garment.

He made his way to the center of the makeshift stalls and laden tables, careful to keep her close. He glanced about. The marketplace was full. A thin line of perspiration beaded his lip. All his nerves were tingling. He looked around again to be sure there was nothing that would compete with him for attention. This was the moment he had been waiting for. He stood to his fullest height and bellowed, "I'm tired of you walking around looking so sour-faced and all. Pull yourself together, woman, and do what I say!"

Izevel looked up with obvious delight.

"Beat her," she said with relish to the angry stares of the other women.

Because the ugliness of her personality eventually began to show in her face, Izevel was overlooked her first two years of marriageable age. Bitter because rather than being the most sought after maiden in her group she had almost ended up an old maid, she finally married Hushai, a well-known brutalizer of women who had invoked the erwat dabar on his previous wife after breaking her spirit so completely that she now maintained silence in the presence of men as fully as if she had been born mute. Rather than herself becoming yet another victim of Hushai's brutality, Izevel had so internalized the hateful definitions that ruled the lives of Hushai and those who thought like him that she became his partner and advocate in the meanness he fomented in the village at every opportunity. Because he was assured that her every public remark would be as hateful and divisive as his own, Hushai did not penalize Izevel for her outbursts. In fact, he so enjoyed her angry taunts and protestations that now he encouraged them.

"Beat her!" she said to the sneers and vigorous nods of Hushai. "Who does she think she is to disobey her man?"

"Move! Now!" said Nahshon.

The crowd hushed as if they shared one muted voice. She looked at Nahshon with surprise, but strangely felt no alarm. There had come, at last, a finality to her. All her life, all she'd known was to be careful and afraid. Now she was through with it. Even if it meant that she would die that very day, she told herself, she would be careful no longer.

"Nahshon, I don't care what you feel or don't feel. I just know that I'm tired. I have bowed my head to you for the last time."

"What did you say, woman?" he bellowed for all to hear. "I know you're not smart-mouthing me. Look at me when I'm talking to you." His tone was dangerous now.

She slid her hand into the pouch at her waist. "I'm through bowing to you. I have bowed enough." There was no fear in her voice.

Her defiance caught Nahshon off-guard. He had not foreseen this; in his self-delusion he had expected the old deference and fearfulness. The white-hot glare of the crowd was upon him, and he knew that the men would like nothing better than to see him publicly disgraced. To hide his feverish recalculating he stared fiercely at her, as if to pounce. It was clear to him that if he was not careful, his whole ploy could back-fire. What passed as honor for Nahshon was wholly at stake now. He could not deliberate long; hesitation would signal indecision—and indecision, weakness, even fear. So he did what he knew: he struck out at her with all the force he could muster.

The blow snapped her head back violently, spinning her, her arms flailing, blood and saliva flinging from her mouth. She staggered, but she refused to fall; she thought her skull would burst from the pain, but she did not cry out. She shook her head to clear it, and turned back to him with a face full of defiance, her hand inching for the knife. It was then that she saw his arrogance and anger turn to fear. She decided then that she would do more than protect herself; she would defeat this man who sought to crush her, to destroy her body and soul, and at the same time vanquish the specters of all the men besides who had so viciously assaulted her spirit. She removed her hand from the pouch, empty. *I'll show him just how weak he is.*

Nahshon saw defeat lumbering toward him. His strongest blows had not reduced her to less than she was. He had staggered her, but she had not fallen. Her mouth dripped with spit and blood, but she had not cried out. His eyes were wide with astonishment and real worry; the woman he had once beaten at will faced him now as his equal. The marketplace was silent of laughter and speech, even the sounds of barter and trade: the dickering and haggling, the creak of the women's overladen baskets, the scuffing of sandled feet and the animated rustle of garments. The still air was flush with expectation. In the quiet every eye was on Nahshon, but the silence of the men did not disguise their amusement. Nahshon knew that if he failed here in their very sight and hearing, nothing would ever count beyond this undoing; the men would vengefully laugh his name and tor-ment him the balance of his days. He was overcome by a cold panic. Before he knew it he had unleashed a desperate frenzy of blows.

The onslaught staggered her. Yet she did not fight back and she did not fall. Nahshon struck her each time she tried to stand aright, praying her knees would buckle. Still she did not fall and she did not cry out. He tore into her again, so viciously this time that he was certain she would drop. But when he had spent his blows, her knee had not touched the ground. Instead, she pulled herself to her fullest height and smiled through teeth red with her blood.

"I told you I'm through bowing to you," she said. "Look at you. Sweating and blowing, and I'm still standing. You're no kind of man at all."

His jaw dropped in shocked incredulity. He frantically cast about, his chest heaving, hoping that somehow the crowd had not heard, but from the buzzing and murmuring it was clear that her words had carried to them.

Nahshon shook with panic. He knew he had to act. He dared not strike her again because for all their force, his blows had accomplished nothing but his own humiliation. He decided to take another approach. He turned his back on her and forced a laugh, scornfully waving his hand.

"Haw. She's just acting crazy because I wouldn't keep that girl-child. I told her not to bring me no girl, and I mean what I say. She went ahead and gave me one anyway, so I got rid of the little squalling thing just like I said I would. Cause I'm a man who means what he says."

He turned and thrust his face at hers. "I did it to that one and if you have the nerve to bring me another girl, I'll put that one to rest, too. I—"

Before she realized it she had buried her knee in Nahshon's groin. He fell heavily at her feet, moaning and gasping for air, paralyzed and held fast by the pain. She was instantly upon him, whipping the knife from its pouch to his gasping throat in one quick, purposeful motion.

"You piece of dirt," she cried. "You rode me like a mule every day until I all but dropped, and I never asked you for anything, not even for the bride-price you never gave me. I did what you said and never caused you any trouble. But that wasn't enough for you. You had to break me, make me feel like nothing. And even that wasn't enough. You had to take the only thing I had, the only thing that would love me, and bury her like some trash. But you're the one who's going to be buried today. You say God doesn't hear a woman's prayers. Let's see if God hears yours."

She yanked his head to expose his throat and raised her arm. A cry rushed from him, hoarse and breathy with pain. "Wait! No! Please! I'm sorry! I'll treat you right, I swear before God I will! We'll have another girl. Please."

His cowardice shocked her. She was overcome with disgust. "Look at you." She spat the words. "You're nothing but a bully. All the time you tried to make me think I was nothing, you were just scared I would see how much of a nothing you are. Look at you. You're not even worth killing."

With undisguised revulsion she pushed Nahshon into the dirt whimpering and sobbing. Bubbles of snot swam on his upper lip. She stood slowly and defiantly. Wiping the blood from her face, she made her way through the throng that was speechless again. Her back was erect. She did not look back. Any man in the crowd might have punished her boldness by custom if not by law, but she was past caring. She had reclaimed herself. She was through with being careful. She was free.

She expected one of the other men to call her to answer for her actions, not to avenge Nahshon's honor but for fear that her boldness left unaddressed might set an empowering precedent for their own wives. But nothing. She walked at a deliberate pace; she was determined not to appear frightened or as if she had done something wrong.

Then she was clear of the marketplace and its astounded voices and its soaring air of astonishment and she felt a sudden lightness. Her steps were unhurried. She realized she was smiling.

T he marketplace was in a frenzy. The thrilled women smiled and quietly celebrated her courage among themselves, careful not to betray too much pleasure. The men were so tickled to see Nahshon humiliated that they neither noticed nor even cared about the women's delight. Bounding laughter and loud talk and feigned sympathies filled the air. The men hovered above Nahshon, laughing, sneering, taunting him without mercy as he lay in the dust locked in painful self-embrace.

"Lord. That's the most pitiful thing I've ever seen."

"Bet there's never been a man so rich who looked poor so quick."

"What good are all your shekels and your lands doing you now, Mr. Think-you're-better-than-everyone-else?"

"Great God in heaven, I'd rather die slow and stay dead than be shown up for a half a man by a woman."

The pain gradually loosed its grip on Nahshon. He rose slowly amid the ongoing laughter and derision, his face twisted with humiliation and rage. He looked to the guffawing men, the women tittering behind their hands, even Kenaz's head reared back in amusement, and he thought the laughter would choke the life from him. In anger and anguish he screamed, "I'm going to kill her! Make me look bad like this. I'm going to kill her!"

His distress only fueled their mockery. "Killing her won't do you any good now. She already showed you up for the little bit of man you are.

You can kill her if you want, but you'd probably do better killing yourself. Haw."

Nahshon knew that retribution could change nothing; no matter what he did, none of the men would ever again take him seriously. The wealth he had spent his life accumulating meant nothing now. There was nothing left for him to do but to salve his pain with vengeance.

"Woman disrespect me like that. I'm going to kill her. I'm going to kill her dead!"

"Be careful, Nahshon," they taunted. "She might beat you really bad this time."

He stumbled away, the laughter and ridicule roaring in his ears. Past the village outskirts he could still hear the chortling and snickering. Nahshon limped along, cursing and kicking dust and weeping more bitterly than he had since the death of his mother. With each step he was more angry. When he reached the yard of his nahala he paused, then turned toward a storehouse. He grabbed the largest knife it held, the one he used to slaughter livestock, and stormed across the yard.

When he burst into the hut she was seated on a mat in a dark corner. She did not move. He stood there heaving and blowing and crying with rage. Finally he raised his knife and started toward her. She stood quickly, her eyes blazing, the same knife she'd held to his throat readied in her hand. He saw the defiance in her face and her limbs, the squaring of her shoulders, the resolute tightness about her mouth, and he stopped short, almost losing his balance. They faced each other without motion, without words, the astounded humiliated man and his determined and unvanquished wife, poised with their knives and their hatred. Several times he tensed to rush at her, then he'd see her unblinking, unyielding unhesitance and he could not move. She was no longer afraid, and he knew it. But he was afraid, and he knew that, too. Each moment his fear grew. He wanted to kill her, to spill her blood, more than anything in the world, but found that he could not. It was not only his fear that stopped him; it was also the futility. He was already defeated. He knew it. Even if he slew her she still had won. He was beyond saving face now. And for all his anger, for all his need to restore his banished honor, the hatred in her eyes had raised an impregnable wall of fear.

She saw it, too. "You've been puffing yourself up all these years, putting everybody else down. But look at you now. You're a coward and a bully. Even with a knife in your hand, you're a coward. And everybody knows it."

Nahshon grimaced and raised his hand to strike once more. He was trembling, trying to will himself through her crippling resolve. When she did not flinch, her whole countenance seeming to blaze before him, he dropped his hand and stepped back. His shoulders sagged, his head bowed. He was finally, irretrievably defeated. Suddenly he raised the knife again, as if hearing a command and answering it. In flagrant and furious repudiation of everyone who had ever laughed at him or denied his beauty or refused to look into his face, he pulled the knife across his throat with a swift repudiative motion. A wound gaped deep and pink, spitting blood like a second mouth. He gasped softly and fell back against the wall of the hut. He slowly slid down to half-sit on the dirt floor, his tunic and sash bunched behind him. His blood spewed wildly, gushing in rhythmic bursts, splashing her garments and her sandled feet, but she did not move; she did not even look his way. This was his death and, like his life, she had no share in it. She did not try to help him and he did not try to help himself. He half-winced, and his blood flowed freely. When he finally raised his hand to staunch it, his tunic was awash in crimson.

"I shoulda . . ." He struggled to speak in his hoarse dying voice. He was sucking the air quickly and unevenly, and he sobbed. "I shoulda"—he coughed now—"loved you better."

The red cascade was beginning to slow. She heard his breathing become more labored, but still she did not look. She was not thinking of him; she was thinking of her own life, what it had been, what it might have been.

The rhythmic spurts had all but ceased. His head slumped forward. There was a rattle in his chest, then only the sound of her own breathing.

"You should have," she said, unaware that Nahshon's dying words were meant not for her but for the woman who could never bear to look at him.

She stooped through the entrance of the hut to the sun upon her face and the dumbfounded stares of the men who had assembled to see her dead, and the women who had come to bear away her corpse.

Part 2

MARYAM

Chapter
32

W hen she emerged drenched with blood, everyone was certain it flowed from grevious wounds that Nahshon had inflicted upon her. The men shook their heads sadly. "Oh, Lord. Look what Nahshon did to her." One woman swooned. But among them Izevel and her scowling husband showed no compassion. Hushai was incensed by her very public audacity. Izevel had never forgiven her for having married, in their turn, both the young man she sought for herself and then the richest man as well. She sniffed, "That's what she gets for being so gibora. I always said she wasn't no good," to Hushai's vigorous nods.

But when the bloodied woman's stride did not falter, when it was evident that there was no rending of her garment or slashing of her flesh, when no cries for help or deliverance issued from her mouth, it began to dawn on the onlookers that things had not gone as they'd supposed. Still, no one was prepared for what they found inside.

"Lord have mercy! The woman killed Nahshon dead. Cut the man's throat and left him to bleed. Cut his throat!"

She had come out of the hut and into their midst as if in a dream, as if stepping into an improvised ritual of slowed motion and unintelligible sounds. A world unfolded before her that she had not seen since she became careful and her colors began to dull. Everything appeared more vivid, moving in a pulsating whirl of hue and light. The fading rays of dusk were upon her face, its reds and oranges and muted purples laid in swaths across the blue reticent sky. She squinted against the light and gasped at the sudden new beauty. As though for the first time she saw greening fields of new barley and millet and emmer, the undulating golden fields of wheat, the leafy beckoning poplars, the brilliant yellow of daisies, the shaded reds of poppies and mountain tulips, the green spread-armed olive trees silently communing in their groves. There were new smells, too: the acrid musty smell of chickens, goats, and cows, but also the honeysuckled air, the sweetish smell of the residue of grapes, the tart scent of the olive press, the clean, fresh scent of the afternoon breeze off the river. Birds sang and the secret rustling of the trees. She experienced all the newness and majestic subtlety as if waking from a long and colorless sleep.

The exclaiming, gesticulating men with their storm-filled expressions and their voices raised in furious cacophony seemed incongruous in her new world of color and light. Her head ached, her lip was swollen, and her left eye was closing. Her tunic was stiffening with Nahshon's blood. Yet, these seemed to her like distant sensations. She felt that she was floating above and away from everything accosting her, drifting past the clenched fists and snarling mouths, heading to the cleansing river to wash herself of blood and every screaming memory. Then someone knocked the knife from her hand and the vengeful din jolted her back to earth.

"Where you going, woman? You think you can kill a man in his own home and walk away like nothing happened? You're not going nowhere. This man's blood has to be redeemed."

Redeeming the Blood was the age-old ritual of retribution that was the traditional right of the family of a victim of fatal foul play. It was accomplished by inflicting death in return or by accepting a blood ransom, a payment made in lieu of the spilling of actual blood. Either act redeemed the honor of the victim's kin. The closest male relative was called owner of the blood; it was his slaying of the killer or his acceptance of the ransom that restored honor to the victim's family. Redeeming the Blood was a crucial rite, for it was believed that without it, the victim's blood would "cry out" as Abel's did until the judgment of

Cain. But if the death was found either to be justified or accidental, thus unworthy of revenge, the blood could lie as it was, without vengeance or hard actions of acrimony to disturb it.

However, even before a determination of guilt was made, all the men called for retribution for Nahshon, for whom they apparently cared more in death than in life.

"Just look at him lying there with his throat cut. This man's blood has got to be redeemed!" they screamed, whipping themselves into a vindictive frenzy. All of them. Except one. His name was Yeshua.

Yeshua was a man of better than average height, broad shouldered, narrow waisted. He walked with a fluid straight-backed stride. His bearded face was full, his lips prominent, his dark eyes intense yet kindly. He exuded a calm but unmistakable strength and a peaceful self-possession that filled the air around him. His skin shone with a smooth brown sheen. His voice was deep and he spoke with gravity and deliberation. He did not laugh easily, but he wore often a beautiful serene smile that filled his entire face.

Yeshua was different from the other men. He was a newcomer to the village, but his difference ran deeper than that. His father, Yusef, who was once greatly admired and respected by all, had been forced from the village by the men's unyielding ostracism when Yeshua was still a suckling. Yusef had committed the unpardonable sin of taking public umbrage with a fellow villager's unkind treatment of the man's own wife. Because this occurred before the epidemic of meanness that was spawned by That Day, the men might have forgiven Yusef save for one thing: he had issued a *public* denunciation of a man in favor of a woman. For that transgression, which men had deemed unforgivable since the time of Abraham if not before, Yusef was so roundly shunned that he was effectively driven away. With great difficulty Yusef resettled his family in a small village to the west. There he kept his opinions to himself and struggled to provide for his loved ones—eventually Yeshua was joined by two female siblings—by working the land of others until he suffered a stroke in the fields and died before his fellow workers could get him home. Yeshua's widowed mother, Sherah, never remarried; she and her own mother alone reared Yeshua and his sisters. It was unusual for a young widow to remain unmarried for any significant period, particularly one as beautiful as Sherah, but she never met a man whose kindness and humility approached that of the husband she'd buried. Her own father had passed away long ago, so she was spared the compulsion of remarriage, which her father surely would have insisted upon. That did not mean that Sherah was a woman unprotected, however. The brothers she'd left behind in the old village thought her odd, and the eldest among them was piqued that she did not ask his permission to remain unmarried. But they did not insist that she conform to their wishes, nor did they interfere with her affairs other than to visit her new village soon after Yusef's death to make sure she had a parcel of land for her subsistence and to let the men there know that she was not without champions.

Yeshua, then, was reared by women, and grew to manhood leavened by the distinctive strength and character of women's humanity. Moreover, his reading of the scriptures was shaped in the safety of a home in which women spoke truths that did not seek the endorsement of men, and which rejected the codes of honor and shame that dominated the lives of men.

Much to the surprise of his fellow villagers, Yeshua expended no effort to marry when he reached the traditional age. Instead he concentrated on the care of his ailing mother and the shepherding of his sisters through their rites of betrothal and marriage. He worked diligently and assiduously and, with little help from his distant uncles, provided his sisters' dowries and kept the hut he shared with his mother well-stocked with food. His peers thought him strange, as they did his father before him, because of his devotion to his female kin and the unremitting self-sacrifice with which he served them. But choosing to remain unmarried was even more than strange to them—it was unnatural. So the men kept Yeshua at arm's length, though he was never the subject of their scorn, because like his father before him, they knew Yeshua to be honest and honorable.

Yeshua continued in this way, serving his kin and denying himself, until his mother died and his sisters were married. He realized then that he had no further reason to remain in the village, so he returned to the birthplace of his parents to work the land his father had left in the care of his uncles, all of whom had passed on without one son among them, thus leaving Yeshua as the sole heir of the family patrimony.

Because he was reared by parents who in their own way questioned and at times even challenged tradition and convention, Yeshua evolved a religiosity that was driven by spirit, not by the doctrines that were often the battlefield on which humanity fought and too often died serving obsessions that had nothing to do with God and, when not causing death, seemed more adept at causing division than engendering peace. In Yeshua's view of the world, God was not a stern and angry dispenser of judgment but a loving creator insistent upon justice as the highest form of love. It was the spirit of justice that engendered in Yeshua, though still a newcomer to this the village of his father, the courage to oppose the rising sentiment of a crowd of strangers possessed by the vengeance that had overtaken their hearts. And so he roused his voice to speak.

"Now, brethren, let's not rush to judgment on this woman. You saw what she went through," he said.

Hushai, the mean-hearted fomenter of the mistreatment of women, said, "What about what Nahshon went through? A blind man can see this woman killed him. She killed him and we're taking her to Abba Samuel to be judged so Nahshon's blood can be redeemed."

Hushai grabbed the woman's arm at the elbow. Sonny Boy felt Oholibamah tense. "Don't you say nothing," Sonny Boy whispered.

"But Sonny—"

"She made her bed, now she has to lay in it."

The embattled woman pulled from Hushai's grasp. "I'm not going anywhere with you. Why didn't you judge Nahshon when he beat me right in front of you? You didn't judge him and you're not judging me."

Hushai was livid. His hand was raised like a viper braced to strike. "Who do you think you're talking to, woman? I will—"

In an eye blink Yeshua stepped between them. "Now wait, brother. How do we know there's blood to be redeemed? Everyone saw how Nahshon was hell-bent to kill her. If she did kill him, she probably was trying to keep him from killing her. The scriptures don't give us the right to shed anyone's blood for protecting themselves."

Hushai's chest heaved with anger. "Get out of my way," he growled.

Yeshua did not move.

Hushai balled his fists. "You challenging me?"

The two men faced each other, their eyes locked in poised ferocity.

Izevel broke the tension. "All this talking and arguing isn't doing a thing. Something needs to be done about a woman that don't respect men. She never did respect men. Been gibora all her life. Went from man to man and now look what she's done."

"She ain't nothing but trouble," Ocran added with a hateful frown. "Did my boy Jalon so bad he ran off to Shechem and never come back. She just ain't no good at all."

Hushai glowered at Yeshua. "We don't need to wait for nothing. We're going to redeem this man's blood right now. We don't need no judging to know that the scripture says an eye for an eye."

The other men muttered their assent.

Hushai turned to the gathered women. "You women go on home," he said. "This is man's business now."

Oholibamah was in a frightful panic. "Do something, Sonny."

"Go on home," Sonny Boy said firmly. "You heard him. This is man's business."

"No, Sonny. Please. That's my sister."

Sonny Boy pulled Oholibamah away.

"But that's my sister," she cried.

"I'm sorry for her, too, 'Bamah. You know I am. But your sister killed a man, and there ain't nothing being sorry can do to change that. Now go on home and don't make no scene." He roughly pushed her into the cluster of women, who pulled her along, whispering their words of comfort and resignation.

"Now wait," said Huldah, who had watched with growing alarm. "What are you men going to do?" The eyes of the departing women asked the same.

Hushai yelled, "I told you women to leave. You better go on now, before you get into trouble of your own."

The women slowly walked toward the village, full of dread and silent prayer, all the while thinking with mixed relief that it was just as well not to be associated with such an incendiary situation. Huldah, however, did not leave. She placed her hands on her hips and thrust out her chin. "I said, what are you men getting ready to do? You can't do anything without a proper judging."

"I said to go home, old woman," Hushai snapped.

"Let her stay," said Yeshua forcefully.

"It's just old Huldah," said Ocran with a conciliatory air. "She can't do nothing."

"Alright. Alright," said Hushai impatiently. "But I'm through with all this talking. We need to redeem this blood right now."

"How you going to redeem it?" asked Kenaz.

Hushai gritted his teeth. "Stone her."

Everyone stopped still. There had not been a stoning in their village in anyone's memory. Pasach broke the stunned silence. "Well, that is scriptural," he said with his perpetual look of puzzlement.

"Fine with me," said Kenaz. "She killed my best friend."

Ocran rolled his eyes. "Friend? You ain't got to go that far."

"Alright. We was drinking buddies. But the man's blood still got to be redeemed, and stoning is the way to do it."

"Now wait," said Yeshua. "This isn't right. Let's take her to the rosh."

"We don't need to do nothing but redeem this man's blood," said Hushai.

The others grunted and nodded and began to look for stones. Yeshua pushed the woman behind him. "I'm not going to let you kill this woman like this," he said. There was no fear in his voice.

"How you going to stop us?" said Hushai with a vicious sneer. "If you don't get out of the way, you might get stoned, too."

Yeshua squared his shoulders. "Then that's what you're going to have to do. May the Lord be my deliverer."

The woman stepped away from Yeshua's shielding body. Her manner was intractable, her eyes ablaze, her swollen mouth tight with defiance.

"If they're going to kill me," she said to him, "let them kill me. But I'm through bowing."

Each man picked up a large stone, and they began to gather around her in a loose circle, though now their righteous indignation was beginning to cool and they were increasingly devoid of eagerness, almost reluctant to proceed. Everyone except Hushai, whose nostrils flared with avid anticipation.

"What kind of God do you worship that can only be satisfied with blood?" Yeshua said.

Hushai sniffed, "There you go with that soft religion, that love and tolerance and all. If it was up to folks like you, God would love sinners as much as us who's living right."

Then Hushai picked up a large rock and fixed his eyes on the encircled woman. She stared back at him brazenly. Yeshua shielded her body as much as she let him. Hushai drew back his arm. "An eye for an eye is what the scripture—"

A booming voice halted him. "Stop!" Mr. Ishmael pushed through the crowd with a cattle goad in his hand. "What do you think you men are doing?"

"Oh, Lord. Here comes that crazy Mr. Ishmael," Ocran moaned.

Hushai gestured for the old man to stand back. "This don't concern you, Mr. Ishmael."

"You're about to stone this young woman and this young man and it doesn't concern me?"

"She killed Nahshon and now we're giving her what the scriptures say to give her."

"Without a proper judging?"

"We judged her already," said Hushai.

"You can't do that. She has to be judged by a knesset council, or at least by the rosh."

"We don't need no knesset and we don't need Abba Samuel. She already judged herself when she killed Nahshon. Now she's going to get her punishment," Kenaz said.

"You know that if she did kill that mean Nahshon, surely he pushed her to it," Mr. Ishmael said as he moved toward her.

Hushai hefted the rock again. "I don't care what he did. A woman can't go around killing men just cause they beat her."

The old man's face was grim, his words harsh with certainty. He looked from face to face.

"Hear me. I will strike down any man who tries to touch her."

"How you going to stop all of us by yourself, Mr. Ishmael?" Hushai sneered.

A voice rang from the rear of the crowd. "Ain't by himself."

The men turned to see Mr. Pop in ancient but formidable battle array: an aged helmet, a breastplate of battered leather over a short, drab battle tunic. Hanging on one side of a drooping leather belt was a dagger in its scabbard; on the other hung a short-handled battle-ax. Two empty scabbards hung from the belt. Mr. Pop held a short sword in his left hand and a long sword in his right. Both gleamed as if recently sharpened. The men froze. They knew his fearsome reputation as a warrior and his celebrated prowess with the weapons of war. Old or not, he was still fearsome.

But Hushai was unmoved. "You think we're going to let two old men stop us from giving her the punishment she deserves? She killed Nahshon and his blood got to be redeemed."

"If she's done wrong, let Abba Samuel judge her. This is nothing but murder. And yes, Hushai, if you don't drop that stone right now I will strike you down." Mr. Ishmael moved toward him.

"You'd kill a man over a woman?" said Hushai.

"If I need to. You men don't want to tangle with us. You want Phinehas to wade into you? We're old, but we're still as strong as any man here. Phinehas," he called. Mr. Pop began to slowly circle the crowd.

The men looked from one old man to the other. No one moved. Without warning Mr. Ishmael thrust the cattle goad just short of Hushai's throat. "Tell them," Mr. Ishmael said. "Now."

A startled Hushai glared at Mr. Ishmael for a moment, then dropped the stone.

"Go on, you men," said Mr. Ishmael to the others. "Drop those stones." The others followed suit.

"Now. Move away from her. Good. Now step back. We're taking her to Abba Samuel." Mr. Ishmael and Yeshua flanked her.

"Not yet." Hushai pointed to a chubby adolescent with a wisp of a beard. "Here's Nahshon's oldest boy. He's the one that's the owner of the blood. If he says go to Abba Samuel, we'll go. If not, we're going to finish our business."

Like his three brothers, Nahshon's eldest son, whose name was Seorim, had never respected or felt any real affection for the man who was more despot than father to them. If the truth be told, Seorim and all his brothers secretly rejoiced that their lifelong tormentor was gone. They held no grudge against this woman. She had shown Seorim and his siblings nothing but kindness, at least as much as their father's tyranny had allowed. But this was Seorim's first act as the new head of the nahala his father left behind; now was no time to stand apart from the will of the men, acceptance into whose ranks he so roundly coveted. Relishing his position as the center of everyone's attention now, Seorim stated his opinion like an edict, in the same self-important, puffed-up tones of his father, his only model for his new role.

"My daddy is dead. As the new head of this nahala I have a duty to see his blood redeemed for the honor of my brothers and me."

Mr. Ishmael visibly stiffened, Yeshua's fists clinched, and Mr. Pop began his circling warrior's dance again. Seorim looked at Mr. Pop's gleaming weapons, Mr. Ishmael's powerful bulk, Yeshua's broad chest and shoulders, and he swallowed hard. "Maybe we should just go let Abba Samuel judge her."

Chapter
33

She walked briskly into the open yard of Abba Samuel's nahala with Mr. Ishmael and Yeshua flanking her and Huldah close behind. Mr. Pop brought up the rear. Both old men still had their weapons in hand. Huldah had wiped the blood from the beleaguered woman's face, though Nahshon's blood still stained her garment. The crowd of angry men followed, kicking dust and shouting at one another.

"Why we let them old men stop us?"

"Seorim's starting out a coward just like his daddy."

"Should've stoned her and got it over with."

Abba Samuel heard the approaching furor and emerged from his hut. "What's going on here? Ishmael. Phinehas. Why do you come here looking like you're preparing for war?"

"Samuel, these men were going to stone this young woman," said Mr. Ishmael.

"Stone her?" said Abba Samuel. "There'll be no stoning or any other punishment without a proper judging. Do you men hear?"

With great emotion, Hushai and several others related to Abba Samuel the horrific scene they'd encountered at Nahshon's hut. They cried mock tears and shook their heads as if the memory was too much to bear. Abba Samuel turned to the object of the men's ire.

"Daughter, we're not here to hurt you. We're trying to do justice. Nahshon is dead. The men say you killed him. What do you say?"

She rubbed her swollen jaw and spoke slowly and deliberately. The men fidgeted at her uncowed manner.

"With all due respect, Abba, I'm going to tell you my truth. Nahshon was a dirty dog and all of you know it. These men watched him beat me near to death, and not one of them raised a hand to help me. They knew when he left the marketplace that he had killing on his mind, but not one of them tried to stop him. And Abba, now you're talking about justice and asking me to answer your questions. But why should I? No man has ever given me justice, except Mr. Ishmael and Mr. Pop and this man here who spoke up for me today. Nahshon killed my child. Where's my justice for that? No. I'm not looking to any man for justice. You keep your justice. If you're going to kill me, go ahead, but I'm through asking men for justice."

The men shouted their indignation. "See, Abba? Does that sound innocent to you? We need to go ahead and redeem this man's blood."

Abba Samuel motioned for silence.

"Daughter, I know you're upset, but if you have something to tell me that's different from what these men say, I need to know so we can have justice here."

"With all due respect, Abba, you married me to five different men and you never called me anything but daughter and woman. How can I expect justice from you when you don't even know my name?"

The old man looked stricken. For long moments he was silent. When he spoke, it was with a tone chastened and contrite. "You're right. I . . . didn't realize . . . I mean . . . What is your name, daughter?"

"Why do you care now? I'm tired of being nothing but *girl* and *woman*. I had four husbands, and now this dead one, and not one of them ever called me by my name. My own daddy never called me nothing but girl. But I have a name, Abba. And none of you men here judging me even knows what it is."

"I'm truly sorry. It's just . . . things have always . . . I guess I never thought about it. But I promise you that I will call you by your name from this day forward."

She stood with shoulders squared, her chin held high. "My name . . . My name is Maryam."

"Maryam," Abba Samuel said.

"Yes, Abba. Maryam."

"Lord, Abba," said Hushai with that soaring voice of outrage. "Who cares what her name is? She's just a mouthy gibora woman who killed her husband. Let's just judge her and go give her what she got coming."

"Hush up, Hushai, and act with the manners your people taught you. Have you forgot that I do the judging around here?"

Abba Samuel turned back to the woman and his face softened. He seemed to be fighting back tears. "I beg your pardon, Miss Maryam," he said.

"Don't be begging her for nothing, Abba. She ain't nothing but a mouthy woman."

"I said hush up, Hushai," the old man snapped. "Miss Maryam, I would appreciate it if you would please tell me what happened in your hut. I need to know the truth."

Maryam struggled to hide her surprise at the gentleness of the old man's response; she was determined not to concede any part of her hard-won emotional ground.

"The truth is that Nahshon was nothing but a coward. You all know that. He wasn't worth killing. He came back to the hut looking to kill me and I wouldn't let him. Then he just killed himself."

The men exploded with one voice.

"Don't nobody kill hisself over a woman!"

"Killed the man, now she's lying on him. She ain't got no shame at all."

Again Abba Samuel motioned for silence. He looked at Maryam, clearly puzzled. "Killed himself, you say?"

"Killed himself."

"But look at all this blood on you. And they said you had a knife."

"When he cut himself his blood spilled on me, too. I had the knife to defend myself if he came at me. I didn't kill Nahshon. He killed himself."

Abba Samuel pondered for a moment, then he asked, "But why would he kill himself?"

Maryam was emphatic. "Nahshon was a coward, Abba. Maybe he couldn't stand that everyone saw what a coward he was. Other than that, I don't know why and I don't care."

Ocran shouted, "That's crazy, Abba. Wouldn't no man kill himself over a woman."

"Miss Maryam, it does sound strange. We never had a man to kill himself before. It just doesn't sound right."

"You asked me for the truth, Abba, and I told you."

Yeshua gestured to speak and the men stared daggers at him. "Abba Samuel," he said, "if the man killed himself, shouldn't we be able to tell if we look in the hut?"

Abba Samuel stroked his beard. "Maybe. Did anyone move his body yet? No? Then let's go see what we can see."

Abba Samuel entered the hut alone. He found Nahshon with the knife still in his hand, his drying blood on the floor and on the wall, even coagulating on a hanging string of onions. His lifeless body was slumped in bloody repudiation. Abba Samuel searched for anything to help him render judgment. He sought signs of struggle but found nothing overturned, nothing out of place. He examined Nahshon's body, the bloody knife in his grasp, and scrutinized the sprays of blood on the wall. When he had thoroughly perused the scene, Abba Samuel emerged with a solemn look.

"I can't see where there was any kind of struggle. If they had fought, something would've been turned over or knocked down. If they knife-fought, I can't see how she could have gotten near him without getting cut herself. And him sitting there with the knife still in his hand and all. . . . This is my ruling: there is no blood to be redeemed here. This man killed himself."

"The man killed himself," he repeated. "Miss Maryam is free of this man's blood. This is my ruling, hallelujah, amen."

The men looked to one another, stunned into a seething silence. Then there erupted baritone complaints and mumbled curses. Hushai was beside himself with outrage.

"Abba, how you going to let this woman get away with killing a man? If you let her go, then they're all going to think they can kill a man every time they get a beating."

"That's my ruling, Hushai. And if it bothers you, then stop the beatings."

"You don't need to be signifying, Abba," said Hushai, so angry that he spewed spittle as he spoke. "But alright. You're the rosh. You say won't be no stoning, there won't be no stoning—today, anyway."

Then Hushai turned to Maryam. "You ain't got away with nothing, woman. You hear me? This ain't over."

"It better be over," Mr. Ishmael said, staring into Hushai's hateful face.

Eventually the men dispersed in a cloud of churning vexation.

Yeshua watched them depart and breathed hard with relief. He stole a glance at Maryam, who was surrounded by Huldah and the two old men. Then he left for his nahala without a word.

Chapter
34

Huldah and the two aged warriors walked in silence, the tension and adrenaline that had gripped and spurred them slowly dissipating. When Nahshon's nahala and its roiling oppression were finally no longer in sight, Maryam was overcome by a rush of emotion. She threw her arms round Mr. Ishmael, then Mr. Pop.

"Thank you," she gushed. "I love you both. You saved my life. Did you see them, Miss Huldah?"

"Did I see them? Looked like they were ready to fight the battle of Jericho."

"Wasn't nothing," said Mr. Pop.

"But I guess we still have it, eh, Phinehas?"

"They were in trouble," said Mr. Pop.

They all shared a laugh.

"But don't forget that brave young man," said Mr. Ishmael. "He left in a hurry, but it sure looked like he was ready to die with you. Who is he?"

Maryam shrugged.

"He's a newcomer," answered Huldah. "They call him Yeshua."

"He sure stood up to Hushai and those men. If not for him, there's no telling what would have happened."

They walked together a bit farther, then the old men bid shalom and turned off the path. When the women were out of sight, Mr. Ishmael breathed deep the pine-scented air and smiled.

"Felt good, didn't it, Phinehas?"

"Sure did," said Mr. Pop.

"When we get home we'd better put these weapons away. You know, violence begets violence."

"Almost begot some today."

Maryam and Huldah walked along in silence. Maryam's mind began to wander over all that had occurred in the last hours and suddenly it dawned on her how close she had come to death. Her whole body began to tremble. Huldah pulled her close and a sob shook Maryam, then another and another until she was wracked with a spasm of weeping.

"Go on and cry," Huldah said. "You've been through something."

Maryam fell to her knees. She cried for each blow, each slight and insult, each moment of emptiness and doubt and loneliness and pain. She cried for her seasons of degradation and years of invisibility, the chattel years when it seemed her every breath was owned by another. Most of all she wept for the child whose face she never saw, whose fingers and toes she did not count, whose tears she never dried. Huldah kneeled with Maryam in the dusty path, caressing her face and her shaking shoulders.

"Go on, baby. Huldah's here."

When Maryam had cried herself out, when her chest no longer heaved and her tears no longer flowed, the shadows stretched a little longer across the path. She wiped her face with her blood-flecked head covering, then she stood.

"Where you going now?" Huldah asked, shaking the dust from her garment.

"I don't know, Miss Huldah. Back to that old camp, I guess. Rather be there than where I've been, though."

"Well, you're welcome to stay with me. Nobody there but me and the spirits. And stop calling me *miss*. All that formality makes me tired. Huldah will do."

"Alright. But are you sure you want someone as scandalous as me living with you?"

"All that'll mean is two scandalous women together. You don't want to go back to that camp, anyway."

"No, ma'am, I don't. Thank you."

"Good. Before we go home, let's stop by the river. There's someone I want you to meet."

At the women's place of meeting with its quiet and its holy, Huldah removed her tunic and motioned for Maryam to do the same. She led Maryam into the shallows, both clad only in their undergarments. With one hand holding Maryam's head, the other on the small of her back, Huldah lowered her into the embrace of the whispering river praying and quoting scripture with more emotion than Maryam had ever heard. The waters engulfed Maryam, dissolving her unsecret blood, and she felt the years of violations and the excruciating vestiges of a life lived on eggshells float away.

"What do you hear?" said Huldah.

"I hear wind and the water."

"Listen again. Do you hear music, soft music coming from the trees, from the river? Listen."

Maryam attuned her ear and there was distant music, fluid, etheric.

"I do," she said in a voice that seemed to come from somewhere outside her.

Then Huldah's words wafting through the pulsating shimmering air, soft, melodic, disembodied. "Do you hear the voice?"

And there it was, a deep booming voice, forceful, declamative. Then the voice metamorphosed and its timbre was the clean, high-toned brilliance of small bells. Then the joyful laughter of infants. Then the holy sound of an old woman humming. Its timbre rose again and now it was more like singing than speech, like the liquid music of the flute, soothing, calm, with an energy and vibration that seemed to match her own. Then it changed again. A voice, sourceless, ancient, not emanating from her but within her; ethereal, yet as real as her blood, a nurturing voice without recrimination or jealous sovereignty that possessed such beauty and suffused her soul with such contentment that Maryam found herself weeping.

"Do you remember?"

Yes. She was a small child at her mother's feet, before her mother's spirit was broken and hope was beaten from her, together at the river with the women cheerfully engaged in their washing, laughing without inhibition, venerating the feminine divine with deep and self-affirming joy.

"Who do you see?" said Huldah in that almost voice.

Maryam beheld her mother as she'd once been, animated and smiling, laughing and carefree, rising each day with joy and happy expectation.

She saw her father in his long-ago youth, a sensitive boy, then a sensitive man, mocked and teased to an impenetrable veneer of hardness and unyielding emotional reserve for the unforgivable transgression of exhibiting the gentle contours of a compassionate heart.

Then there was Ma Tee, young, buoyant, joyous on the eve of her wedding, an excited bird poised for flight, filled with jubilant hopes for blissful days and nights that never came.

Then Huldah's voice again, floating, evanescent. "Look deeper now. Do you see yourself? Look close."

Suddenly Maryam appeared to herself in colors. A blue light emanated from her heart in brilliant pulses and her face shone like gold in the sun. Her body was permeated with stars, glowing garments floated and hovered about her, and she twirled and danced and floated in laughter. She felt an inviolate indomitability, something within her like iron or even stone, not in their cold inscrutability, but in their strength and illimitable durability.

"I have taken it all," she said, "and I am still here. I am free."

She flowed with the river, its currents coursing her veins, cleansing her, washing her, as she bathed in the ecstasy of the divine within her. She lost track of time and space as she communed with the elegant spirits of ancestor women, drinking in the wisdom of their words lying whispering on the waters.

Then it was over. Maryam was sitting in the twilight shoulder to shoulder with Huldah on the bank of the talking river. They did not speak. They did not have to.

Chapter
35

Living with Huldah was a balm for Maryam. With the meeting of their spirits and their hearts, Huldah's gruff exterior fell away, and Maryam found that Huldah was the nurturer she needed. With Huldah she felt a freedom she had not known before. When Maryam was brusque and irritable, Huldah laughed her back to good humor. When Maryam provoked frowns by loudly laughing in public, Huldah laughed louder still. Where Ma Tee had taught pliancy, Huldah privileged strength. Huldah taught Maryam to forsake shadows and dwell in the light. Huldah taught her to walk only when it was her choice and to run just because she could. Huldah taught Maryam to give beauty her own name. Huldah taught her to love herself.

Huldah was a pillar of the river community of woman God-lovers that had flourished in Maryam's earliest years. A young wife with three young children, Huldah's life revolved around family and woman-talk of God. Praying together, reciting and celebrating together, the women looked into the face of God and saw themselves. Then came the pitiless contagion that brought death to some homes and spared others with bewildering caprice, leaving in its wake fresh graves and stupefied mourners. Fearing the women's ministrations had brought the disfavor of God upon them all, the men forcefully disbanded the worshiping community that the women had built of joy, a singing river, whispered visions of God, and the hope of wholeness. In the aftermath of the men's desperate repression, the name of Hokmah was exiled to secret prayers and fearful quiet.

For Huldah, the toll exacted by the cruel disease was more than the demise of her spiritual community; it also took her family. Her husband, loving and selfless to the last, died first, then their three children, one by one. Huldah never again married, refusing ever to revisit the terrain on which such pain could occur. Instead, she resolved to soothe the pain of others. She donned the mantle of midwife and from that vocation derived her joy.

The contagion also wrought another change in Huldah. In the agony of her despair she called on Hokmah and was delivered from her crippling grief by a divine dance of transcendence that turned her sorrow into joy. When the dance ended, Huldah was healed of her debilitating pain and determined to share the fruits of her wondrous experience with every woman whose heart could hear. Maryam fell heir to this vow. Huldah shared with Maryam her own inner realizations and regaled her with warming tales of the community of woman worshipers. She told glowingly of the joy and satisfaction that characterized their assemblies and recounted the glories they shared.

"Miss Puah—she's dead now—she came to the river after her mean old husband Hatil had beat her something fierce. All the women were crying with her and praying and calling on Hokmah by name. And I remember how it seemed like a misty cloud came down on us, and the breeze began to blow and everybody could swear they heard the wind calling Puah's name. The sun was shining, except it wasn't shining at all, but there was a shininess to everything. Then everybody seemed to glow and I heard wind whooshing past my ears like I was ascending, like going straight up to heaven. And I looked around and everybody's face was peaceful and upturned; Puah's, too. And she wasn't crying anymore; she was happy and glowing and her bruises were healed. Everything seemed light, like floating in this cloudy mist that was all around us, and the women's feet didn't even seem to be touching the ground. That was holiness.

"Those were some times, I tell you. If the men had just left well enough alone, we'd all have been better off. Loving the woman-side of

God wasn't hurting anybody. If Moses' wife Zipporah had gone up on Mount Sinai with him, she could have brought back the instructions to women that Moses didn't have the ears to hear. Then we wouldn't have to sneak around to worship in a way that affirms us. The men oppose women acknowledging the woman-side of God because they're afraid we won't worship in the way that keeps men in control. Always calling God *He* and acting like God thinks and feels just like men, punishing and killing and slapping down everyone who doesn't think like them. If men just opened themselves to the compassionate womb of God instead of always talking about God's sternness and might, there would be a lot less pain in this world."

Maryam's resolute stand against Nahshon, her victory in the face of imminent death, and the subsequent cheerful change they witnessed in her demeanor invigorated the women. The once cowed and careful soul they had watched ground almost to dust now lived life on her own terms more fully each day, each day less encumbered by the judgments of men. The women gloried in her growing confidence and clarity, and vicariously experienced the soaring freedom of her spirit.

It was not so with the men, of course. For some weeks after Nahshon's demise, in their secret circles they rejoiced that she'd rid them of the rich braggart who had humiliated and dispossessed so many of them. Despite their private admiration, however, no man dared to speak well of Maryam, and certainly not to desire her; her association with public defiance and the blood of a man far outstripped any attraction she might possess.

After the novelty of her deed receded into memory, some of the men settled into a mundane equilibrium: they simply ignored her as unworthy of further notice. Others coalesced into a venomous faction led by Hushai that harbored an undiminished rage toward Maryam for having escaped the punishment they believed she richly deserved. None of these attitudes constricted Maryam's movements, however, because of her association with Huldah. Having birthed their children and their grandchildren, too, without the least hint of indiscretion, Huldah was regarded by the men as possessed of a proven sense of propriety in spite of her eccentricity. This allayed the men's fears of Maryam's defiant spirit poisoning their homes as long as Huldah was her mentor. For that reason Maryam was able to move through the village unencumbered by the enforced social exile that would otherwise be expected for one with Maryam's transgressions to her credit.

Chapter
36

In her unrestrained movement through the village, Maryam sometimes encountered Yeshua in the marketplace or as she hurried
with Huldah on her midwifery rounds. In the days following his cham-
pioning of her, Maryam had thanked Yeshua effusively. Now when she
came upon him they exchanged pleasant greetings but little else
because for Maryam all had been spoken. Yet even as he walked away, a
part of Yeshua always seemed to linger. In his few words and in his
silences, too, there seemed to be much that was left unsaid. She thought
perhaps he felt she had not expressed sufficient appreciation for his
bravery, so she made sure to thank him again and especially, but that
was all. Yet little by little, their meetings lost the character of chance.
Yeshua found himself traversing the village, passing Huldah's hut often
for whatever pretended chore for no other reason than to search out
Maryam's face. Maryam neither noticed his interest nor expressed any
interest of her own.

In the weeks that followed, Yeshua began to find any pretext for
interaction with Maryam. In his awkwardness he engaged her on whatever topics came to mind: the vagaries of the weather, the rising height
of his wheat, the sprouting greenness of his lentil shoots. When she was
near and unaware of his gaze, his eyes stayed upon her, studying her,
straining to see into her, endeavoring to understand the very workings

of her mind and heart. When apart, he fastened upon her in his nightly meditations and tried to hear the song her spirit was singing. Sometimes it seemed he could decipher the very utterances of her heart. Other times she remained a mystery to him, as remote and inaccessible as a cloud. In the deep nights of his solitude he spoke to her as if she was there with him; he shared with her his aspirations, his hopes, his vision of the life they'd have together, the depth of the devotion he was prepared to offer her. When sleep overtook him he saw her in his dreams, smiling, laughing, dancing, her heart as open as any door.

As his affection for Maryam deepened, Yeshua's spirit began to leave him nightly to traverse the far regions of the world within her, seeking to enter the deepest parts of her, reaching for that part of her, that special thing, that spark or phrase that explained her. At those times Maryam could feel the yearning of his spirit. If she was awake, thoughts of Yeshua suddenly encamped in her mind as if she had at that very moment chanced upon him, as if she'd just heard his voice or someone speaking his name. If she was asleep, he took abrupt residence in her dreams, leaving a strange residue of perplexity and desire that lingered long after she awoke.

Maryam was chagrined and baffled by this startling pattern of emotions and thoughts that intruded upon her days and her nights; the last thing she wanted was a man on her mind. So to guard herself from even the slightest temptation to embark on what she was certain would be yet another marital debacle, she began to avoid Yeshua whenever she could and shied away from him when she could not, finding some task or matter to divert her attention whenever he drew near.

But Yeshua was not to be deterred. He communed more deeply with Maryam in his meditations, calling her name and envisioning the secrets of her heart spilling into his hand. In his dreams he was even bolder. Loosed as he was from the galling constraints of time and space, in his unfettered state he declared to her soul in the most poetic terms the growing affection that no part of him could any longer doubt or deny.

Yeshua's visits to Huldah's hut became more frequent, too, accompanied by gifts of sweets or flowers. He also began to venture to the women's clandestine gatherings at the river. In his initial visits the women viewed him with awkwardness and disquiet, but it was not long before they felt at ease enough that they no longer waited for him to depart before laying bare their hearts.

At first Yeshua sat among the women for no other reason than to drink in the presence of Maryam, but he found that the women's worship nourished him like nothing he had known. He prayed with them, commiserated with their anguish, celebrated their small triumphs, and raised his hearty baritone in solemn recitation, easy laughter, and enthusiastic song. What moved him most was that in the serenity and contentment of these moments he found himself reliving his times in the loving embrace of his own family. In his mind he saw his father delighting in his daughters with a shining pride men usually reserved for their sons, happily instructing them, against all tradition, in the recitation of scripture and ritual supplications. The image of his father's dignity and calm came to him on these occasions, and he could hear his father's weekly admonition that he must not only protect the women in his life but honor them, too, for Abraham was the father of many nations, but it was from the wombs of Sarah and Hagar that they sprang.

His most moving recollections were of the precious hours spent alone with his mother, Sherah, after his father had died and his sisters were married. How in sudden and hastening decline, prostrate upon her deathbed, as her body became less, her spirit became more. Though his mother's voice was reed-thin by then, neither the frequency nor the lilting ring of her laughter lessened. She had no fear of death, as is the way of those who have lived faithfully and well, yet as she grew too weak to walk, rather than accepting her hard-earned final rest, she wanted nothing more than to regain her strength to honor God in new and greater ways. "If only I could get well," she said over and over, "I could serve God better," which she uttered with a passion and boundless sincerity that still moved him. When her pain and weakness increased and she could barely raise her arms, and she had begun to see things around her that others could not, in her few moments of lucidity and relief she used her every labored breath to praise the name of God and to instruct Yeshua to help their neighbors who were sickly or infirm, none of whom she ever forgot in her prayers though none of them was as ill as she. Her last night on earth was spent singing hymns with joyous celebration, although her voice was barely a whisper, and praising God with even greater conviction than before the advent of her spiraling decline.

The evocation of these edifying remembrances by the women's gatherings with their laughter and joyous sacramental air accounted for Yeshua's astonishing comfort as the only male among them. The older women soon came to dote over Yeshua, the young marrieds to cherish him as a brother, and the maidens of their number to be held captive to giggling crushes.

It was in these women's assemblies that Yeshua fell in love with Maryam. He'd long known that he was fond of her, but now he was certain that his heart sprouted the wings of love, for it seemed to him that she became more beautiful with each rising of the sun. Having returned to the village just months ago, he had observed only the final days of Maryam's years of mistreatment and pain. What appeared to him now in its fullness was her triumph: the courage and unfaltering dignity, the erect bearing, the growing self-confidence, the deeply held respect the women accorded her. He watched in secret awe and wondered at the source of her resilience.

When Yeshua first saw Maryam her face was drawn and sunken and her eyes shone with the intensity of a cornered rodent. Her shoulders then were stooped and slightly rounded, her footsteps unsure. In the wake of the death of Nahshon, for some time her face was angry, her body language rebellious and dismissive, the shining cinnamon of her skin dull and ashen. Her gait was stiff with obstinacy and rage, her chin thrust out with affected arrogance. Her head covering was thrown on with obvious abandon, and at times she looked absolutely disheveled. But as soon as she'd been embraced by the women and immersed in Huldah's towering love, her anger began to ease. The hard lines in her face softened, her mouth was no longer a tight line, the sheen returned to her skin. Her stride was now more fluid and relaxed. She adorned herself with Huldah's decorative stones and amulets, and her head coverings were of brightly colored cottons culled from the meager possessions of

Rafca and Petronelah and others of the older women who took pride in Maryam's flowering.

These thoughts eased through Yeshua's mind as he sat with the women in worship, as was now his regular practice. In flowing testimonies women testified to and gave thanks for their growing self-realization and the changing circumstances of their inner lives. Then Maryam rose to tell how her own journey had brought light to her darkness. As she spoke, Yeshua became aware of a radiance emanating from her and suddenly he could not see her face, so bright was the incandescence that obscured it. The volume of her voice had not changed nor its tone nor its timbre, yet somehow her voice was different. Then Maryam began to pray and he felt the unmistakable presence of God. It was then that he knew that his wait was over: without a doubt he had found the woman he had been waiting for. The next day he began an inspired regimen of prayer and fasting to ready himself to ask her to be his wife.

A month later, fortified by his nightly prayers and solitary communion with God, Yeshua was ready to lay himself on the unsteady altar of Maryam's attentions. She was still ensconced in self-protective reserve from him, but Yeshua ignored her reticence and at every opportunity engaged her in energetic conversations in which he shared with her his thoughts, his experiences, his dreams, the very trajectory of his life, and invited her to share her own. He was determined that nothing would stop him except a clear and unsubtle revelation from God.

Surprisingly, Maryam did not meet Yeshua's increased attentions with increased resistance now. In fact, in Yeshua's undeterred insistence Maryam secretly found the comforting security of constancy. She looked forward to Yeshua's weekly disquisitions at Huldah's hut in which he delved into the meanings and significations of yet another verse of scripture. Maryam could be sure that after Sabbath services Yeshua would accompany her and Huldah on the path to their home, discussing Abba Samuel's Sabbath message and its implications for his own life and theirs. She knew with certainty that he would ask to sit with her at the sacred place at the river when the others had gone, observing for her in the water's flow some new aspect of the inexorable grace of God.

"You see, you can't have the same river twice; it's already moved on. If you try to hold on to it or get it back, you just waste your time. That's why you can't worry about the past, Miss Maryam. Just like that river, life keeps going. Just let your river go and God will give you a fresh stream of blessings. But you have to let the river go."

Yeshua spoke to Maryam of his mother, his sisters, his courageous loving father, the arid years of his own aloneness. He exposed the deepest parts of himself to her without reserve or hesitation. Inspired and freed by Yeshua's earnest openness, little by little Maryam began to speak to him of her own life, her own thoughts. Before it dawned on her that she had lowered the insuperable barrier around her heart, she was already baring parts of herself that sometimes were as revelatory to her as they were to Yeshua. Her increasing openness to him at first alarmed her, but because of the emotional satisfaction she derived from their growing friendship she did her best to keep her fears at bay. A bond flourished between Maryam and Yeshua that became so natural that neither felt the need to name or define it.

That did not stop the women from naming it. To them it was clear that Yeshua and Maryam were in love. Speculating when Yeshua would ask for her hand became a major topic of discussion. But when they playfully approached Maryam with their excited conjectures, she dismissed every word as unfounded gossip.

"How do you know Yeshua is sweet on me?" she said with a voice full of exasperation. "You all are just talking. After what happened with Nahshon, no man in this village is ever going to want to marry me again. And that's fine with me, because I don't want any of them. If Moses himself walked in right now I wouldn't want him either. I don't plan ever to be another man's property. Ever."

"Now, Maryam," said Rafca, a mother of three grown sons who delighted in Maryam as if she was the daughter she never had, "I'm old enough to know when a man has a fancy for a woman. But the kind of fancy that Yeshua has, well, he's got something special in his heart for you."

"What do you want me to do? I told you I'm not interested in any man."

"Nobody's trying to tell you what to do, Maryam," said Phumiah, a tall woman whose lean frame belied her advancing years. "We're just saying that God moves in mysterious ways, is all. When a special man has a special feeling for you—well, something that rare and special can be God speaking. Just make sure you don't say no to sweet today just because yesterday had some bitter in it. You might miss your blessing."

"Listen, all of you. I'm not thinking about Yeshua and Yeshua is not studying me. Even if he was, I'm not interested in any more sandals next to my bed mat. I've already paid my marriage dues."

"Well, Miss Huffy," said Huldah, "all we're saying is you should give the man a chance and listen to what Hokmah says to you."

"I don't have to give Yeshua a chance. I'm just not going to be any man's property. Period."

In the ensuing days Maryam continued her denials, but the truth was that she was beginning to feel the unspoken essence of Yeshua. This both gratified and troubled her. Finally, after weeks of disavowals, she had to admit to herself that she had become attuned to Yeshua's vibration. Without fail she knew when their paths would cross in the courtyard, she could sense almost to the moment when he would appear at Huldah's hut or walk into the women's midst at the river gatherings, and without looking she knew when his eyes were upon her. These realizations so made her heart flutter that she reproached herself severely at the thought of being seduced into yet another marriage. Still Yeshua visited her thoughts with greater frequency and each time lingered with her longer. Then she awakened one dawn to find that she was possessed of a ravenous need to hear his voice. When she realized that even in this small way she had again become dependent upon a man, the tottering edifice of her old fears and ruinous hurts fell in on her.

That night Huldah was aroused from a deep sleep by the sound of fevered tossing and loud sighs.

"What is it, Maryam?" she said. "You haven't been yourself for a good while now. What is it that has such an upsetting hold on you?"

"I didn't tell you the truth. It's Yeshua. It seems like if I'm not thinking about him, I'm dreaming about him."

"And that's a problem for you why?"

"Because I don't want to think about him, not like that. Not him or any man. I told you, Huldah. I'm through with men and marrying and being somebody's property and being ordered around like a slave."

"You know Yeshua isn't like that."

"Maybe not now. But how do I know that he won't change when he's got me? I don't want my happiness to depend on how a man decides to treat me."

Huldah dipped a gourd into her years of wisdom and shared it in little sips.

"Tell me, is Yeshua a good man?"

"I believe he is, but—"

"Do you respect him?"

"Yes, ma'am. I do, but—"

"Could you love him?"

"Why are you asking me that? What's love got to do with it?"

"Could you love him, Maryam?"

"I . . . I think I could—"

"But you don't want to."

"That's right. I don't want to. Now or never."

"You're afraid. Because of all you've been through."

"Wouldn't you be?"

"So it's not Yeshua, it's feeling vulnerable that's bothering you. I understand. After all you've been through, you'd be a fool not to protect yourself. But Yeshua is good and kind. He's a man with a womb-spirit if there ever was one. He's the kind of man you can trust. And a good thing, too, because Yeshua is inside you now. Anytime you think of somebody day and night, when you hear their voice when they've not spoken and see their face when they're nowhere near, and the thought of them fills you up and warms you, then they're in your soul. Yeshua is in your soul. You're never going to be any good without him. So you might as well go ahead and be with him."

Maryam sat up in the dark. "What do you mean?"

"I mean just be with him."

"You mean just live with him?"

"Yes."

"Without being married?"

"I'm saying it's worth thinking about."

"How can I just be with a man without being married? I know I'm already scandalous, but that's too scandalous even for me. Abba Samuel would have a stuttering fit."

"Maryam, you refused to bow down to a man and now he's dead. You're always going to be scandalous." Huldah laughed. Maryam did not.

"You can't let what other folks think rule your life. As long as you know you're right with God, you have to live the way your heart tells you. Don't let the way men have debased marriage keep you from a good life. The way they do marriage these days is not God's way. Anyway, customs and traditions and rituals are made by folks to serve their own needs. So make your own custom."

"Huldah, why are you so set on me going to live with that man?"

"Cause I think it's the right thing. Also, I'm old and I'm not going to be around forever. You're young. Lord knows you deserve some happiness. And some babies, too."

"Well, I don't care how scandalous I am, I'm not going to just move in with a man. That's not right."

"You don't have to do it just like that."

"You sound like there's another way."

"There is."

Unhampered now by Maryam's denials, at last her relationship with Yeshua began an ascent freed from fears and frustrations. They opened wide their hearts and together uncovered thoughts and feelings they had kept hidden even from themselves. They spoke of their pasts and every aspect of their present. Yet they never spoke of a future; what had gone before was still so painful for Maryam that she could not bring herself to venture what was to come. For his part, Yeshua had no doubt that Maryam was to be his wife, but he awaited a clear and unambiguous prompting from God as to when.

. . .

After nine months had passed since his return to the village of his birth, Yeshua's parents appeared to him in a dream with their arms extended wide in welcome, and he knew this was his sign. He awoke already in motion, washing and dressing in the predawn dark before starting down the path. He stopped only to gather a bouquet of wild roses in the gray light. The sun was still just hinting its rise when Yeshua reached the hut of Huldah.

"Miss Huldah, shalom," he called. His voice was firm. "Miss Huldah, I need to talk to Miss Maryam."

He heard a voice husky with sleep. "Who is that? Yeshua, that you?"

"Yes, ma'am. I need to talk to Miss Maryam."

He heard the bustling within, the whispers, the rustle of clothing, a small splash of water. Maryam quickly emerged with an expression of curious anticipation. Yeshua's face was all seriousness. His eyes blazed with resolution. He did not smile. The two stood facing in the beginning light.

"What is it?" Maryam asked, her brow furrowed with concern.

Yeshua motioned to her. "Sit with me for a moment, Miss Maryam, if you please."

Under his arm was a blanket that he unrolled on the dew-wet ground. Maryam sat upon it and Yeshua sat beside her. "These are for you," he said, handing her the bouquet. Then he cleared his throat and spoke with his eyes averted.

"Miss Maryam, in my life I've spent a lot of time alone, but I never knew I was lonely until I met you. I knew I was missing something, but I never knew how rich life could be until I came to know you. When I first saw the strength of your spirit, standing there with your head held high even while all those men were calling for your blood, that's when I got lonely. Then when you began to flower, and your flowering brought all that joy to women who have been feeling put down all their lives, that's when my heart started to hunger for you."

He slipped his hand over hers. "When I'm not with you and I can't see your smile brightening up everything and everybody, loneliness gets all inside of me. All these years I never touched a woman because I was waiting for God to speak to me. I didn't just want a wife, I wanted the woman God had for me in divine order, the woman in whose eyes I could see the face of God. I got to know you and respect you and I thought for sure you were the wife I had waited for, but I still had to hear from God. Last night my mama and my daddy came to me in a dream. They nodded at me and smiled. That's all; just nodded and smiled and opened their arms. But that was enough. I knew that was my sign from God that you are the one and now is the time."

Now Yeshua's eyes met Maryam's.

"So I'm asking you to be my wife now and forever in God's holy name. I'm asking you to be a helpmate to me and I'll be a helpmate to you. I'll be your comfort from the storm and your strong arm when you're weak. I mean it. I'll hold you up when you lean and catch you when you fall. I will cherish you all the days of my life as my solemn duty to our God, hallelujah, amen."

Yeshua's words hung between them as they sat as still as the cloudless sky. The sun was rising and a faint mist hovered over the ground as the dew lifted. Just as the silence became overwhelming, Maryam replied.

"Yeshua, I would be proud to be your wife. I never knew that I could feel about a man the way I feel about you. You're a good man. The women call you a womb-spirit, and they're right. You respect women and you're not afraid to call on the feminine side of God. I believe we could have a good life together. But I can't marry you. Not in the same old way with its erwat dabars and men lording over women. I won't ever do that again."

"But Miss Maryam, you have to know that I'm not like the other men. Marrying me wouldn't be anything like what they do."

"I've given it a lot of prayer and thought and I mean what I say. I'm willing to share your life and share your home, but never again will I be a man's wife in this same old way."

"What are you saying, Miss Maryam? That you'll live with me but you won't marry me?"

"Not in the same old way, I won't."

"If you trust me enough to make a home with me, why don't you just marry me?"

"It's not you, Yeshua. It's just that marrying you would make me into something I don't want to be: the property of a man. What if you change and start thinking like the other men? I'd end up ruled and mistreated all over again."

"Miss Maryam, all my life I have tried to do right. I'm a grown man and I have never touched a woman. I didn't want a woman just to have her; I wanted a woman the way God says. I believe deep down in my spirit that God has sent you to me. But my mama and daddy both would roll over in their graves if I spent even one night with a woman without a wedding consecrated by the God of Abraham."

"I didn't say I didn't want a wedding. I said I didn't want to get married in the same old way."

"How else could we be married?"

"If we married invoking the name of Hokmah, that would be a new kind of marriage, a marriage of a man and woman as equals. I would marry you that way, but that's the only way I would marry you."

"How could we do that?"

"We could marry at the river with the women and consecrate it with the blessing of the feminine divine. If we don't marry according to the customs of the scriptures, then there's nothing to say that I'm your property."

"How can we get married without the scriptures? That doesn't seem right."

"It would still be consecrated by the scriptures; Hokmah is in the scriptures. They just wouldn't be the scriptures that tell women to obey men like children, that let men throw women away and feel like they have the sanction of God."

"You know Abba Samuel wouldn't perform a wedding ceremony like that."

"I know, but we won't ask him. We can have some of the women say new wedding sentences."

"But how will the men know we're married? I'd be proud to be your husband and I'd want everybody to know. I don't want folks to think ill of you, like we're doing something sneaky or wrong."

"The women will know, God will know, and we'll know. That's all that matters."

"Just doesn't seem right somehow."

"Well, that's the only way I'll marry you, Yeshua."

Yeshua was silent for a long time. Then he looked deep into Maryam's eyes.

"I want to spend the rest of my days serving God and loving you. All I need to know is that you love me. If you love me, I'll do whatever it takes to be together. Do you love me, Maryam?"

"I do. In the deepest part of me I do."

"Well, if you'll be my wife I'll be proud to be your husband, and together spend our lives serving God."

Chapter

37

The community of women was electrified by the news.

"Girl, Yeshua finally loosed his stammering tongue and popped the question to Maryam."

"For real?"

"Yes, he did. But Maryam said she wouldn't marry him under Moses' law because she's not going to be anybody's property. You know how Maryam is since she scared that ugly Nahshon into his grave."

"She has been a ball of fire."

"But you know how Yeshua is, too, always insisting on doing the honorable thing before God, so you know he had to have some kind of ceremony."

"You know he did."

"He told Maryam, 'I don't like sneaking around. Doing something in private looks like we're too shamefaced to let folks know about it in public.' So we're all going to get together and Huldah's going to say some words, and Maryam and Yeshua will do the rest. Girl, I can't wait."

The women assembled at their river place of meeting shielded by trees, rocks, the incline of the riverbank, and the pretense of having gathered for "women's work." Some brought bundles of clothing and suckling infants as their means of subterfuge. Others simply stole away without explanation or notice. A cool breeze blew across the whispering river, swaying the bowing branches of the willows and stirring the poplar leaves in delicate dance. The late-afternoon sun dappled the grass and smooth pale rocks, glittering off the water with the brilliance of jewels.

Maryam sat beneath a willow surrounded by Oholibamah and the other proud attendants fussing over her, chatting gaily, arranging in her hair scented flowers and beads of bright colors. A striped reddish tunic of soft cotton adorned her, wound with a mantle of even brighter red. Tiny bells hung from a white cotton veil that covered her hair and draped her shoulders.

Yeshua waited a little further downstream, where he was tended by Petronelah and Keturah, the latter of whom reminded the women for the rest of the day that the garland covering Yeshua's head was the work of her hands. He wore a striped yellow-brown tunic tied with a mantle of yellow. A white kaffiyeh cloaked his head and framed his face, with one end tossed over the opposite shoulder.

The bustle and excited laughter gave the gathering a festive feeling. In fact, the celebration began even before the ceremony. Songs and spirited paeans to the feminine divine filled the air:

> Hokmah is better than jewels,
> and all that you may desire cannot compare with her.
> I, Hokmah, dwell in prudence . . .
> I have counsel and sound wisdom,
> I have insight, I have strength . . .
> My fruit is better than gold, even fine gold,
> and my yield is better than choice silver.
> I walk in the way of righteousness,
> in the paths of justice.

The riverbank was decorated with bunches of flowers. Decorative grasses tied with brightly colored woolen strings were implanted in the soft soil and draped from the overhanging branches. Children sang and clapped with the water at their heels and bright feathers in their hair. A cluster of women talked buoyantly while another little group hummed and swayed and nodded in quiet contentment. Huldah stood proudly among them clothed in a white linen tunic, dignified and erect in her proud role of priestess for the day.

The ceremony itself was a curious balance of whimsy and sobriety. There was a hush as Oholibamah and two young women escorted Maryam to the spot where Huldah stood. Yeshua followed with the preening older women fussing over him so much that he almost tripped on their feet. There were admiring glances and delighted whispers. A spontaneous song erupted:

Y-e-s, we have a mighty good Lord, a mighty good Lord, a mighty good Lord.
Y-e-s, we have a mighty good Lord, who brought us all this far.

Someone started to pat a tambourine and the song took wing. The women sang until they were wordless, then they hummed, clapping and swaying; hummed themselves into a frenzy of low moans and sudden bursts of feeling. One of the older women, then another, stepped forward to raise their gnarled hands in praise. "Glory! Go-lory, Lord! You been a mighty good God! Thank you, Lord, for all you've done for me!"

Arthritic knees, sore and weakened, suddenly carried stooped old women to dance like children. Spinning, whirling, twirling women, experts in the art of spirited praise, seemed hardly to touch the ground. Then one by one the women fell, overcome with ecstasy, raptured and writhing, crying out to God as they lay prostrate in the grass, their faces turned to heaven. Then furious fanning by the few women still standing, comforting their laughing and crying sisters stretched out upon the ground.

When their frenzied spirits were satiated, the rejoicers gradually came back to themselves and began to speak in their old voices and walk in their old skins. Yet there remained in each of them a newness, for they had felt the presence of God intimately, intensely, and the evidence remained.

Then there was only humming and swaying. On cue little Diata, prim and smiling, her skin the golden color of peach flesh, her hair

arranged in tight little copper-brown plaits, stepped forward to recite a
Hokmah text from the Book of Proverbs that she'd learned in secret
sessions carefully conducted by her mother out of earshot of her father,
for the unavoidable reason that the religion of the Samaritans frowned
upon any scripture not found in the Five Books of Moses, and just as
much upon any woman learning even those.

The little girl cleared her throat, smiled in the way that children do
when they know they are about to please adults, and spoke with great
affect in a voice that was tiny, yet clear.

> *Does Hokmah not call?*
> *Does discernment not lift up her voice?*
> *On the hilltop, on the road,*
> *at the crossways, she takes her stand;*
> *beside the gates of the city,*
> *at the approaches to the gates she cries aloud:*
> *"O people: I am calling you;*
> *my cry goes out to the children of humanity.*
> *You ignorant ones, study discretion;*
> *and you fools, come to your senses.*
> *Listen, I have serious things to tell you,*
> *and from my lips come honest words.*
> *My mouth proclaims the truth . . .*
> *All the words I say are right,*
> *nothing twisted in them, nothing false,*
> *all straightforward to the one who understands,*
> *honest to those who know what knowledge means.*
> *Accept my discipline rather than silver,*
> *knowledge in preference to gold.*
> *For Hokmah is more precious than pearls.*

There was applause, proud smiles, and hearty amens.
"Look out, Huldah."
"That girl is something else."
"She sure is smart."

With a solemn air Huldah called forth the beloveds to a buzz of cheerful expectation. A low stool and two clay bowls half-filled with water were placed before them.

Huldah waited for full quiet. Then she said with all the formality she could muster, "When traditions and rituals no longer serve us, we must start new ones. This man and this woman have decided that the traditional way of marriage commits the blasphemy of giving men rights that women are not allowed, so they've chosen instead to utter wedding sentences from their own hearts."

Yeshua spoke first.

"I love the Lord. The Lord has been my rock and my salvation from my earliest times. I was blessed to have a good, God-fearing daddy. He showed me how to make the sacrifices to our God and to pray prayers with power. I watched him love my mama like a friend and a helpmate. He never raised his voice to her that I ever heard, and he cherished her like she was a piece of gold. When my daddy died, I saw all those silly men coming around trying to court my mama when all they wanted was a field worker and a bed warmer. But she wouldn't settle for less than my daddy gave her. This is what I've seen all my life, and neither will I give less or settle for less."

He paused to order his thoughts.

"I believe that when the spirit of God really gets you, it makes you love folks and treat them right. I believe that. You can know every jot and tittle of scripture and still not treat people right. I know the scriptures, but I know the spirit of God, too. Maryam, the scriptures say that marrying me makes you my property, but the spirit says you belong to God alone. I'm going to follow the spirit and work every day of my life to love you like God says I'm supposed to: like my own flesh. So in the presence of this assembly of sainted women, in the presence of the spirit of my mother and my father, in the presence of God and angels, I declare that I will love you and respect you and be your helpmate and your friend. I will never try to rule you or boss you. I will be your shoulder to cry on and your strong arm to lean on. And I welcome the same from you. I will love you with all my heart and soul, and I will hold you up on every leaning side until my last living breath."

He kneeled and motioned Maryam to the stool. He tipped the clay bowl over each of her feet, then dried them with the cloth Keturah handed him. When he stood he said, "I've washed Maryam's feet because I plan to love her and serve her all the days of my life."

Now Maryam stood.

"I never really saw love between a man and a woman. My daddy never paid attention to my mama unless she did something he didn't like. All I ever saw was women that were afraid and unloved. I was scared to death myself; you all remember that. But Hokmah has healed me and I'm not afraid anymore. I am a full woman now with all my strength intact. With that strength I will stand beside you, Yeshua. I will love you with a strong love, a love that strengthens you and helps to keep you strong. I'll try to be all that you need me to be. But most of all I will be myself, for that is the most precious thing I can give you: myself, just as I really am. If you look, you'll find me. If you call my name, I'll always answer. I'll stand by your side until God calls us home, then I'll stand beside you before the heavenly throne."

When Maryam completed the ritual of washing and drying, she and Yeshua faced Huldah, who held her hands as in prayer and spoke her words with the gravity of pronouncement.

"Maryam, Yeshua, you are one flesh now. Love each other. Protect each other. Serve each other like it's God you're serving. And call on Hokmah, for Hokmah is the mercy of God. Mercy isn't just a feeling; mercy is an act. To be merciful is to be as good to folks as you can. Serve God and be merciful to each other, strengthening and inspiring each other to make a world where everybody can be happy and free.

"Now, Yeshua, take the hand of your wife. Maryam, take the hand of your husband. In the name of Hokmah, the wisdom and mercy of the God of Abraham, I declare that you are one flesh, hallelujah, amen."

Chapter
38

Before the day he wed, except when he held the hand of Maryam, Yeshua had never touched a woman who was not his kin. Yet his first desire on his wedding night was not to caress the naked softness of Maryam, but to protect and assure her. He held her head to his chest stroking her face and her hair, listening to the wondrous sound of her breathing and the exultant beating of her heart. They had lain this way for some time, fully dressed, still and calm in each other's arms, when it dawned on Yeshua that Maryam was now flesh of his flesh and bone of his bone, not only in formal ceremony but in every way, and his breathing began to quicken. He kissed her cheek, then her lips. Her exquisite and instantaneous surrender awoke in him a strength of passion that surprised them both. He pulled her body to his with such hunger that it took her breath. As he touched and kissed every part of her, it seemed that the newly uncovered wellspring of his love overflowed through his encircling arms. The lovers traveled deeper and deeper into each other, not only in body but in spirit, too, meeting on planes and in dimensions they'd dare not dream. They loved with their singing hearts, their soaring spirits, with every part of themselves, fueled to even greater heights by their happy surprise that loving could be as satisfying to body and soul as this.

The passion that enveloped them on their first night set the tone for their days to come. Some mornings they awoke so filled with love that they glided through the day invoking blessings in their hearts upon everyone they met. Other days they were overcome with a feeling of holiness that made them look upon everything with awe.

The women thrilled to see the loving couple hand in hand, their heads tossed in laughter or bowed in thoughtful discussion. But the men, knowing nothing of their promises before God, thought their public displays of affection were disgraceful.

"Look at that. That is about the most shameful thing I have ever seen. It's bad enough that they live in the same hut without being married. Now they're walking around in front of everybody touching and carrying on. Sure is shameful."

Weeks of angry talk about the couple's apparent disregard for social convention finally brought the men to confront Yeshua at the close of synagogue service.

"Yeshua, what are you thinking about? You act like that woman has worked roots on you or something. She's already killed one man and now she's got your name out here in ruination. You need to get free of that woman before she messes up your life for good."

"Yeah, man, you're scandalizing the whole village living with that woman. Abba Samuel is real hurt you didn't come to him to tie the knot up, especially since you're always throwing the scriptures in everybody's face."

Yeshua was not surprised by the confrontation; he only wondered what had taken the men so long. His voice was firm but free of anger. "Gentlemen, this is not just some 'woman' you're talking about. She's my wife."

The men reacted with predictable indignation. "Your wife? If you had a wedding we all would know about it. That's what marrying is: you make a public announcement that now the woman belongs to you. But you ain't told nobody nothing."

Yeshua measured his response. "Well, seems to me like that might be the problem. The way you men see marriage is a man owning a woman. I don't want to own Maryam; I want her to give herself to me the same way I give myself to her."

He stabbed the air for emphasis. "And please, brethren, let's be clear.

Me and Maryam are married. We didn't marry at the synagogue, but we married the way we believe God wants us to: pledging to love each other in God's name so we can help to bring a little more heaven on this earth."

Now the men really raged, accosting Yeshua from all sides with accusations and recriminations.

Yeshua choked back his rising anger.

"Listen. You know how I feel about the scriptures of God, hallelujah, amen. But you men have made women afraid of the scriptures because you've used them to serve yourselves, and you've been real mean about it. My daddy didn't want any part of the way you all do things and I don't either. Now, I'm telling you that Maryam is my wife. I expect every man here to treat her with the same respect that I treat yours. I hope I don't have to tell you again. Gentlemen, shalom." He hurried away before his fraying self-control came completely undone.

Hushai watched Yeshua depart and spat on the ground. "See. That's what crazy ideas about women do to a man: get him all confused. Now look at him, all shacked-up with a woman that kills men. That fella needs help."

Chapter
39

From the first there were few spaces in their togetherness. Together in the fields and in the marketplace. Together at Sabbath services. Together at the river meetings, clapping and chanting, encouraging and consoling. Then home to laughter and loving. They meditated together. Studied the scriptures together. Prayed together.

A few weeks after their wedding when they'd finished the midday meal in the shade of their hut and were preparing to return to the tending of their crops, Maryam noticed that the water jug was nearly empty. "I'm going to the well for water to take with us to the field," she said as she donned her head covering.

"I'll go with you," said Yeshua, brushing the crumbs from his lap.

"No need for both of us to lose sunlight. Don't worry. I'll be back as quick as I can." She blew him a kiss as she left.

The thrusts of Yeshua's hoe into the rich earth were rhythmic. His heart was filled with gladness, his mind was at rest, his body was satisfied. His life was so endowed with happiness that he felt as if he had fallen headlong into the hedge of God's blessing. He had a loving wife, his own hands worked his own land—yes, his life was the stuff of song and thankful celebration. He stood in symmetry now, in balance, his emptiness and struggles swept away in the wake of his satisfying new life. His heart leapt and sang, his hoe rose and fell. In the happy wanderings of his mind, he thought he heard God calling his name. He struck the earth and he heard it again. *Must be Hokmah,* he thought with excitement, *because it's a woman's voice.* The call grew louder. Then something about the voice seemed incongruous, earthbound, even alarmed.

"Yeshua! Yeshua!" the voice said. "Come quick!"

He looked up to see Phumiah running toward him. Yeshua dropped the hoe and ran to meet her. "What happened? Is Maryam alright?"

Phumiah fell into his arms, gasping for breath. "Yeshua," she panted. "Something . . . something is wrong with Maryam."

His heart leaped into his mouth. "What is it?"

"Nobody knows," Phumiah panted. "She's talking all out of her head."

"What do you mean? Did something happen to her?"

Phumiah shook her head. "Nobody knows," she repeated. "We saw her talking to this man at the well, and the next thing we know she's running around talking all out of her head."

Yeshua's eyes grew wide. He asked slowly and fearfully, "Did he . . . did he do something to her?"

"Nobody knows anything. She's not making sense."

Yeshua took her arm. "Come on. Take me to her."

The women had half-carried Maryam to Huldah's hut, but the midwife was not at home. They seated Maryam on the ground with her back leaned against a palm tree. They stood over her, their faces grave, fanning her with their head coverings and loose palm fronds.

Maryam was locked in an alternating cycle of loud weeping and hysterical laughter. She was talking, yet all that could be made out was, "I have to find him. I have to find him."

They asked, "Find who, Maryam?"

"I don't know his name," she said through her laughter and tears, "but I know who he is."

"Then who is he?" they asked.

She gave the same answer: "I don't know, but I have to find him."

"How are you going to find a man you don't know?" they asked, becoming more worried by the minute.

Finally Huldah arrived in a huff of concern. All the women started talking to her at once.

"You all move now. Stop crowding the child," she said; then under her breath, "What happened to her?"

Rafca shook her head. "Don't nobody know what happened. One minute she's at the well talking to some strange man, the next minute she's walking around talking crazy."

"What did he say to her? Something mean or ugly? Did he threaten her?"

"Nobody knows. He did look kindly, though. Smiling and polite and all. He was a Galilean—I could hear that Galilean twang to his speech—but he was nice, not condescending like most Galileans and Judeans."

"That's all?"

"Well, I just saw him from a distance, but he seemed to talk to Maryam like she was a man. You know, with respect. And he was listening to what she said, not like these men around here."

"If that's all, then what upset this child so bad?"

Everyone shrugged.

"Alright. Alright," said Huldah. "Hush up and let Maryam tell us what she's trying to say."

She stroked Maryam's cheek and said gently, "Tell Huldah what happened, child."

Maryam looked into the worried faces and words rushed from her in a torrent. "I've never seen . . . it felt like God . . . the man was . . . he . . ." She burst into tears again.

Huldah tried to appear unruffled, but she was worried, too. Never had she seen Maryam like this, not even when she faced death. Had she suddenly broken from the weight of her struggles? Huldah placed her hand on Maryam's brow and prayed. "O Lord God of Abraham, Hokmah the wisdom and mercy of God, please help your child. She's been through a whole lot, but she's still praising your name."

Yeshua arrived with Phumiah, his eyes wide with fear and concern. Maryam brightened as he pushed past the women. He took her hand and knelt at her feet.

"You alright?" he asked.

She nodded.

Yeshua kissed her hand and held it against his cheek. "I'm here, honey. Everything's going to be fine. Just take your time and tell us what happened."

Chapter

40

Maryam breathed deeply. Her eyes alternated between the faraway look of recollection and the plaintive look of needing to be believed.

"Honey, when I left you I went straight to the well. There was a bunch of men sitting around talking. I could tell they weren't Samaritans; you know, the way they talked."

The women nodded knowingly.

"I walked up carefully, watching them out the corner of my eye. I don't know why, but I started feeling like there was something special about this one Galilean sitting in the middle of them. He was big and strong-looking with a deep powerful voice, but there was something real quiet and gentle about him, like a lamb or something. That's what it was: he was big and strong, with all the men looking to him like he was the leader—and they were a rough-looking bunch, too—but he seemed innocent and pure as a little lamb. He had this face that was sort of dusty brown, brown like clay dirt after a rainfall; a smooth, soft kind of brown. There was, I don't know, a glow to him. And his eyes—Lord, his eyes! They just seemed to look right through you, right into your soul. They were dark, almost black. When he looked out those eyes, it seemed like he was seeing everything and everywhere. All the men were talking to him and he was listening and answering them, but when he looked at me it was like I was the only person in the world."

Rafca interrupted. "Maryam, hush your mouth, talking about a man like that in front of your husband."

"It's alright. I trust my Maryam. Go ahead, honey. Tell your story."

"But that was just it," Maryam choked back another sob. "It wasn't like he was talking to me; he didn't seem to be thinking about anything in this world. I mean, he was talking to me, but all the time it seemed like his eyes were on God."

The women asked impatiently, "So what happened?"

"The rest of the men got up to leave, saying they were going somewhere to break bread. I was dipping water so I could get back to the fields with Yeshua. The man saw me with my jug, so he asked me to dip some water for him."

The women were incredulous. "He asked you to give him water? He got some nerve. Like he's your husband or something."

"But I keep telling you, it wasn't like that. I mean, he did speak to me familiar, and with any other man I would have been offended. But with him it was a different kind of familiar, like I was his sister or something. His daughter even. It just seemed like I knew him all my life."

The women urged her on. "So what did you do? Did you pour him his water?"

"Well, I didn't want him to know I was feeling all of this, cause I didn't know who he was. He seemed godly, but he could have been one of those lecherous charlatan preachers for all I knew. So I didn't pour him anything. I said, 'Why are you, a Jew, asking me, a Samaritan and a woman at that, to draw water for you? You don't know me.' He just smiled and said, 'If you knew who it is you're talking to, you could ask me and I would give you living water.' Well, you could have knocked me over with a feather. I didn't have the first idea what he was talking about, but I knew it was true. I didn't know this man from Adam, but I knew in my heart that what he was saying was truth straight from the mouth of God."

"So what is this *living water*?" Phumiah asked.

"That's what I asked him. I said, 'This water comes from the well of our father Jacob. Are you saying that you have better water?' He just smiled that soft lamb smile and said, 'If you drink this well water, you'll be thirsty again. But whosoever drinks of my water will never thirst again.' Up to then I was just testing him, acting like I was only half interested in what he was saying. But the way he was talking about this living water, I just couldn't hold back. It sounded like heaven or something. So I said, 'Sir, what is this living water?' He said God gave it to him to raise the people up to just and righteous living."

"Then what?"

"Then I said, 'Sir, I would like to be closer to the Lord. Could you give me some of this living water?'"

Old Rafca waxed indignant again. "Maryam, why would you ask a strange man for anything?"

"Hush up, Rafca," Huldah snapped. "Go on, child. Rafca don't seem to know that she can't talk and listen at the same time."

Rafca crossed her arms and rolled her eyes. "I am listening," she said. "Scripture don't say nothing against asking questions."

"Go on, Maryam," Huldah huffed.

"So when I asked him for some of the living water he said, 'Alright. Go get your husband.'"

"I said, 'Some folks would say I don't have a husband.' And you know what he said?"

"What?" the women asked in unison.

"He said, 'You're right. . . .'" She swallowed hard. "'You've had five husbands and now you're living with a man that you didn't marry under the law of Moses.'"

"He said all of that sure enough? He was reading you like a page out of scripture. How did he know all that about you?"

"That's what he said. I don't know how he knew. He wasn't a magician or a root doctor; I felt too much God in him for that. I believe he knew because he has a mind of God. The feeling I got from him, I just believe he has a mind of God. And . . . and, I know he's not a Samaritan, but I believe he's the Messiah. He has to be. Nobody could have that much God in them but the Messiah."

Yeshua raised up. "You mean the Messiah everyone's waiting for to deliver us from the kingdom of Caesar into the kingdom of God? What makes you think this man is the Messiah?"

Maryam touched her forehead. "Cause he has a mind of God. I

didn't feel even a little bit of a man's mind in him. Even after he told me all about myself, I didn't get the feeling he was judging me or anything. It was like he was telling me that he knew all I've been through, all my pain, all my hurts. My little girl dead at that devil's hand. All those years I was just a shell, too afraid to live and too afraid to die. I could see in his eyes that he knew all about it, and that it pained him, too. I just started crying and I told him, 'I know you're a prophet and a man of God. But why have you, a Jew, come to Samaria? Why aren't you in Jerusalem?' He called me child—he said, 'My child, there is no difference between Jew and Samaritan or anybody else in the sight of the Most High. We're all God's children. No need for me to be in Jerusalem when I can be right here.' He said, 'It doesn't matter where you worship; what matters is how you worship. The true worshipers are the ones who worship God in spirit and in truth.' And his voice. Lord. Sounded like doves cooing and thunder clapping at the same time."

She started to cry again. "The man had such a womb-spirit that it seemed like I was talking to the feminine side of God. And love . . . have mercy! Ma Tee loved me. Yeshua loves me. Huldah loves me. You all love me as strong as anybody can love in this world. But the love I felt from that man is nothing like I've ever known. It's so strong it's like it's not even of this world; so much love that you can feel it all over, like somebody dipped you down in the river. That's what his love is like: sweet, pure, peaceful water. One minute it feels like it's lapping at you with that soft feeling like a gentle stream. Next minute it's rushing all over you like a river, washing away all your pain and fears. The minute after that, it's like a fine soothing mist that gets inside and soothes your heart. I never felt as much love as I felt from that strange man."

She took Yeshua's hand.

"Honey, the man knows God in a whole new way. He's the Messiah, I just know it. We have to find him and drink of his living water, so we can know God in that new way, too. Not just a God that men use for control or women call on for mercy, but a God of spirit and truth that is all of that and more."

"Where is he now?" asked Yeshua.

"Last time I saw him he was going south," said Maryam.

"Then I guess we have to go and find him," Yeshua said.

The women were agog. "The Messiah," they said. "Imagine that."

"You sure it was the Messiah?" Petronelah asked.

"There's not a doubt in my mind."

Yeshua helped Maryam to her feet. Her knees were weak and her face tearstained, but she had regained most of her composure. She hugged each of the women, each of whom was surprised at how much Maryam trembled.

She and Yeshua had already departed for home when Maryam stopped and excitedly turned back to the women. "His name. Now I remember. The men with him called him Jesus. Yes. That's what they said. Jesus."

After she'd told her story to the women; after she'd cried them a river; after Yeshua helped her to her feet; after they left for home together; after she'd said she did not seem the same; after he said he felt different, too; after she'd cried that she thought she was losing her mind; after they'd collapsed on the path many times to weep; after they'd prayed in fear and wonder; after she told him of the water that troubled her thoughts like locusts; after she'd shrieked, as if stricken, that she'd seen the eyes of God; after they'd all night pondered spirit-drenched waters and lambs and soul-searching eyes, it was as plain as the sun that they could know no rest until they saw him—this Jesus—to find if through him God could quench their thirsting souls.

Maryam and Yeshua left the next morning at the first light of day, carrying a small bag of provisions and the prayers of many women, to seek this strange man who had seen into Maryam's heart and raised in her an insatiable yearning.

They traveled as quickly as they could, hoping to overtake Jesus and his party on the road. They stopped only to consume quick meals of dates and barley loaves and sips of water and diluted wine, and to ask of travelers coming north if they had passed a group of Galileans with one among them whose eyes burned like fire.

The first night they camped in the rocky hills away from the road and the prowling night bandits that stalked it. The cold was an imperious master as they huddled beneath their blankets from dusk to daybreak, the fire unlit for fear of intruders. They warmed themselves by mingling the heat of their bodies, whispering their love and humming the hymns of the faith of their people. At first light they found a little brook. They drank from its pleasant coldness, filled their water skins, and continued on their search.

The second day they spent as the first, steps quick and purposeful, stops for short meals, brief inquiries, and mumbled thanks. With dusk near and the prospect of another achingly cold night before them, they spied yet another traveler, an old man in an empty oxcart.

Yeshua raised his hand in hopeful greeting. "Shalom, sir. Have you seen a bunch of Galileans around here?"

The old man cocked his head and squinted at them curiously. "Were there about eleven or twelve of them? One of them got eyes that look right through you?"

"Sounds like them."

"He is got some strange durn eyes, don't he? I saw the bunch of them in a grove of beeches yonder just past that rise. Making camp. If you step quick you can get to them before dark do."

They saw the fire first. Around it the inhabitants of the little camp joked and regaled one another with tall tales. Several lay on the ground, doubled up in laughter. Others howled and hooted, wiping tears of mirth, offering mock appeals for mercy.

"Come on now. Don't say another word. Puh-lease! You're killing me. I'm about to bust over here. Oh my stomach. Oh my stomach."

In the middle of the merriment was a man who was all arms and animation.

"Phillip, you know my tales don't have a thing to do with your stomach. You're about to bust because you eat like Jonah's whale. Eat so much I get full watching you."

The men howled like hot grease had splashed on them. They fell into one another in a backslapping, stomach-grasping, doubled-over heap.

The scene surprised Maryam and Yeshua, who had expected to find solemnity and bowed-head piety.

"You sure this is them?" Yeshua asked as they cautiously approached, hand in hand. "They just seem like a bunch of regular fellows having fun."

"I can't tell," said Maryam. Then the main jokester looked her way and Maryam's heart jumped. Her knees felt weak; she steadied herself on Yeshua's arm. "That's the man," she whispered. "The one talking."

They drew slowly near, calling out "Shalom" as they entered the glow of the fire. Several yards away a second fire flared. Around it sat a group of women, set apart from the men at night according to traditional notions of propriety, but enjoying themselves no less. Then everyone turned to look at the visitors and the laughter seemed to hang in midair.

Jesus raised his hand in greeting. He was tall and well muscled and strapping, with a large head and large hands. His piercing eyes blazed like black suns in their orbits, and he had a long, wide nose that flared when he spoke. He wore a drab, colorless tunic that was frayed at the hem. His skin was the color of burnished brass and his dark hair was thick like lamb's wool. An energy emanated from him that seemed almost to crackle.

"Shalom," said Jesus. His smile was wide and welcoming. The women waved and the men spoke short greetings. A big broad-shouldered young man eased next to Jesus. He had rough, callused hands and an enormous face that was all seriousness. He eyed the visitors suspiciously.

Jesus brushed past the man and said, "Good to see you. Make yourselves at home. And don't mind Peter. He's just protective sometimes."

With a note of playfulness, without taking his eyes off the visitors, he said, "This is the sister we met at the well back at that village, and this must be the husband she's not married to."

The men chuckled loudly. The women shook their heads as if at a wayward child. "Don't mind that Jesus," they said. "He just loves to keep something going."

Yeshua's face felt hot. The muscles around his mouth tightened.

Jesus noticed the change in Yeshua's demeanor. He touched Yeshua's arm and Yeshua was instantly calmed.

"Brother, we're just having fun, that's all," Jesus said gently. "I know you're her husband. I can see in your spirit that you're a good husband and a good man, too. But we can talk about that later. For now, come on in here and have some of this fish Peter and Andrew caught in that stream yonder."

Thomas, a wiry man with a voice as coarse as sand, said, "They caught it alright, and they burned it, too."

Little John piped in through a mouth filled with food. Still a teenager, with a soft brown face sporting hair that resembled the fuzz on an unwashed peach, he was the youngest of the group, most of whom were younger than Jesus, who was himself barely thirty. "It's burnt alright," John chirped. "But it still tastes good."

"See, that's why I call John *beloved*," Jesus said. He patted the boy's head. "Because he looks through what seems to be, to see what really is. What he's showing us is the simple nature of God's loving grace: no matter how bad things seem, just beneath the ruined surface is the goodness that God has waiting for us. When it's burnt but it's good anyway, that's God's grace."

Jesus' smile turned into a grin. "And God is going to have to give us a whole lot of grace on this fish, cause Lordy, it sure is burnt."

The men and women erupted again in chortling and guffaws.

Jesus rubbed his hands together with great exaggeration. "Well, I'm going to eat some of this fish and see how much grace God gives us today."

He bowed his head in mock prayer. "Lord, if ever we needed you before, we sure do need you now." Everyone laughed but Peter.

"Nobody's making you eat it," Peter said without a trace of humor.

Jesus turned to Maryam and Yeshua and handed them a fish on an unshaven stick that served as a spit. "Come on now, you two get some of this fish, too. Don't let us be the only ones to suffer through it."

He laughed again with his contagious laughter, and finally Peter did, too.

The men and women settled around the fires, which were dancing and bright against the enveloping night, to eat and swap new tales. As Peter looked on with protective vigilance, Jesus took Maryam and Yeshua apart from the others to sit at the edge of the fire's glow.

They ate without words. It was not a brooding silence or a distant silence, but a placid hush that seemed to well up about them. Jesus' smile was not really a smile at all now; his face was still and glowing.

Maryam, her spouse, and Jesus sat together half-eating fish and listening to the low murmur of the meal-talk and the quiet of the night, and a holiness set in upon them. Maryam sensed it, and Yeshua, too. They looked at each other with stunned expressions that asked, *Do you feel it?*

Jesus sat motionless, his head high, peering straight before him, eyes opened wide as if beholding the world for the first time. Occasionally, he nodded to the distance and smiled. Otherwise, he was silent and still. To the woman and her spouse who had walked far to find him, the world suddenly seemed to revolve around this strange man they flanked, cross-legged in the dark.

There beneath a tree in a grove under the stars in the fire-split night, it was to them as if they were being reborn. Led by a silent guide. Borne by a man possessed by superior spirits. A God-man. Flesh conversant with angels, this purveyor of new horizons, this smiling healer reposed on thrones of devotion, this laughing lover of all things. This God-intoxicated man, singing perfect harmonies, mouth closed, eyes closed, singing nonetheless. Enthroned in kingdoms of wholeness, reeking gentle moments, reeking divine demeanor, reeking of God, this Jesus: he is of us and he is not. A God-man. Everywhere God. In him. Around him. In his eyes. In his hard hands. God in his breath. God in his coarse hair. In his dusty feet. In the rude sandals he half-wore. In the fish grease on his ragged tunic.

They felt the sprouting of wings. Smelled the scent of fruits and the fragrance of blossoms. Hardened flesh washed from their hearts. Suns rose before them. Worlds of beauty, oceans of love, a new and loving nomenclature.

Chapter

42

Maryam and Yeshua awoke from a deep and peaceful sleep to find Jesus' threadbare cloak covering them. Jesus himself stood off in the near distance, barely visible in the last of the moonless night. His back was to them, his arms outstretched in suspended embrace, his face lifted to heaven, basking in something only he saw and heard and felt. They did not know how long he had stood that way, but sweat glistened on the nape of his neck despite the predawn chill, and his arms trembled as if they had been raised for some time. Maryam and Yeshua watched light gather about him. They watched him softly glow. They saw the air move around and through him, his arms outstretched, his face upturned, and the air moved faster, surrounding him in a dance of wind and whirling motion. They witnessed stars encircle him, a revolving eddy of pure light, glistering orbs and the exploding colors of dusk, and the world moved around him, enfolded and counted him as its center: there where Jesus stood was the Messiah of God. There, in the space his spirit filled with unstrained perfection. There within him, where heaven and earth embrace. There, in the whirling vortex, the funneling of light they could see but could not see—there, in that place, flowed grace and truth that knew no ebb. Hovering in majestic suspension, fully immanent yet somehow far away, his arms splayed in ethereal embrace, his face raised and uplifted, basking in something only he knew and saw and heard and felt.

Then Jesus dropped his arms, lowered his head, and he was simply flesh again. The stars regained their orbits and the sun its horizontal throne. The air loosed its flourish and the vortex its whirl, and suddenly there was peace so profound it seemed the whole world was at rest. He exhaled and he was with them again.

"We thank our God for this morning," he said with slow solemnity. Then he winked at Maryam and Yeshua and said, "How was your journey?"

Mary Magdalene was a stout, middle-aged, plainspoken woman with streaks of gray in her thick hair and creases of old grief in her thin, honey-colored face. She was called Magdalene—that is, from Magdala— to distinguish her from Mary the wife of Clopas, the other Mary in the camp, and Mary the mother of Jesus, who sometimes traveled with them. Mary Magdalene was the eldest of the women, who also included Salome, Lydia, Susanna, and Joanna, the disowned wife of Herod's steward Chuza. In fact, Mary Magdalene was older than any of the disciples. She was the closest confidant and adviser to Jesus, who relied heavily on her proven good judgment and maturity. It was she who looked after the material needs of the group of men and women and made sure things ran smoothly. She was a no-nonsense woman who mediated disputes and issued directives that were never questioned or resented. She counted it as her calling from God to support Jesus in every way and to free him from the mundane so he could engage in his spiritual exertions and his ministry of transformation unfettered by quotidian cares. When Jesus retired to the hills to pray alone, sometimes for days at a time, it was Mary Magdalene he left in charge.

Phillip and the two Marys—the mother of Jesus did not accompany them on this journey—were busily laying out breakfast. Everyone, including Jesus, took turns in groups of three serving the morning and evening meals. Other than prayer, table fellowship was the group's only ritual. Jesus insisted upon it as an enactment of the radical fellowship of equals—servants serving servants—that would characterize the coming kingdom of God.

Everyone was assembled when Jesus and Maryam and Yeshua joined the breaking of the morning bread. No one sat casually or reclined on the grassy ground; their legs were crossed and their backs held straight. Jesus placed his hands upon his knees, his palms turned upward in open receptivity. Everyone did the same. He closed his eyes and offered words of thanksgiving that became a stirring prayer to invoke the spirit of God among them anew. Then the camp settled into silent meditation that enveloped everyone. No one moved or spoke, and there seemed to be no self-consciousness about them. For some time the men and women sat without shifting or movement of any kind, without coughing or complaint from their limbs or their joints. At last, Jesus said softly, "This day we recommit ourselves to the establishment of your kingdom on earth as in heaven. Thank you for the nourishment of our bodies. Bless this food and grant us the grace that we might be strengthened to serve you with faith and thanksgiving. Amen."

Each of the men and women disciples emerged from their interiority beaming and ready to eat. With mouths full of food and small talk, they turned one to the other in their friendly morning banter. Jesus beckoned Peter and Andrew to sit with him and Maryam and Yeshua. When they had settled in a little circle, Jesus said to Maryam, "You and your husband have come far. What would you ask me?"

Maryam responded without deliberation. "At the well you offered me living water."

Jesus smiled. "That's a good place to start." His expression became serious. "Living water flows from the river of God that runs through us all; it's the river of God's presence within us."

"God is within us?" asked Maryam.

"Yes. Have you not heard in the scripture that you are gods, because the light of God is in you?"

"I never heard it," said Yeshua. "And I've been listening to priests and preachers all my life."

"You have not heard these things because there has come upon the world a famine, not of food or drink, but of hearing the voice of God.

Men and women are possessed of this light, but they don't let their light shine. Because of the impoverishment of their spirits they hide behind their obsession with the outer forms of worship. They utter unintended blasphemy by calling emotionality *spirituality*. They are so preoccupied with the sound of tambourines and cymbals that they cannot hear the quiet music of God; they are so in love with the sound of their own voices that they can no longer hear God's still voice. You see, the men of religion don't want you to hear God; they want you to hear them. Priests and preachers bray like donkeys; the people shout and fall out in self-induced ecstasy and call that the movement of God, offering the utterances of their mouths and the flailing of their limbs as proof of their spirituality. But true spirituality not only makes you feel differently, it makes you act differently. There are those who cry and go about with long faces and offer that as proof that they are communing with God. But the evidence of true spirituality is that you love your neighbors and do justice to them. How can you say that you love God whom you have not seen when you don't love God's children whom you see every day?"

"How are we supposed to show love for our neighbor?" asked Maryam.

"A holy hug and nice words are not enough. Even charity is not enough. Yes, the people must have food and clothing, security and safety. But that only treats the symptoms of festering need. The truly spiritual are those whose love of God moves them to look beyond symptoms to instead take up the struggle against the causes of the people's suffering: the injustice and greed of principalities and powers and unjust rulers in high places. The truly spiritual heed the prophet's call to let justice roll down like waters and righteousness like a mighty stream; love takes them beyond self-centered worship to selfless service. I tell you: there is no greater love than this, that you give your life so others might have life more abundant."

"But what if your neighbor doesn't love you? Are we supposed to love everybody? Even Romans?" Yeshua asked.

"Yes, you must love even Romans, because they are brothers and sisters who have become sick with evil. They act like they believe themselves to be greater than others. But in truth, they fear that they are not as good. They construct laws and governments, rulings and everyday sayings to convince everyone—especially themselves—that they are superior. They build huge edifices as monuments to their own greatness. They treat war like it's a thing of honor. They hold themselves up as the standard of beauty, and thereby reveal their own ugliness; they enslave others and thereby themselves become less human. They paint pictures of God in their own image to induce others to join them in the worship of themselves. They are a sad, sick, godless people. That is why we must struggle to help purge the evil from them that they might find God within. Men and women of love and justice must stand against them, not to punish them but to free them from themselves. Yet even as we struggle against their evil, still we must love them. We must help them to see that there is one who is God of all. Doesn't matter if you're Samaritan or Judean, Galilean or Roman, no one is better than another, no one has the right to lord it over anyone else."

Yeshua cradled his head in his hands. "My Lord. This sure is different from what we've been taught."

"I know, my brother. The proud men who sit in Moses' seat would not teach against themselves, for too many of them are engaged in the exploitation of their own people. Priest and rabbi used to be just roles. They were important roles, but just roles like any other that made life run smoothly. But now the men of religion act like they are possessed of more than a role; they strut among us as if they have a privileged status. And even that's not enough. Now they all want to be called a chief priest or some other self-important title as a sign of the exalted status they believe to be theirs."

Peter broke in. "That's right. Why can't they just be priests? Why they always looking to be honored as big-time big shots? Cause everything now is for show, that's why."

Jesus nodded in agreement.

"No real substance," Peter continued. "Just show. It's got so bad that it seems like every priest is calling himself doctor now: Doctor of the Law of Moses or Doctor of Scripture-ology or Doctor of Sure-Can-Make-You-Shout or whatever they can come up with to make themselves sound more important. Got to have some kinda big-shot title because they've forgot that what they're supposed to be is servants of God."

"And that's all we're here trying to be: servants of God, just like the scriptures tell us," said Andrew.

"That's the honest truth," said Peter. "We just want a pure religion. Folks are tired of all these big shots and pretenders. Our people are sheep without a shepherd. We need us some real shepherds. The priests ain't doing right, so God sent us a Messiah anointed to free our people from their oppression, hallelujah, amen."

Jesus wore a look of pride. "My brothers have spoken rightly. Truly I say to you that the greatest among you is the servant of all. I am among you as one who serves."

"Are you the Messiah?" Maryam asked, her eyes full of excitement.

"That you must judge for yourself. But remember this: you will know a tree by the fruit it bears. What I say has no meaning if my actions say otherwise. If my words are liberating, if in the name of God I stand against the oppression of the people; if I stand against the religious establishment, the blind guides and greedy hypocrites who reduce the proclamation of God's kingdom of justice to a narrow teaching of individual piety and personal covetousness—if I stand against this and call men and women to do likewise, my deeds will bear witness to who I am. Yet, if I am the Messiah, King Saul and King David were Messiahs before me. They, too, were anointed to free their people from the heavy yoke of oppression."

"You are the Messiah. I know it," Maryam said. She began to prostrate before him.

Jesus reached for her. "Rise, Maryam. If I am the Messiah that doesn't mean you should bow down to me. Messiah is a role, too, not a status. I don't ask you to bow down to worship me; I call you to worship God the father. Follow me, believe that what I say and do and teach are from God, but worship God alone. I know that there are some who would make a god of me, but it is only because they have become drunk from the wellspring of God's saving truth that I have tended.

"I ask you, is it the carrier of the gift or the giver that is worthy of praise? The messenger deserves thanks for willingly sacrificing himself, for he does it out of love, but it is the giver who deserves worship, for it is from the giver that all good things come. Did the son create himself? No. So you must worship the Father, not the son. You may thank me, you may admire me, you may strive to serve God as you see me serve. You may even extol my love for you and the service it inspires in you. But do not worship me. Worship only the Father which is in heaven."

By then the soft light of dawn had given way to the brightness of morning. Jesus suddenly stood. The others were already preparing to break camp. They packed their few provisions into their woolen cloaks, which they rolled tight and slung over their shoulders with lengths of flax twine.

"Come with us," Jesus said to Maryam and Yeshua.

"Where?" asked Yeshua.

"Wherever God leads us."

They crossed a meadow and reclaimed the main road, the men in their knot of laughter and conversation, the women in their own, Jesus laughing and talking and teasing in the midst of them. Theirs was the unhurried pace of those for whom the journey is its own destination.

About midday they saw the low boxlike stone dwellings of a village rise into view.

"We shall bring the word of God to these people," Jesus pronounced. "Prepare yourselves to be vessels of love."

"How do we do that?" asked Maryam.

"Behold the light of God within yourself and you will see it within others," he said with a reassuring smile.

Jesus uttered blessings and warm greetings as he and his disciples entered the low-slung village with its huts of mud and clay and crudely cut stone. Dust billowed about their feet as dogs, lean and lethargic and hang-tongued from the heat, tiptoed in their wake. Those in the huts— the recumbent elders, the women with hands filled with spindles and carded wool, shy little ones barefoot and inquisitive, bits of bread held fast in their moist, dirty hands—stared without speaking. Only the proud old men nodded, speaking their greetings through toothless smiles. The word quickly carried to the workers in their fields of the strangers gathered in the courtyard in the heat of the day. Soon a crowd had tramped in from their labor, wiping dust and sweat from their faces. The villagers collected under the watchful eye of Peter, who stood at the right of Jesus, alert and protective. Drawn by the shining smile of the Galilean and his inviting manner, the children ringed about him, chattering gaily and reaching to touch him, as delighted as if they had been given a gift of sweets. Jesus playfully lifted each of the youngsters and engaged in their laughing games: hide and seek, spurts of foot-racing, kissing the doll baby. Their parents tried to shoo their little ones aside, but Jesus continued his play until he had in some way shared himself with each happy child. Only then did he open himself to the questions of their parents and the needs he sensed in them.

After he had taught for some time a villager said, "Rabbi, your teachings are so different. Would you have us pray differently, too?"

"Yes, I would. When you pray, pray like this: Our father in heaven, hallowed be your name. May your kingdom come, may your will be done on earth as in heaven. Give us our daily bread and forgive our debts as we have forgiven the debts of others. And do not lead us into temptation but deliver us from evil."

The man asked, "What kind of prayer is that? That's not a personal prayer. What does all that mean?"

"I'll explain it to you. You should pray 'us' and 'our' because you must want for your neighbor what you want for yourself. When you pray, you should pray for the deliverance of everyone, not just those you count as your own.

"And whose name is hallowed throughout the land? Caesar. In whose kingdom do you experience such pain and unrequited need? Caesar's. That is why we must pray that God's kingdom of love and justice replaces the unjust kingdom of Caesar that serves the few and leaves the many to starvation and disease and ignorance and fear. In Caesar's kingdom there is hunger and want, so pray for God's kingdom, for there the people will always have bread.

"And debt. In Caesar's kingdom the poor are crushed beneath the weight of those who enrich themselves at your expense, but in God's kingdom the people give rather than lend; there are no rich and no poor, and no one has a greater right to the fruits of the tree of life than another. Finally, because evil and greed are so seductive, you must pray that you do not succumb to the temptation to imitate those who oppress you."

Another of the villagers said earnestly, "I see the truth in your teaching, but seems to me that talking like that will get you crucified."

"My brother, I must speak as my father in heaven commands me. I have come to comfort the afflicted, yes, but also to afflict the comfortable. You cannot have the warmth of fire without the burning of fuel."

Jesus taught until the sun slumped onto the horizon. He laid hands on the sick of body and consoled the sick at heart. He encouraged the discouraged and gave hope to those in despair. He played with the children and embraced the old and infirm. When he had given something of personal value to everyone assembled, he prayed a prayer of blessing and begged of them his leave. The grateful villagers pleaded for him to stay among them, but he bowed deeply and, invoking heartfelt blessings, departed with his party to the hospitality of the countryside. There they found a dry streambed and prepared to share their evening meal.

Chapter
43

After the talk and laughter of another shared evening repast, Mary Magdalene took Maryam aside in the gloaming. Mary Magdalene sat slowly, straight-backed and stately and effortlessly genteel, smoothing her tunic primly. Her manner was dignified and formal, her every move and gesture and her facial expressions, too, marked with grave and proper decorum. Her diction was precise and elegant, her manner of speaking refined.

"My sister, I know you are here for the same reason as the rest of us: you were never the same after you sipped the living water of Jesus. It awoke a thirst in you that you never knew was there, and you had to find him so you might drink more. That is true, is it not?"

Maryam nodded.

"That is what brought me to him, too. I was married to a well-to-do trader of fabrics and woven goods. We had a good life, my Othniel and me. Better than most. We had a stately nahala with beautiful gardens, orchards of grapes and olives with a dozen workers to tend them, a handsome two-story dwelling that faced the Sea of Galilee, and we were blessed with two sons of whom we were very proud. We looked forward to their marriages and the gift of grandchildren, but their detestation of the oppression of our people was stronger than the call of wedlock, so they chose instead to join a rebel band in the hills and make a vocation of fighting the Romans. We did not hear from our sons again until one afternoon months later when they rushed home begging us to hide them. Before we could move, Roman soldiers arrived at a gallop. They burst into our home cursing and shouting. We cried, 'No! Take us! Take us!' but the soldiers just laughed and tied our hands. They dragged our boys into the yard and flogged them until every inch of their backs was bloody and raw and their voices were hoarse from screaming."

Mary Magdalene paused. She breathed deeply. A slight quickening of her breathing and momentary pursing of her lips were the only indications of the pain of her remembrances.

"The soldiers nailed crossbars to the terebinths and crucified our sons before our eyes. I can still hear their screams. Then they turned on Othniel and me. The soldiers beat my Othniel until he was too broken to stand, then stripped me naked and took turns upon me. While they assaulted me they hoisted my Othniel from the ground, crucified him with our sons, and set fire to the three of them. The soldiers held my face and forced me to watch the only man I ever loved and the only children I ever bore writhe in their screaming agony, the flesh burning and blistering and melting from their bones. They left me naked beneath the charred remains of my loved ones.

"From then I was consumed with anguish. I was inconsolable. I talked to no one and listened to no one. All I wanted was to die. Demons of grief possessed me day and night. For weeks I stumbled through Magdala shrieking and calling my loved ones' names. It was while I was in this state that I encountered Jesus. He was passing through with Peter, Andrew, and Thomas. He heard my cries and came to me and consoled me with his gentle love. I looked into his beautiful eyes and immediately I was soothed and comforted and a peace came over me. With his love and care Jesus freed me of my demons and the torments of my memories. When he was readying to leave Magdala I retrieved my husband's hidden cache of gold and silver and left with him. I've been with Jesus since that day. And you?"

"He found me when I was ready, I suppose."

"So it is with us all."

. . .

Yeshua sat across the little camp from Maryam in wide-eyed thrall as Jesus moved among his followers. Peter sat next to him.

"Feeling kind of overwhelmed, huh?" Peter said.

"Yes, sir," said Yeshua. "My head's been spinning since we found you all."

"I know how you feel. When I first saw Jesus, me and my brother Andrew were casting for fish on the Sea of Galilee, down at Capernaum. Now, I'm big and strong; I'm not impressed by too many men, and certainly not no weak man. But when Jesus walked up I felt his strength right away. He felt strong, but he felt gentle and loving, too. I could feel it. It was not that fake, whiny kind of love. It was a strong love, a bold love, so pure and strong that I wanted to cry. He looked at me and Andrew and said, 'Follow me and I'll make you fishers of humanity.' We didn't know what that meant, but we looked at each other and dropped our nets at the same time. A part of me said I shouldn't leave my work and my livelihood, but I couldn't help it. When I looked in Jesus' eyes I felt something inside me stir that I didn't even know was there. I told Andrew that I was going with him and Andrew said, 'Don't leave me,' and we been with Jesus ever since."

Peter smiled at the memory, then the smile ceased. "Jesus kids about me being protective and all, but what he doesn't tell you is that he's a wanted man. The Romans are looking for him and the greedy priests are, too, because he challenges their power. Can you imagine if everybody prayed the way Jesus teaches? It would empower folks to bring down these unjust principalities and powers who lord it over us. The Romans and the priests know that. That's why they want to kill Jesus: because he threatens their power."

Peter thought for a moment, then he sighed sadly. "Jesus says someday his enemies will get him. You can be sure that I'll fight with every bit of my strength to keep that from happening, but folks in power will do anything to stay in power. Jesus has made it clear, though, that no matter what happens to him, we who love God have to continue Jesus' struggle to change this world. He teaches us *Blessed are the peacemakers,* not the peace*keepers,* the ones who keep the false peace of an unjust world, but the peace*makers,* those who struggle to make a world of real justice and real peace, hallelujah, amen."

"Do you really think they'll kill him?" asked Yeshua.

"Well, you've had priests who killed their own kin cause they threatened their power. And the Romans will kill anybody. So . . ."

Peter shook his head sadly and moved away.

In the days that followed they trekked with Jesus and his band of disciples from dusty village to dusty village healing, loving, playfully engaging, proclaiming the good news to everyone they met, pouring living water for all who would drink. Each night when they had eaten, and the merriment and good-humored fun had wound down, Jesus ministered to the thirsty spirits and hungering souls of Maryam and Yeshua. He instructed them in the interpretation of the scriptures of God and taught them the inner meaning of prayers and spiritual postures, how to leave their sleeping bodies to traverse the inner realms of spirit and the lower precincts of heaven. Their meditations became deep and satisfying, and they learned to discern the voice of God within. Beneath it all, what Jesus taught Maryam and Yeshua was love; he took them beyond feeling love to offering love to radiating love to living it. But especially Maryam, for it was she whom Jesus had chosen.

Two weeks into their journey as the camp prepared to sleep, Jesus beckoned Maryam to him. The night air was cool and the sky starfilled.

"There's something you've wanted to ask, but you feared it might be too private," he said after she had settled next to him.

"Yes, sir, there is." Jesus' ability to discern the thoughts of those around him no longer surprised her. "I've just been wondering, why hasn't a good man like you ever settled down and married?"

A sadness seemed to cover Jesus' face. "It wasn't like I never wanted to marry; I did. A man and a woman becoming one flesh is a holy thing. But I grew up seeing little people treated like dirt." His eyes narrowed. "The Romans killing us at will and the men of religion seeming not to care about serving anything but their own greed and their hunger to be important. I grew up seeing all this, and I always knew God wanted me to do something about it. I knew I had the spirit of the prophets inside me, Jeremiah and Elijah and Amos and all of them that spoke God's liberating truth against the rulers of their times. But I also knew I was different from them. They were prophets, but I am more than a prophet. Ever since I could remember I've known that God has set me apart for something special. So I fasted and prayed and meditated and dwelled alone in the desert to prepare for my service. I don't have much education, I don't have any wealth, I don't even have a place of my own to lay my head. But what I do have is this special calling to speak the truth of God in season and out of season, to the rich as well as the poor, to the comfortable and the comfortless, to bring new life to this world dying beneath the weight of its own evil and greed and terrible injustice. Yes, I would like to marry, but I can't put all that struggle and danger on a wife and children, so I just keep holding on to God."

With a sweeping motion he gestured toward the men and women in the camp.

"And look, because I have been faithful, God has given me a wonderful family. Even have some Samaritans in the family now. Isn't God good?" He laughed heartily.

"But why did God choose you, a poor man? Why not a priest or an educated person that people could look up to, instead of poor folks like us?"

Jesus patted the ground. "Because poor folks are the salt of the earth. It's nothing new. God has always loved poor folks. Most folks are poor. Most of the prophets have been poor, too. Even Moses had to leave Pharaoh's house before he could become a prophet of God. The rich want us to think that rich folks are special, that it's my father's natural will that they should live better than everyone else. But most rich folks are going to be in trouble in the kingdom of God because they pay more attention to shekels than to the needs of people. The rich stay rich only because they don't share enough with others."

They sat in silence again while Maryam ruminated over Jesus' words. Then she said, somewhat sheepishly, "With all due respect, why do you call God *father*? And why isn't God *mother,* too?"

His eyes took on that faraway look. "The people in the village of my youth didn't understand the circumstances of my birth, so to them I was a *mamzer,* a bastard son. My brothers James and Joseph and Judas and Simon all called my mother's husband, Joseph, father; they were the fruit of his loins. Joseph also accepted me as a son, but my fellow villagers never let me forget that he was not my father. I had Joseph and my loving mother; still I felt the absence of an earthly father acutely. So I cleaved to the only real father I could claim. That is who God is to me: my heavenly father. That is how I experience God. If you experience God like a mother, then call God mother. The men of religion would say that you blaspheme, but I would not be offended, because even the scriptures equate the mercy of God with the nurturing womb of a woman and call the wisdom of God by the female name of Hokmah. But no matter how you experience God, know what is true, that God is neither male nor female, and more than mother or father. God is spirit, the creator of all, in all and with all, possessed of a greatness and majesty beyond all your imaginings."

Then Jesus clapped his hands. "Now it's my turn to ask something of you. I know your village has suffered a great hurt; I could feel it as soon as I entered. It's a hurt that's repeated in every town and every village under the heel of Roman oppression. That is why I spoke to you at the well and compelled your spirit to seek me out: so I could prepare you to be an agent of your people's healing."

Maryam touched her hand to her chest. "Me? Why? How?"

"I chose you first because you're a woman, and it's time for men to stop seeing women as less in the sight of God. That is another great blasphemy spoken in the heavenly name: that women can't be priests and ministers of God. But there is another reason I chose you: because my father has healed you in the midst of great pain. What better agent of healing than one who is a witness to God's healing power? This is what God has destined for you, that you will heal the people of your village by sharing with them the living water of divine love and truth as I have shared it with you."

·   ·   ·

The next morning Maryam and Yeshua awoke to find Jesus sitting on his haunches before them, running his fingers through his thick beard and smiling his radiant smile. Beside him lay a small bundle bulging with food.

"This is for you," he said. "You have been a joy to me, but now it's time for you to go. You have listened with your hearts and learned what I have taught you; you've gone everywhere I've led you and seen the glory of God in the beauty of your own spirits. You are ready."

"Are you sure, Jesus?" said Maryam. "There's still so much we have to learn."

"You are ready," Jesus said. "Have faith in yourselves as I have faith in you. God will make a way."

He hugged Maryam, then Yeshua. "I thank God my father that you have blessed us with your presence. You've both been a joy to my spirit. From now on I will call you friends and you will call me brother. Go my friends and spread the truth of God. Share the life-giving words I've spoken to you with everyone that thirsts, no matter who they might be. If sometimes the words don't come, call on my spirit and I will pray that you will be sent another comforter: the holy spirit, the spirit of truth, who will teach you all things. Now go in peace to change the world."

Chapter

44

The sun stared down from a cloudless sky. Maryam and Yeshua walked the dusty, rutted road hand in hand, pensive and unhurried and unfaltering. Not the bloom and sway and elegant greenery of orchard and field, nor the unregenerate bulk of the aeon-sculpted configurations of rock and stone and sun-baked earth, nor even the putrid carcasses of skinned and eviscerated camels and sickened livestock, left to bloat and rot where they fell, against every scriptural protocol, caught the smallest thread of their attention, for remembrances of their encounter with the Messiah lodged in their every sense and sensibility. A starless night had already descended when they noticed that dusk had presented its profusion of colors and withdrawn them unannounced. They spent that night in a dry streambed huddled in meditation and prayer, oblivious to the cold and dark, filled with the unmistakable feeling that they were now living in a wholly different world.

The next day they walked along as ensconced in their thoughts as on the first. That is why they did not see the lone man on the dusty road until they had almost overtaken him. The man turned to them with an expression that held more curiosity than suspicion. His face was deeply lined and both the hair of his beard and his uncovered head were speckled with gray. One eye was scarred shut and he walked slowly with a pronounced limp. He carried on his shoulder a camel-skin bag that appeared all but empty. They greeted the stranger almost in unison.

The man returned the salutation with a smile as he took measure of them with his good eye.

"Where you folks heading?"

"To the next village down the road, about half a day's walk."

"Sure enough? I'm on my way there, too."

"That's home for us."

"You don't say. I was born there. Lived there."

"Really? What's your name, sir?"

"Yoram."

"The rosh of the village? I remember . . . when they took you. I'm Aridai's daughter. His youngest. Maryam."

The man's craggy face lit up. He clapped his hands and leaned toward her. "You mean that little spunky thing who used to run through the village? You weren't knee-high to a goat when I saw you last."

"Yes," Maryam chuckled. "That's me."

Yoram hugged Maryam hard. Then he backed away, slightly embarrassed. He pointed to Yeshua. "Excuse my manners. Who is this?"

"This is my husband, Yeshua."

"Husband?" Yoram pumped Yeshua's hand and took measure of Maryam again. "All grown up and married. I guess it has been a long time," he said. "It's so good to see you. See you still have your spunk, too."

"It's more like I got it back," she laughed.

The three began to walk at the slow pace of the older man.

"The men back home said you were dead," said Maryam.

Yoram noticed her fix on his scarred eye. He fingered it.

"I guess in a way I was. I was so full of hate after the Romans took me that I didn't have room for love at all. I joined Barabbas and his band of fighters and killed many a Roman. I thought killing Romans would satisfy me, but the more I killed, the emptier I felt. Then on one raid I got injured bad. Took a sword in this eye. My fellow fighters carried me away, up into the hills, and we came across a camp of travelers. They gave us food and drink and let us take rest. I had lost a lot of blood and was so weak that I resigned myself to die.

"They laid me in the shade. We knew the Romans were hunting us, so after a few hours the others in our band started getting me ready to move. One of the strangers kneeled beside me. He looked at me and said, 'This man is hurt bad. Leave him here with us. We'll look after him.' That man nursed me back to health like I was his own brother, almost like I was his child. He fed me with his own hands and brought me cool water to drink. When they broke camp he carried me on his back all by himself alone. Wouldn't let nobody help him. Didn't matter that I was a Samaritan and he was a Jew. That man just took care of me with all the love and gentleness you could ever imagine. Living under his kindness and care for those weeks, all the hatred and anger I'd been carrying around all those years just started to fall away, and before I knew it a strange kind of peace came over me and it's never left. I've been a changed man ever since."

Yoram was quiet, then he said softly, "Now I'm going home. I'm ready to love my folks again."

He took a fearful breath and touched Maryam's arm. "Are they still alive?"

"They were fine when we left."

"Thank God." He exhaled in relief. "By now my children are all grown like you. Some of them are even older than you," he said thoughtfully. Then he hesitated. "Did my Phebe . . . did she marry again?"

"I don't think she ever did," Maryam answered.

Yoram loosed a sigh and slammed his fist into his hand. "If she takes me back I'm going to love her right. Love her like I never did before."

The village shimmered in the sun-singed windless air tinged with the thin wafted scents of smoke, freshly turned earth, and the mingled smells of living. The nahalas spread out before the wayfarers, their orchards as neat and orderly as soldiers, the greens of the verdant fields broken only by the open brown uncrowned yards denuded of grass and vegetation. Sheep stood almost motionless in the heat. Clutches of cows gathered in the scant shade of the occasional clump of shrubs and huddles of trees dotting the pastures. The toiling workers appeared tiny in the expanse as they engaged in the eternal dance of wresting their livelihoods from the earth. Maryam and Yeshua and Yoram beheld it all with a mixture of emotions.

"Home," Yoram breathed. "Home." He sat heavily and wept into his scarred, callused hands, tears streaming from his good eye. "It's just that it's been so long. So long. You all go on. I . . . I'll be along."

Maryam brushed Yoram's thick hair with her fingers.

"It's alright. You take your time. Come when you're ready, Mr. Yoram."

She kissed his forehead lightly, and she and Yeshua started down the road hand in hand.

"Don't tell them I'm here," he called. "I just need a little time is all. I'll be along."

Maryam and Yeshua descended to the village with mounting excitement, but with apprehension, too. They were coming back transformed, but the village to which they returned was unchanged. Half of their neighbors—that is, the men, and some of the women, too—had bitterly resented Maryam and Yeshua's presumption to determine the contours of their own lives when it was only the lives of Maryam and Yeshua that were at issue. What could they expect returning with a message for the lives of others, too, a message asking them to reach into parts of themselves they had worked so diligently to hide away?

"Maryam, you sure you're ready? You know how folks feel about us. And you know these men aren't used to listening to a woman."

"I'm ready. I've faced it all my life without a shield or a breastplate or a shred of self-belief. I certainly can face it now. Just stand by my side, my love."

Yeshua drew her close. "You know I will."

When first they departed the men had laughed harshly. At the river and at the marketplace, too, they ridiculed the sojourn as foolish and bereft of all hope and reason, for even if by some inexplicable turn the stranger at the well was the Messiah, surely he'd have nothing to do with a brazen murderess and her friendless consort openly living outside the bounds of moral propriety. In their gleeful retelling of

Maryam's meeting at the well, she had either lost her mind or, worse, had succumbed to the seduction of a demon spirit—which, in their estimation, was a fitting consequence for her transgressions. Smoldering beneath the men's shared derision was the unspoken resentment that on her journey Maryam might indeed encounter the Messiah and be touched by him, too, while those left behind remained implanted in the same unyielding earth, locked in their unremitting anguish and tireless wrath by the spiteful stagnation that masqueraded as their lives.

In the days that followed, the men's private rancor increasingly flared until it engulfed them in a flame of collective bitterness that a woman—an audacious and irreverent one at that—might actually usurp the blessings that rightfully belonged to them. Yet as the men's hostility rose so did the most secret of their hopes, that Maryam might come back into their midst with a life-changing word that would both empower and liberate them, not only from the hands of those who with their gleaming swords and imperial decrees and twisted notions of heavenly fiat ravaged the age-old patrimonies of Samaritans and Jews alike, but also from the spiritual malaise and unwellness forged in their souls by the oppressive weight of Caesar's will.

For although none gave voice to it, in their deepest selves each man hungered for the return of their former days of grace. They simply were tired of being unhappy. They wanted their old lives back, the selves they'd once been, the lives that were theirs before the advent of their shame. Yet even as they yearned for change, they feared it, too. What would it mean for the world they had so carefully constructed and controlled? If their defenses were peeled away, could their hearts, raw and unprotected, endure the pain of it? Torn between the certainty of the pain they knew and the uncertainty of the lives they longed for, the men cursed Maryam's journey even as they looked forward to her return, and hoped for her failure even as they prayed fervently for her success.

The women were afflicted with ambivalence of another sort. They hoped the stranger's selection of a woman to hear his truth, particularly a woman so vilified by men, was an omen of better days to come. If indeed he was the Messiah, they thought, his choice of Maryam as his returning messenger would be unchallengeable, indisputable evidence that women had a higher standing in the household of God than their men were willing to admit, a status and stature that not even the *erwat dabar* could negate. But these hopes were denied their full flight by the encumbering fear that if Maryam were to reappear without life-altering testimony to preach and proclaim, the conspicuousness of her failure would only make the men's hearts harder, dashing the women's nascent hopes and whatever validation their spirits had begun to claim.

Even the children awaited Maryam's return, alternately fearful and excited in the way that young ones are. Having heard their fathers' contentions and their mothers' secret hopes, without understanding either they assumed their elders' contagious air of suspense and expectation. The children awoke each day with their eyes on the horizon and made a game of vying to spot the familiar figures traversing the incoming road. Each hoped diligently to be the one to announce it. Though it was not only the children. The men and women, too, stole frequent glances at the horizon to see if Maryam had returned to ease their waiting and want.

After weeks of watchfulness the thrilled children spied their distant approach and trumpeted their arrival.

"They're back! They're back!" the children called as they whizzed from one field to another, breathless with excitement.

The villagers struggled with their different postures of response as they hurried to the courtyard. The men attempted to bridle their anticipation and fear while sharpening their ridicule and their simmering resentment. The women tried hard to temper their hopeful longing and hold at bay their annoyance and pique that Maryam had brought a new layer of uncertainty to their lives.

All of them left their midday endeavors with a fecund air of curiosity and wonderment, expecting either a word from God or a public display of insanity. Both possibilities promised a rare and unique event that no one wished to miss, for there had not been a holy man or a truly crazy person in their village for quite some time. Moreover, those still harboring anger that Maryam had not been stoned imagined that the scene unfolding before them held a further possibility: that this might offer the occasion to gloat publicly over her madness and point to her sorry state as final proof for their harried wives that to disobey their husbands was to court a sad and tragic end.

Maryam and Yeshua entered the familiar cluster of basalt huts and hard-packed dirt and crude ovens of rock and clay with the sun at their backs and a retinue of their gawking neighbors in tow. Huldah was among those making their way from diverse points as if pulled along by a single thread of inquisitiveness. She entered the dirt expanse with her ear inclined to hear what had drawn farmers from their fields and fishers from their nets—in her hut she had not heard the children's cries—when she saw Maryam in the middle of the flurry of words and movement. Huldah felt a prick of fear, then she noticed Maryam smiling. She was almost upon Maryam when she stopped, speechless and still. When Huldah spoke again, it was in a voice filled with awe.

"I see it in your face," she said. "You found him, didn't you?"

Maryam beamed.

Huldah shouted "Glory!" and embraced Maryam with such jubilation that every head turned. Huldah sensed the heated stares and suddenly felt an unaccustomed self-consciousness. She lowered her voice conspiratorially and spoke directly into Maryam's ear. "I knew you would. Did he say anything about Hokmah?"

Maryam leaned away just enough to lock eyes with Huldah.

"I saw him. We stayed with him. And he told me not only women need to know Hokmah, but men, too. He said, 'Hokmah is justified by all her children.'"

"Really?"

"He did. He said everybody knows God's conquering strength, but if men are to know the fullness of God, they must know God's nurturing strength, too. And Jesus has a womb-spirit, Huldah, a real compassionate softness to him. Sometimes he fussed and called the men of religion a brood of vipers. Other times he held his heart and lamented, 'O Jerusalem, how I wish I could gather you to my truth as a hen gathers her young.' In him is joined strength of body and strength of spirit. He's softness and might, compassion and conviction. In him the masculinity and femininity of God come into balance. With him there's no need for women to meet in secret and call on the woman-side of God to validate us."

A voice spoke from the crowd in caustic challenge. "If you have something to say, say it to everybody."

Huldah shot the man a sideways glance. "Maryam, I think we'd do better to talk later."

She squeezed Maryam's hand. "You go on and teach us, child. You hear?"

The courtyard throng parted a little as Mr. Ishmael and Mr. Pop strode toward Maryam; the two old men were given a wide berth since their afternoon of heroism. Maryam kissed each on his bearded cheek.

"My friend-girl, I hope you have glad tidings for us," said Mr. Ishmael.

"Want some good news," said Mr. Pop.

"Don't worry. That's what I have: good news for everyone."

Others now drifted into the courtyard on the undercurrent of murmuring. As they milled about, casting scornful, wondering glances at Maryam and Yeshua, a man pushed through the crowd gesturing furiously and barking angry words. Hushai stomped into the dusty expanse, his every step betraying the storm of rage within him. He shoved aside the several villagers standing in his way.

"You old crazy woman. Who do you think you are, calling folks from their work and all and making a fuss?"

He took another menacing step as the throng looked on with acute and noiseless attention. Yeshua tensed and instinctively placed himself before Maryam, his legs spread wide, his shoulders squared, the hands at his sides clenching into fists. Then Maryam whispered to Yeshua and his shoulders and fisted hands relaxed. He stepped aside and Maryam leveled her eyes at Hushai.

"We have been to see the Messiah," she said with an astonishing crispness of voice and manner. Nothing about her betrayed apology or even reserve.

Izevel screeched, "Lord have mercy! Listen to this woman blaspheme. What in the world would a Messiah want with her?"

By now Hushai shook with rage. "Messiah? Who you talking about, that ragged Galilean at the well you had no business talking to? You saying that ragamuffin was the Messiah? You're nothing but a fool. God wouldn't choose no raggedy man for a Messiah. And if he is the Messiah, why would he talk to you and not to us men? You're just lying and blaspheming."

The men with their clinging garments of unanswered perplexity and fresh outrage stomped their feet and shouted.

"Blaspheming on the name of the Messiah!"

"The woman don't have no kinda shame!"

"We need to rid this village of this evil woman once and for all."

Yeshua cast about at the men's faces, glowering and distended with fury. He whispered emphatically, "We need to go."

Yet Maryam's countenance in that rising storm of self-induced indignation was perfectly calm. She said to Yeshua in a steady voice, "Just stand beside me."

Abba Samuel had watched the unfolding scene from the back of the crowd, but now he pushed forward.

"Hear me. I don't know if I believe Miss Maryam talked to the Messiah or not. I have to hear what she has to say. But if the man at the well is the Messiah, him not speaking to you men might have something to do with how you've been living."

"What you mean, Abba?" Hushai said, hot with indignation.

"I mean that you men have become so hardhearted that you can't hear anything but the sound of your own anger."

Hushai's mouth curled with rage. "Now wait a minute, Abba, you can't—"

"Lower your voice, Hushai, and show some respect."

"Tell this woman to show some respect, Abba. She's lying and you know it."

Kenaz added his own offended voice to the exchange. "Abba, there you go protecting her again. We should have stoned her when she killed Nahshon. Now look at her, blaspheming right out in the open."

"I say stone her now," said Hushai.

"Yeah, stone the hussy," screeched Izevel.

The crowd roused to a dangerous pitch. Yeshua was beyond uneasy now. He took Maryam's arm. "We got to go. Now."

"Not yet," she said, calmly slipping from his grip.

"Quiet!" Abba Samuel exclaimed, invoking the weight of his age and authority upon the rapidly rising clamor. But before he could speak further, Maryam did.

"Hushai," she said with a firm voice.

The crowd was immediately tongueless, as if silence had fallen abruptly from the sky. Yeshua shifted his weight, his eyes fixed on the snarling man who seemed as baffled as he was angry, as incredulous as he was baffled, captive to a soaring rage.

"Hushai," Maryam said more softly. "It's time to let go of your anger."

Hushai's face was distorted with venomous surprise. He opened his mouth to speak, but no words came out.

Maryam's face was tranquil and composed. "It's time to let go of your anger so the peace of God can come in."

Hushai's furious expression turned to befuddlement. His lips moved soundlessly.

"Let go, Hushai."

Then Maryam looked into the motionless faces of the dumbfounded men around her. "Aren't you tired of being angry, of arguing and acting mean and holding your pain inside? Aren't you tired of treating your wives and your daughters like enemies? Aren't you tired of having to maintain a facade of coldness and meanness and constant control?"

Hushai raged in his skin, snarling beneath his every breath, dribbling hot spittle down his beard. But Maryam was undaunted. She had already begun her ascent to that realm beyond reasoning in which jangling words of discord are discerned, nakedly and without judgment, for the utterances of fear and abject cries for help that they are.

"The Messiah said to me, 'Feed my sheep.' That doesn't just mean food for your bellies; it means spiritual food, too. It means sharing the living water of God's truth and love. The Messiah's name is Jesus, and he gave me a message for you."

A great air of certainty came over Maryam. Her entire countenance was changed. The sudden authority in her speech and in her motioning limbs mesmerized her hearers.

"He told me to tell you men that he saw the pain in your eyes, in your spirits and souls. He knows what the Romans have done to you and to all our people. He knows your shame and humiliation at Roman hands, how they've used every law and weapon to beat you down and make you feel like less than you are. He feels your mourning over all you've suffered and lost. So he sent a special word to you."

She cleared her throat, clasped her hands before her, and lifted her chin.

"Now hear the words of the Messiah: 'Blessed are you that mourn.'"

She looked from face to face. "Blessed . . . are you that mourn. All your transgressions are forgiven. Every one of you.

"For all your failures, real or imagined, you are forgiven.

"For every time you've been unkind, you are forgiven.

"For every time you lashed out at the ones who with open hearts look to you for solace and love, you are forgiven.

"For every time you treated your families like enemies and declared war on them in your hearts, you are forgiven.

"And for every time you struck your wives, or brutalized their spirits, or humiliated them in the presence of their children, or turned your backs on them, or treated them as less than the gift that they are, God has forgiven you. In the name of the Messiah, you are forgiven."

The men stood stock-still, too stunned even to breathe, mortified, unmasked, held in unrelenting thrall by the confrontation between the legacy of their corrosive self-indictment and the confounding promise of divine release. None could formulate language for their lips or for their limbs, so they did not speak or move; even their faces remained immobile.

Hushai felt his heart flayed raw. Among the men he alone stirred. He shut his eyes, his shoulders sagging, his lips pursed tight and quivering, seized by a sudden and overwhelming terror that the barrier to the passions he'd kept locked away was about to be breached. Unwilling to face his grief and shameful memories, indeed unable to admit even to himself that he could feel anything so deeply, and admitting no need for forgiveness from heaven or from earth, Hushai retreated to the emotion with which he was most at home: anger. And not just simple anger, but a measure of hate commensurate with the terror that threatened to consume him. He raised his fists and rushed at Maryam, shouting "No!", reaching for her throat as if to choke the life from her.

Rapidly and with one motion Yeshua threw himself into Hushai's path, thrusting his forehead into Hushai's chest and wrapping his muscled arms around his thick waist. Hushai flailed and struck Yeshua with his arms and hands as Yeshua strained to hold him. Hushai bellowed at the top of his lungs. "No! What she know about my mourning? I don't want to hear it! No!"

Yeshua held Hushai tight, absorbing the blows with his head and his shoulders, speaking softly. "Hush now, Hushai. It's alright. It's alright."

The compassion in Yeshua's voice pushed Hushai deeper into terror, and he fought even harder to vanquish the threat to the protective hardness of his heart. The two wrestled fiercely, Hushai bellowing and Yeshua speaking to him steadily and softly, kicking up dust and loose stones, until Mr. Ishmael caught Hushai's arms in his massive grip and the others shook off their shock and wrestled Hushai to the ground.

"No! No! She got no right!" Hushai thrashed and shouted, writhing mightily, tossing his head from side to side, cursing and yelling.

"No! I don't need no forgiveness!"

Then his fury left as suddenly as it had convulsed him and he went limp in the men's grasp, whispering tiredly, "I won't let her. I won't."

His breathing slowed. He sat up, pulled his knees to his chest, and hid his face and his throbbing temples in the hollow his knees made.

"I'm alright. I'm alright," he said, shrugging the men's hands from his shoulders with a voice that sounded of resignation, but was more of anger that was by no means vanquished, just withdrawn. He was not apologetic, he simply stilled.

Hushai's sudden violence had thrust everyone but Izevel into an openmouthed silence. Now it was as if the deluge of emotion that had lifted Hushai suddenly descended upon the other men. They began to call out in voices juxtaposed, almost alien.

"You better mind your business."

"We don't need you to tell us a thing!"

"Ain't nobody mourning about nothing."

"And don't nobody need forgiveness, neither."

Abba Samuel's voice rose through the din. "Quiet. Let her have her say. What if she has been with the Messiah? You want to take a chance on ignoring the truth from the Messiah's own mouth?"

If the men heard Abba Samuel it did not show. They still screamed their strident, anger-laden disclaimers, caught in the rising current of their own passions. The clamor grew and many of the men were not even forming words now, just shouting and crying out. Still Maryam was unmoved. The greater the cacophony, the greater her calm.

"Blessed are you that mourn. Blessed. All of you," and her voice could have been a trumpet.

The men cried and shouted more loudly still. Then they began to drop their heads, some hiding their faces in their hands, their torsos heaving and trembling, trying their best to conceal their tears.

"Don't nobody know how we feel."

"Even our dreams torture us."

"Can't nothing take away our pain."

"Love can," Maryam said.

The men were suddenly quiet.

"Love can take it away," she repeated. "Love can heal you."

The quaking edifice of the men's dread of their own emotions abruptly gave way and there was a sudden tumult of weeping as they wailed out the pain they could no longer contain. They wept and pounded the dust, crying for every hurt they had endured or witnessed or simply feared, bringing great moans from the deep inner places in which they had hidden them. For many, these were their first tears since their passage from their mother's son to their father's. Men screamed and stretched out in the dust oblivious to shame and embarrassment.

Each time it seemed the tears might subside they flowed again. The women wept, but not as the men; they, too, were beset with grief but had much less shame and self-loathing to exorcise from their souls. The children of the village, frightened and confused, watched fearfully, huddled behind the trunks of the palm trees and sycamores.

The pain and humiliation and hurt flowed like a river. Everyone in the village wept for something, the men for the legacy of shame that ate at them like cancers, the women for their years of enduring the bitterest fruits of the men's unbridled self-loathing. Everyone wept, even Huldah, who yet mourned the husband and children who had left her more alone than Hagar in the desert, and Abba Samuel, who wept quietly and with great dignity for the pain of all the others. Mr. Ishmael cried for Elisheva, the lost love of his life. The tears of Phinehas were for his many comrades lost in battle and the children he never had. They all cried, each of them, until they were tearless, until the worst of their pain had been screamed and pounded away.

They sat exhausted, almost quiet and a bit sheepish and unsure, with only occasional whimpers and wisps of moans escaping their mouths. Finally there were heavy breaths of release, and the children gratefully reclaimed the reassuring laps of their mothers. A blanket of tranquillity descended upon everyone that soothed and quieted the riotous noise of their inner struggles and raging contentions. There was a lightness in the air and a pleasing new calm. Yet the men and the women, too, found themselves confused by the sudden and almost unfathomable absence of the tension that for so long had been a defining factor in their lives. They interrogated their thoughts for the cause of their confusion. When nothing presented itself that could be named or defined, they could do no other than conclude that what they were experiencing was that thing with which they had become totally unfamiliar: peace within and among them. The perpetual scowls of the men disappeared; replacing them were unaccustomed half-smiles, innocuous and benign, the foreignness of them a source of actual bafflement. The men stole sheepish glances at the women, unsure of what to do with their new and unexpected feelings of tenderness. The women sensed the change in the men's collective demeanor, but they averted their eyes and tried to purge it from their minds, afraid to offer such an unprecedented development even the smallest welcome, unable as they were even in their imaginations to conceive of it as anything but fleeting and impermanent. When the shocking novelty of these changes and the initial bewilderment of trying to fathom them had subsided, and the people could again hear something other than the tumult of their own old griefs and overflowing emotions, Maryam rose again to speak.

Some of the men seemed genuinely moved by the forays into the inner regions of their hearts. Others felt varying degrees of resentment that Maryam had dared to stir the embers of their suffering. Nonetheless, all prepared to hear. Even if they did not understand, they knew they were witness to a power that could change their lives forever. Even Hushai listened in silence, though he squinted suspiciously, his mouth twisted and tight beneath his beard.

"The Messiah has said that you who mourn are blessed. But to claim your blessing, you must love, for love is its own blessing. It is only love that will bring back your happiness and joy. It is only love that will sustain you. Open yourselves to God's love and you will know a peace beyond all understanding.

"Love is more than a feeling. It's a practice, a way of life. You love by treating folks right. You love by making sure everyone has enough to eat. You love by treating everyone like someone. You love by comforting, by protecting, by lifting up on every leaning side. Man. Woman. Samaritan. Jew. It doesn't matter. Treat everyone like you want to be treated. That's the love the Messiah teaches.

"But most of all you must be just; justice for God's children is the highest expression of love for God. Do not return evil for evil. Don't let the meanness and shameful injustice of the Romans make you mean and unjust, too. What they do is evil, and we must resist their iniquity, but not out of anger. Stand against the structures of evil because of your hunger and thirst for the righteousness of God, and your faithful recognition of the heavenly mandate to let justice roll down like waters and righteousness like a mighty stream."

She paused to catch her breath. Every eye was upon her.

"My brothers, you must forgive yourselves, for it's only then that you can love yourselves. But you can't love yourselves without also loving your women, we who are your mothers, your daughters, your wives, for we are yourselves. You are the issue of our wombs, and we are flesh of your flesh and bone of your bone. Doesn't God cause the sun to shine on male and female alike? If it is so with God, then it must be so with you, for it is the will of God that you love your women and accept us as your equals in the sight of heaven.

"And you, my sisters. You have suffered pain that is immeasurable. You know the hurt of constant heartache. Your spirits have been trodden upon, your precious worth devalued as pearls cast at the feet of swine. And now many of you harbor secret enmity in your hearts because of it, and angry fears consume you. But there is a balm in Gilead. You women must forgive your men. Forgive them, love them, yes, but do not bow down to them; that is blasphemy. There is only one alone who is worthy of obedience and worship: that is the Lord God Most High. Sisters, if you insist on your own worth, your men will be forced to acknowledge it. Then they will know that they cannot dishonor you without dishonoring God."

Maryam stilled like a sower pausing to discern if her seeds were cast on fertile ground. In that lull Huldah stood.

"You've told us how the Messiah says men and women should treat one another. What does he say about divorce?"

The crowd stirred. Men and women leaned forward.

"I asked the Messiah that very question. He said in my hearing that the erwat dabar is a stench in the nostrils of God. What was meant to alleviate irreconcilable strife has become an instrument of terrible pain and sorrow. Divorce is given in the scriptures to be used only in the most grievous cases, for when two have become one, God would have it remain so. But if there must be a parting, then women must have the same rights of divorce as men, for we, too, are children of God."

With Maryam's assertions of the equality of female and male, Hushai had begun to fidget and fume. But when she challenged the erwat dabar, the right of men Hushai had seen in the scriptures with his own eyes, he could bear no more. He stood brusquely and said with reclaimed arrogance, "Your words are moving and nice and all, you got everybody all worked up and crying, but how do we know that what you're saying comes from the Messiah of God? How do we know you're not making up all this stuff about women and divorce?"

In the spontaneous emotion that had consumed the crowd, Ocran had cried as hard as anyone, but now his sneering malice recovered its course. "That's right. How do we know the Messiah really said all these things?"

The other men's instinctive distrust welled up again in a fuming welter. Into the midst of the shouts and recriminations and footless fury, a lone figure limped into the courtyard unnoticed. He searched the agitated crowd as if looking for someone. He listened intently and unobserved. Then he spoke.

"What she says is the truth," the man said loudly. "I heard the man say some of those same things myself, hallelujah, amen."

Everyone turned to look. Ocran exclaimed, "Great God in heaven. I think it's Yoram."

Yoram picked his way through the stunned, gawking villagers to stand at Maryam's side. He rubbed his scarred eye.

"I left here and let my family mourn me for dead because I was full of hatred and shame. I spent all my time killing Romans or planning to. But no matter how much killing and how much revenge, I never had peace, not even for an instant. Then I met this man with eyes like fire. When I lost my eye he cared for me and healed my body and my soul. He gave me strength to stand against evil without being evil. He brought me back from the living dead and taught me to love again. His name is Jesus. He's got so much God in him that he has to be the Messiah."

Yoram fell silent and scanned the stunned crowd until his eye fell on a woman whose countenance spread wide with the terror of recognition. She was fleshier now and her face, which was half-hidden behind splayed fingers pressed to her lips, was lined with the well-formed wrinkles of her advancing age. But it was her, it was his Phebe, wide-eyed and openmouthed, unsure if she should laugh or cry.

"I know how to love now," Yoram said aloud. "And I'm ready to love my family right if they'll let me." His good eye was filled with pleading.

There was a moment of perfect stillness. Then as though on cue the men rose, embracing Yoram with shouts of welcome, laughing and patting his back. Yoram accepted the warmth, yet his eyes never strayed from Phebe, her fingers pressed to her unpursed lips, her eyes still wide with amazement. Slowly she moved her hand and a thin smile crossed her mouth. She beckoned to Yoram. He pulled away from the men and rushed through the throng as rapidly as his limp allowed, falling into the open arms of his tearful wife and the now-grown offspring who had thought him dead.

The appearance of Yoram and the sight of him in the arms of his loved ones were so enervating that the women and men rocked on their heels and swayed, struggling to preserve what was left of their fragile composure. Maryam's face took on a new intensity. She closed her eyes and the air began to stir. She stretched forth her hands and orbs of light rested upon them. Her face shone with a sudden new incandescence and she seemed to speak with a new voice.

"You have seen the miracle of Yoram. Now all of you, ask God to heal your hearts. Now. It is only through love that you will be healed."

A gust of wind fluttered her garments and snatches of light glittered and swirled around her head.

"Love one another as God loves you," she boomed and her voice seemed to resound from every direction. The villagers felt her words take breath within them and there occurred a miraculous thing: men suddenly embraced men, their tears mingling from cheek to cheek. Before they'd realized it the men had found their tongues and turned to the shocked women in unreserved openness, crying in their arms and begging their forgiveness. Husbands embraced wives, sons kneeled at the feet of mothers, fathers held daughters close.

In the midst of it Hushai and Izevel sat shoulder to shoulder with their arms folded, struggling to retain their crumbling armor of resistance. They did not reach out to their neighbors and they did not reach for each other.

"I don't want to hear it!" Hushai sobbed. "I don't! Leave me alone!"

Hushai tried to stand but his legs buckled and he fell to his knees. He threw handfuls of dust and bellowed into the air. "Leave me alone!" he cried with amazed futility. But in the end the spiritual contagion was too much. His resistance and illimitable juxtaposition at long last eroded, Hushai crawled on all fours and laid himself at Maryam's feet.

"I need to be blessed," he cried through gulping sobs and great flowing tears. "I'm so tired. Bless me with the Messiah's blessing. Please bless me."

Izevel fell at his side and grasped the hem of Maryam's tunic. Her face was tearstained and anguished.

"Maryam, I-I . . ."

Maryam rested her hand on Izevel's head. "It's alright, Izevel. Ours is a God of forgiveness."

"Bless me with the blessing of the Messiah," cried Hushai. "I need you to bless me. Please. I want to change."

Others heard Hushai and began to implore the same in an instantaneous panic of unrequited desire and frightful need long domiciled and intensified by the brooding weight of waiting. Huldah, Ritzpah, Mr. Ishmael and Mr. Pop, Oholibamah and Sonny Boy, Ocran, Phumiah, Keturah, Petronelah, and the rest, even Abba Samuel, all kneeled at the feet of Maryam.

"Bless us!" they cried, and that was all that could be heard. "Bless us! Please bless us!"

A thickly built man with reddish skin and reddish hair shot now with gray gingerly picked through the crying supplicants sitting and lying prostrate. He led along a stooped woman who appeared much older than himself. The old woman did not lift her gaze as they approached Maryam. The man's lips quivered as he spoke.

"I . . . I went to get your mama." It was Aridai, her father. He dropped his head and stared at the ground.

The old woman hugged Maryam, whimpering and moving her mouth wordlessly, as the man stood by, awkward and unsure. Maryam held her mother close. She felt the old woman's fear and fragile frailty but something more, too: the strength of the fallow yet undiminished love her mother had nurtured and held for her like a seed in a battered husk, and Maryam's heart overflowed for this soul broken and confused and debilitated and aghast, yet still pulsing with love in spite of the viciousness of life's onslaughts against her. Maryam blessed her mother in the fullness of her spirit and prayed upon her the abiding peace of God.

"I thought you might want to see her," her father said, his voice cracking.

She looked past her mother into the river of his eyes and saw there a boy derided by his own father and bullied by his peers until he was shamed and hardened into a creature who felt no love even for himself. Staring into his eyes now, she did not feel or even remember his myriad assaults against her spirit. Instead, she was filled with a great tenderness and thanksgiving for the return of his love. "Thank you, Daddy," she said gently.

Aridai studied Maryam's face, raised his hand as if to touch her, then pulled his hand away. He continued to contemplate her face. "Bless you, Maryam," he said at last.

He took his wife's hand, helped her ease her stooped frame to sit among the others, seated himself carefully beside her, and again bowed his head. The old woman stared a faint smile at Maryam, rocking and talking softly to herself.

Maryam looked at Yeshua, his tearstained face upturned in prayer; she considered those she had known all her life lying prone at her feet, crying out to her for deliverance and absolution. She closed her eyes and the panorama of her life passed before her, its harshly dark and disjointed intervals melding into a fluid continuum of gold and brilliant yellows, and there appeared Ma Tee, her ebony countenance restful and serene and triumphant. She smiled at Maryam, blew a kiss, and nodded.

There, suspended between eternity and time, Maryam understood.

READERS' GUIDE TO
LIVING WATER

PLOT SUMMARY

In a village in biblical Samaria—the region north of Jerusalem and south of Galilee—a contingent of Roman soldiers subject the local men to indescribable brutality in the tearful sight of their wives and children. The ongoing memory of that terrible event births in the men a sense of humiliation and self-loathing that spirals into a tragic cycle of spousal abuse and general mistreatment of women.

In this pain-filled setting grows a little girl with a "gibora" spirit—a spirit of boldness—that the men angrily decry as a challenge to their domination of the village women. After the girl's father strikes out at her in a brutal rage, her grandmother, Ma Tee, tearfully vows to protect her from the men's ire by breaking the little girl's spirit. By the age of betrothal the now young woman is deemed as sufficiently obedient to be a wife, and is thrust into what becomes a succession of soul-wrenching marriages. After five marital disasters, the death of a child and a bitter trial for the murder of her fifth husband, she has a life-changing encounter at the village well with an extraordinary stranger from Galilee who offers her "living water." It is then that she finally reclaims the fullness of her spirit and becomes the vehicle for the healing of the broken men and women of her village.

OBERY HENDRICKS ON LIVING WATER:

Living Water is an African American retelling of the New Testament story of the woman at the well who was married to five successive husbands at a time when women did not have the right to choose either marriage or divorce. With Living Water I tried to imagine that woman's life, pushed and pulled from one painful relationship to another; how she might have felt, her fears, her anger, her hopes. I also wanted to imagine the five husbands whose property she had been, and who conspired in the oppression of her spirit. Although the issues that the story treats are universal, *Living Water* is an "African American retelling" because it reimagines the woman's life and struggles and ultimate triumph through the lens of African American culture and issues and social concerns.

I began *Living Water* ten years ago as a high school graduation gift for my eldest daughter, Tahirah. The tale of the woman at the well who endured five spirit-breaking marriages to become Jesus' apostle to the Samaritans embodied the spirit of perseverance and triumph that I wanted Tahirah to take on her journey to college and beyond. But what I thought would be a ten-page story took on a life of its own. Soon I realized that as I described the woman's husbands, to varying degrees I was writing about myself. Looking back over my own life and surveying the emotional wreckage I have left in my wake, I realized that in many ways *Living Water* is not just about the struggles of women; it is also about me and men like me. The journey of the woman at the well to be free of male domination and mistreatment was also my own journey to free myself from the roles of dominator and mistreater.

Some might say that a novel that portrays such naked oppression of women caricatures or even demonizes men. Yet one has only to look to certain rural areas of India where wives are burned alive on the funeral pyres of their husbands; or to the ritual female genital mutilation in some parts of Africa; or simply to the rising rates of abuse and even murder of women at the hands of men in the "enlightened" United States, to know that only in the historical details is this story different from those of so many women in the world today.

Living Water has been an extraordinary experience for me. I have learned much about myself and my relationships, healed rifts and reconciled with family and loved ones, and made many meaningful new friends. Yet I am only beginning to draw from the spiritual well from which *Living Water* springs for it contains much wisdom that I have yet to learn and to put into practice in my own life. I am not nearly as loving, tolerant and understanding in my relationships, or as far along in my journey to God as I could be, or should be, for that matter. The great blessing, however, is that despite the imperfection of the earthen vessel through which it has come—me—*Living Water* is still a well that contains within it currents of self-realization and divine guidance that can nourish all who drink of it. It is my hope that readers have found *Living Water* to be a fulfilling reading experience. The following questions are provided as a guide for further individual reflection and group study.

TOPICS FOR DISCUSSION:

1. In childhood, the girl who would become the woman who encountered Jesus at the well was rejected as having a "gibora" spirit, that is, as being too bold and self-confident for the comfort of men. When have you exhibited a gibora spirit in your own life? How did those around you respond? Were there times when your gibora spirit was repressed or broken? How did you reclaim it?

2. While explaining to her granddaughter the meaning of *erwat dabar*—an arbitrary declaration of divorce—Ma Tee impresses on her that to avoid facing *erwat dabar* herself she should, "Always be careful how you live." Consequently, "careful" becomes her defining approach to life. What factors in your life might have made you careful, that is, afraid to take risks in life? How might you overcome them?

3. On page 18 we read, "Into the abyss of the little girl's questioning creeps the ravenous self-doubt that eats at too many women from girlhood, subtly, quietly, until they come to regard themselves as forever unworthy of the fullness of life." What causes this self-doubt? How can it be counteracted? How can girls and young women be protected from it?

4. On that day the village men were subjected to soul-crushing brutality and public humiliation. As a result, the men descended into self-loathing that hardened their hearts and practically destroyed their ability to experience emotional intimacy. Many men today have similar difficulty with intimacy because of social factors and circumstances. What are some of those circumstances? What are some of the ways that the feelings resulting from these circumstances manifest in the lives of men? How can boys and young men be protected from these feelings?

5. On pages 22 and 23 there occurs this exchange after Yoram's abuse by the Romans:

"I'm going to kill every Roman the good Lord sends my way."

. . . "But you can't make all Romans guilty for what Caesar and his soldiers do."

. . . "If they benefit from the evil, but don't stop the evil, how can they not be guilty?"

Are those who derive benefits from injustice guilty even if they don't actively commit the injustice themselves? Why?

6. The women of the village pray to Hokmah, the "woman side" of God. What does it mean to believe in a feminine side of God? What are of the implications of this belief with respect to religion and society? Your personal belief and practice?

7. Tragic loss made the character Man afraid to love. What kinds of things can raise fear barriers against showing love? Are you afraid to love? Why? How does that fear manifest in your behavior and relationships?

8. How does the Jesus of *Living Water* differ from the traditional picture of him?

9. What was the cause of Nahshon's anger toward women? How can men like Nahshon overcome their anger toward women?

10. Maryam refuses to marry Nahshon under the Law of Moses, that is, according to village tradition. Why? Does this have significance for the way marriages are performed and lived out today?

11. What was the basis of the bond between Big Mama and Jalon?

12. Why was Maryam accused of murdering Nahshon? What were the men trying to protect by calling for her stoning?

13. After the death of Nahshon, Maryam had an experience at the river that changed her forever. What was the nature of that experience? What role did Huldah play in it?

14. Although he was a charlatan, many people believed in Parshandatha the "holy man." Why? Do we see this attitude toward religious and social leaders today?

15. What role did Mr. Ishmael and his friend Phinehas play in Maryam's life? Has there been someone who has played a similar role in your life? How?

16. How did Yeshua's attitude toward women differ from the attitudes of the other village men? What experiences in his life might have accounted for that difference?

Acknowledgments

Thanks and gratitude for their encouragement and support to my agent, Wendy Weil, to my editor, Gideon Weil (no relation; no collusion), and also to my readers, who include Bishop Vinton Anderson, Morial Asiel, Stephanie Berry, Akili Buchanan, Tahirah Hendricks Cannon, Debra Chambers, Dr. Gwendolyn Childs, Ishmael Childs, Dr. Heather Elkins, Dr. Ann Elliot, Donna Epps, Mari Evans, Dr. Rochelle Garner, Jacqueline Glass, Kathleen Henderson, Linda Hendricks, Rochelle Hendricks, Shirley Magee, Opal Moore, Niamani Mutima, Lisa Rhodes, Henry Rock, Denise Stinson, Vonya Thornton, Beverly Todd, Velma Union, A. J. Verdelle, and Diana Winter. And a special word of thanks for their months of kindness to the crew at Border's Book in Dayton, Ohio.